Looking for Leroy

Books by Melody Carlson

Courting Mr. Emerson
The Happy Camper
Looking for Leroy

FOLLOW YOUR HEART SERIES

Once Upon a Summertime
All Summer Long
Under a Summer Sky

HOLIDAY NOVELLAS

Christmas at Harrington's
The Christmas Shoppe
The Joy of Christmas
The Treasure of Christmas
The Christmas Pony
A Simple Christmas Wish
The Christmas Cat
The Christmas Joy Ride
The Christmas Angel Project
The Christmas Blessing
A Christmas by the Sea
Christmas in Winter Hill
The Christmas Swap
Christmas in the Alps

Looking for Leroy

MELODY CARLSON

Revell

a division of Baker Publishing Group
Grand Rapids, Michigan

© 2022 by Carlson Management Company

Published by Revell
a division of Baker Publishing Group
PO Box 6287, Grand Rapids, MI 49516-6287
www.revellbooks.com

Printed in the United States of America

Library of Congress Cataloging-in-Publication Data
Names: Carlson, Melody, author.
Title: Looking for Leroy / Melody Carlson.
Description: Grand Rapids, MI : Revell, a division of Baker Publishing Group,
    [2022]
Identifiers: LCCN 2021029332 | ISBN 9780800739751 (paperback) | ISBN
    9780800741136 (casebound) | ISBN 9781493434237 (ebook)
Subjects: GSAFD: Love stories.
Classification: LCC PS3553.A73257 L655 2022 | DDC 813/.54—dc23
LC record available at https://lccn.loc.gov/2021029332

Baker Publishing Group publications use paper produced from sustainable forestry practices and post-consumer waste whenever possible.

22   23   24   25   26   27   28   7   6   5   4   3   2   1

Chapter 1

Early June
Portland, Oregon

"Hey, if you want to believe in fairy-tale endings, go for it." Brynna Philips paused to wave goodbye to a cluster of her third-grade students as they walked across the grassy lawn in front of the school. "All I'm saying is it's not for me." She forced a smile for the sake of her two younger colleagues.

The three teachers were visiting on the sunny front steps of the grade school while saying last-day-of-school goodbyes to their students. Tasha and Gwen seemed determined to convince Brynna to join their summer escapades of finding Mr. Right. But Brynna was not having it. Tasha elbowed her. "Seriously? You've completely given up on men and dating?"

"That's right. But I wish you two the best of luck." Brynna watched as little Taylor Thompson raced toward her from her mother's parked car. Bouncing precariously in Taylor's hands was a potted plant.

"I have something for you, Mrs. Philips!" Taylor yelled happily. Then, just a few feet away, she tripped—falling forward onto the plant.

"Oh, Taylor!" Brynna rushed over to help her. "Are you okay?"

"Yeah, but I ruined your flowers," Taylor sobbed.

5

"No, no, they're not ruined." Brynna helped the girl to her feet, trying to repair the bruised and broken flowering plant. "It'll be beautiful, Taylor." She smoothed the girl's mussed hair. "This was very thoughtful."

"I asked Mommy to get pink flowers." Taylor frowned down at the bruised blossoms.

"Thank you. I'm sure I'll enjoy more pink blooms throughout the whole long summer."

"I wish school wasn't over." Taylor hugged Brynna tightly. "I don't see why we need a summer break. I'm gonna miss you so much!"

"I'll miss you too. But I hope you get in lots of reading." Brynna patted Taylor's head. "You've become such a good reader. I want you to go to the public library a lot. Just like I used to do when I was your age."

Taylor nodded, jumping at the sound of her mom's car horn as she called out for Taylor to hurry up. "I gotta go, Mrs. Philips."

Brynna thanked her again for the plant, then waved as Taylor jogged off.

"Bittersweet, isn't it?" Tasha said quietly. "The last day of school."

"Not for me." Gwen laughed. "I'd like to be doing the Snoopy happy dance right now."

"Save it," Tasha warned. "Here comes Sergeant Bart."

"And here I go." Gwen winked as she made her exit.

Brynna grimaced, wishing that teachers didn't treat Jan Barton like the plague. It wasn't easy being vice principal. And, other than being a little bit brusque sometimes, Jan did a good job.

Jan greeted them as she glanced across the school grounds. "Looks like the place is nearly cleared out."

"Speaking of clearing out, I better go attack my room. Our last-day party got a little messy." Tasha's smile looked nervous. "I know you say no food in the classroom, Jan, but Jessie's mother sneaked in cupcakes and punch. What could I say?"

Jan grimly shook her head. "Well, the janitor will probably complain about ants again."

"Sorry." Tasha took off.

"So, what were you girls gossiping about?" Jan asked Brynna.

"Oh, nothing. They were just telling me their summer plans."

"Anything special?"

Brynna chuckled. "They think this will be their summer of love. They've joined a dating app. They actually wanted me to join it too."

"And?"

"No thanks." Brynna firmly shook her head.

"How long have you been divorced now?" Jan asked.

"It's been a few years."

Jan studied her more closely. "I used to worry about being alone. But over the years, I've gotten used to it."

Brynna knew Jan was single but not much more than that. "I'm getting used to being alone too. Although I considered getting a cat until I found out my condo's homeowner's association forbids pets. So maybe I'll take up gardening."

"Gardening?" Jan frowned at the broken plant in Brynna's hands. "Is that a sample of your green thumb?"

"Well, this one took a little tumble."

"How do you garden in a condo?"

"I have a little terrace. I thought I'd use planters. Get lots of pretty-colored flowers. Maybe some veggies. Put a little bistro table and chair out there. String some lights."

"That sounds nice." Jan didn't look convinced.

"What about you? Any summer plans?"

"As a matter of fact, I've got a little plan." Jan's lips curled into what seemed a genuine smile, one somewhat out of character for the stalwart vice principal.

"A plan?" Brynna's curiosity piqued.

"Take a look at that." Jan pointed to the parking lot across the street where an old-fashioned red-and-white trailer was parked behind a shiny red SUV.

"You mean that car and trailer?" Brynna frowned. "Won't the owner get a ticket for parking there?"

"Nope. And for the record, it belongs to me!"

"Really?" Brynna cringed with embarrassment. "Uh, is it for camping? Is that what you call an RV?"

"Yep. It's a super lightweight camp trailer." Jan's voice grew enthused. "As you can see, it's a vintage style, but brand-new. State of the art too. It's compact but with all the modern conveniences and comforts." Jan actually chuckled. "Can you tell I've studied the brochure backward and forward?"

"You do sound like an expert."

"I sort of am." Jan let out a dreamy sigh that sounded so out of character, Brynna couldn't help but stare at the older woman. "The best part is that this trailer is so lightweight I can actually tow it behind my Yukon."

"Your Yukon? Didn't you drive a Corolla before?"

Jan smiled yet again. "I did but I traded it in for something bigger. Doesn't it look handsome in front of that sweet trailer? Quite a pair if I do say so."

"Oh, yeah . . . nice." Brynna nodded like this all made perfect sense, but the truth was, she'd never had the slightest interest in that sort of thing. In fact, she'd never even been camping. Her ex-husband, Dirk, used to talk like they would try it someday . . . but someday never came. And now it was too late. Still, it was amusing to see Jan going on like this about it. So happy. So unlike her. It was kind of sweet.

"That particular trailer's been nicknamed 'the single girl's getaway.' I first saw it at the big RV show at the state fairgrounds during spring break. I knew it was meant for me. Well, except their show model was pink instead of red." Jan wrinkled her nose. "Pink's not really my cup of tea. But I was sold on the idea so I went ahead and ordered mine in red. Isn't it a cutie pie?"

"Yeah . . ." Brynna couldn't help but smile at Jan's unexpected gushing. But to mask her amusement—and not risk offending

Jan—Brynna kept staring across the street, studying the trailer closely. "So you can actually do that yourself? I mean, you know how to pull that trailer behind your car? And you go camping and everything? By yourself?"

"You bet." Jan firmly nodded. "But I have to go back to the dealership to have some things checked. Then I'll be ready to rock and roll. I can't wait."

"Well, that's very cool, Jan. I'm happy for you."

"Yep, I plan to head out for some serious camping. I have it all mapped out with campsite reservations and everything. I'll start out along the Oregon coastline and then head down to the Redwoods, and eventually I'll stay in Yosemite National Park."

Brynna looked down at the pot in her hands, then propped up a broken flower stem only to watch it fall again. "You'll really camp all by yourself? Out there with wild animals and bugs and everything?"

"Absolutely." Jan shook a warning finger at a boy sliding down the front steps banister, then turned back to Brynna. "Why not?"

"Well, I admire you for that. That's really brave."

Jan grinned as she pulled a faded Dodgers ball cap over her short, graying hair. "Braver than teaching a bunch of whiny fifth-grade girls PE all year long? Hopefully our budget will cover a real PE teacher next year so I can get back to my real job."

Brynna laughed. "Yeah, I sometimes overhear the girls' complaints. They make it sound like they've been through boot camp." She wouldn't go into the details with Jan, but she had given the disrespectful girls more than a couple of stern warnings. Not that it ever helped.

"They hate the circuit-training unit and endurance test, but I rather like it." Jan turned to go back inside the school with a gleeful cackle, as if torturing fifth-grade girls made up for the additional work placed on her.

Brynna chuckled to herself as she followed Jan into the building. Well, if anyone could get students to toe the line, it was Sergeant Bart. Not that Brynna approved of that moniker for her colleague.

Of course, no one said it to Jan's face. Not only was the six-foot-tall woman a force to be reckoned with but as second in command, she wielded a lot of power. Most of the staff shied away from unnecessary encounters, and even Principal Parker backed down around her. But Jan seemed to appreciate the distance. She didn't appear to need friends.

Yet, for some reason Jan treated Brynna a little better. Probably because Brynna had always tried to be respectful. Not that it was easy. Especially if Jan was in a bullying mode. But to be fair, her victims usually asked for it. Like earlier in the week when Mr. Reynolds punished Ty Lampton for stealing Drake Stein's basketball shoes. As it turned out, Jan had been spot-on. Ty had been innocent. Drake had staged the whole crime himself to get Ty into trouble. And Mr. Reynolds still hadn't heard the end of it.

As Brynna returned to her empty classroom, she cringed to imagine Jan camping out there in the wilderness—all by herself—in that flimsy little trailer. It seemed a little crazy, not to mention scary. What if some wild animal or, even worse, some crazy person decided to attack in the middle of the night? Out in the middle of nowhere? Then again, if anyone could fend off an assailant, it was probably Jan. And more power to her for it! As she tossed old papers into the trash, Brynna actually longed for that sort of courage.

She used to think of herself as fairly strong and gutsy. She'd survived the loss of her parents in college. Yet she'd continued with her schooling, getting her degree and a good job afterward. She'd even supported Dirk while he finished his master's degree. She might be slight of stature, but she'd always considered herself a confident woman.

But after being beaten down by Dirk's betrayal three years ago, she hadn't quite been herself since. Sure, Dirk had moved on and remarried, but Brynna sometimes felt stuck. Maybe she just needed to accept that she'd never be that same strong, gutsy person again and that this was a different era for her. But that didn't mean she had to roll over and die—did it?

Chapter 2

Sonoma County, California

Leroy Sorrentino slowly stood, letting the clumped soil in his hand trickle through his fingers down to the vineyard floor. "Needs loosening for better drainage." He gazed out over the rolling vineyard hills in an effort to avoid his daughter's eyes. "You want to be a vintner so badly, Gina. Well, then, grab a rake and get to work."

Gina tapped his chest. "*Listen* to me, Dad. I'm trying to tell—"

"I did listen to you. Doesn't mean I have to agree with you."

"It's *my* life. If I want to quit college, it's *my* choice. Not yours."

He locked eyes with her, wishing he could make his impetuous daughter see reason. After only two years of college, she was determined to never go back. Nothing he said seemed to get through. Now they were having a stare down on the north hill of the family vineyard. Still, he couldn't help but feel amused to look into her stubborn, blue eyes. Despite the fact that both her parents had dark brown eyes, Gina's were a deep ocean blue, and far more intense than usual today.

"I know it's your life . . . and your choice," he said more gently. "And I understand and appreciate your love of the vineyard. But if you really want to help out here, you should stay in school. Finish your business degree and—"

"We've been over this," she snapped. "I know kids with business degrees who can't even get a job at Starbucks, Dad. I grew up here. I understand the industry. I know how to do this. I don't need college."

Leroy wanted to tell her she was too young to know what she didn't need. But he knew just where that would get him. The grape didn't fall far from the vine where he and his youngest daughter were concerned. He leaned down to pat his dog's head. Babe was a faithful old yellow lab, who still loved to chase her ball now and then. Other than slowing down in her old age, she never gave her owner a bit of grief.

"Come on, Dad." Gina's pleading voice brought him back to the moment. "Just listen to me. Give me a chance."

"I was giving you a chance—a chance to get more education." He scowled at her. At twenty, she wasn't even old enough to legally taste wine—and yet she thought she could run a vineyard? Why couldn't she see the value of a college degree? And besides all that, where'd she get the idea he was too old to run this place on his own? Good grief, he wasn't quite fifty.

"Well, you know Sophie's expecting again," she continued, "and she's already got enough going on with Lucy and Addison. How's she going to manage the office and keep books with three little rug rats underfoot?"

"I already put out word that I'm hiring for—"

"Don't you get it, Dad? I'm here. I can help."

"Gina, I've told you before about how I had to give up school to run the vineyard when my father got sick—"

"I know, I know . . . you've told me your tale of woe before . . . and you were even younger than I am. That's just my point. You've done just fine without college. I will too."

He removed his straw cowboy hat, then ran his fingers through his shaggy hair. He knew he was overdue for a haircut, but time was precious right now. Besides, he liked it long.

"How about *this*?" Gina placed her hand on his arm, peering appealingly up at him—just like she'd been doing since she was old enough to manipulate him. "Let me take one year off from school. And during that year, let me take on more responsibilities here. Just see how it goes."

He considered this as he picked up Babe's ball and gave it a good chuck down the road to the house, watching as the elderly dog took off after it with surprising speed. The truth was, he really could use more help around here. Not only in the office but out in the fields as well. The section that got scorched by last fall's wildfire was in dire need. In fact, he should be working on it right now. Of course, he'd already arranged for seasonal workers. They would show up as soon as school was out. But he'd never find anyone as trustworthy and dedicated as Gina. She loved the vineyard. Still, he hated to see her give up her education and get trapped into the family business.

"What do you think? Couldn't you at least give me a chance? Let me take on more managerial tasks? Let me show you what I can do?"

He rubbed his chin, trying to think. "How about this—I'll give you this summer to prove yourself. But you need to understand the bar's going to be set high. I'll treat you like a real employee. You won't be running to the lake with your friends when it's hot. You can't take off for a concert weekend or shopping trip whenever you please."

She pursed her lips. "I can live with that."

He frowned. "You sure? You're still a kid. Don't you want to enjoy it?"

"You were a kid, too, when you took over for your dad."

"Yeah, but times were different then."

She crossed her arms. "Different how?"

"Well, computers . . . technology . . . we didn't have all that to deal with. We still did everything the old-fashioned way."

"Which is exactly why you need me. I know computers. And I can do things like social networking. I can build and maintain a website for us. Do you know we're one of the only vineyards in the county—maybe the world—without a website?"

"So I hear." He shrugged. "But our uniqueness is that we're still just an old-world winery. We don't host big fancy weddings or tasting parties. We don't have a B and B or—"

"But maybe we should, Dad."

He groaned. "You sound like your aunt."

"Well, maybe Aunt Sherry's right. Damico's is only half the size of our vineyard, but they seem to be doing better than us."

He frowned. His brother-in-law's socially driven business plan might be fine for them, but it wasn't what Leroy wanted for Sorrentino's.

"Even Grandma's been bragging about how many events they have scheduled for this summer. She says we're missing out."

"I guess that's my choice." He leaned down to pat Babe's head. "Good girl."

"Even if it's the wrong choice?" She scowled at him as he stood.

He scowled back. "If you're so impressed with how they're running Damico's, why not go work for them?"

"I'd rather go to school than work for Aunt Sherry," she protested. "You know she drives me nuts. And my spoiled cousins are even worse."

He concealed his amusement. His baby sister drove him nuts too. But she was family. Still, he was thankful that his mother had chosen to live with Sherry instead of him. His mother left primarily because she hadn't gotten along with Leroy's late wife, Marcie. Ironic considering she had set him up with Marcie in the first place. But that was all water under the bridge now.

"So, tell me, Gina. What's your general philosophy for running a vineyard? If we're going to partner like you're suggesting, it might be important to make sure we're like-minded. You know I don't want to do things like Damico's—or most of the vineyards around here—so what do you think?" He studied her closely. Did she know this was a test?

"Well, I think our vineyard has room for improvement." Her expression was slightly defiant, her chin stubbornly tilted upward.

"Such as?" He grew defensive. Was she criticizing him?

"Naturally, I'm not talking about what you manage, Dad. That probably doesn't need improvement."

He softened. "So what kind of improvements would you bring to the table?"

"Well, among other things, I think we should have on-site tastings. We'd offer flights and case discounts to visitors. That would introduce new vintages, as well as help with sales."

He couldn't help but feel impressed. Gina was doing her homework. "Maybe so. But to have tastings, you'd need a special room," he pointed out.

"What about the barn? We don't use it for much of anything besides storage. And most of the stuff in there is just old junk from the family. Anything of value could be moved up to the loft, and the rest could be used to furnish a tasting room. I mean, it would be rustic, but that would be pretty cool."

"And you honestly think you could manage to organize all that?"

"*Can I?*" Her eyes lit up. "You mean, you'll let me?"

"I'll still expect your help in the vineyard."

"And can I design us a website? And promote tasting parties on it?"

Already he was regretting this whole thing, but she was so enthused, how could he say no? "Just remember, I get final approval. That means the right to reject anything that doesn't seem right to me. And don't forget that we're an old-world–style vineyard. You need to respect that. It's something that sets us apart."

"Believe me, I know. I've heard the story . . . my great-great-great-grandfather established Sorrentino's back in eighteen—"

"Okay, okay." He held up his hands to stop the lecture. "I get that you get it."

"And that's something we should celebrate. I was looking at

the winery origin plaque in the barrel room. Do you realize this summer is the 140th anniversary of our vineyard? That's a pretty big deal."

"I guess so." He shrugged. "But not as big as our hundredth anniversary. I was a boy at the time. But my dad and grandpa threw a big party. I'm glad we did since Grandpa passed away the next year."

"Can't we do something like that too?"

"Huh?" He frowned. Did she think he was going to die?

"I mean have a big celebration?"

"I don't know, Gina." He slowly shook his head. "Everything you're talking about takes money. After the fire damage to the south hill . . . well, we're already scraping by as is."

"I know. That's exactly why I want to work for you. And why we need to do these things. This vineyard is a commercial venture. And it takes money to make money. We need to make the winery a profitable one."

"And you've only had two years of college?" He tried not to look overly impressed.

She chuckled. "Yeah, well, don't forget that I grew up in this biz. And I've been doing a lot of research lately."

He smiled. Maybe his daughter was sharper than he gave her credit for. "Okay then. You can go ahead and check into these things. Just keep me apprised of what you're doing and, more importantly, how much it's going to cost."

She threw her arms around him. "You won't be sorry, Dad."

But as he and Babe went one way and Gina the other, he wasn't so sure. He hated letting her think she was getting out of college so easily. But this summer would be a learning experience—probably for both of them. If it fell apart, maybe Gina would be convinced to return to school, after all. And if things got really bad, he could always consider his brother-in-law's offer to buy out Sorrentino's. Tony Damico had tried to talk him into selling after last fall's fire, but Leroy had refused.

As he walked between the grapevines, with Babe patiently following, he breathed in the sweet fragrance of blossoms. The morning sun warmed his shoulders, and he could hear birds chirping in the giant oak tree next to the barn. He couldn't imagine ever wanting to give up on what so many folks—especially the ones who didn't understand the actual work involved—imagined to be a *dream life*. Oh, sure, there were ups and downs, but sometimes, like this time of year, it did seem pretty dreamy.

Although, to be honest, being a vintner hadn't been his dream. Because he was the only son of an only son, his family had assumed it should be. Though for whatever reason—probably from watching *LA Law* as a kid—he'd dreamed of becoming a lawyer. But in Leroy's second year of college, his father had gotten ill. Naturally, Leroy came home to help.

The plan had been to take over until his dad got back on his feet. But that never happened. The Hodgkin's disease, linked to Agent Orange exposure in Vietnam, was relentless. After three long years of battling, his father lost the war. By that time Leroy's younger sister, Sherry, was old enough to start college. To help cover her tuition expenses, Leroy continued to run the vineyard. And his mother, determined to make sure he stuck around, encouraged him to marry his good friend Marcie Edwards.

Had he settled? Both in life and in marriage? He sometimes wondered. But he'd loved Marcie. And he'd been thrilled at the arrival of each of their three daughters. And when Marcie passed away from cancer nine years ago, his grief had been distracted by the demands of single parenting three daughters—as well as having a vineyard to run. But now the girls were grown. Sophie, his firstborn, had married young and was expecting her third child in August. Luna, his middle child, was in law school. And Gina, the baby and light of his life, seemed determined to replace him as vintner of Sorrentino's. He chuckled at the thought. Babe, hearing him laugh, wagged her tail and dropped her ball at his feet again. He gave it a good throw, down toward the barn this time.

As he walked to the barn, trying to ignore the sight of the peeling paint, he didn't think too many would conclude that he'd "settled." Sure, he'd had his disappointments, but all in all, it hadn't been a bad life. Good grief, despite Gina's insinuations he was ready for the rocking chair or worse, he was in pretty good shape. And not unhappy. Over the years, he'd grown to appreciate the blessings of running the family vineyard. Nothing was better than being up with the sun, breathing fresh air, working the land, growing healthy vines, harvesting the grapes, and going to bed tired.

Oh, sure, he probably still wondered at times . . . had he missed out on something? Was there something more? And sometimes, like after a long hard day of working the vineyard, he wondered if Gina could be right about him aging. Because he did feel old. Or was he simply lonely?

Chapter 3

On Saturday morning, Brynna got up early with a new kind of energy. It felt sort of like she had real "vim and vigor," words her mother used to use. And perhaps the June sunshine streaming through her window was helping. But for a happy change, Brynna didn't want to sleep in until noon. Not this morning! Because today she had a plan.

As she hurriedly made her bed, she suspected she'd been motivated by hearing Jan's plan the day before. Although Brynna's plan wasn't nearly as daring, and it did not involve trailers or camping. More likely it was inspired by a dog-eared vision board residing in the back of her coat closet. She'd put the board together in earnest last winter, but the timing had been wrong because what she'd wanted most of all was to grow things. And today she would begin!

Brynna started her morning with her usual coffee and yogurt, followed by a bit of housecleaning and laundry. Her reward when done would be to pay a visit to Riverside Gardens—hopefully while the morning air was still cool and fresh. She'd noticed this new business back in April. Located by the river, the attractive nursery had a big sign that boasted of native Oregon plants, miniature trees, water features, and an authentic Japanese tea garden. There was even a colorful coffee kiosk in the parking lot. She couldn't wait to see it all up close and personal.

But she didn't plan to just window-shop. She would begin by choosing some handsome pots and planters. Not too many containers since her condo deck was small, but enough to make it feel like a real garden. After selecting containers, she would load lovely plants into one of those cute little nursery wagons. She'd collect a combination of small shrubs, perhaps a miniature tree, and lots of flowers and herbs. Maybe even some salad veggies. And she'd also get bags of soil. Somehow she'd pack it all into her small car, then she would happily drive home and spend the rest of the day just planting and arranging everything.

As she went down to her car, she realized it would be hard work hauling everything up these stairs, but the results would be well worth the effort. And, really, it was about time she enjoyed some sort of garden. Despite city living in a condo unit that she and Dirk had purchased years ago as a starter home, Brynna had always nurtured a dream of owning real land someday. At first she'd imagined a quaint little farm with sprawling gardens, beehives, laying chickens, and maybe even a goat or two, like her friend Amy raised. But thanks to Dirk's lack of interest in any agriculture, her dream had been reduced to the idea of a little house with a big yard. But even that had resulted in arguments. Dirk had no interest in spending his weekends maintaining a yard and didn't believe her promises that she would tend to it all herself.

Of course, that was just one of the many things she and Dirk couldn't agree on. Not in the beginning and not after twenty-some years of trying to persuade him otherwise. In fact, it seemed that the more she'd pressed him about life beyond the condo, the more he'd resisted. He ultimately pulled away completely. Sometimes she wondered if, like he claimed, the divorce really was her fault.

Perhaps if she'd been more content with city living and their status quo, maybe they'd still be together. But no, there had been Ashley to contend with. The pretty student teacher at Dirk's high school had shown up just about the time Dirk was headed for a midlife crisis. Ashley was young enough to be their daughter, but according to Dirk, the infant made him feel younger. "Young and alive again," he'd told Brynna. Whatever!

Anyway, Brynna was determined not to think about him today. In fact, she felt she'd reached a place where she truly wished Dirk and his young wife nothing but blissful happiness. At least, that's what she told herself. Some days were easier than others. As she entered the Riverside Gardens parking lot, which was quickly growing crowded, she knew this was a day for sweet pleasures. By sundown, she expected to have dirty fingernails and a lovely patio garden to enjoy. And maybe someday, when she was feeling really bold and confident, she would consider selling her condo unit. She'd heard that real estate values were on the rise in her neighborhood. Her new terrace garden might even help sell the place. She might have enough equity to purchase a charming little fixer-upper, one with a big yard outside of the city. Her old dream of having a farm was probably too much for a single career woman to manage, but she wouldn't give it up completely.

Brynna parked near the coffee kiosk on the edge of the parking lot. As she waited for the barista to make her latte, she admired the pretty window boxes overflowing with pink geraniums, variegated ivy, and delicate bleeding hearts. Lovely! She wondered if she could grow something like that in the shaded corner on her patio. She knew she'd mostly need heartier plants that were able to withstand the afternoon sun. Perhaps she'd put up a sun umbrella like her neighbor Ella had done last summer. She could imagine herself at a little table, enjoying her morning coffee . . . or in the evening, with some lanterns or string lights. It could look sweetly romantic.

As she picked up her latte, her mind wandered back to the conversation she'd had with her colleagues the day before. Perhaps she hadn't given up on men entirely. There might still be one or two good guys out there. Who knew? Her heart felt light and bright and hopeful as she strolled through the open gates of the nursery's entrance. She claimed one of the last wagons and, inhaling the scents of earthy growing things, headed toward the area where pots and planters were displayed. Spotting an aromatic section of lavenders, she paused, bending down to simply breathe it all in. She'd definitely come back for some of these later. Oh, what a wonderful way to launch a perfectly delightful summer!

"I don't *want* Russian sage," a woman's shrill voice insisted. "I want petunias. I already told you we're planting nothing but petunias in the strip in front of the lawn. Purple petunias. That's what I want."

"But this tag says they'll have purple flowers, Ashley. And it says they'll get nice and tall, and they're low-maintenance," another voice countered.

"But I already told you. I want purple petunias, Dirk. Just like my mom's house. *Remember?*"

The hair on the back of Brynna's neck bristled and she stood up straight. She recognized not only her ex-husband's voice but his new wife's too. They had to be here today? Arguing over flowers? Really? Brynna glanced over her shoulder, hoping to be invisible. To her relief, her ex and his young wife had their backs to her. But as they continued to disagree over flowers, Brynna's flip-flops seemed adhered to the asphalt beneath them. Like witnessing a train wreck, she felt slightly sickened by the sight but couldn't stop staring.

Ashley had on a pretty pink floral sundress and delicate white sandals with kitten heels. Not exactly gardening garb, but fairly typical for the slightly frivolous young woman. Meanwhile Dirk wore khaki shorts, an OSU T-shirt, and Adidas. Nothing unusual about that. But what did seem noteworthy was the fact that Dirk and Ashley were at a nursery together, *picking out plants.* Since when had Dirk given a hoot about landscaping? Or spending a precious Saturday at a nursery?

Although aggravated at having her fun day interrupted by them, Brynna was surprised that she wished them no ill will. Pretending to sip her latte, she inconspicuously watched the couple head for the colorful section of annuals. Really, purple petunias? How

22

conventional and unimaginative. But as Ashley turned to pick up a small tray of blooms, Brynna felt as if the wind was knocked out of her. So stunned, her latte slipped from her hand, tipping and pouring down the front of her white tee. Oblivious to the hot liquid, she simply gaped in disbelief at Ashley's very rounded midsection. Unless the young woman was hiding one of Dirk's soccer balls beneath her sundress, Ashley was very, very pregnant. Like she could have the baby any minute!

With wobbly knees, Brynna turned away from the sight and, leaving the spilled coffee and garden cart behind, hurried from the nursery, across the parking lot, and straight to her car. Her hands trembled so violently, she couldn't even manage her key fob to unlock it, so she just leaned her forehead against the driver's side window and quietly cried. How could he? It was bad enough that Dirk was planting stupid petunias in his yard, but the same man who'd refused to have children with her was about to become a dad! *How could he?*

Chapter 4

Brynna was still crying when a shadow crossed over her and someone tapped on her shoulder. She jumped in surprise, looking up to see Jan Barton staring down at her.

"Are you okay, Brynna?" Jan demanded, though her tone held concern.

Blinking in shock, Brynna wiped her wet cheeks with her hands and attempted to appear perfectly normal. "Yes, yes, of course. I'm fine." She stood straighter.

"You don't look fine to me." Jan frowned. "What's going on here?"

"Nothing." Brynna finally managed to click her fob, unlocking the door.

Jan pointed to Brynna's brown-stained and still soaked T-shirt. "What happened?"

"Just a little accident. It's nothing." Brynna opened the door.

Jan continued to pester her with questions. "What are you doing at the nursery?"

"I was, uh, getting plants and things."

"Where are they?" Jan glanced over Brynna's shoulder into her car. "Your plants and things?"

"Well, I, uh, didn't get any."

"Is that why you're crying?" The woman's head tipped to one side as her tone grew sarcastic. "Were they all out of pansies?"

Brynna's pain morphed into anger. "If you must know, I just ran into my ex and his pretty new wife. And she is *pregnant.*"

Jan's dark brows arched. "And that bothers you? That she's pregnant?"

Brynna's hands balled into fists. "Of course it bothers me. Dirk *never* wanted children. For years I begged him. I nagged and pushed and prodded—everything I could to convince him. But he always rejected the idea of fatherhood."

Jan looked surprised but said nothing.

"And you know what he did for his thirtieth birthday? *He got himself a vasectomy!*" Brynna couldn't believe she'd disclosed this much, but it was too late to reel it back now.

"Hmm . . . must've gotten it reversed."

Brynna's eyes filled with angry tears. "I'm just so—so—enraged about it. I feel like my head's going to explode. I'd like to throw something or hit something or spit or—"

"Go ahead. *Spit.*" Jan looked amused.

Brynna actually considered it then slowly shook her head. But now her tears were flowing again. "I better go before—before they come out here. They didn't see me, and I don't—don't want them to see me like *this.*"

"You're not fit to drive." Before Brynna could protest, Jan took her keys. "Friends don't let friends drive enraged."

"But I—"

"Come on. Come with me." Jan closed the driver's side door, locked it, then took Brynna by the arm. "You can cool off, and we'll come back for your car later."

Without arguing, Brynna let herself be led to Jan's bright red SUV. She climbed into the passenger side. "Nice car," she mumbled. "Still smells new."

"Of course. So do you remember I told you my trailer's getting checked out at the dealership? I'm on my way to get it now. You can come with me."

"But I—"

"They're expecting me around ten thirty." Jan started the engine.

"Then why were you at the nursery?" Brynna buckled her seat belt.

"I wanted to nab myself a pot of red geraniums—you know, to go with my new trailer." Jan chuckled as she pulled out of the parking spot. "I thought it'd be fun."

"Oh . . . yeah. Sorry to distract you from it. Do you want to go in and get them?"

"I can do that later." She drove through the parking lot.

"I just wanted some plants and flowers," Brynna said glumly.

"For your little condo garden? Well, you can always come back later too. After you calm down."

"I guess." Brynna sighed. The truth was, she no longer had the slightest interest in her terrace garden. She looked down at her stained shirt, slowly shaking her head. "What a stupid mess."

"Your shirt?"

"My life." She took in a shaky breath. "And I was feeling so hopeful this morning."

"So just because you saw your ex and his pregnant wife, your life is now a stupid mess?"

"Maybe mess is the wrong word. It's off track or derailed or something. I'm sort of lost at the moment." Brynna felt tears coming again.

"I guess we've all been there." Jan's tone softened. "I mean, feeling lost. And if we haven't been there, we will be . . . someday."

"So you've been there too? Lost?"

"Of course. Burt and I weren't together as long as you and Dirk, but I felt lost for a while as well. Actually, for a long time."

She felt caught off guard by Jan's transparency. Sergeant Bart had never spoken of her deceased husband. Brynna didn't even know how to respond.

"To be honest, I never expected to be alone at this stage of life," Jan continued. "It certainly wasn't in my original plans."

"But you seem okay with it."

"Well, you learn to live with things. And I've learned I can live without a man. Like I said yesterday, I've come to like it."

Brynna glanced at Jan. She probably wasn't that much older than Brynna, but her no-nonsense short, graying hair and lack of makeup, combined with her mom jeans, clumpy tennis shoes, and baggy T-shirt—well, it all seemed to suggest she really had given up on attracting the opposite sex. Hadn't she said as much just yesterday? Hadn't Brynna said so as well? So why, just because she'd seen Dirk, was Brynna so upset now? Oh yeah, the baby thing. She felt the angry lump in her throat again. That dirty rat! Her eyes filled with angry tears. Why did he have to ruin everything?

"Don't get me wrong, Brynna. I probably felt similar—at first. Like life had dealt me a bum hand." She sighed. "Of course, my situation was different. And to be honest, I can sort of relate to Dirk because I never really wanted children either."

"If you don't like children, why'd you become a teacher?"

"It's not that I don't like children . . . ." Jan sighed. "But when I learned motherhood wasn't possible, well, I accepted it. I told myself I had plenty of kids at school. That was enough for me."

"And your husband?"

"Burt said he was okay. Later on, though, I think he may have felt differently." She shrugged. "But what can you do?" She turned into a big RV dealership. "Well, here we are. Want to come in with me and look around?"

Brynna glanced down her front at the coffee stain. "Not looking like this."

Jan nodded, tugging her Dodgers ball cap onto her head. "Suit yourself."

After Jan was gone, Brynna wished she hadn't agreed to come here with her. What was she doing at an RV place, stuck in Jan's car, in the middle of a parking lot filled with motor homes, trailers, boats, and campers? Sitting like a sniveling child in her soiled

T-shirt, Brynna wanted to leave, but her car was too far away to walk and home was even farther. She pulled out her phone and was about to call for a taxi when Jan returned with a bag and a grin.

"I got you something." She opened the door and tossed the bag on Brynna's lap. "Change your shirt and come inside. Something you gotta see in there."

Jan went back into the building and Brynna opened the bag to see a pale-yellow T-shirt with a picture of Smokey the Bear on the front. The words above his picture read ONLY YOU CAN PREVENT FOREST FIRES and below it, TAKE ME CAMPING! Grateful for the tinted windows, she ducked down and struggled to pull off her soiled shirt and put the new one on. Then she tucked her new shirt into her frayed and faded jeans, readjusted her long brown ponytail, and got out of the car, feeling slightly better. Just because her life was a mess didn't mean she had to be. She checked herself in the side mirror, using a wet fingertip to rub off some smudged mascara, and even paused to apply a bit of lip gloss. If Jan was kind enough to rescue her and get her this T-shirt, the least she could do was try to act like a normal human being.

Still feeling a bit alien and far out of her comfort zone, Brynna entered the big RV building. It appeared to be a giant showroom with several shiny RVs parked around a faux campsite, complete with fake grass, trees, and shrubs. Several camp chairs were even gathered around a surprisingly realistic-looking campfire that, on closer inspection, was actually fake flames flickering from a fan beneath.

"Come here, Brynna. You gotta see this," Jan called from a miniature wooden bridge. Brynna followed a rock-lined path to join Jan on the bridge and, looking down, saw that there was an artificial stream with rushing water, rocks, and plants. "See those?" Jan pointed down. "They even have small trout in here."

"You're kidding." Brynna stared in wonder as several brown fish zipped under the bridge.

"Farm trout. The salesperson said when they get bigger, they'll relocate them to a big lake on the owner's property."

"Interesting." Brynna nodded.

Jan turned to her. "Looks like the T-shirt fit okay. They're really for kids. But I figured you're not much bigger than a full-grown kid."

"Thanks." Brynna didn't admit that she still felt pretty childish. "I'm glad I came in to see the fish."

"Me too. Now you hang out here while I check on my trailer." Jan chuckled. "You can *pretend* you're camping."

Brynna sat down in one of the camp chairs and thought about that. Pretend you are camping? Pretend you are happy? Pretend you are making a garden on a teeny-tiny terrace? Pretend your students are your children? Pretend you don't mind being single? Pretend you are living? Was that all Brynna could do—pretend? With fresh tears stinging her eyes, she decided to slip outside to wait. Sitting on a bench in the bright sunshine, she put on her sunglasses and let her tears fall freely.

"What's wrong now?" Jan asked when she found her ten minutes later.

"Nothing." Brynna stood up, wiping her cheeks.

"Doesn't look like nothing to me." Jan studied her closely.

"I just got tired of pretending I was camping," Brynna snapped at her. "Like all I do is pretend."

"I have the answer." Jan held up a finger.

"What's that?"

"You will not pretend to camp, you will go for real. I am taking you with me on my camping trip, Brynna. What do you think of that?"

Brynna was speechless.

"So, it's agreed upon. You're coming with me. No more pretending for you. Camping is about as real as life gets."

Jan continued to talk about all they would do and see and what Brynna was to pack to take with her. By the time Jan dropped Brynna back at her car, it seemed to be set in stone. Brynna was going camping with Sergeant Bart!

Chapter 5

Despite his daughter's claims and promises, Leroy never expected Gina to be so driven. After just a few days, she had the barn nearly cleared and cleaned. "I'm impressed," he told her as she walked him through, explaining her plans to reuse old pieces of wood and corrugated metal to transform the space into a rustic tasting room.

"I also want to recycle a lot of those old furniture pieces." She pointed to a bunch of family "heirlooms" that were stacked against the back wall—a motley selection of tables and chairs and other family castoffs. "But first I want to put a clear finish on the pine floors. And make chandeliers from wine bottles. I saw a great tutorial on YouTube." She waved her hands excitedly toward the roof as she spoke. "I'll hang them from the center beam, as well as lots of strings of white Edison lights along the rafters. And there will be seating areas with tables and chairs." She faced a side wall. "I'm going to put the tasting counter over there. I'll make it from more wine barrels with some old planks of wood for the top. I already salvaged a bunch of stuff from behind the barn. Reduce, reuse, recycle." She beamed at him.

"I like how you're thinking, Gina. This all sounds real interesting." He tried to imagine it. Hopefully it wouldn't be a waste of her time and energy. What if no one came out here? "It's a lot of work though. You sure you want to do this?"

"Absolutely. And it's really fun work, Dad. I've dug out so many treasures to use. It's going to be really cool. There's this amazing old trunk just full of photos and memorabilia—stuff I can use for the tasting room and the website and even the anniversary celebration."

"A trunk?" He rubbed his chin.

"Yeah. It's so old, I'll bet it came on the ship with our Italian ancestors. Anyway, the deeper I dug, the more I found. Like going through a time warp. It even had some of your stuff too."

"My stuff?" He frowned, then recalled the antique trunk that used to sit next to the stairway when he was a kid. But what had he put in it?

"Yeah, I set your stuff aside for you." She led him back to the stack of dusty furnishings and picked up a large manila envelope. "I'm pretty sure this belongs to you." Her brows arched as she held it toward him.

He blinked and, fully aware of what was in the envelope, took it from her. "I thought I threw this stuff away."

"I hope you don't mind that I took a peek inside." She peered curiously at him. "Who's Brynna Meyers?"

"Brynna Meyers?" He slowly repeated the name, feeling an odd tightness in his chest. "Nobody, really. Just an old friend."

"An old *girlfriend?*" She drew out the last word.

"Just a girl I met at camp a long time ago." He peeked into the envelope to see that the letters and an old Kodak folder of snapshot photos were still there.

"Sounded like she was more than just a girl from camp, Dad." Gina's blue eyes twinkled with far too much interest. "Come on, tell me, who was she?"

He shrugged, trying to appear nonchalant. "Just a girl from a summer camp that I attended after my senior year of high school. It was up in Oregon. On the coast. A really spectacular location."

"Yeah, the background in the photos looked pretty."

"Uh-huh." Leroy hid his irritation. She'd obviously gone through all of it.

"Yeah. And that girl—the pretty brunette with the big blue eyes was in almost every photo—was *that* Brynna Meyers? Your girlfriend?"

He shrugged again. "Yeah. We had a little camp romance. Nothing more." He peered at her. "Did you *read* the letters too?"

She glanced away, fiddling with a dog-eared stack of old sepia-toned photos, then barely nodded.

"You did?"

"Just one. Sorry, I didn't think it was a big deal."

He looked down at his boots. "It's not."

"Was she your first love?"

"Oh, Gina." He tugged one of her pigtails. "You're just a hopeless romantic." Then, without giving her a chance to question him further, he slid the folder under his arm and turned to leave. "Keep up the good work in here." He called out to his dog, who'd been lying in a shady spot by the barn, as he strode back out into the sunshine—as if on some official business, but really just trying to escape his nosy daughter.

As he continued toward the house with Babe at his heels, Leroy felt divided. On one hand, he was surprisingly eager to dig into the old envelope and study every bit of it . . . but on the other hand he wished he'd tossed the whole thing decades ago. For the time being, this blast from his past would have to remain securely tucked in his master bedroom—safe from the snooping eyes of his overly curious daughter. And not just Gina either, since Sophie often took it upon herself to help with the housework. How she found the time was a mystery, but he knew how she poked around. Maybe even worse than Gina! Of course, Sophie did it in a nurturing sort of way, asking why he hadn't taken his vitamins or worn the new socks she'd put in his drawer. Just like her mother.

Similar to Marcie, Sophie loved domesticity and organization. Apparently the double-wide she, her husband, Garth, and their two kids occupied over on the back slope of the vineyard wasn't enough to keep her busy. She claimed housekeeping for her dad allowed her time in the old family home. Leroy knew that, like him, Sophie loved the serene view overlooking the vineyard. And she probably appreciated a bit of solitude and quietness in lieu of her normal routine of chasing two noisy youngins. Of course, she claimed the kids needed "daddy time" with Garth when she headed over to clean.

As he peeked in the kitchen, sadly overdue for Sophie's touch, Leroy knew he should be grateful for his daughter's help. His housekeeping was pretty slack—he'd become too good at ignoring dust and dog hair and clutter. And he hated doing laundry the "right" way. Who cared if his whites turned gray? Well, besides Sophie. Unless she was in the back of the house or upstairs, she didn't appear to be around at the moment. That was good. He hadn't liked Gina snooping into his past. He didn't need Sophie sniffing around too.

Just to be safe, he tiptoed up the back staircase. He felt bad for being secretive with his girls. He had no doubts Gina had only his best interest at heart. His daughters had all been fiercely protective of him after their mother passed and news spread around that he was a bachelor. Within months, "well-meaning" matchmakers came crawling out of the woodwork. But the attempts at setting him up usually fell apart. Partly due to mismatches . . . and even more so to the "loving" intervention of his devoted girls. They were a picky bunch! Eventually he quit trying. Dating was not for him. He had had enough on his plate raising his three girls and keeping the vineyard afloat. There'd been no room for romance. And bachelorhood agreed with him. How many guys could traipse through the house with muddy work boots and not get yelled at?

His master suite was quiet and undisturbed and, to his relief, still messy. Sophie must not have been here at all. Hopefully she wasn't in the office either. He'd told her to stay home and put her feet up. Hopefully she was doing just that. Naturally, this was just one more reminder that he needed to start interviewing office managers. The sooner, the better.

He studied the thirty-year-old folder for a long moment, tempted to dump its contents onto his unmade bed and just stare . . . and wonder. But, hearing a vehicle coming up the gravel driveway, he suspected the truckload of new vineyard workers had arrived. They would need his direction for getting started on the scorched south hill. So he opened the bottom bureau drawer and slid the envelope beneath a stack of old blue jeans. He knew he'd have to deal with the letters and photos later—maybe in a ceremonial fire. Because, really, he didn't need the distractions of an old romance—and a broken heart—to haunt him again. He just didn't have time for that right now.

Chapter 6

Brynna felt strangely at ease as Jan navigated the twisty highway toward the Oregon Coast the following Saturday morning. Surprising since she'd had a full-blown panic attack just last night. After a full week of trying to concoct a viable excuse for bailing on this odd camping experience, while getting her classroom packed away, she'd been unable to come up with anything convincing. In fact, each time Brynna had raised the subject—only when other teachers weren't within listening distance—Jan would quickly derail her with packing suggestions, dietary questions, and details on arranging where to meet up on Saturday to avoid getting her vehicle and trailer stuck in Brynna's parking lot—apparently Jan wasn't too confident about her backing-up skills yet. Finally the day arrived and Brynna realized she didn't want to disappoint her friend.

So when Jan had pulled up with her red SUV and matching trailer at eight o'clock this morning, Brynna had been groggily waiting next to the street and, feeling like a sleepy transient with her overly stuffed duffel bag, she climbed in. After a brief greeting, the morning had passed quietly. With Jan intent on driving, Brynna—still suffering from her sleepless night—took a nice, long nap. When they reached the coast, Jan found a cute little coffee-house right on the water.

Sitting outside on a wooden deck overlooking the sea, Brynna removed the lid from her steaming latte, taking in a delightful sniff. Suddenly she felt inexplicably happy she hadn't pulled the plug on this trip. "The ocean looks so beautiful," she told Jan. "I'm really glad I came. Thanks for inviting me."

"Well, I know you had some doubts." Jan seemed overly focused on her blueberry muffin, meticulously breaking off a small piece.

"Really? What made you think that?" Brynna spread cream cheese on her bagel.

"Well . . ." She looked at Brynna. "I realized this trip would be way out of your comfort zone."

Brynna nodded. "That's true."

"And I'm aware that I'm not the most popular faculty member at our school."

"But you're respected," Brynna said quickly. "Maybe that's more important."

"Maybe." Jan sipped her coffee. "And besides that, you have to admit we make a pretty funny pair."

"Why's that?"

"Well, I'm sure most people would see us as complete opposites. You're usually cheerful and sweet. The children love you. The teachers too. I'm sure you could win the Miss Congeniality award at school."

Brynna rolled her eyes. "I've always been a people pleaser. I'm sure I try too hard. But I'm working on it. I want to get tougher."

"You shouldn't. Being thoughtful and kind makes you a good teacher. I hope I can learn some of that from you on this trip." Jan chuckled. "Wouldn't it be funny if I showed up at school in the fall, all goodness and light? The staff would be stunned."

"Or suspicious."

Jan nodded. "They'd probably assume I was up to something. Might be funny."

"We could make it even funnier—what if I showed up acting like you? It would be like that movie *Freaky Friday*. We could really get everyone confused."

Jan's eyes twinkled as she chuckled, and in that moment she looked about ten years younger.

"I actually don't think we're all that different," Brynna said. "We probably have more commonalities than we realize." She took a bite of her bagel.

"Maybe, but you have to admit we make a pretty funny-looking pair."

Brynna considered their appearances as she chewed. In a way, Jan's baggy jeans, oversized red sweatshirt, and white athletic shoes weren't all that different from what Brynna had on. Yet Brynna knew her faded skinny jeans, navy hoodie, and sleek Nikes looked more stylish. But who really cared? "I don't think we're a funny-looking pair. We're just campers, out on the road, enjoying the day."

"We look like Mutt and Jeff."

"Mutt and Jeff—what's that mean?" Brynna watched a line of seabirds gracefully flying over the rolling blue waves.

"They were old cartoon characters. My grandma used to tease me and my best friend. She called me Mutt and my friend, Grace, was Jeff. Grace was about your size and I was, well, as tall as I am now." Jan shrugged. "It wasn't easy being six feet tall in junior high. I wasn't just bigger than all the girls, but the boys too. I hated being such an amazon."

"I used to hate being only five feet tall. Always the shortest."

"But being small is cute and sweet. For a girl, anyway. Some of the kids used to call me Moose. That was fun." She rolled her eyes and sipped her coffee.

"Kids can be mean. And being short was like an invitation for them to treat me like a baby. It didn't help that I was perennially cheerful. I got so sick of being patted on the head or called a 'good little girl.' Even Dirk did that."

"Yeah, I've noticed some of the teachers at our school do too. Men particularly. But I don't think they're putting you down. More likely they're flirting. Like Rick Reynolds. I know he's had his eye on you."

"And that's another thing. I hate it when guys think that I need someone to take care of me. Like, *Let's help the little woman.* It's infuriating. Even if I get mad, some guys think I'm just trying to be cute. I get so sick of it!"

"So maybe being petite has shortcomings too." Jan grinned. "Sorry for the pun. I can see how your height might be a challenge, after all."

"And not just for reaching things up high. As an adult, I have often been mistaken for a child—forced to show ID." She paused to sip her coffee. "I'll admit it's more flattering as I get older. But not always."

"Being tall has gotten easier with age. It probably earns me some respect."

"That must be nice. Being short is still a pain. And ever since my divorce, it seems to invite the wrong sort of men."

"What do you mean?"

"Well, I actually made some attempts at dating this past year." Brynna grimaced to think of some of the situations she'd been in. "Some were setups from friends—at least, I thought they were friends. And I even joined an online Christian dating site. But almost every date was a disaster."

"And you blame that on your height?" Jan looked confused.

"Sort of. It goes like this. Everything might sound good online or texting, and then I actually meet the guy. Oh, he'll give me a compliment, but it's always tied to the fact that I'm short. One guy even said I was 'cute as a bug.' He said it a few times. And then it will feel like they think they have the upper hand. They might get patronizing or protective. Like my size makes them the big man. It's so irritating. It's why I just don't care to date anymore. I'm almost convinced that all men are jerks."

"Oh, they can't all be jerks," Jan said, then finished her muffin.

"I know . . . my brother's okay. And my dad was a really good man."

"And so was my Burt." Jan looked out over the water with a dreamy expression.

"You mean, early on . . . *before* you split up?"

"Split up?"

Brynna felt confused. "Aren't you divorced?"

Jan slowly shook her head. "What made you think that?"

"I don't know. I guess you never really spoke about it before. I just assumed."

"Well, I like to keep my private life private. At least at school." She sighed. "Burt died about ten years after we were married."

"I'm sorry. I didn't realize."

"Yes, well, it's not a story I like to tell."

"Then I won't ask." Brynna picked up her coffee.

"Thank you. So, back to Mutt and Jeff," Jan said lightly. "I've come to accept there's an upside to being tall. Pun intended. But even more so after hearing about your troubles. I had no idea."

Brynna nodded. "Be thankful you don't have to put up with that kind of nonsense from men. I have to admit that I'm envious of how the opposite sex seem to respect you. I know it's partly because you're tall. Maybe they're afraid you'll deck them."

"Maybe that's why they call me Sergeant Bart behind my back." Brynna grimaced. "You know about that?"

"Of course." She smiled. "But it doesn't bother me. After all, I really was a sergeant."

"Huh?"

"I was in the army. Both Burt and I came from lower-income families, and we were academic but we couldn't afford college tuition. We actually met at an army recruiting meeting at our high school. We started dating after that, and then we both decided to enlist. We'd do our time with Uncle Sam and then get help with our tuition bills."

"I had no idea."

"We went in straight out of high school. After boot camp, we were both deployed in the Middle East to different units. But we stayed in touch. We got married after our terms ended, then came home and did college. Burt became a CPA, and I started teaching. We bought our house and, for a while, thought we had the world by the tail." She finished her coffee. "Then the tail came off." She glanced at her Fitbit. "Well, if we want to stay on schedule and reach our campground by four like I planned, we better skedaddle."

Back in the car, Brynna considered what Jan had just disclosed. She'd been in the army, maybe even active service. And she was widowed, not divorced. There also seemed to be a tragic tale concerning Burt's death. They'd had a good relationship but it was cut short. So sad. There was obviously a lot more to Jan than Brynna had realized. She wondered if she'd hear the rest of it before this camping trip ended.

Chapter 7

The manila envelope had resided untouched at the bottom of Leroy's jeans drawer for a full week now. A very full week. Every single day had been busy from sunup to sundown. Sunday had been his nephews' high school graduation party. The twins, Taylor and Tyler, had graduated last Friday, but the family celebration at Damico's had taken up the better part of the day. Then, first thing Monday, Leroy began interviewing for the office manager position. Unsuccessfully. Added to that, he'd spent time training and supervising the new vineyard crew. Plus, he'd helped Garth organize an export shipment of pinot noir. And now perhaps most concerning, he had to ensure that Gina's new tasting room, which Garth had dubbed the Pour House, didn't actually land them *in* the poor house.

"New plumbing and electric?" he asked after Gina shared the contractor's estimates she'd just received. "I thought this was going to be a *rustic* setup. Just a few visitors tasting some wine in the barn. No big deal. Why do we need new wiring and plumbing?"

"Because right now, we only have two electrical outlets and two wired-in lights in the whole barn. And for water, we have the hose outlet *outside.*"

"So, what's wrong with that?" He glanced over to where Babe

was comfortably situated on a new dog bed that Gina must've tucked into a back corner. Nice touch. "This is a barn, after all."

"Seriously, Dad?" Her eyes gleamed with irritation. "I thought you understood the plan. It's a barn that is being renovated into a tasting room. *Remember?*"

Instead of responding, he glared down at the barn's shiny wood floor then over to a corner where Gina had already arranged a few pieces of furniture. He couldn't deny the place was looking pretty good. And the display of wine bottles on the back wall behind the tasting counter looked like a work of art. But these bids for work were not only unexpected, they were downright exorbitant.

He shook the bids at Gina. "Is this what it really costs to put up a few more lights and install a sink for washing glasses? Because it's perfectly ridiculous!"

"I got several bids. They're not that much different from each—"

"Well then, I'm in the wrong business, Gina. I should be a plumber or electrician. And, really, if I had more time, I could probably just do it all myself—for free! But I'm too busy. Besides this is supposed to be your project."

"It is my project, Dad. And I'm trying to handle it. And FYI, the bids aren't just for lights and a sink. They also include restrooms and a—"

"Restrooms? Are you kidding? If we actually get anyone to come out here to visit the tasting room, let 'em use the outhouses—"

"*Dad!* You can't expect guests to use the work crew outhouses."

"This is getting too elaborate, Gina. And way too expensive. There's no reason it should cost this much." He handed the bids back to her. "My answer is no."

Gina took in a deep breath, signaling this battle wasn't over yet. "The other reason these bids are so high is because this includes a kitchenette. With a fridge and dishwasher and—"

"We do not have that kind of a budget." He knew his voice was too loud, but he couldn't help it. Gina might be stubborn, but so was he. He'd already told her that the vineyard's finances were extra tight this year. "You do understand that I still need to hire a new office manager and the south vineyard won't produce—"

"But don't you understand that we're building for the future, Dad? In order to do that, we have to invest in the present. It's just a business fact."

"Where are you getting your business information, anyway? The *New York Times*? *Forbes*? This is Sonoma, Gina. Not Bordeaux or Tuscany. We'll never be able to compete with places like Chateau Montelena. We're not a fancy vineyard, and that's the way I like it." He ran his fingers through his hair, lowering his voice. "I'm sorry, but we'll just have to make do with a *rustic* tasting room. Seems to me that's what you said it would be originally."

She frowned but said nothing.

"Or *no* tasting room at all," he said firmly.

"Fine. I guess it'll just be a rustic old-world tasting room with no modern conveniences whatsoever." She brightened slightly. "Hey, maybe that's what I'll really call it. Sorrentino's *Old-World* Tasting Room. And I'll keep everything in there old-world and rustic."

"Yeah, that's what I thought you were doing." He felt relief rush over him.

"It is. I plan to enlarge some of the old photos too. Get them stretched onto canvas to put on the walls," she said. "Unless you think that's too expensive."

"That's probably okay." He knew he needed to give her some concessions.

"And I'll still recycle a lot. I can probably rig up some kind of makeshift sink. Maybe use an old metal tub. But I'll have to bring the glasses into the house to wash in the dishwasher. Do you mind?"

"Not if it saves me tens of thousands of dollars." He smiled. "And who knows, the rustic bit might be a novelty for your visitors."

She rolled her eyes. "Yeah, I'm sure they'll think that using an outhouse is really novel."

"Well, for now, it'll have to do."

"For now." She nodded with a determined look. "But someday, Dad—you'll see. We'll bring Sorrentino's into the new millennium." She grinned. "Without sacrificing the good old days."

"Well, I'll be impressed if you can make this work. I mean, with what you have to work with. And if it doesn't, well, at least I got my barn all cleaned out. Could always use this space to store barrels. Garth would like that. He mentioned he needs more room."

"That's so not happening." She made a face and socked him in the arm. "Speaking of Garth, Sophie was just in here. She left Lucy and Addison with Garth this morning. She plans to attack your house."

"Attack?" He tried to conceal his alarm.

"Yeah, she saw how filthy it was the other day. In fact, she raked me over the coals for how nasty the laundry room has gotten since I came home. Like it's my fault." She rolled her eyes. "She seems to think that part of my job description should involve keeping house for you, but I told her I've got enough to do out here."

"Well, she's probably right. We've been living like a couple of pigs, Gina. We could both stand to brush up on our domestic skills." He remembered the manila envelope in his drawer. Hopefully Sophie hadn't put any freshly laundered jeans in there and spotted it. "Well, maybe I should go talk to your sister. It's sweet she wants to help, but she shouldn't overdo it. I'm not looking for a new office manager just so that she can become our full-time housekeeper."

Going into the house, he wondered how he'd explain the letters and photos to Sophie—if she'd discovered them. Of all three daughters, Sophie had always been the most intrusive when it came to his love life. Not that he'd had much of one this past decade. But the idea of being questioned by Sophie about an old romance . . . well, he just didn't need that at the moment.

She wasn't in the laundry room or kitchen when he checked, although she'd clearly been there. As he hurried up the stairs, he heard her music drifting from the master suite. As usual, she had her iPhone playing her favorite tunes while she cleaned. She reminded him of Marcie in that way—a love of music and house-cleaning. It was actually rather sweet.

"Hey, Sophie," he said as he found her plumping a bed pillow. "What's up?"

"Just some much-needed housecleaning, Dad." She tossed the pillow against the headboard. "Man, you and Gina are hopeless. And helpless."

"That doesn't mean you have to step in and rescue us. The reason I agreed to hire the new office manager was to give you some downtime before the baby comes." He glanced to the bureau and the empty laundry basket next to it. "I don't want you overdoing it." He picked up the basket. "Did any of my jeans get washed? I'm down to the last pair."

"They're in the dryer right now."

He felt relieved as he gathered up the pile of dirty sheets and towels she'd heaped by the bathroom. "Well, let me get these for you."

"Thanks, Dad, but it's not like I'm an invalid. I'm just pregnant." She peered curiously at him.

"I know, honey, but I really don't want you thinking you're the maid—"

"I *love* coming here. And Garth was happy to keep the kids today. You guys were so busy that he barely saw them all week. Cleaning your house doesn't really feel like work. There's no one tugging on me or distracting me . . . it's quiet and peaceful." She smoothed the comforter. "Please, don't say I can't come here to clean, Dad."

He sighed. "As long as you don't wear yourself out."

"Well, I wouldn't mind if you and Gina picked up a bit," she said as she was heading out. "The laundry room was almost impassable."

"We've had a busy week." He followed her downstairs, setting the laundry basket on the kitchen island.

"And the dishes in the kitchen sink looked like they'd been there awhile."

"Sorry. I'll tell Gina we have to do better." He smiled. "Thanks, Sophie. You're a treasure."

She pushed a caramel-colored curl away from her face and sighed. She was so much like her mother. Not that he planned to say as much since she never seemed to appreciate the comparison.

"Well, I'll leave you to it." He thanked her again, then shot back up the stairs, closing and even locking the master bedroom door. Then he went straight to his jeans drawer and, relieved to see the envelope still beneath the last pair of clean jeans, he pulled it out.

"Brynna Meyers," he said the name aloud as he dumped the contents onto the freshly made bed. "Wonder what she's up to these days."

Chapter 8

As Jan drove south on Highway 1, she went over their camping itinerary, telling Brynna exactly how long they would stay at each campground, how many hours of traveling time in between, and the various sites she hoped to see along the way. They made several pit stops along the coast—lighthouses, blowholes, and other points of interest that Jan had marked on her map. They had lunch in Depot Bay, enjoying some whale watching from the bridge. As they walked back to the SUV, Brynna offered to drive, but felt relieved when Jan declined. She made it look easy to drive with a trailer trailing behind them, but Brynna wasn't so sure.

Finally, it was midafternoon and something about the stretch of road felt familiar. "Either I'm having déjà vu or I've been down this road before," Brynna said as a rocky strip of coastline came into view again. "I feel like I've been in this very place."

"I thought you said you'd only vacationed up north." Jan slowed down so a motorcycle could pass them.

"That's right. Mostly the Cannon Beach area. And Dirk took me to Seaside a couple of times. But I did go to a camp in high school. It was before my senior year . . . in late August." Brynna tried to remember. "It was somewhere on the coast, but I honestly can't remember where. Mostly I recall the long, horrible drive in a crowded van with a bunch of rowdy church kids—and being totally miserable."

"Why were you so miserable?"

"It feels pretty silly now." Brynna rolled her eyes. "But I was pining away for Dirk."

"Dirk your ex?" Jan glanced at her.

"Yep. He was supposed to have gone on the trip with me. In fact, he was the only reason I was going at all. But at the last minute, he canceled without even telling me. To make matters worse, he gave his friend Rod a note to hand-deliver to me, but he told him not to give it to me until we were safely on our way. It was a break-up note."

"That's real classy."

"Yeah. So there I was, trying not to cry in front of a bunch of kids I barely knew. They were Dirk's church friends and naturally, they wondered what was up with me, and why Dirk wasn't there."

"Uh-huh."

"Fortunately, Rod tried to cover. He made up some story about Dirk having to work for his dad to make some last-minute college money. Dirk was about to leave for OSU. Rod admitted to me later that Dirk was actually having a summer fling with a cheerleader friend of mine. Jenny Maxwell. At least, I'd thought she was my friend."

"And you still married the guy?"

She sighed. "It's embarrassing to admit that now."

Neither spoke for a few miles, and Brynna tried to wipe the negative Dirk memories from her mind. What a waste of brain space!

"So, anyway, you think that camp was around here somewhere?" Jan asked.

"It really seems like it. But honestly, it's one of those things I've tried to forget. I can't even recall the name of the camp."

"How long were you there?"

"Two weeks."

"So you stayed for the whole session?"

"I didn't really have a choice. My parents had taken a cruise that coincided with the camp dates." Brynna's memory seemed to light up. "But there was one bright spot during those two weeks. Something I'd almost forgotten."

"What was that?"

"A boy." She sighed to recall the sweet guy who'd befriended her.

"Dirk's friend? Rod?"

"No. Rod was a total goofball. It was Leroy."

"Leroy." Jan chuckled. "Sounds like a hillbilly. Or an old man."

"That's exactly what I said the first time we met. But he told me his mom named him after some French ancestor, and that she pronounced it *Lah*-roy." Brynna laughed. "He hated that so I would jokingly call him Lah-roy with a French accent. At first he got mad, but then it became our private joke. 'Oh, *Lah-roy*,' I'd call out. And that darling boy would just come a'running."

"So Leroy was your bright spot."

"Yeah . . ." Brynna sighed again.

Jan glanced at her. "That should help dispel your 'all men are jerks' philosophy."

"Yeah, I can't imagine that Leroy ever became a jerk." Brynna felt surprised she'd nearly forgotten about him. To be honest, Leroy had been more than just a bright spot . . . but that was so long ago.

"Well, I'd really love to hear more about your *Lah*-roy boy, but that's the exit sign for our campground up ahead." Jan slowed down. "Sounds like we'll have lots of stories to share 'round the campfire tonight."

"For sure." Brynna gazed curiously around as Jan pulled up at a log cabin with a CAMP REGISTRATION sign in front. Something about this place felt familiar. But as Jan went to check them in, Brynna began obsessing over thoughts of Leroy. It was as if some secret chamber inside of her had opened and memories were flooding in.

What a fun couple of weeks they'd shared together! At first Leroy had seemed the perfect remedy to recover from selfish, arrogant, egomaniac Dirk. Really, she couldn't imagine two guys being more total opposites. But it didn't take long for her friendship with Leroy to transform into something more. And when the camp session ended, it was hard to say goodbye. But they promised to stay in touch. Leroy gave her his college address and she gave him her home address.

They even talked about the possibility of attending the same college after she graduated high school. They'd assured each other it was only a temporary parting, and yet, as fate would have it, the separation was permanent. About thirty years permanent by now. But still, she wondered . . . what had become of sweet Leroy?

Chapter 9

Leroy took his time going through his envelope of memorabilia. He started with the bright-yellow Kodak folder, removing the prints one by one, closely studying each one, then laying them out across his bed in what felt like a chronological order. At least, to the best of his memory, which seemed pretty clear at the moment. Even though it had been almost thirty years, it was all rushing back to him.

The first print in the lineup was a candid shot of Brynna with what looked like a notebook balanced on her knees. The pretty brunette was sitting on a bench outside the mess hall with her knees pulled up to her chest as she chewed on a pencil. He later learned that the book was her journal and that she loved to write and hoped to someday become a journalist.

"Who said you can take my picture?" she'd snapped at him when she saw his camera aimed at her. Even when she glared, there was an unmistakable sweetness to her face. He'd seen her earlier that day, but she seemed sad and withdrawn, as if she didn't want to be at the camp. For that matter, he hadn't wanted to go either, but it had been a graduation gift from his grandmother. She'd sent Leroy's dad there years ago—for his own graduation. And the camp was actually pretty cool. Situated by a coastal lake, the camp offered boating and fishing. And there were surfboards available for those who wanted to take on the ocean, plus a nine-hole golf course, and a number of other activities. But it was the petite brunette girl who'd really captured his attention.

Leroy smiled, feeling sheepish as he approached her, first apologizing, then quickly explaining how he'd gotten the 35-millimeter Canon for graduation and that he really liked photography. "You looked so photogenic sitting there on the bench with the old building behind you. But my apologies. I should've asked first. Forgive me?"

She had softened and, setting her journal down on her lap, smiled up at him. And that was it—he'd been smitten. That sparkling smile and those incredibly blue eyes—and he was a goner.

He picked up the next photo. It had been taken just moments later. This time with her permission. Fully cooperating, she'd posed next to a tall carved bear statue on the porch of the mess hall—making a face like she was terrified. By then they'd exchanged names and she'd teased him about his name, saying it sounded like an old man. Then he'd told her about his maternal grandfather and how his name was Leroy Boucher, but feeling silly, he'd pronounced it like his mom often did, with an affected French accent. *Lah*-roy *Booshay*. Of course, Brynna thought that was hilarious and started calling him *Lah*-roy—with an accent too.

He studied the photos of Brynna on the beach. What a day that'd been. He'd lured her out with the excuse of needing a subject for some seaside pictures, taking her ankle-deep in the surf and posing her on a huge piece of driftwood. He remembered dragging a slimy piece of seaweed toward her with a menacing expression. There was a photo of her back, sitting in the front of the canoe he'd been paddling—and another one, probably moments later, when she'd turned around and stuck out her tongue.

He looked at photos of her eating ice cream and one where she'd posed like Robin Hood, complete with the hat, at the archery range. There were several shots of her in a swimsuit with a surfboard, and even one of him that she'd taken. They were both dry and smiling. Then the picture of them together after a day of surfing lessons, where they looked wet, cold, and bedraggled. There were several good shots of Brynna by a big bonfire on the beach. And then there was one that someone had taken of the two of them dressed up for the last-night-of-camp dance. She had on a pretty sundress the same color as her eyes. She was tanned and smiling and beautiful. With her hair pinned up, she looked older. That was the night when he'd kissed her . . . and not just once.

"Dad?" It sounded like Gina. By the way she was pounding on the master bedroom door, it had to be urgent. "Dad! Are you in there?"

"Coming!" He grabbed the photos and the envelope, shoving them beneath a pillow before he hurried to open the door.

"What's wrong?" he demanded. "Is the place on fire?"

"No." She held up his phone. "But Luna's been trying to reach you all morning. She finally texted me and said you weren't answering your phone, which I found on the counter in the bottling room." She thrust it at him. "Please, call her ASAP." Her eyes seemed to light up to something on the floor. "Oh?" She zipped past him and snatched up a photo that must've slipped out in his rush. "Aha—taking a sentimental journey, are we?"

He scowled then, focused on his phone, and called his middle daughter. Hopefully Gina would take the hint and make herself scarce. But as he talked to Luna, relieved to hear there was no real emergency, Gina remained fixed in his room. Still holding the picture, she went over to the easy chair by his big window and made herself at home, humming quietly like she was in no hurry.

"Well, that's fine," he finally told Luna. "Thanks for letting me know." He told her goodbye, hung up, then turned to Gina with narrowed eyes.

"Is everything okay?" she asked in a playful tone. She'd obviously heard the conversation.

"Luna just wanted me to know she won't be here tomorrow like she'd planned." He folded his arms across his chest, studying his daughter and wondering if she already knew all about her sister's plans. "In fact, she won't be home all summer. She's been offered a job in a law office in San Francisco and—"

"I know, Dad." Gina grinned. "Just messing with you." She held up the photo of him and Brynna, dressed for the dance. She waved it in the air like a victory flag. "She really was pretty. So, tell me, were you in love?"

He gave her his sternest warning look. "I thought I taught my girls to respect their parents and—"

"I do respect you."

"Then respect my privacy."

"I do. I'm just curious. And FYI, I didn't even tell Sophie or Luna about your mysterious romantic past."

"Thanks, but there's nothing mysterious about it." He went over and plucked the photo from her hand. "Don't you have work to do? What am I paying you for, anyway?"

"Yeah, right." She stood. "But when the boss runs off without his phone, I get distracted from my work. And I have to run over here to—"

"Fine, fine, little Miss Nosy Pants." He tweaked one of her pigtails. "Then why don't you get back to it before your boss gives you your walking papers."

"You can't fire me. I'm family." She smirked as she left. Yes, Gina could be irritating and nosy and a little too mouthy, but she was his baby girl. And at least she hadn't mentioned anything about the envelope's contents to her sisters. That was worth something. Some stories were meant to be kept private.

He retrieved the rumpled envelope from beneath the pillow, carefully sliding the pictures back into the Kodak folder, but as he put them away, he thought about those letters from Brynna . . . Did he really want to read them again or would that just stir up old hurt? And what was the point of that? Except that it aggravated him that Gina had read one. He wanted to read them again just to know what was going through her overly active imagination. He started to pull one out, but hearing Sophie yelling up the stairs for him—wanting to know what was going on with Luna—he knew this wasn't the time to continue this "sentimental journey," as Gina had put it. Daughters! Can't live with them—wouldn't live without them.

"Coming, Sophie," he called back. And since his bed had already been neatly made, he slid his "mystery" packet under the mattress, reminding himself he'd need to find a better hiding place soon . . . maybe the fireplace later this evening. But only after he knew that Gina was safely to bed.

Chapter 10

As Jan slowly drove through Surfside Shores Campgrounds, Brynna experienced an increasing sense of déjà vu. And then she saw it—the same old dining hall with the tall carved bear on the porch. Except now the sign hanging above the front door said CAMP STORE AND RESTAURANT. But everything else looked exactly the same.

"This is it!" she shrieked—and Jan hit the brakes.

"What?" Jan looked around in alarm. "This can't be it. We're not even to the campsite section yet. What're you talking about?"

"I'm sorry, Jan. I mean, *this is the camp*. This is the same camp! The one I told you about, where I came in high school. This is it!"

"You're kidding. The camp with Lah-roy?"

"Yes." Brynna nodded in amazement. "I recognize the dining hall and the bear on the porch. And there's the flagpole and the wooden bench and—" She pointed to the right. "Even the original cabins are over there. I stayed in Seahorse Cabin."

"Yes. I saw those on the website. They rent them for fifty dollars a night, but they looked pretty rustic. My trailer's much nicer."

"I can't believe it. This is the *same* camp."

Jan continued to drive. "Was it called Surfside Shores then?"

"No. But that's close." Brynna tried to think as she looked

around. Some things looked familiar. Some not so much. "Camp Surfside. That's what it was called. And they even had surfing lessons. I spent a whole day trying to master it, but nearly had hypothermia by the time I gave up. Fortunately someone had a big bonfire going on the beach." She sighed. "It was really a fun time."

"Okay, I want to hear more about it later." Jan was navigating the narrow road that meandered through the RV camp spots. "But for now, I want you to watch for space 53."

"This used to be a wide-open area." Brynna tried to imagine the sports fields as she watched the site numbers. "Room for soccer and softball and archery . . . They even had an amphitheater."

"Sounds like a fun place. Wonder why they changed it to an RV park."

"Probably more profitable." Brynna pointed to an empty site. "There. Space 53."

"Great. Now I need you to help me back in. They told me it's a pretty tight squeeze."

"Sure." Remembering how she helped Jan park at Depot Bay, Brynna felt a bit more confident as she got out. She directed her with waves and hand signals, and after a couple of crooked attempts, the trailer was finally in place.

"Thanks." Jan checked to make sure the trailer was well situated. After emptying some things from the Yukon, Jan unhitched the trailer, then handed Brynna the keys. "This space is so small, they told me to park in the lot near the entrance. We're supposed to pick up a parking pass at the general store. Why don't you take care of that while I set up camp? Feel free to check the place out on your way back."

"You don't need my help?"

"Nah. I'm sure you're curious about your old stomping grounds." Brynna nodded. "Might be interesting."

As she drove to the general store, Brynna took in her surroundings. Much had changed, but there were some familiar spots. The swimming pool was still there, but the old craft shack had been transformed into a cute coffeehouse. After she parked the Yukon, she decided to use the restroom, but as she walked by the busy pool, the sounds of kids' voices and splashing was like slipping through a time warp. Had it really been nearly thirty years? At the store, she got the parking pass as well as a souvenir carved wooden bear, a miniature of the one on the front porch.

As she walked toward the lake, she felt that same insecure seventeen-year-old girl lurking inside of her . . . as if no time had passed. She almost looked over her shoulder to see if Leroy was running to catch up with her, calling out for her to wait up. She remembered the first time Leroy had bashfully reached for her hand, keeping his eyes downward. It was on this very same path to the lake. After they got into their canoe and rowed out to the middle of the water, he'd shyly confessed he'd had only one girlfriend before. It hadn't been serious—just a girl his mom had pressured him to take to prom. Their families were friends, and the girl was nice . . . but he'd assured her he had no interest in her.

In return, she'd told him a bit about Dirk. Not much though. She purposely kept it brief since she was determined to wipe her unfaithful boyfriend out of her memory once and for all. After three years of off-and-on dating—and too many tears—she was finished. And that's exactly what she'd told Leroy.

Today the lake gleamed in the afternoon sunlight. Several rowboats, canoes, and kayaks lazily drifted by the docks. After giving up on their less-than-successful surfing lessons, she and Leroy had gotten interested in canoeing. And he didn't even mention her wimpy paddling skills, but she noticed how he compensated with his own more muscular strokes—two for her one and changing sides more often. In fact, Leroy was the only guy she could recall who hadn't made a big deal about her small stature. Despite being a full foot taller, he never made her feel childish or small. He never teased or attempted to take the upper hand. He'd always treated her with respect.

These memories were surprisingly pleasant, but Brynna knew

it was time to get back to their campsite. She shouldn't have abandoned Jan to set up camp alone. But as she hurried back to the RV camp area, Brynna felt glad—once again—that she'd agreed to come on this trip. Oh, sure, it still felt a bit weird to be camping with Sergeant Bart. But something about the conversations today, then being here at this old familiar camp, remembering a happy couple of weeks of her life . . . well, it felt strangely cathartic.

By the time she reached the campsite, Jan appeared to have it all under control. She was even chopping kindling and tossing it into the small firepit. And the trailer's striped awning was out, with a pair of matching red camp chairs beneath it. Even the picnic table looked nice with a checkered tablecloth secured from the sea breeze by the two geranium pots Jan had gotten at Riverside Gardens.

"Nice campsite you got here." Brynna grinned.

"Thanks. Home sweet home." Jan sank the small ax into a large piece of wood. "And we made a friend."

"*We* did?" Brynna blinked.

"Apparently this guy—Mike—passed us on the highway a couple of times today. He has a royal blue Harley. I'm calling him Motorcycle Mike." She chuckled. "Anyway, it seems he followed us here."

"Followed us? Like a stalker?" she teased.

"No. He seems safe enough." She nodded to her right. "He's camping over in the tent area."

"Uh-huh?" Brynna wasn't sure where this was going. It seemed unlike Jan to be friendly with a motorcycle dude.

"Anyway, he brought us this firewood." Jan pointed to the small pile, then lowered her voice. "And then he asked if he could visit our campfire later on." She pushed messy damp hair away from her brow. "I didn't know what to say."

Brynna frowned. "That seems kind of forward." Maybe he really was a stalker.

"Yeah, I sort of thought so too. But he told me his campsite doesn't have a firepit."

"So?"

Jan shrugged. "So, I agreed."

"And you're okay with it? You're not worried he might be a creep or something?"

"I know how to defend myself." Jan picked up the ax with a threatening look.

Brynna felt her eyes grow wide.

"Just kidding, Brynna. But, no, I'm not worried. He seems okay. And he did give us this firewood." She returned to chopping kindling. "So did you enjoy your walk around the campground? Was it a real blast from the past?"

"It was pretty interesting." Not ready to talk about it, Brynna glanced around the well-organized site. "Looks like you got everything under control, but is there anything I can do to help?"

"Not out here. I got the trailer jacks down and everything leveled and the wheels secured. The water and electric are hooked up. Easy breezy."

Brynna didn't think it sounded that easy. "Well, next time I'll be sure to stick around and learn how to do that stuff."

"That's probably a good idea."

Brynna felt guilty. "I don't want to be a freeloader. There must be something I can do to help."

Jan's brows arched hopefully. "How are you at cooking?"

"Cooking?" Brynna considered this. "To be honest, Dirk didn't appreciate my cooking skills. But, then, he was a very picky eater. He'd prefer powdered protein drink to a hot bowl of homemade chili."

"You're kidding. I love chili."

"Me too." Brynna smiled. "And I actually *like* to cook."

"Well, I hate it." Jan made a face. "How about you take that chore?"

"Okay . . ." Brynna glanced toward the trailer with its pint-size kitchen.

"Really?" Jan brightened. "You wouldn't mind?"

"Not if you don't." Brynna couldn't handle any more criticism over her culinary skills. It was one of the best things about Dirk leaving.

"I'd be relieved to leave the cooking to you," Jan assured her. "The kitchen is all stocked. Well, at least enough for a few days anyway. We can hit grocery stores along the way as needed. And there's a camp store here if you're missing anything vital."

Brynna still felt uncertain. What kind of expectations would Jan have? What if she was used to fine cuisine? Or worse, what if she was a picky eater like Dirk? "Honestly, I haven't cooked much. I mean since my divorce. And I've never been what you'd call a serious foodie."

"That's okay. And I don't mind doing dishes. That's how Burt and I used to do it. He'd cook something great, and I'd clean up afterward."

Something great? What did that mean? Brynna flashed back to Dirk and how he'd throw a fit if she cooked something with onions or garlic or celery. Plus, he hated all vegetables. Sometimes he'd even claim food allergies just to get out of trying a new recipe. It made her hate the kitchen. "So, uh, are you a picky eater?"

"No, not at all. Burt had a rule. If I complained about the food, I'd have to cook the next meal. I learned to keep my mouth shut. But honestly, I like almost anything."

"That's reassuring."

"And if you like to grill, there's a little fold-down propane barbecue right there." She pointed to the side of the trailer. "Grilling was Burt's job too. Not because I didn't try. But when I grilled, the food either turned out raw or blackened. Burt finally told me to forget it."

"Grilling sounds like fun." Brynna suddenly felt hungry. "Guess I better check out the kitchen."

"It's small."

She laughed. "The whole trailer is small."

"I figured we can do our eating outside. After all, we are camping."

"Works for me." Brynna stepped into the trailer to see that Jan had already transformed the small dining area into what appeared to be a fairly comfortable bed, complete with a couple of pillows and a fluffy plaid comforter, with Brynna's duffel bag on top.

Soon, she was poking around the kitchen, seeing that it really was nicely stocked. Jan might not like to cook, but she was good at getting the right stuff. The fridge had milk, eggs, several cheeses, yogurt, deli meats, hamburger, veggies, fruits—and the cupboards had staples like pancake mix and syrup, oatmeal packets, cans of soup, containers of rice and beans, and lots of other things. There was even a small spice rack. They certainly wouldn't starve. But what to cook for their first night out?

Seeing it was already close to six, Brynna decided on a meal that wouldn't take too long to cook. Who didn't like burgers on the grill? And instead of just making two burgers, she made several patties. Leftovers could make for a good lunch tomorrow. Then she threw together a pretty fruit salad. Next, she sliced tomatoes, onions, pickles, and lettuce, making a topping plate for the burgers. It wasn't easy working in the tiny kitchen with limited counter space, but she knew she could get used to it in time.

With Jan's help, they got the grill set up, and as the burgers started to sizzle, Brynna brought the rest of the meal and place settings outside to the table.

"This all looks just great." Jan nodded in approval. "Plenty of food too."

"I made extra so we could have leftovers for lunch tomorrow."

"Good idea. This cooking arrangement is going to be perfect."

"Thanks." Brynna turned to check the grill and was just flipping the burgers when she heard a man's voice calling out a greeting.

"It's Motorcycle Mike," Jan said.

Brynna turned around to see a large guy approaching. He had

a full beard and an armload of firewood. "Thought I should bring some more wood for tonight's fire."

As he set the wood down, Jan introduced them. Although he seemed friendly enough, Brynna wasn't sure. Her first night of "real" camping put her on high alert, and Motorcycle Mike's multiple tattoos, man bun, and single gold earring weren't helping.

"Man, something smells good." He leaned over Brynna's shoulder to peek at the smoking grill.

"Just burgers," Brynna said quietly.

"Well, you ladies know how to camp." He walked around the small site then went over to where Jan was seated in a camp chair. "Nice little setup you got here."

"We've got plenty of food." Jan glanced over at Brynna. "Maybe we should invite Motorcycle Mike to join us."

Brynna tried to hide her doubts. After all, this was Jan's trailer and Jan's food. Who was Brynna to object? "Sure, why not?" She forced a smile, glancing at the hatchet still by the woodpile. Hopefully Jan wouldn't need it for self-defense.

"Brynna's in charge of cooking," Jan told Mike as he sat down in the other chair. "I'm on cleanup crew."

"Nice arrangement. Wish I had a cook to travel with me."

"On your motorcycle?" Brynna asked him.

"It's big enough for two." He winked. "Especially if the rider's not too big."

"How do you pack camping gear?" Jan asked.

"I have some compartments and saddlebags. Just have to make sure to roll my tent and sleeping bag up tight then pack it all just right."

As Brynna set the plate of burgers and an extra place setting on the table, Mike grinned at her. "Looks good enough to eat, Half Pint."

Brynna grimaced but said nothing.

"Brynna doesn't like being teased for her small stature," Jan told him in a no-nonsense voice—as if her inner vice principal had just been reawakened.

"Oh, my bad." Mike apologetically tipped his head to Brynna. "Please, forgive me. You see, when I was a kid, I used to watch *Little House on the Prairie* with my single mom. She loved that show. To be honest, I did too. I used to imagine that Michael Landon was my dad." He shrugged shyly. "And I liked how he called Laura Half Pint."

Brynna felt herself warming to Mike as they all sat down. He suddenly reminded her of a big, sweet teddy bear. "I used to watch reruns of that show after school. I guess Half Pint's not such a bad nickname."

He brightened. "It's actually a compliment. I had a major crush on Laura Ingalls aka Melissa Gilbert."

"I had a thing for her brother Albert." Jan laughed as she dipped a spoon into the fruit salad bowl. "This looks great, Brynna."

"Thanks." Brynna reached for the topping plate.

"How about I say a blessing first?" Mike said quietly. Both Brynna and Jan looked at him in surprise, but Jan agreed that was a nice idea.

"Dear mighty lord of the universe," Mike began in a deep voice, "we thank you for all your good blessings. We thank you for the summer sunshine and tall pine trees and the big, blue ocean. We thank you for our safe trip on the road and our nice campsites. We thank you for our newfound friends and a good campfire tonight. We pray your blessings on this fine meal and on the hands that prepared it. Amen."

As they began to eat, Brynna felt bad for the way she'd misjudged Motorcycle Mike earlier. It seemed he was a genuinely nice guy who took his faith seriously. Besides the relief that Jan wouldn't need to defend them with her little hatchet, it was refreshing to meet a man who wasn't a jerk.

Chapter 11

Leroy had barely lit a fire in the big stone fireplace when Gina came padding down the stairs. Past eleven and she wasn't asleep? Without looking her way, he stashed the envelope of Brynna memorabilia beneath a throw on the ottoman. Hopefully she was headed to the kitchen for a late-night snack.

But no such luck. In her plaid pajama shorts and a raggedy T-shirt, Gina peered down at him with a curious expression. "What's up?" In one hand she had her e-Pad and in the other her cell phone. "Mind if I join you?"

"You're welcome to, but I don't know about your electronic friends there." He frowned at her gadgets.

"Oh, Dad." She rolled her eyes as she flopped down on the worn leather sofa right next to him. "A summer fire?"

"The house felt a little chilly." He glanced nervously at the throw concealing the envelope. "So, what brings you down here this late?"

"Well, I heard you thumping around and thought you might be interested to see the website. I was just doing some final tweaks, and I'd like to launch it." She smiled. "With your approval."

"Right now?"

"Come on, Dad." She held up her pad. "Just take a peek."

He nodded reluctantly, waiting as she turned her e-Pad on then handed it to him. Navigating him through the site, she explained how she'd arranged it and why she'd kept it simple. Although he wanted to keep this short, he was impressed with how good everything looked. "And you removed those old pictures of me—like I asked?" That had been one of his conditions. He hadn't liked seeing himself plastered all over the website. Especially since the photos had been taken years ago.

"Yeah, yeah. But you better let me take some new ones soon. The website should have at least a couple of you. After all, you're the star."

"Sorrentino's is a *family* business," he reminded her.

"I know, I know." She yawned. "Just tell me whether or not you approve. It's late, but I really want to launch this tonight."

"What's the rush?"

"For starters, it's tourist season. Then there's the anniversary celebration and our new tasting room to promote. Seriously, we should've had this site up ages ago."

He quickly skimmed through the "Our History" section, looking at old photos of their ancestors. "Well, it really looks great, Gina. Nice work."

"And check this out." She reached over to click something. "We'll even have an online store. I already talked to Garth about it."

"A store?"

"Yeah. It won't go live yet, but hopefully in a week or so."

"And who's going to manage that?"

"Garth and our new office manager and me. We can handle it, Dad. You don't need to worry about it."

"Uh-huh." He paused to admire the lighting of an interesting photo taken in the barrel room as Gina grabbed the throw from the ottoman, causing his hidden envelope and its contents to tumble to the floor.

"Aha!" Gina scrambled to pick it all up. "So this is what you were really up to . . . going down memory lane by the romantic firelight. Wow, this girl must've really meant something to you."

"I was planning to burn the whole thing," he growled.

"Burn all of it?" She looked horrified, clutching the envelope to her chest. "After you saved this for so long? Why would you burn it now?"

He tried to think of a sensible answer. "Because there's no reason to keep it."

"But doing it like this? All alone late at night? Am I interrupting some kind of ceremony?" she persisted. "Do you need this moment alone to burn these old memories on the sacrificial fire?"

"No, of course not!" How did she manage to aggravate him so much?

"Want me to throw them in for you?" She gave him a challenging look, like she knew he really wasn't ready for this. And the truth was, he wasn't ready. He hadn't even reread the letters yet. His plan had been to read them in order, then toss them, one by one, into the flickering flames. End of story.

"Gina . . ." He tried to soften his approach. "You need to respect my space."

"I'm sorry. But it's just because I love you."

"Uh-huh." He couldn't help but be amused by this kind of love.

"If I didn't love you, I wouldn't put up such a fuss. But I just can't help myself. I know you're troubled by these memories, and I really think you need someone to talk it through with—you know, to sort of work things out. That's all I want to do." Her eager expression reminded him of Babe when she was waiting for him to throw her ball. But right now, Babe was lying quietly and obediently by the fire . . . bothering no one. Training dogs was much easier than training daughters.

"There's nothing to talk through, Gina." He reached for the envelope, but she still stubbornly clung to it.

"Then just tell me about her. Who was this Brynna? What was she to you? I know it was more than just a camp romance. You

67

wouldn't be acting like this if that were true. You two were in love. I just know it. I could tell by those photos. But what happened? Did she break your heart? Or did you break hers and now you feel guilty about it and just want to forget?"

"Why don't you go to bed?" he said in a weary tone.

"I'm not sleepy."

"Then go launch your website." He pointed to her devices. "You have my approval."

"Great." She nodded, wrapping the throw around her with her knees pulled up to her chest and eagerly watching him. "But first, tell me about Brynna."

He ran his fingers through his hair. "I thought you read the letters. You should already know."

"I told you I only read *one*," she said defensively. "And I think it was the first one. Brynna wrote it to you right after camp. It did sound like she was in love, so what happened?" Her eyes grew wide. "Did she die?"

"No, she didn't die." He paused. "Well, not that I know of anyway."

"Then what? What *happened*?"

He knew his only way out of this would be to just spill his story. And who knew, maybe it would be therapeutic. Then he could read the letters and burn them.

He began to tell her a condensed version of how he and Brynna had met, how he used photography as an excuse to get acquainted, and how over the course of two short weeks, they fell in love. "The way only teenagers fall in love," he said without emotion. "Like a flash in the pan. Now you see it, now you don't."

"But you promised to write each other," Gina pressed. "And then what?"

"Well, I did write to her. From college. Not as often as she wrote to me, but it was my freshman year and there was a lot going on. Plus, she was a better writer than me. She wanted to be a journalist."

68

"Cool. But why did you quit writing each other? When did it end?"

"When did it end . . . ?" He considered this. "It was right before winter break. I'd been saving up to take a trip to Oregon to visit her at Christmastime."

"Did you go?"

"Nope."

"Why not?"

"She sent me a letter," he said. "It seemed that her old boyfriend came home from college for Thanksgiving. They'd been together for several years, but he'd broken up with her right before we went to camp." Leroy smiled sadly. "I suppose I was just a rebound romance."

"Oh, I don't believe that."

"I do." He leaned back. "Anyway, her old boyfriend apologized for everything and even gave her a promise ring."

"A promise ring?" Gina wrinkled her nose. "Why?"

"His promise that they'd get married. And I guess, well, Brynna must've really loved him, because she told me it was her last letter, and she asked me not to write anymore."

"And you didn't?" Gina looked truly disappointed.

"Of course I didn't. What would be the point of writing after that?"

"But it's so tragic. Were you brokenhearted?"

He rolled his eyes at her, but only for dramatic effect. Because he had been brokenhearted. "I didn't really have time to dwell on it much," he continued quietly. "My dad got sick not too long after that. I had to quit school and come home. My hands were full."

"Oh, Dad." Gina threw her arms around him. "I'm so sorry. First this girl breaks your heart and then your dad gets sick and dies. And you were only my age. Man, it really was tragic, wasn't it?"

He barely nodded. "Yeah, it was a tough era."

"But then you found Mom." Her expression seemed uncertain. "And you had all of us girls and life got way better, right?"

"Absolutely." Nodding, he attempted a smile. "And now I'm

going to burn all these silly photos and letters and forget the whole silly thing."

Gina stood, reverently handing the envelope back to him. "And I am going to give you your privacy." She set down the throw and picked up her electronic devices. "And since you approve, I think I'll go launch our new website."

"You really did a great job on it, honey. I'm proud of you." His smile was sincere now. "Keep up the good work."

She hugged him again. "Thanks, Dad. That means a lot."

As she ran back upstairs, he opened the folder, ready to chuck the contents into the flames piece by piece . . . but somehow, he just couldn't. Suddenly he felt more tired than ever, and for some reason, his chest was aching. He couldn't be having a heart attack, could he?

———

Brynna stared into the flickering campfire flames as Motorcycle Mike rambled on about his plans to take a road trip clear up to Alaska—all by himself.

"On your bike?" Jan asked with wide eyes.

"What else?"

"Camping in a tent?" Brynna frowned at him. "Aren't you worried about wild animals? I thought Alaska had grizzly bears and wolves and things."

He chuckled as he threw another piece of wood on the fire. "Well, it's crossed my mind, but that's just part of the adventure. Anyway, it's on my bucket list. It's not like I'm going next week."

"Maybe you should wait until you're eighty or ninety," Brynna teased. "Then if the bears get you, at least you've enjoyed a few extra decades of life."

"Good point." Mike laughed. "How about you, ladies? What's next on your traveling agenda?"

Jan explained about their reservation to camp in the Redwoods and her desire to see some of Sonoma. "After that, it's Yosemite."

"I'm headed to California too," he told them. "Maybe our paths will keep crossing."

"Sonoma," Brynna said the word out loud. "You know, now that I think about it, I'm pretty sure that's where Leroy was from."

"Leroy?" Mike turned to her. "Who's Leroy?"

"Her old true love," Jan said lightly.

"Well, not really. I mean, he was sort of a boyfriend," Brynna admitted. "But only for a short time. A very short time."

"They actually met right here," Jan told Mike.

"Right here?" Mike looked confused, so Brynna told him a quick version of her story, trying not to show how deeply the memories had stirred her today.

"That's crazy wild," Mike said. "What're the chances that Jan picked this camp and it's the same place where you fell in love? Like kismet or something."

"Yeah, I was pretty shocked," she confessed. "It felt like real-life déjà vu. Now it's hard to shake it out of my mind."

"Interesting." Mike slowly shook his head. "So, Leroy's the guy who got away?"

"And you really think he was from Sonoma?" Jan asked Brynna.

"Yeah. When you mentioned Sonoma, I had this vivid flashback to when Leroy told me about his family. They were into agriculture. I think it was a vineyard that—"

"Leroy's family owns a vineyard?" Mike poked Brynna's shoulder. "Hey, we should look this dude up. Maybe we can camp on his property."

"Wouldn't that be fun?" Jan tossed another log onto the fire.

"What's the dude's last name?" Mike asked.

Brynna felt her face warming. Was it from the fire—or the memory? "I, uh, I can't really remember."

"Seriously?" Jan raised her brows.

"I honestly don't recall." Brynna frowned, trying hard to think. "I always just called him Leroy. Sometimes Leroy Boucher, but that was just a nickname."

"You really don't know his last name?" Mike looked disappointed.

"I'm totally blank. Except that I think he was Italian." She tried to remember. "I'm not sure, but I think it ended with a tini or bini or—"

"Martini?" Mike tried. "Bambini?"

"Rusini?" Jan tried.

"Or maybe it was a tino." Brynna held up both hands.

"Valentino?" Jan suggested. "Augustino?"

"No, no . . . that's not right." Brynna closed her eyes, trying to force the name to the surface.

"Farrentino? Martino?" Mike threw even more names out, and the more Brynna heard, the less able she was to concentrate.

"This isn't helping." She stood up. "Give me time, maybe it will come to me. And, really, what difference does it make? It's not like I plan to look him up."

"Why not?" Mike asked.

Jan crossed her arms in front of her. "Yeah, why not?"

"What would be the point? I'm sure he's happily married and living his life. He doesn't need some old girlfriend popping in." Brynna backed away from the fire's heat.

"But it might be interesting," Jan said. "You could see how he's doing, catch up . . . like a mini reunion."

"And maybe we could camp at his vineyard," Mike said again.

"You mean his family's vineyard," Brynna added. "Because I do remember Leroy saying he planned to become a photographer. He had no interest in working for the family business."

"That's too bad." Mike looked seriously disappointed. "But maybe his family's vineyard is still there."

"It probably is." Brynna came closer again and sank back into her seat at the picnic table. "I remember now that Leroy mentioned it was one of the oldest ones in that part of the country."

"We should try to figure this out," Mike insisted. "It'll be like solving a mystery."

Jan held up her cell phone. "I'm going to start doing an online search of Sonoma vineyards—and the name Leroy." She glanced at Brynna. "Just for fun, mind you."

"Whatever." Brynna just shook her head.

"It's like fate." Mike leaned toward her, elbows on his knees. "You're here in the camp where you met and then you're going to Sonoma where his family has a vineyard. What if you actually meet up with him down there?"

"Yeah." Jan looked up from her phone. "Maybe you two are meant to be together, Brynna. What if that's why you came on this trip with me?"

Brynna couldn't help but laugh now. "I hardly think that's possible. Maybe in fairy tales or Hallmark movies, but not in real life."

"Why not?" Mike pressed her. "Stranger things happen all the time." He told them about his older sister Leah and the way she discovered an old boyfriend online a couple years before. "They hadn't seen each other for almost fifty years. Dan and Leah got married last year and have been living in Mexico ever since—happy as clams."

"Well, I'm sure Leroy already has a life and a family." Brynna was ready to end this conversation. "And besides, I don't see how we can find someone when I don't even know his last name. It's not just ridiculous, it's impossible."

"What if it isn't?" Mike challenged her. "What if we could find him?"

Brynna laughed. "And what if pigs could fly?"

"It would be an adventure to try." Mike threw another log onto the fire. "But maybe you're not the adventurous type." He winked at Jan. "I know you are an adventurer. But maybe Brynna is more of a bystander."

"I'm not a bystander," Brynna shot back at him. Although, to be honest, she had spent most of her married years feeling like one. But it wasn't who she really was. Not really.

"So are you a risk taker?" Mike asked.

73

She considered this. "Well, I came on this camping trip with Jan. And I'd never been camping before."

"And how are you liking it so far?" Jan asked.

"I actually do like it." Brynna smiled as she poked the fire with a stick.

"So are you an adventurer? Are you a risk taker?" Mike fixed his gaze on her, the campfire flames reflected in his eyes.

"I guess I'd like to be."

"Then here's to all of us having a risk-taking, adventurous summer." Mike held up his cocoa cup in a toast. Jan and Brynna joined him.

"We can be like the Three Musketeers," Mike added with a jovial laugh.

"Here's to the Three Musketeers," Jan said.

Brynna feigned enthusiasm but felt surprised at how easily Jan seemed to be pulled into Mike's way of thinking. It seemed very un-Jan-like. And yet, Brynna was beginning to realize there was a whole different Jan underneath the no-nonsense vice principal facade.

"The only thing wrong with this evening is no s'mores," Mike said.

"Yeah!" Brynna agreed. "Jan did such a great job in stocking that kitchen." She turned to Jan. "I can't believe you forgot the ingredients for s'mores."

Jan slapped her forehead. "I didn't forget to *get* them, Brynna, I forgot to pack them. They're back home sitting on my kitchen counter right now."

They all laughed. Mike started to talk with enthusiasm about some coastal sights they should all see the next day. By now, it seemed he had fully included himself in their plans. And Jan seemed perfectly fine with it. In fact, unless Brynna was reading something into this, it almost seemed as if Jan was enjoying Mike's company—and his attention. Could it be that Sergeant Bart had found her man? Brynna couldn't imagine what the other teachers would say if they could see them now.

But really, Brynna would be happy for Jan if something came of this. Nothing wrong with a little romantic interest. And it probably would go nowhere anyway. Still, it made Brynna wonder about her place in all this. What if she were about to become the odd woman out? She hated to admit it, but the thought of being displaced or replaced or rejected was seriously disturbing. Maybe she'd been mistaken to join Jan on this journey. Maybe Jan didn't need her company after all.

Chapter 12

A couple of days passed without Leroy disposing of the Brynna envelope. It seemed the longer he procrastinated, the harder it became until he finally put it in the old family safe that he rarely used for anything—just to get it out of sight and out of mind. Except it wasn't really out of mind. The problem had come with reading the letters. That had been a mistake.

As Leroy and Babe came in from the south vineyard in the late afternoon, he could see several cars parked in the area that Gina had designated for visitors. He suspected this meant she had guests in the tasting room. Hopefully with Garth's or Sophie's assistance since they all knew that Gina was not old enough to host. Even though Sophie was on prematernity leave, she'd been spending more time than ever at the vineyard lately. And not only in the house.

For some reason Sophie had taken great interest in Gina's new tasting room. So much so, she'd utilized her artistic talents to make an attractive sign that Garth had set out on the main road. And Sophie had even offered to step in for Garth if he was ever too busy. But Garth seemed to like this added responsibility. He claimed it forced him to be on his toes regarding elements like tannin, body, aroma, and color, instead of simply focusing on taste like he usually did. But Sophie, not wanting to be left out since she'd always considered herself the expert in describing their vintages, made sure she was available as well.

Fortunately for her, Leroy's mom didn't mind staying with her great-grandkids for an hour or two in the afternoons. Impressive considering his mom would be turning eighty-five soon. The thought reminded him that Sherry wanted his help planning a party for their mother. Maybe he could sic Gina on that. Now that the website was up and the tasting room running, she could probably use a new challenge.

Not wanting to be conspicuous, especially since he still had on dirty work clothes, Leroy stuck his head in the barn to see Garth playing the role of host and vintner. He was explaining the difference between a cabernet sauvignon and a pinot noir, with Sophie standing nearby, ready to correct him if necessary. But as Leroy listened for a moment, curious to see how well Garth—a man who spent more time mixing grapes than mixing socially—could pull this off, he was impressed that his son-in-law was eloquent, informative, and surprisingly entertaining. The small crowd seemed appreciative as they clapped and eagerly asked questions. Perhaps Gina had been right about this whole thing. Maybe it had been a good idea, after all.

As he headed over to the house to clean up, he saw Gina standing on the front porch with an oversized basket, full of clean wineglasses, looped over one arm.

"Hey, Dad." She gave him a sly look. "Did I just catch you spying on the guests in the tasting room?"

"Just checking things out. Seems to be working out nicely."

"Yeah. Garth and Sophie say they're loving it. It's so cool. I mean I barely launched the website and already I've made two reservations for group visits. Isn't it exciting?"

"Yeah, exciting. Garth told me this morning the tasting room is already boosting sales." He patted her head in a patronizing way just because he knew she hated it. "Nice work, princess."

"Thanks a lot." She smirked back at him. "Ready to make me your business partner now?"

"Don't push your luck." He smirked. "This could be a long summer."

"Okay, but tell me the truth, don't you think it was worth it? I mean my work on the tasting room and our social networking and everything."

"Time will tell." He rubbed his chin. "Now that you're not so busy setting these things up, you can help your aunt Sherry with your grandma's eighty-fifth birthday party. Remember, it's in late July."

"Really? You're shoving that off on me?" Gina scowled.

He shrugged. "Or you can come work in the vineyard. That'll give me more time to help your aunt."

"That's fine with me." There was a challenge in her tone.

"I mean in the burn area, Gina. Restoration over there is hard labor, and it's been really hot. It's exhausting and dirty." He held up his soot-stained palms like a visual aid, certain she'd back down.

"No problem." She shrugged. "I'd rather get dirty than be stuck helping Aunt Sherry." Without giving him the chance to renege, she ducked off to the barn, but he was pretty certain he wouldn't see Gina working the burn area anytime soon. For that matter, he wouldn't even want her there.

"Well, that serves me right," he muttered to Babe as they went inside. "Give that girl an inch and she'll take a mile." But at least she wasn't bugging him about turning their house into a B and B today. That had been her latest harebrained idea. She'd actually suggested they create living quarters above the barn—where she and he would stay in order to rent out his comfortable house to guests. She'd even calculated the income it would bring them. But he was not having it. Not at all! His house was his kingdom, and he did not intend to be dethroned for a bunch of noisy tourists traipsing in and out. Sure, they might be tightening their belts this season, but they were not destitute. Not yet anyway.

Brynna couldn't deny that Sonoma County was beautiful and well worth seeing. Everything was so green and beautiful this time of year. Really, this part of the country was amazing. From castle-like estates to gorgeous sprawling haciendas, the properties they'd visited in search of Leroy had been magical. But by the third day, and umpteenth vineyard tour, Brynna was fed up. Not at the gorgeous vineyards they were driving through but at Jan's and Mike's diehard persistence that they locate her old camp flame.

Yes, Mike had remained with them. And for some reason, Jan hadn't objected when he'd set up his camp right next to her trailer at the Sonoma RV Park a few days ago. And the day after that. And the next night too. According to Jan, her only interest in Mike was friendship. She later confided to Brynna that Mike reminded her of her dad. Sure, he was a nice guy and Brynna liked him well enough. He was helpful and lighthearted and just plain fun. Even so, she wondered how long he'd continue to tag along with them.

On the first day of touring wine country, Mike had jokingly titled their little road show "The Three Musketeers Looking for Leroy." He even made up a song about it. At first Brynna had been amused, but with each additional day, and the multiple winery tours they took in pursuit of their quest, she grew increasingly aggravated. Mike was clearly obsessed with finding Leroy. So was Jan. And it seemed they were only fueling each other.

Today, their third day, and what Brynna hoped would be the final day of the Three Musketeers tour, she sat in the back seat of the SUV, wishing she was somewhere else. Anywhere else! As usual, Jan and Mike sat up front discussing the afternoon's itinerary. And as usual, Brynna felt like a third wheel. Even worse, she felt like a child—like the kid in back with the parents up front ignoring her. She wanted to shout out "Are we there yet?" *again*, but she knew they were tired of that joke.

And she was tired of this! So tired that she'd put her foot down this morning, insisting she planned to remain at camp instead of traipsing off to one more vineyard. It would be another hot day and their RV park had a nice swimming pool. She wanted to lounge by it with a good book and a cool drink and forget all about vineyards and Leroy. She'd actually begged them, but Jan and Mike wouldn't hear of it. "This is our last day to look for Leroy," Jan had told her. "You're coming with us!"

Their obsession to *find Leroy* had turned into a real-life *Where's Waldo?* game. They'd mapped out all the vineyards Jan had found on the internet. Anything remotely related to an old Italian family-owned vineyard or the name *Leroy* had made Jan's looking-for-Leroy list. Surprisingly, she'd found quite a few suspects. But after two long, hot days of driving and touring various vineyards, they'd come up empty-handed. Well, except for the wine collection that Mike had stashed in the back of Jan's SUV. But Brynna was sick of this game.

"You guys *do* realize there are more than four hundred vineyards in Sonoma County," Brynna reminded them. "And that Jan's reservation at Yosemite is just two days away now. You *do* understand you'll have to give up this wild-goose chase."

"Yeah, yeah, we know." Jan pulled into a gravel parking area outside of what looked like a Spanish mission home. "But we still have a couple of hours to look."

"And who knows." Mike opened her car door. "*This* could be the place."

"When have I heard that before?" Brynna stretched as she got out, glancing around the immaculately landscaped property. She couldn't deny it was pretty here, and apparently it was popular too. Visitors were crawling all over the place. But something about this vineyard felt too commercial for her taste. It seemed highly unlikely that Leroy could be here. And that suited her just fine. She had no real interest in crossing paths with him, and by the end of the day, she'd happily put all this behind her. By tomorrow or very early on Sunday at the latest, they'd have to resume Jan's travel schedule and journey toward Yosemite. End of story. The Leroy story anyway.

"Clementino's goes back several generations." Jan read from her phone as they strolled toward the stately buildings. "It's one of the larger vineyards in the area and—"

"Any mention of a Leroy?" Mike interrupted.

"No, but the website doesn't really have much information about the owners or their history. Mostly it's about the wines and accommodations and such. Their B and B is very highly rated."

"And so the hunt for Leroy continues." Mike sounded like a tour guide. "Let's hope our mystery man lives here."

"Don't count on it," Brynna said, her tone terse.

He just chuckled as he elbowed her. "Hey, don't give up, little lady. We're determined to get our man. I mean *your* man."

As they did the usual winery tour, Brynna had to admit that it was very educational. By the time their hunt for Leroy ended, she expected to be something of an expert on vineyards and wine production. As they were led about the property, Mike and Jan persisted with their usual line of questioning. First Jan would ask the tour guide how old the vineyard was, how long the family had owned it, and finally, Mike would boldly inquire if anyone named Leroy was part of the family. Brynna always wanted to hide when he did this. But once again, and not surprisingly, the answer was no. Brynna was hugely relieved . . . and just a tiny bit disappointed. But at least they could move on now.

"Any chance we could stop for an iced coffee?" Brynna asked as they drove away from the vineyard.

"Sounds good to me," Jan said. "Let me check my phone for something nearby."

"I saw a sign earlier for a town a few miles ahead." Mike was driving now. He and Jan had been taking turns. Another thing that surprised Brynna since she knew how much Jan loved her Yukon. Apparently she trusted Mike behind the wheel. Very interesting.

"Hey, I just found something!" Jan exclaimed.

"A coffeehou—"

"No, a vineyard," Jan interrupted Brynna. "It looks like a new website. Or new to me. I don't remember seeing it the other night when we made our touring list."

"What makes it so interesting?" Mike turned onto the main road.

"The name, for starters. It's called Sorrentino's. But that's not all. There's a historical section on their webpage." She held up her phone so Brynna could see an old sepia-toned photo of a couple of grim-looking bearded men standing by wine barrels. "It's been family-owned for generations."

"Sorrentino." Brynna repeated the name.

"Does it ring a bell?" Mike asked eagerly.

"I'm not sure. I've heard so many names lately . . . I might just be imagining it, but Sorrentino does seem familiar."

"Where's it located?" Mike asked Jan.

"I'll turn on Maps."

As Jan waited for the map to load, Brynna's stomach knotted in angst. She felt fairly sure Sorrentino was the right name. *Leroy Sorrentino*. The more she ran the name through her head, the more certain she felt, but she didn't want to admit as much to Jan and Mike She hoped that the vineyard was so far away, it would be impossible to go. Right now they were at the south end of the county, and their RV camp was about an hour's drive away. If Sorrentino's was way up north, it would be impossible to visit it and return to their campsite at a reasonable hour. At least she hoped so.

"It's only nine miles from here," Jan proclaimed. "And it says their new tasting room is open until five."

"Well, it's past four now," Mike said. "Maybe we should skip coffee."

"Yes," Jan agreed. "And step on it."

Suddenly Brynna's stomach wasn't just twisting—she felt sick. She'd never dreamed that they'd really find Leroy. He was like a needle in a haystack. What on earth would she do if they actually found him? What would she say? How embarrassing would it be to show up after all this time? She had to put the brakes on.

"I don't know about this." She leaned toward the front seat, feeling even more childish and possibly carsick too. "It might not be such a good idea—"

"It's a *great* idea," Jan insisted. "This could be the one, Brynna. You admitted the name's familiar."

"Yeah, and we've already spent three days on this search for Leroy," Mike reminded her. "We can't stop now. Not when we're this close."

"That's right." Jan pointed a finger upward. "No stone unturned. Remember?"

"The Three Musketeers Looking for Leroy!" Mike boomed. "We found our man."

"Well, let's not start celebrating yet," Jan warned him. "We don't know for sure."

"Yeah . . ." Brynna slumped back against her seat, closing her eyes and trying to breathe deeply . . . trying to slow down her pounding heart. She tried her best to relax. Meanwhile Jan and Mike were chattering away like they were the next best thing to Nancy Drew and the Hardy Boys.

After a couple of minutes of internal dialogue and self-therapy, Brynna felt somewhat reassured. It was highly unlikely this particular winery had anything to do with Leroy. Most likely, it belonged to a relative. Hadn't he said it was a family business? Leroy was probably off working for some important marketing agency far away from here. She remembered when they'd shared their aspirations. Leroy, with absolutely zero interest in wineries, had longed to be a photographer in a big city. And she'd hoped to become a journalist for a newspaper. Maybe her dreams had been cut short, but Leroy had been very determined. He was probably living out his dreams in New York or LA . . . or perhaps Zimbabwe.

Chapter 13

Despite her earlier resolve, Brynna experienced what felt like the onset of a panic attack as Mike turned at the Sorrentino's Vineyard sign. What if Leroy really was there? What would she say? How would she act? What if she lost her lunch?

"Hey, you guys," she said weakly, "I, uh, I don't think I can do this."

"Sure, you can," Jan reassured her.

"But I—"

"You're just nervous," Mike added. "That's only natural. But relax. Remember you're with friends here, and we've got—"

"But you don't understand," she protested. "I hurt him. Hurt him badly. I wrote him that final letter. It was so cold—telling him not to write me anymore. I just cut things off without any explanation. With no concern for how he might feel. I was a horrible, selfish person, and I'm sure he must hate me." She rolled down her window, but the fresh air did nothing to soothe her. "I can't do this."

For a long moment, no one said a word. The SUV just bumped along a rutted gravel road between row after row of grapevines. There was no place wide enough to turn around and go back. No escape from this madness.

Finally Mike spoke up, but this time his tone was serious. "Maybe this is your chance to make things right with him, Brynna."

"That's a good point," Jan said quietly.

"But what if he doesn't want things made right?" Brynna countered. "What if this is all just a great big stupid mistake? Like the mistake I made with him thirty years ago. What if seeing me is awkward and painful and just plain weird for him? How can I just strut in and throw the past in his face like this? I am a horrible, selfish—"

"You need to chill out, Brynna." Jan used her vice principal tone now. "You're working yourself into a frenzy. Take a deep breath and calm down."

"But I have no right to hunt him down like this, Jan. Like a stalker. Straight out of the blue—"

"Look, we're just tourists out looking at vineyards," Mike said firmly. "That's all. If you should cross paths with an old friend, well, what's wrong with that? You'll say hello, how are you, goodbye. No big deal."

"Yes, that's right." Jan shifted in her seat to face Brynna. "You're blowing this all out of proportion."

"Chances are this isn't even the right vineyard," Mike said lightly.

"Even if it is, he might not be here," Jan added just as some buildings came into view. "You might not see him at all."

"If it is Leroy's place, it looks a little run-down," Mike said. "Not near as fancy as the other wineries we've visited."

Jan pointed to the parking area. "And there's only a couple of cars here. They're probably about to close up shop."

"Yeah." Mike started to slow down as they approached the other cars. "How 'bout we take a quick peek around and call it a day. No biggie."

Brynna knew they were both just trying to placate her by downplaying it all . . . and maybe they were right. For some reason it was hard to imagine the Leroy she'd briefly known so long ago could actually live here. It was too surreal.

"Sorrentino's might not be as impressive as the other vineyards we visited"—Jan sounded like a schoolteacher now—"but it might just be older. The website says it's having its 140th anniversary this summer. That would mean it began in the 1880s. Transcontinental railroads would barely have been running."

As Jan continued her brief US history lesson, Brynna studied the two-story stone house on the knoll and the vineyard hills gently rolling away from it. Here and there were old oak trees and a variety of buildings of different sizes. She couldn't dispute that the property did seem old and perhaps a bit in need of some attention, but it wasn't unattractive. Not to her anyway. "I actually think it's rather charming," she admitted quietly.

Mike pulled into the roped-off parking area, which was actually just packed-down dirt next to a big red barn. He turned off the engine. "You gals ready for this?"

"I am," Jan declared.

Brynna's stomach twisted. "I'm not."

"Now don't you worry, Half Pint." Mike opened the back door and waited for her to get out. "We got your back."

"Hopefully Leroy won't want to slip a knife into it," she muttered.

Mike laughed. "No way. We won't let that happen."

"Come on." Jan linked her arm into Brynna's. "Pull on your big-girl pants and let's do this. We won't let Leroy hurt you."

As Brynna walked, she felt deep inside of her that even if she were to see Leroy, he would not be rude to her. He just couldn't be. Leroy was a true gentleman. At least, he used to be. Okay, she had no way of knowing what he was like now. People could change. She certainly had. Besides, he probably wasn't even here. And yet, she had the distinct and unexplainable feeling gnawing inside of her that he was associated with this place.

Flanked by Jan and Mike and feeling like the proverbial sheep headed for the slaughter, Brynna approached the barn. Above the big double doors was a sign that read SORRENTINO'S OLD-WORLD

Tasting Room. As they entered the dusky space, Brynna decided that she probably deserved to be scorned and despised by Leroy. And if he were truly here, she hoped that he'd just get it over with as quickly as possible. Then they could get out of here.

A small knot of people hovered around a counter where a young man was holding up a glass of red wine. "As you know, our family vineyard is one of the oldest in the county," he said. "We do things differently here. We take pride in the old, slow processes, using the original techniques of our ancestors."

"Do you have folks stomping the grapes with their bare feet?" an older man called out.

"Not usually." The young man behind the counter chuckled. "That's actually been outlawed in the US. But sometimes in the fall, my mom and some of her girlfriends will stomp on some grapes. Just for fun. And they have a pretty good time too."

"You actually use *that* for wine?" a woman asked, sounding concerned.

"Sure, but not for public use. It's only for family," he assured her.

"Do *you* really drink that?" She pursed her lips.

The young man smiled. "My parents do. To be honest, it's not my thing. But that old process was proven to be perfectly sanitary in Spain. The delicate balance of acid, sugar, and alcohol prevents any human pathogens from surviving in the wine."

"Wouldn't it taste like dirty feet?" the old man called out.

"You'd have to ask my parents." He laughed. "But back to your question about crushing and pressing. We do still use an old-world process. After the grapes are crushed in oak racks, we use a batch press. That's a wooden basket where the crushed grapes are tightly packed to separate the juice from the skin and debris. It's considered a gentler way because there's less movement and stress to the grapes. And it results in a gentler wine."

"You know so much about this," a white-haired woman said. "Where did you learn everything?"

"I did take some courses at University of California." He winked at her. "But most of it was learned from growing up in the vineyard. I've observed my parents and grandparents making wine for as long as I can remember. I guess it's in my blood."

The old man made a joke about having wine in his blood, but as Brynna studied the fair-haired young man in front, clean-cut and sober, she thought he looked nothing like Leroy. And yet it seemed possible. Based on what he'd just said about his family, he could be Leroy's son. And that bit about his mom stomping grapes . . . well, it just seemed to confirm that Leroy was happily married with a family. She felt more intrusive than ever. What on earth was she doing here? And what was the best and quickest way to escape?

With Jan and Mike seemingly transfixed by the young man's monologue about old-world wine making, Brynna decided to slip back to the car. Even if it was locked, she could sit on the bumper and just wait. Anything to get as far from here as possible before it was too late.

Yet as she slipped out of the barn and into the bright afternoon sunlight, she didn't want to go cower by Jan's SUV. Something about this place intrigued her. She glanced around but didn't see a soul anywhere, and everything out here felt quiet and peaceful. The house and other buildings appeared quiet too. So, with no one around to notice her presence, she decided to poke around a bit. Not snooping, exactly. Just exploring. She wasn't quite sure what she was looking for but suspected she hoped for a peek at Leroy's wife. Just out of curiosity.

Instead of heading toward the tall stone house, like she wanted to do but knew was too risky, she strolled in the other direction. Trying to appear casual, she walked past a large storage building that she suspected was used for wine. And then she passed a smaller building with a sign that read OFFICE AND SALES. Like everything else, it seemed deserted.

"Can I help you?"

Brynna spun around to see a young woman peering curiously

88

at her. She had dark curly hair and big brown eyes. Beneath her floral sundress, she was clearly expecting a baby.

"I'm sorry." Brynna started to back up. "I was just looking—"

"Oh, you must be here for the job." The woman's countenance brightened.

For some reason Brynna just nodded. Hoping to look less suspicious and nosy, she forced a friendly smile.

"Great." The woman stepped forward and stuck out her hand, which Brynna shook weakly. "I'm Sophie. My dad was supposed to do the interview, but he had to go to a meeting at my aunt's house. So I'm going to handle it for him." She unlocked the office door. "Come on in. We got AC last year, so it's lots cooler in here. Believe me, I need it." She patted her belly. "This little guy gets me pretty heated up."

Unsure of how to get out of this, and yet exceedingly curious about this young woman, Brynna followed her inside. But before she could clarify the situation, Sophie took over the conversation.

"And just to reassure you, I know what we want for our office manager because it's been my job the last eight years. I started the year after my mom died. Just a year before Garth and I got married. He's five years older than me and a real expert. His family used to own a small vineyard up north, but sold out when he was studying to be a vintner. Dad hired him as our winemaker and right now he's playing host at the tasting room. He loves that." She continued to talk nonstop as she adjusted the blinds and eased herself into a chair behind an oak desk. The only information Brynna latched on to was that Sophie's mom had died. If Leroy was the dad she spoke of, did that mean he was a widower now? She shook her head. Even if he was, what business was it of hers?

Sophie leaned back in the chair, locking her fingers over her rounded midsection. "Dad didn't think I was old enough to handle this job at first. I mean, I was barely twenty, but I'd taken some business classes at community college and then I took more online. Anyway, I sort of figured everything out and I set up a new system and managed to bring our winery into the new millennium—and it was about time too." Her cheerful expression faded. "I'm not trying to put my mom down. Not at all. She used to handle everything in here. And she was really good at it too. Mom was organized and meticulous, but she did it all the old-fashioned way—you know, with books and ledgers." She sighed. "Super time-consuming and convoluted."

"I can imagine." Brynna nodded, wondering how to get out of this . . . and yet at the same time fascinated at hearing this family's story.

"I guess I should be asking you about yourself." Sophie grinned. "Dad always calls me the chatterbox of the family."

Brynna smiled nervously, trying to think of a transition that could lead to a graceful exit. "When's your baby due, Sophie?"

"Early August. But I'm big as a house already. I guess it's because it's my third pregnancy."

Brynna was surprised. "You have other children?"

"Yep. Two other rug rats. Lucy is five going on fifteen, and Addison just turned three."

"Wow . . ." Brynna tried to imagine the Leroy she remembered as the grandfather of three—it seemed impossible. Maybe they hadn't really found him, after all. Perhaps this place was run by another family member. "You really do have your hands full."

"That's for sure. My grandma's watching the kids right now. It was my way to keep her occupied while my aunt and Dad plan her surprise birthday party. She's going to be eighty-five in a couple of weeks."

"Sounds like there's a lot going on in your life." Brynna glanced to the door. "I hate to take up any more of your—"

"Don't worry about it." Sophie waved her hand. "In fact, that's why it's so important that I talk to you now. Dad really wants to fill this position." She picked up a pencil, studying Brynna more closely. "So, tell me about your qualifications. About your education and job experience?"

"Actually, I'm a teacher." Brynna grimaced.

"Oh?" Sophie tipped her head to one side. "A teacher?"

Brynna nodded. "Elementary. Third grade. For quite a while too—in the same school." She felt like a runaway train. How could she stop this thing? Derailment?

Sophie leaned forward with interest. "But you want to change jobs? Teaching doesn't appeal to you anymore?"

Brynna actually considered the question. "Yeah . . . maybe. Sometimes . . . I guess I do."

"Huh?" Sophie set down her pencil. A confused frown spread across her face.

"I'm sorry. I don't want to waste your time." Brynna started to stand.

"No, no, that's okay. You seem like a nice person. And it's fine that you've been a teacher. In fact, it's probably good. You've obviously finished a college degree if you've been teaching. Tell me, though, do you know anything about business management or bookkeeping?"

"I use an online bookkeeping program . . . and I suppose teaching a classroom of lively kids requires some management skills." Brynna smiled sheepishly. "But not what you'd be looking for." Now she actually did stand. "I'm really sorry, Sophie, I do hope you find someone more suitable for—"

"No, no—please, don't go yet. My dad will think I blew this interview. And we *really* do need an office manager. I mean ASAP." Sophie dug through a messy stack of papers. "Dad said your résumé was here on the desk. What was your name again? Or did I forget to ask? Garth keeps teasing me that each pregnancy reduces my brain cells. I'm probably running on empty by now."

"My name is . . . Bree." Brynna cringed, feeling deceptive. She couldn't give her real name, and Bree was what her dad used to call her—a name she hadn't used in ages. "Bree Philips." She watched nervously as Sophie shuffled through the papers, still searching.

She eventually gave up. "Well, I can't seem to find it. Garth is probably right about that maternity brain cell thing."

"No, you seem very intelligent to me. I'm impressed you started running this office at such a young age. Kudos to you."

Sophie brightened. "Well, thank you very much. See, I knew I liked you."

"Anyway, you won't find my résumé because it's not there." Brynna remained standing.

Now Sophie stood, but her brow was creased. "That's okay. You still want to apply for the job, don't you? To be honest, you might be one of the best applicants we've had show up. Dad said all the others were too young or inexperienced. Like they thought working at a vineyard would be a fun summer vacation. But it's not. It's a lot of hard work. And sometimes it's tricky to get good employees way out here. As you can probably tell, we're not a fancy vineyard. Not like some of our competition."

"I haven't seen much of Sorrentino's, but it seems lovely. I'd think people would be eager to work out here."

Just then, the office phone rang. "Excuse me for a moment. I need to take this."

As Sophie talked to someone about an order, entering information onto her computer and compiling a varied list of wines—everything from chardonnay to cabernet—Brynna stared out the window. Mesmerized by the beautiful view, she gazed longingly at the rolling green hill before her. Row upon row of lush grapevines, healthy and carefully tended, so neat and orderly. It was indescribably soothing and peaceful.

A tiny impulse inside of her hinted this might be her perfect opportunity to make a clean getaway. But a much larger part of her felt paralyzed. Maybe it was this gorgeous view, or the soothing feel of cool AC on the back of her neck, or maybe she simply didn't want to hurt Sophie's feelings. Whatever the reason, she was unable to move a muscle.

Chapter 14

Just as Sophie's phone conversation wound down, Brynna returned to her senses, almost as if someone had snapped their fingers and woke her from a hypnotic trance. She glanced around the office and wondered what she was doing there. Why had she left her phone in the SUV? She could've used it as an excuse to get out of this mess. And what about Jan and Mike? What would they make of her strange disappearance?

"Thank you so much." Sophie spoke into the phone with a cheery business voice. "We'll get your order right out, Mrs. Walker. And best wishes for your daughter's upcoming wedding." She hung up the phone and smiled at Brynna. "See how easy that was?"

"Yes, of course. I'm sure it could be interesting to work in a place like this, but I really should be—"

"It's definitely interesting, but it can also be boring too. And it's not for everyone." Sophie looked eagerly at her. "So what about you, Bree? Would you enjoy working at a vineyard?"

Brynna sighed longingly. "Oh, I'm sure I would, but—"

"Then you're hired." Sophie hurried around the desk, reaching out to shake Brynna's hand. "Dad will be so happy."

Brynna caught her breath, staring at Sophie in shock. "*What?* But you don't know anything about me. You can't just offer me—"

"Then tell me more, Bree." Sophie leaned against the desk. "Let's see, where to begin . . . Tell me—are you very organized? On a scale of one to ten, with one being you're a total mess, where do you fall?"

Brynna pursed her lips. "I hate to admit it, but my ex used to tease me for being hyper-organized, so I'm probably a nine or ten."

Sophie grinned. "My sisters have said that exact thing about me. So that's good. You said your ex? Does that mean you're single?"

"Yes. Very single." Brynna sighed again.

"Kids?"

She glumly shook her head.

"Oh . . . okay." Sophie rubbed her swollen midsection with a thoughtful expression. "So, anyway, what bookkeeping program do you use?"

Brynna told her and Sophie confirmed it was compatible with their program. "Seriously, Bree, if you can keep a room full of third graders in line, I'm sure you can keep our little family business on track. This is going to be great. You'll be perfect for the job!" Sophie beamed. "I'm so relieved to have you. Dad's gonna be thrilled."

"But I can't do—"

"You don't want the job?" Sophie's smile vanished. "What's wrong?"

"I actually would love the job. But I, uh, I don't live here. You see, I live in Oregon and I'm—"

Sophie blinked. "You live in *Oregon*?"

"Yeah. I'm just here for the summer." Brynna wondered why she'd said that. Not that it was a lie exactly . . . but it wasn't quite true either. Or was it?

Sophie frowned. "So you mean you just want to *try it out* down here? To see if you like Sonoma County? Like, if you want to live here permanently?"

"Yeah, I guess." Brynna caught herself. "I mean, no, I'm not really sure."

Sophie tilted her head to one side. "So where *are* you staying right now?"

"Staying?" Brynna considered this. "I'm actually camping with a teacher friend. She has this little trailer, and we've been visiting vineyards." It was time to backpedal her way out of this.

"I know!" Sophie held up a finger. "We have this guest cottage out behind the main house. It was a caretaker's cottage, but my mom fixed it up about ten years ago. Anyway, Garth and I used to live there, back before we had babies and it got way too small for us, so Dad put a manufactured home on the backside of the property. Now the cottage mostly just sits there empty. My sister Luna stays there sometimes, but she's working in San Francisco this summer. And Gina won't mind. She never uses it." Sophie paused to check something on her phone.

Brynna wondered if Gina could be a stepmom. Why wouldn't Leroy have remarried? And if so, what difference did it make? Brynna still needed to get out of here. Even if it turned out that this vineyard had nothing to do with Leroy, Brynna had no business here. Her curiosity got the better of her though. "Gina?"

Sophie looked up from her phone "Gina's my baby sister. She just dropped out of college. Dad's not too happy about it either."

"How many sisters do you have?" Brynna asked meekly, at the same time questioning why she was prolonging this bizarre job interview. She felt more and more like *Alice in Wonderland* or *Through the Looking Glass* or just plain crazy. It was so hard to imagine the boy from camp with grown daughters and grandchildren. "Two younger sisters. Luna and Gina." Sophie set down her phone with a quizzical expression. "So now I'm thinking if you lived in our cottage, could you take less pay? We're running on a pretty tight budget just now. We lost a lot of valuable vines to wildfires last fall, so if you agreed to a smaller salary in exchange for rent, it would be helpful. Would that seem fair?"

"Of course, it's fair," Brynna heard herself saying.

"Great. Then it's settled." Sophie dug through the paper piles again. "I can't believe how quickly this place goes to pieces when I'm not here. Hopefully you'll whip it into shape in no time."

Brynna couldn't believe she'd just agreed to a reduced salary for a job she had no intention of taking. What was wrong with her? Besides being certifiably nuts!

"Here they are." Sophie handed Brynna some official-looking forms. "Just fill these out. I'll need to make a copy of your driver's license, and then we'll be all set."

Brynna stared down at the papers, wondering how to unravel this mess without hurting this sweet young woman's feelings. Sophie seemed so happy about everything. What if she got upset? Would it be bad for the baby? Brynna didn't want her to go into labor. "How about if I take the papers with me and, uh, get back to you?"

"I guess you could. But wouldn't it be easier to just fill them out right now? It shouldn't take you long." She held up her phone, which was buzzing. "That's my timer. If you'll excuse me, I need to get to the house. I put something in the oven for Dad and Gina's dinner. Those two live like bums without my help. I'll be right back."

"Okay." Brynna slowly nodded. This was her chance to escape.

"And when I get back, we'll go look at the cottage." Sophie opened the door. "You're going to love it here, Bree. I just know it."

Brynna waited a full minute after Sophie left, then hurried outside. She needed to find Jan and Mike—and they all needed to make a fast getaway. She glanced toward the tasting room, which was closed up, and then over to the little parking area. Other than Jan's SUV, the place was deserted. At least they hadn't left without her, which wouldn't have surprised her if they thought it would link her up with Leroy.

As Brynna hurried toward the SUV, she saw Jan and Mike coming from around the barn with confused expressions. She called out, waving and running toward them. "We need to go," she exclaimed breathlessly as they met in the parking area. "Now! Let's get going!"

"Where were you hiding?" Jan demanded. "We've looked all—"

"I wasn't hiding." She glanced toward the house, hoping Sophie wasn't done in the kitchen yet.

"I told Jan you probably found Leroy." Mike winked at her.

Jan's eyes grew wide. "Did you?"

"No. But we need to go. *Now!*"

"But we solved the mystery, Brynna. We found your Leroy. We discovered that this whole vineyard belongs to none other than Leroy Sorrentino!"

"Okay, fine, whatever." She bit her lip.

"You didn't see him anywhere?" Jan asked. "His son-in-law, Garth, in the tasting room—he told us that Leroy is here somewhere."

"No, I did not see him." Brynna tugged Jan's arm. "Come on, let's get—"

"But you *have* to see him," Mike insisted, not moving. "That's why we came."

"I don't *want* to see him." Brynna kept trying to pull Jan toward the SUV. "I want to go. Now!"

"What's the big rush?" Jan asked with a furrowed brow.

"Yeah," Mike said, "these people seem real nice. And their vineyard is nice too. It's an old-world winery. Pretty interesting."

"Sure, it's all very nice and interesting, but they're trying to hire me." Brynna shook Sophie's paperwork in the air as if to prove her point.

"Hey, that's great." Mike slapped her on the shoulder playfully. "What a fun place to work."

"Then *you* take the job," Brynna told him. "I want to go." She tried the door on the SUV only to find it locked. "Come on, you guys, *please.*"

"Slow down, Brynna." Jan's grin grew slightly mischievous as she folded her arms in front of her. "First you need to tell us what happened."

"Yeah." Mike nodded. "You really didn't see Leroy?"

"No, I didn't."

"Then who offered you a job?" Jan asked.

"His daughter. Well, I assume it's his daughter. Now that you say you know Leroy owns this vineyard, it probably was." She looked over her shoulder. "Can we go now?"

Jan ignored her question. "What kind of job did the daughter offer you?"

"Picking grapes?" Mike teased.

"No. Managing their office. Sophie—that's the daughter—she really wants me to work here. She even offered me the guest cottage—"

"Way to go!" Jan patted Brynna on the back. "That sounds perfect."

"Perfectly crazy!"

"Not so crazy." Mike held up a hand. "I think it's a God thing."

"Me too." Jan pointed to the forms still in Brynna's hand. "Do you need to fill those out?"

"Yes, but—no, I mean *no.*"

"What are you so afraid of?" Jan locked eyes with her. "What are you running from, Brynna?"

"I—I don't know." Brynna felt strangely close to tears now. "It's just that I don't belong here. I never should've let Sophie think I'd take that job. I just want to go."

"You shouldn't be fighting this," Mike challenged her. "It's like I said before—*it's kismet.* Remember, I told you how God works in mysterious ways."

Brynna sighed. "But I can't do this. I just want to go. Please—"

"Is that the daughter over there?" Jan nodded toward the house, and Brynna turned in time to see Sophie strolling toward them. Happily waving, she was completely oblivious to Brynna's distressed demeanor. She had no idea who she'd just hired or what her father might think if he knew. Hopefully he never would.

Brynna smiled weakly as she waved to Sophie, but her stomach felt like she'd ingested cement. She tried to come up with an explanation that wouldn't be too upsetting, but before she could say a word, Jan and Mike cheerfully introduced themselves to Sophie. The two took turns complimenting Sophie on the vineyard and winery and her husband's great hosting skills in the tasting room. Clearly, Brynna's friends would be of no help in this matter. So much for the Three Musketeers' motto of "all for one and one for all." Jan and Mike were their own team of two with their own agenda. Their *Looking for Leroy* game had been seriously annoying, but finding him would be much, much worse.

Leroy knew he should love his baby sister—because she was his baby sister. And he did love Sherry, but sometimes he didn't like her very much. Like today. He'd been trying to bite his tongue as she rambled on and on about her high expectations for their mother's "surprise" eighty-fifth birthday party. Expectations that seemed to mostly involve his efforts . . . and bank account . . . and property.

"Do we really need two hundred guests?" he asked her.

"They're all Mom's friends and fellow vintners," Sherry protested. "I've already told a lot of them we're doing this. I can't uninvite them, Leroy."

"But when you asked me to host, I assumed it would be an intimate gathering of friends and family." It felt like the tenth time he'd said this today. "Maybe you should just host it here."

"But Sorrentino's has special meaning to Mom." Sherry had a slightly sly expression on her face. "After all, that's where she married Dad and had her children."

"I know that, but there's the burn to deal with, and the house and yard are a little neglected. I'm not sure I can get it together in time."

"Are you saying you feel overwhelmed?" Sherry leaned forward with arched brows and a bit too much interest.

"I'm saying I'm already stretched thin and we've got a lot going on at Sorrentino's right now."

"Sophie told me about Gina's *improvements*. I thought you were too strapped to improve anything, Leroy. And that burned section, I assume you're just letting it go for now." Sherry's eyes narrowed slightly, making him wonder if this was really about him hosting the party, or if it was Tony's way to pressure him into selling. Sherry's husband just wouldn't give up on his attempts to purchase Sorrentino's—like they were having a "fire sale" after the burn damage. Was Tony behind this nonsense with Sherry today?

"I have a crew working on the burn area," Leroy said calmly. "It's not as bad as I originally thought. Thanks to our wet winter, about half of the roots appear to be alive. And, as for our so-called improvements, Gina's tasting room is pretty much a bare-bones operation. It didn't cost much."

"And what about the Sorrentino anniversary celebration Garth told me about? That can't be cheap."

"Gina claims it'll be great advertising. She's certain we'll make up what we spend in increased sales, and she might be right. We're already filling more orders than last year around this time."

"Yes, I noticed your fancy new website. It looks expensive." Sherry studied him closely.

"The website was pretty much free, Sherry. Gina made it." He masked his growing irritation, now convinced Sherry's "party-planning meeting" was more about Tony's desire to own Sorrentino's than Mom's big birthday bash. Well, whatever!

Sherry's brows arched. "Impressive. Maybe I should get Gina to update our website."

"Gina's pretty busy these days." He ran his fingers through his hair, wishing for a quick end to this conversation. "We all are." He decided to just bite the bullet. "Okay, Sherry, I'll host the birthday party at Sorrentino's. No problem."

"You will?" Her expression suggested this wasn't the answer she wanted. "Are you sure?"

He nodded firmly. "Yep. I'm positive. Gina's new tasting room can hold a lot of folks, and the weather should be good enough to be outside anyway. We'll set up a tent if necessary."

"But if you don't want to—"

"No, I *want* to do this." He stood up to signal this was over. "After all, it's for our mom. She deserves a good party. And Sorrentino's is the perfect venue. Like you said—that's where she married Dad and raised her children. It's a special place for her."

"Yes, I know that's true, but—"

"Don't worry. Everything will be just fine. Gina's full of ideas and energy. She'll probably get the place looking great in no time." He picked up his straw cowboy hat, hiding a satisfied grin from his slightly manipulative sister. Sure, it was going to be a lot of work to host this crazy birthday party, but it was almost worth it to see Sherry squirm like this. She'd probably wanted to host the whole thing herself right from the beginning!

Sherry started to protest again, but he cut her off by pointing to her backyard. "Gotta pay my respects to Mom and the grandbabies." He winked at his now-glowering sister. "Sophie had Mom babysit to keep her from snooping on our meeting." Before Sherry could object, he slipped out the patio door. He'd barely made his appearance before he was mobbed by Lucy and Addison, both of whom were squealing with joy.

"Hey, it's my two favorite little people!" He scooped them both up in a giant bear hug, swinging them from side to side and making them squeal even louder. "Have you worn out your granny yet?"

"Granny?" His mother, Dorothy Sorrentino, gave him a look of disapproval, which he knew was only skin-deep. "I told you not to call me that, *Grandpa*. I am *Great Gran*."

"And he's not Grandpa," Lucy corrected. "He's *Pappy!*"

He chuckled. "I do beg your pardon, *Great Gran*." He turned to see Sophie coming through the house and into the backyard. "Looks like your mom's arrived just in time to rescue you." He set the kids down and, not surprisingly, they acted unhappy to see their mother. But he knew it was just because they didn't want this play session to end yet.

Sophie hugged her grandmother. "Thanks so much for running herd on these two, Gram. And sorry for taking so long. I was having a fun interview for the office position."

"Not at all, dear. But if you'll both excuse me, my naptime is calling." She reached for her iced tea glass and magazine and went into the house.

Sophie turned to Leroy. "That interview went great, Dad."

"Great? That's a switch. Tell me more."

She beamed at him. "She was absolutely perfect."

"*Perfect?* I'd settle for just plain good at this point. So did you offer her the job?"

"I did. I hope you don't mind. But, really, I think she'll be great. She's got good energy."

"Good energy?" He frowned. "Hopefully she's not a kid. I never had a chance to really go over today's résumé."

"She's not a kid. I mean, I don't really know her age. But I know she's older than me because she's been a teacher for a while. I'm guessing she's like thirtysomething."

"A teacher?" He rubbed his chin. "Does she have any office skills?"

"Yes, of course." Sophie called to her kids to get ready to go.

"And you're sure she'll be a good fit?"

Sophie nodded as she grabbed Addison's hand. "I really do, Dad. And I'm willing to take total responsibility for her." She reached out for Lucy's hand too. "And here's another good thing. Bree needs a place to live so I offered her the guesthouse. She's willing to take less pay in exchange for rent, so we'll save some money."

"That's good." He scratched his head. "Wait, Bree? I thought today's interview was with a Susan Baxter."

Her grin looked sheepish. "Well, I guess I got my wires crossed. You see, Bree showed up early. I mean, I *thought* she was early. And then I couldn't find her résumé—I mean Bree Philips's résumé. I did see Susan's file on the desk like you said, and really it wasn't that impressive. Anyway, I went ahead and interviewed Bree. She's so right for the job, I couldn't *not* hire her. Susan showed up about five minutes after Bree left, and I gave her a quick interview and promised to get back to her. I'll nicely tell her that the position's been filled."

Leroy was confused. "You're certain Bree is really right for us?"

"Positive." Sophie smiled as Lucy and Addison both started to tug on her, saying they were hungry and begging for pizza for dinner.

"Okay, honey." He opened the side gate for them. "I guess I'll have to trust you on this."

"And I'll train her and get her settled into the guesthouse and everything," she called out as her kids pushed and pulled her out to the driveway.

"When can she start?" he asked as he followed the kiddie parade. "Soon, I hope."

"Yeah—she said soon. Or maybe that's what her friends said." She struggled to unlock her minivan.

"Her friends?"

"Yeah, they were really nice. And they love our place. They've been visiting vineyards all over Sonoma County, and they said ours was the best by far." She helped Addison into his car seat.

"Okay then." He bent over to help Lucy buckle her seat belt, giving her a peck on the forehead. "Sounds like you have it under control—and not a moment too soon." He closed the door then turned to his daughter, talking quietly so the kids couldn't overhear. "Don't tell the kids, but we're hosting your grandma's surprise party."

"At Sorrentino's?" She blinked. "I thought Aunt Sherry wanted it here at Damico's. I heard her tell Uncle Tony what great publicity it'd be for their vineyard."

Leroy chuckled. "Well, I think your aunt outsmarted herself this time."

"Huh?" Sophie's brow creased.

"No worries, honey. We'll figure it all out. Hopefully your new employee is good at helping to organize birthday parties and anniversary celebrations and all the other activities your baby sister might still have up her sleeve."

"Oh, I'm sure Bree can handle it. She seems very capable."

He gently patted Sophie's overly round belly. "Good. Because you, my dear, need to slow way down. For your sake as much as for our little bambino here. And I'm not just saying that because you promised to name him after me either. And, don't forget, I'm not holding you to that. It hasn't always been an easy name to live with."

She nodded with a twinkle in her eye. "Well, I guess you'll just have to wait and see."

He opened the car door for her, making a silly face through the window for his grandkids as Sophie eased her bulky self behind the wheel. So much like her mother, so organized and maternal—and overly busy. She really did need to slow it down, and he was determined to make sure she did. Leroy smiled, waving both hands at the kids as Sophie drove away. Hopefully this wonder woman Sophie had hired wouldn't disappoint. They had a big summer ahead, one that had just gotten bigger, thanks to Sherry. Everyone at Sorrentino's would have to pull their weight—and then some.

Chapter 15

In the middle of a mostly sleepless night, Brynna figured it all out. In the morning, she would call Sophie and apologize to her, saying she had changed her mind and was unable to accept the generous job offer. She would wish Sophie well and that would be that. Sure, it was the coward's way out, but the idea of facing Leroy—as his new employee—was just too overwhelming. She promised herself, when she got home to Oregon, she would write Leroy a long honest letter including a long overdue, heartfelt apology. End of story.

But at breakfast time, when she told Jan and Mike her plan, they went ballistic. "You can't do that," Jan insisted. "Not after all we did to help you find Leroy. We won't allow it!"

"That's right," Mike agreed. "Running away like that is like running away from God."

"Running away from God?" Brynna blinked.

"Well, that might be overstating it some, but I can't help feeling that God ordained this whole thing." He rubbed his bearded chin. "Okay, I take it back. You might not be running from God, but it's kinda like slapping kismet in the face."

Brynna couldn't help but laugh. "Seriously? Does kismet have a face?"

He shrugged. "It's a metaphor."

For a long moment, no one said anything. Then as Jan refilled her coffee cup, she quietly spoke. "The whole thing really did seem meant to be, Brynna. I mean, what were the chances we'd really find your Leroy?"

"He's not *my* Leroy."

"You know what I mean." Jan frowned. "After all our work, and after Sophie offered you a job, well, it seems you could at least give Sorrentino's a try."

"But I—"

"In all the years we've taught together, you never seemed like a cowardly person," Jan said, using a firmer tone. "I honestly thought you were braver than this."

Brynna considered this. It was easy to appear confident at school, where she knew the rules and was respected. But Dirk had taken a huge toll on her courage. Not only because he usually shut down her dreams, which made her stop dreaming altogether, but the divorce had been the final blow. Oh, she'd wanted to return to her old self, not that she'd made much progress. But taking a job at Leroy's vineyard? Well, that was just too much to expect of anyone. In fact, it was perfectly ridiculous.

"Where's your spirit of adventure?" Mike paused from cleaning bugs off his motorcycle to look at her.

"Good question," Jan chimed in. "Remember how we all agreed that this was a summer for adventures and risk taking?"

"Yeah, the Three Musketeers," Mike added. "Remember?"

Brynna closed her eyes, trying to think of a way to shut them both up. She could see their point . . . and yet. "Okay." She wanted to be honest. "Maybe you're right about being courageous and taking risks. I do want to be like that. Part of me would love to work at the vineyard . . . and maybe even get reacquainted with Leroy. But the truth is, I'm just plain scared."

Suddenly they were both talking at her, taking turns encouraging her, telling her it would be okay, creating worst-case scenarios, and assuring her it wouldn't be so bad. Finally, she held up her hands. "I just need to think about this. I want to take a nice, long walk."

"Not so fast." Jan held out a hand.

"What?" Brynna stared at her.

"Hand over your phone."

"What?"

"I don't want you sneaking off to call Sophie before you've really given yourself time to carefully consider the whole thing."

"Yeah!" Mike heartily agreed. "Good thinking, Jan."

Brynna sighed, but Jan's hand remained out. "Come on, Brynna," she said. "Just think about your decision before you burn that bridge."

"And why don't you try praying about it too," Mike suggested. "Ask God what he thinks about this whole thing. Maybe you'll be surprised."

"Fine." Brynna slapped her phone into Jan's palm. "I'll take a walk. I'll think and pray. But when I come back, you can't keep hounding me like this. Even if you don't agree with my final decision. *Okay?*"

They reluctantly agreed and Brynna took off for her walk. But with each step, she felt it was useless. Her mind really was made up. She was not going back to Sorrentino's to take that job. She'd stick with her midnight plan. Sure, Mike and Jan would be mad and probably call her a chicken, but it was her life.

Still, she reminded herself as she walked through a shady grove of old nut trees, she had promised to think and pray it over. Fine— she would do just that. She would pray for God to put an end to Mike's and Jan's relentless bossiness!

———

With his field crew already on task and working only a half day, Leroy decided to spend his Saturday sprucing up the exterior of his house. Admittedly, it had been sadly neglected for nearly a decade now. Probably around the same time Marcie first got sick and life got overly busy.

With Gina's help and their early start to the morning, they managed to mow all the lawns, trim the hedges, and mend a sagging fence. And now Leroy was repairing some loose boards on the front porch. Meanwhile Gina, who'd brought home several flats of blooms to brighten things up, was putting the final touches on the oversized terra-cotta planters flanking the front door. Leroy had just secured the last plank when he noticed a shiny white Escalade pull up the driveway. At first he assumed it must be the new office manager, but wondered how she could afford such a pricey car on a teacher's salary. Then, seeing more than one person inside, he grew curious.

"Hey, Gina," he called to his daughter. "Is the tasting room open already?"

"Not until three." She looked up from planting a geranium, then chuckled. "Help has arrived."

"Huh?" He stood, watching as an older woman and two younger ones got out of the SUV. They waved to Gina and then began to unload luggage from the back. Leroy hurried over to his daughter. "What're you talking about? What help?"

"I didn't want to say anything because I wasn't sure they were really coming today, but after you said Grandma's party was going to be here, I decided to get some reinforcements." She yelled out a greeting to the women as she dusted off her hands. She turned back to her dad. "And I knew just who to call."

"Reinforcements?" He lowered his voice. "We can't afford to hire—"

"We're not hiring them, Dad. It's just Mara and her sister, Cassie, and their mom. They're taking a 'working vacation' here. We won't pay 'em a penny."

He tossed his hammer into the toolbox. "Even so, we're not set up for guests. You can't just go around inviting people without telling—"

"Don't throw a hissy fit, Dad. FYI, they don't expect to be treated like guests. Besides, *I'm* handling it." Without another word, she skipped over to greet her friends. But Leroy was so aggravated that, instead of being polite and staying outside to meet them, he grabbed his toolbox and hurried around back.

Gina had gone too far this time. She had no right to invite three guests—even "working" guests—into his home without at least discussing it with him. And all women too. Plus, judging by the car and their bags and clothing, they were wealthy. They might claim they were here to help, but he had serious doubts.

As he shoved his tools into the shed, he imagined the women leisurely lounging on his back terrace, playing with their iPhones, painting their toenails, giggling excessively, and driving him nuts! He had no illusions—he knew most people assumed a vineyard was just a pretty place to relax and play—a place to take a vacation from the real world. He laughed out loud, but not with real cheer. A vineyard—his vineyard, anyway—was just plain hard work. If anyone needed a vacation, it was probably him!

He stormed over to the burn area to check on his crew, with Babe trotting alongside him, ball in mouth and tail wagging as if to say "Chill, dude." His pace soon slowed. He gave her ball a couple of good tosses, and his attitude shifted gears. He pulled in a long, slow breath of fresh air. It was cooler here today than yesterday. And working in the fragrant green vineyard, outdoors on a sunny summer day, well, it was sort of like a vacation. Albeit a working vacation. But then he'd always enjoyed a good hard day of work.

Really, what did he have to complain about? Three extra women in his house? Well, he wasn't looking forward to that, but he could just stay out of their way. He could work all day then use the back stairway to slip up to his room. He never spent much time in the house this time of year anyway. With all he had to accomplish in the next couple of weeks, he could easily make himself scarce.

Relieved to escape Gina's friends, he happily spent the rest of the day working with his field crew. He was impressed with the progress these workers had made on the burned section. Already the plants were looking much healthier. By next year at this time, these vines would probably be ready to bear fruit. Maybe the best yield ever.

"Hey, Dad." Sophie stuck her head out the window of her minivan, yelling down the slope to him. "Got a minute?"

He wiped his hands on his jeans as he hurried up the hill toward her. She didn't usually interrupt his work like this. Hopefully nothing was wrong. Her baby wasn't due until August. "What's up?" he asked when he reached her.

"Gina told me you were mad."

"Mad?" He pulled out his bandana to wipe dust from his face, then he remembered Gina's female friends. "Oh, yeah, I guess I was a little irked. But I'm over it."

"Well, she shouldn't have invited Mara and her family without your permission," Sophie said in his defense. "Anyway, I thought maybe you'd want to join us for dinner. I'm making Mom's spaghetti."

"Mom's spaghetti?" He felt his stomach rumble. "Sounds great." He looked down at Babe. "But we're on foot and dirty."

"That's okay. Hop in and I'll give you a ride." As he helped Babe into the back of Sophie's van, she explained how Garth had finished the wine-tasting session then offered to stay with the kids. "So I got to make a bread and salad run." She chuckled as he got in on the passenger side. "My excuse to get out of the house without kids."

He glanced at his work clothes. "Sorry I'm dirty, honey. Hope I don't get your van—"

"It's already dirty, Dad."

"Well, I don't need to be called twice to come to dinner. Not when it's Mom's spaghetti." He smacked his lips. "I'm ravenous."

"I've had the sauce simmering all day. Just need to cook the pasta."

Relieved not to go home to a houseful of noisy women, Leroy

rolled down the window and yelled goodbye to his crew as Sophie drove off. It was nice to see her in such good spirits. Hopefully her workload was about to lighten.

"When's your new office manager coming?" he asked as she drove up the knoll toward her house.

"Bree just called me. She said she'd be here tomorrow morning. Early."

"Great." He nodded eagerly. "She can have Sunday to get acclimated and then start work on Monday."

"Yeah. And she said she'll be arriving by motorcycle."

"Motorcycle? That's, uh, different."

Sophie just laughed. "Who cares how she gets here, Dad? As long as she comes!"

He wasn't so sure about that but didn't want to rain on her parade. Hopefully this Bree person wouldn't turn out to be some kind of wild child. If so, he'd have no problem letting her go.

Brynna's plan to tell Jan and Mike that her mind was made up and that she was passing on the job offer quickly fell by the wayside. In fact, it seemed that while she'd been on her "think and pray" walk, they'd been plotting against her. Besides accusing her of leaving poor Sophie in the lurch, "slapping kismet in the face," and being a coward, they both seemed determined to be rid of her.

"You'll do Sorrentino's while we do Yosemite," Jan said when she got back to the RV.

"But I—"

"Just do it," Mike cut her off. "Try it for a few days. What can it hurt?"

"What about Yosemite?" she pleaded. "I want to see—"

"You can do that anytime," Jan said sharply. "I checked the map, and it's only five hours from Sorrentino's."

"And Yosemite's only four hours from here," Mike added.

"Which is why we've decided to take you on my motorcycle to-morrow."

"Take me where on your motorcycle?" Brynna demanded.

"To Sorrentino's." Mike sat down in a camp chair. "Aren't you listening?"

"You're not listening to me!" She put her hands on her hips.

"Here's the plan, Brynna." Jan sounded like an authoritarian again. "Mike will drive you to Sorrentino's in the morning. Meanwhile I'll head to Yosemite. I want to arrive early and get a good campsite."

"You're just going to dump me there?" Brynna asked, turning to Mike.

He answered with a shrug.

"It's all settled then." Jan turned to Mike with a soft smile, continuing to ignore Brynna.

"You bet. I'll join you at Yosemite by midafternoon." He winked at her.

"So you two will be long gone, and I'll be stuck at Sorrentino's." Brynna could see where this was going.

Mike nodded. "What a great place to be stuck."

"What if it doesn't work? What if Leroy throws me out?" Even as she said this, she couldn't imagine sweet Leroy doing such a thing. But then, she had hurt him . . . One could build up a lot of resentment in thirty years.

"You can call me if it falls apart," Jan assured her. "We're only five hours away."

"It'll make for a long day, but I'll be glad to come and get you," Mike promised. "As long as you give it a fair try. If it doesn't work out, I'll bring you to Yosemite myself."

"Give it a couple of days at the very least," Jan urged her.

"Yeah, and remember to take it just one day at a time," Mike said gently.

"Who knows, maybe you'll make it a whole week." Jan looked hopeful.

"A week?" Brynna tried to imagine seven days of awkward humiliation.

"And after that, if you really don't want to stay at Sorrentino's, I can just pick you up on my way back to Oregon. Then I'll deliver you home to your predictable, ho-hum life. You can hole up in your stuffy little condo for the rest of your long boring summer. Maybe you can get yourself that goldfish for company. Wasn't that your summer plan, Brynna?" Jan locked eyes with her.

Despite Jan's grim but startlingly honest prediction, Brynna wasn't quite ready to give in to their pressure. But then they pulled out the big ammo. Whether it was really true or just a way to manipulate her, they suggested their need for some *alone* time—hinting that Brynna truly was a third wheel when they announced their plans to go to the coast on Mike's motorcycle—without her.

Brynna slumped down in a camp chair and thought hard about everything that had just transpired. And now she did what she hadn't really done earlier. Not in earnest, anyway. She prayed. She sincerely asked God to help her figure this mess out. She asked him to give her the strength to do the right thing. As she prayed, she considered what Mike liked to say—that God worked in mysterious ways. Maybe it really was true. Maybe God really was behind all this. And maybe she'd just been too stubborn . . . and proud . . . to figure it out.

As she said "amen" Brynna felt a strange sense of peace. For the first time since this madness had begun, she felt God really was at work here. And she felt adventurous enough to get to the bottom of it. But first she took a nap. A nice, long, peaceful nap.

Brynna woke to the sound of Mike's motorcycle. Jan and Mike were already back from their ride. As soon as they got off the bike, Brynna told them of her change of heart and even thanked them for encouraging her.

"It was sort of tough love." Mike looked slightly sheepish as he set down his helmet. "But our intentions were good."

"Well, I think it will be an adventure," Brynna told them.

"I'm so proud of you." Jan actually hugged her.

Mike gave her a high five. "You're a real trouper."

"Uh-huh . . ." Brynna wished that were more true.

"I guess I can trust you with this now." Jan's smile seemed somewhat sheepish as she handed Brynna her phone. Keeping her childish retort to herself, Brynna called Sophie's cell phone number and told her the good news.

"And I'll be there early in the morning," Brynna said. "If that's okay."

"That's not just okay. That's fabulous!" Sophie sounded so happy that Brynna felt even more sure she'd made the right choice. "I'll have Gina unlock the guest cottage for you. And I'll stop by to check on you as soon as we get back from church tomorrow."

"Sounds great." Brynna tried to match Sophie's enthusiasm, but it was probably hopeless.

"You're a real godsend, Bree."

Brynna winced at the name *Bree*, but knew she'd need to keep up her charade for a bit. She glanced over at Jan's and Mike's grinning faces, not surprised they were eavesdropping, but wondering why they weren't doing the Snoopy dance.

Before hanging up, Brynna warned Sophie that she'd arrive by motorcycle. She wasn't sure that it mattered, but since it would be early morning, she didn't want to disturb anyone. Particularly Leroy. As she pocketed her phone, she considered the fact that she'd never in her life been on a motorcycle! Normally that would terrify her, but it seemed the least of her concerns right now.

Chapter 16

On Sunday morning Brynna felt like someone else as she donned the bright blue helmet and climbed onto the back of Mike's Harley. Not that she imagined herself some kind of motorcycle mama or anything like that. More like an actor in a sci-fi flick. Because, seriously, everything about this morning felt surreal. Even the fact that Jan had already broken camp, hitched her trailer, and was about to depart for Yosemite. Without Brynna.

"Let me know how it goes." Jan held up her phone and Brynna just nodded. Then Mike took off, and Brynna held on for dear life. The upside of being horrified over a crash that could result in death or bodily injury was that it provided the perfect distraction to the growing anxiety gurgling deep down inside of her. Maybe death would be preferable.

And yet, about an hour later, Mike turned onto the Sorrentino property, and she felt a strange sense of peace. Okay, it was a confused sort of peace. The vineyard land was so beautiful and serene. With a misty fog dissipating in the golden morning sun, it was deeply soothing. But perhaps it was a faux tranquility—the result of being completely numbed from the frightening, bumpy motorcycle ride. At least it was nearly done.

She pointed Mike toward the guest cottage that Sophie had

shown her on Friday afternoon. She'd seen only the cottage's quaint exterior since Sophie hadn't had a key on her, but Brynna had been blown away by its charming Tudor style. "It reminds me of a fairy tale. Kind of like the cottage in *Snow White*," Brynna had said. Then Sophie had joked about the need for seven dwarfs to help get the work done around the vineyard.

Despite her delight over the Snow White cottage, Brynna had been disappointed over its close proximity to the family home. Situated to the rear and off to one side, it sat in plain view of the large stone house's back windows. Right now her only goal was to get safely inside without being noticed. Not that this was likely—having made her entrance on the back of a big, noisy Harley. Just the same, the moment the motorcycle stopped rolling, she hopped off. Hurrying to remove the helmet, she opened Mike's saddlebags to retrieve her things.

"Thanks for the ride," she muttered as she tugged out her duffel bag.

"Fun, huh?" He pulled out her grocery sacks with a wide grin.

"Yeah, I guess." Motorcycles were probably an acquired taste, but she didn't want to seem ungrateful.

As Mike walked her up the pavestone path to the cottage, he gave her a final pep talk, reminding her of kismet and God's mysterious ways. "Man, is this place ever cool." He whistled. "A lot of folks would pay big bucks just to stay here."

"Uh-huh." She opened the wooden door, eager to disappear inside for a while.

"You're going to be okay." His eyes were sincere as he set her groceries on an antique oak dining table. "I'll be praying for you every day."

She thanked him again and nudged him toward the door, afraid that she was about to beg him to take her back, despite her general reservations about motorcycles. After he left, she closed and locked it—leaning her back against the thick solid wood in an attempt to calm herself and breathe evenly. She could do this.

"Time to put on your big-girl pants," she gently scolded herself. "Just take it one step at a time." She started by putting her perishable groceries into the candy apple red fridge. It was a vintage reproduction and fairly roomy—and looked perfect in the old-fashioned kitchen. The cupboards were painted a creamy white, and the countertops matched the fridge. The tiny gas range really was vintage, complete with a shiny teakettle. And when she tested a burner, it worked.

From the cheerful braided rug on the pine floor to the rich golden stucco walls where mullion windows were curtained with red-and-white checks, it was all just perfect.

The living room area next to the kitchen fit an easy chair and ottoman, slip-covered in old-fashioned calicos, as well as an antique wooden rocker that was positioned in front of a small stone fireplace. She carried her duffel bag to a cozy but charming bedroom that was furnished with a white iron bed topped with a cheery patchwork quilt in shades of blues and yellow. Above the bed hung an original seascape. Leroy's late wife had not skimped on anything.

Everything about this guesthouse felt like perfection, and Brynna was reminded of what Sophie had said while pointing it out to her the other day. "Mom started to refurbish it a couple of years before she got sick. We girls were all in school at the time, and I guess she needed a project to keep her busy so she had it completely gutted. Then she redid the interior. Dad wasn't too pleased about the expense, but he gave in. Mom wanted everything perfect for when her mother came to visit. But Grandma Jenson passed away before she could ever make it here . . . and the next year Mom got sick." Then they'd both stood outside the little cottage without speaking. Brynna had wanted to tell Sophie that she understood since she'd lost both her parents at a young age. But she'd been so obsessed with getting out of her predicament that she'd been unable to even form the words.

Now, after completing her full tour of the tiny guesthouse's interior, Brynna paused to examine an intricate cross-stitched piece hanging by the front door. It had the image of a Tudor cottage quite similar to this one. But it was the words that got to her.

Brynna read them aloud. "'By wisdom a house is built . . . and through understanding it is established; through knowledge its rooms are filled with rare and beautiful treasures.' Proverbs 24:3–4."

For a long moment, she stood there thinking on the meaning of that Scripture, focusing on the three substantial words. *Wisdom, understanding, knowledge.* Weren't those the sort of qualities she hungered for in her own life? Perhaps those were characteristic of Sophie's mother—Leroy's wife. Brynna suddenly wished she could've known this woman whose life had been cut short. She felt certain she would've admired her. As Brynna turned away from the wall hanging, gazing out the window that overlooked the lush green vineyard slopes, she felt a cool wetness on her cheeks. She was crying. But these tears were not for herself.

Leroy felt aggravated by the loud rumbling noise disturbing his quiet morning coffee. He'd gotten up early, brewed a quick pot of coffee, then slipped out to his front porch. Partly to avoid the houseful of yammering women, but more so to enjoy the peaceful serenity of a gorgeous, golden morning. But that confounded motorcycle headed down the vineyard road was spoiling everything.

He stood, indignantly staring down the bike that dared steal his peace. If this was his new office manager's main mode of transportation, her employment might be short-lived. The idea of an employee tearing around the vineyard on a noisy Harley was disturbing. He watched the shiny blue bike as it turned down the graveled driveway that led to the guesthouse, confirming it was the new office manager. But why were there *two* people on the bike? One looked like a big bear of a man, and the other one wasn't much bigger than a kid.

As the bike disappeared from Leroy's sight line, the engine noise quieted to an idle. After a couple of minutes, the loud machine roared again, and the bear man drove down the road toward the main highway. *Good riddance!*

Leroy was still shaking his head in disgust when Gina padded out in her bare feet and pajamas, holding her own mug of steaming coffee. "What was that awful noise?" she asked him.

"I assume it's the new office manager," he grumbled back.

"Sounded more like a motorcycle to me." She took a sip, peering down the road where a trail of dust was still faintly visible.

"It *was* a motorcycle. A Harley." He sat back down.

She pulled the other rocker near his. "Our new manager has a Harley?"

"No. At least, I don't think so. Although Sophie mentioned a motorcycle. The Harley arrived with two and left with one. A great big guy driving it. I guess he just dropped off our new manager."

"So our manager's got a motorcycle man?" Gina chuckled.

Leroy shrugged. "Sophie said she's not married."

"Maybe the motorcycle man is her boyfriend." Gina's brows arched. "Does that mean he'll be living in the guest cottage too?"

"Good grief, I hope not." Leroy felt a fresh surge of aggravation. "Sophie wouldn't have okayed that . . . *would she?*"

"I don't know, Dad. She seemed pretty eager to hire this chick."

"Well, I'll put my foot down if she did. That guy is not going to be living here." Leroy set his coffee mug on the side table with a thud. "And if the new manager thinks he is, I might as well go tell her right now. Before they get all settled in and—"

"Oh, Dad." Gina put a firm hand on his shoulder. "Don't be so old-fashioned."

"Call me old-fashioned, but this is *my* property, Gina. And I can maintain my standards on my property. I wouldn't let my girls have live-in boyfriends here, and I sure won't have an employee doing it either."

"*Please*, Dad. Don't make a scene. You don't know what's going on. What if you charge in there and scare the poor woman to death?"

"All I'm gonna do is make sure that guy doesn't think he's coming back here to stay." Leroy started to stand, determined to nip this thing in the bud.

"Wait." Gina held up her phone. "Sophie should handle this. She's the one who hired her."

Leroy sat down again to consider her reasoning, but before he could respond, Gina was already on the phone with her sister. From the sound of it, their new hire had simply gotten a ride from the motorcycle man.

"Okay," Gina assured her sister, "I'll make sure Dad doesn't go off half-cocked." She pocketed her phone with a satisfied smile. "Sophie confirmed that Bree is single and never mentioned a live-in boyfriend. She's certain there's no problem. The motorcycle guy probably goes with the trailer lady."

"Huh?" Leroy scratched his head.

"That's what Sophie said. So don't worry, okay?"

He shrugged. "As long as it's true."

"Of course, it's true. Sophie promised to ask Bree about it, just in case. So why not let her handle it?"

"Fine. Sophie can handle it. Speaking of handling things, where's your little work crew? Sleeping in?"

"As a matter of fact, they were all just getting up. And Judith is fixing us breakfast."

"Judith?"

"Mara's mom. Remember, I told you all about her." She sounded aggravated.

He tried to think. "Well, I do remember Mara was your room-mate—before you dropped out of school." He gave her a dismal look. "But I honestly don't remember anything about a mother or sister."

"Well, Mara's sister is Cassie, and she's seventeen. Mara's mom is Judith. I'm not sure how old she is, but she's been divorced a

120

couple of years. Judith and Cassie live in Palo Alto. I spent a few weekends with them last year. Do you remember *that*?"

"I guess I have a lot going on in here." He tapped the side of his head. "Sorry."

"That's okay. Anyway, I've been wanting you to meet Judith for a while. She's really nice, Dad. Hopefully, you'll remember your manners today. You know, those same manners you taught to your kids. How to congenially meet someone without acting like a social outcast." She poked him in the chest. "I had to make your apologies yesterday. I told them you were just *so busy*."

"I *am* busy." He polished off his coffee. "In fact, I have a full day planned—"

"It's Sunday, Dad. You don't usually do real work on Sunday. You always used to say that it was a day of rest."

"And it usually is. But there's a Bible verse about this guy whose ox has fallen in a ditch on the Sabbath, saying even though it's hard work, it's okay to rescue the ox."

"You don't have an ox, Dad."

"This vineyard is my ox. And there's so much to do right now to rescue it, well, I think God will understand." He stood.

"But don't you want to have breakfast with us? Judith plans to make something special. I think she's going to serve it on the back terrace and everything. Mara wants to make fresh-squeezed orange juice, and Cassie's setting the table up real nice. And they all want you to join us."

Leroy let out a low groan.

"Judith's a great cook. And she loves French cuisine. She's making crepes with fresh berries, cheese blintzes, and I can't remember what else."

Leroy considered the granola bar and banana he'd stuck in his denim jacket pocket. "Well, okay then. I guess I could join you ladies for breakfast. Just don't expect me to sit around and chew the fat all morning."

Gina laughed. "There won't be much fat, Dad. Judith's a vegetarian."

He rolled his eyes. "So no bacon and eggs, then?"

Gina punched him playfully. "Come on, Dad. Be a good sport, okay?"

"I'll do my best," he assured her. "In the meantime, I need to go check on the south slope drip lines. I noticed water was puddling in the low section." He reached for his hat, then shoved it onto his head. "I've got my phone. Let me know when it's time to eat."

"And you'll really come this time?" Gina looked skeptical. "You won't blow us off like you did last night?"

"I'll be there with bells on." He winked.

"Skip the bells, Dad. Just be there."

He nodded somberly. "You have my word."

She grinned then took his empty coffee mug and went inside. Now Leroy knew that, as a man of his word, he'd have to join the females for their fancy French breakfast and try to act like a gentleman—but he could eat fast.

Chapter 17

Even though the guest cottage was sweet and charming, a closer look revealed that it hadn't been thoroughly cleaned for some time. And so Brynna decided to spend her Sunday giving it a good deep clean, starting with the windows, which held years of grime and dust. She found cleaning products and rags beneath the small farmhouse sink, then rolled up her sleeves and went to work. Something about making the thick old panes sparkle and gleam made Brynna happy. As if she could see clearer now too. And, like Snow White in the old movie that she'd watched on a VHS tape as a child, she even started to whistle while she worked.

Her spirits continued to rise as she scrubbed the bedroom window. Because this room was in the rear of the cottage, it had a direct view of the main house. With the lace curtains pushed away, Brynna could clearly see a small gathering on the house's oversized back terrace. Four females appeared to be setting up a rather fancy breakfast with a colorful tablecloth and a big bouquet of fresh flowers. It all looked festive and fun. As she scrubbed the window, Brynna studied the group, curious as to who they might be. The blond woman with short, stylish hair seemed older, but the other girls were younger. Perhaps they were Sophie's sisters or friends. But Sophie didn't appear to be with them. Although the window was closed and she couldn't hear them, they all seemed to be having a good time. Off to one side of the patio was what looked like a nice outdoor kitchen, but they didn't seem to be using it. Still, it was a nice setup and Brynna imagined it would be fun to use to fix a meal outside.

The partiers' attention turned to the oversized sliding glass door just as a man emerged onto the terrace. Brynna came to attention too. Dropping her cleaning rag, as well as her jaw, she openly stared for a long moment. Then, feeling self-conscious, although no one was looking her way, she pulled the curtains back over the window. But, like a child with her nose pressed to the toy store window, she continued to gape through the lacy holes in the curtain, spying on the social gathering, watching as the group grew even merrier.

The four women, smiling and laughing with fresh animation, clustered around the man as he removed a straw cowboy hat and ran his hand through his wavy hair. It was medium brown and a bit longish, but it was his face that knocked the air out of Brynna. She would've recognized him anywhere! An older version of the exact same Leroy she'd met thirty years ago. Leroy wore faded jeans, brown boots, and a pale-blue Western shirt with sleeves rolled up to reveal tanned forearms. And his smile was just as handsome as ever! Unless she was mistaken, he'd gotten even better looking.

With her heart pounding, Brynna watched as Leroy greeted the women and even exchanged some hugs. Then the blond woman took him by the arm, leading him to the head of the table. The other girls sat around him, almost as if he were holding court. The blond woman began to serve food and one of the girls poured his orange juice. The scene was like something out of an old movie. Everyone jovial and lighthearted, enjoying a picture-perfect breakfast on a lovely summer morning. But nothing about this picture felt pleasant to Brynna. In fact, it made her feel so sick that she was glad she hadn't eaten breakfast.

What am I doing here?

With trembling hands, she smoothed the curtains, hoping that no one had noticed their snooping neighbor. As she stepped away, trying to catch her breath and slow down her racing heartbeat, she asked herself again—what *was* she doing here? And how could she possibly make a graceful exit? Call a taxi? Hitch a ride with visitors from the tasting room? Sneak out on foot in the middle of the night? Pray for vanishing powers?

Still feeling unsteady, she went into the tiny bathroom and ran cold water into the little sink, splashing it on her face. She needed to snap out of this. To get ahold of herself and stop acting like a silly adolescent. And then she needed to make a plan.

"It's no big deal," she told herself. Why shouldn't Leroy entertain women in his backyard? Or even in his home? And even if that blond woman *was* his girlfriend, what did it have to do with Brynna? For all she knew, the blond was his fiancée. And why not? Leroy was probably still a very nice guy—and would probably make a great husband. He was a good catch and fair game. And it was none of her business! As she towel-dried her face, Brynna wondered why he hadn't been remarried by now. Women must've lined up at his door. But really, what was it to her?

Trying to calm herself, she gazed around the bathroom. Like the bedroom, it had delicate white lace curtains that also looked toward the family home—not that she planned to look! She inhaled a slow, deep breath, taking in her surroundings. Clean and serene. Several small original seascapes graced the pale blue walls. Above the petite claw-foot tub hung a metal rack filled with fluffy towels and some lavender bath salts in a glass mason jar. If she wasn't so intent on escaping, a soothing soak would be tempting.

Just like the rest of the cottage, this tiny bathroom was perfection. One more treasure left behind by Leroy's deceased wife. Brynna wished she knew this woman's name. She must've been a very happy woman and a wonderful wife . . . but her life had been cut short. For the second time this morning, Brynna cried. And this time, it was partly for herself. But even more than that, it was for Leroy . . . and for the loss of his wife.

Somehow she felt she understood why, after all these years, he had never remarried. It just seemed to make sense. No one could measure up to his dearly departed wife, the mother of his three girls. And although that was discouraging to her on one level, it was deeply satisfying on another.

Leroy truly was a good man—loyal to his sweet wife, both in life and in death. This image of him made Brynna feel stronger. She no longer wanted to run and hide. What did it matter? Even if Leroy didn't hate her, he would not be interested. In fact, he would probably be completely neutral. And that, strangely, felt like a relief.

Besides, she reminded herself, she'd made a commitment to Sophie. She owed it to her to be of some help. Hopefully, she could lighten her load. Even if only for a few days. And she would refuse to accept a penny of pay. Just staying in the cottage and being here was worth free labor. And it was satisfying to know she would leave the guest cottage in better shape than she found it. Because she knew her time here would soon end. Once Leroy figured things out, it would be time to go. And fine, she would be ready.

In the meantime, she would just enjoy this sweet little respite in the guest cottage—and tomorrow, she would work super hard. Even Jan and Mike wouldn't be able to fault her for not giving her best try. Not that she planned to call and interrupt their time in Yosemite. No, as she hung the towel back on its bar, she decided she would simply arrange to get home another way. End of story.

By coming to this realization and making this decision, she felt free inside. Whatever would be would be. She would do her best to help Sophie. The rest was out of her hands. Whether it was kismet or God, it would all work out . . . in time.

⌒

Leroy didn't have to put himself out to participate in the conversation around the breakfast table. Judith, her daughters, and Gina filled in so much of the space, there was barely room to insert a word or two. And that was fine with him. In fact, accustomed to being the only male in a houseful of women, he was used to it. Plus, it allowed him to eat quickly, without being rude.

And, although the picture-perfect meal Judith had fixed was palatable enough, it wasn't his favorite sort of fare. He'd never been into fancy food. It had taken awhile to make Marcie understand he was a meat and pasta man. Eventually she'd accepted this fact and had even collected some of his family's recipes, including the meat and mushroom marinara sauce that she'd made her own.

"Would you like some more?" Judith extended the platter of cheese blintzes toward him with a wide smile.

He held up a hand. "No, thank you. Like those blintzes, I'm stuffed." The women politely laughed at his lame attempt at a joke. Then he stood. "Thanks so much, ladies. Everything was delightful, including your company. But I've got a lot to get done today, so if you'll excuse me."

"We have a lot to do too," Gina told him. "I'm going to keep working on the landscaping and planters, and Mara and Cass are going to start painting the doors and trim on the barn. Won't that look nice?"

"Yeah, it hasn't been painted in years. What color?" he asked.

"Well, it might sound weird, but I got this really deep espresso brown."

"Brown? With red?" He rubbed his chin. "The trim's always been white."

"But red and white is so provincial." Gina dropped her napkin on her plate. "Plus, the white gets dirty and looks dingy. To be honest, I'm not a fan of the red, but we can't afford to change that right now."

"Your mother picked the red," he reminded her.

"I like the red," Judith said, butting in. "It's like a fine cabernet."

"Thank you." He nodded to her. "That's exactly what it was supposed to be."

"Yeah, but the white trim makes it look like you should have chickens and cows inside," Gina protested.

"I wouldn't mind having chickens and cows. Good way to get my milk and eggs," he shot back. Gina's friends chuckled.

"Trust me, Dad, the espresso trim is going to look just great."

"It will be like cabernet and coffee," Judith suggested.

He wasn't so sure but didn't want to keep arguing. "I guess we'll see." He reached for his hat. "You ladies have a good day."

"Leroy, before you go, tell us. Will you be joining us for dinner?" Judith stood with a hopeful expression. "I'm making something very special."

"Well, I—"

"Of course he will." Gina started to clear the table. "He'll be here with bells on." She shot him a warning glance. "Right, Dad?"

"Well, you heard her." He tipped his hat to the group. "See you all later." Then, trying not to feel overly irked at his youngest daughter's strong will, he hurried on his way. Give that girl an inch and she'd surely take a country mile. A brown-and-red barn? Who'd heard of such a thing?

———

Brynna jumped at the sound of a knock at the door. What if it were Leroy? She'd felt ready for this earlier, but after several hours of serious housecleaning and still feeling grungy from camp life, she longed for a bath in the sweet claw-foot tub. She wasn't ready to meet him now! Even so, she tugged the bandana she'd used to tie back her long, in-need-of-shampoo hair and crept to a side window to see who was at the door. To her relief, it was Sophie. "Coming," she called, hurrying to open the door. "Sorry," she said, swinging it open wide. "I was in the midst of some housecleaning." She leaned against the doorframe. "Not expecting guests."

"You're cleaning? On your first day here?" Sophie came in and deposited a basket on the kitchen table. "I brought some provisions for you. In case you didn't have time to get anything. But now I feel bad that you felt the need to spend the day cleaning the place."

"Oh, it's not like it was terribly dirty." Brynna tossed her dusting rag into the sink, hoping Sophie wouldn't see how dark it had become.

"It's just that I assumed you'd be out enjoying the gorgeous weather. It's the first day it hasn't been stinking hot in a week."

"It does look nice out there." Brynna looked longingly out the front window. She would've loved to feel free to roam . . . "But cleaning's good therapy for me." Plus, it delayed the inevitable—bumping into Leroy.

"I get that." Sophie laughed. "I'd probably do the exact same thing. Come to think of it, I don't know when it was last cleaned. Luna stays here sometimes, but she's not into housekeeping."

"It's such a darling cottage, dirty or clean. I just love it."

Sophie smiled at Brynna. Her jaw dropped a bit as she took a look around the room. "Wow, I can't remember the last time I saw these windows so clean." She sighed. "Probably when Mom was alive. She always kept it up."

"You mentioned your mother put this place together." Brynna wanted to tread carefully here. "I just have to say that it's absolutely perfect. I have the greatest respect for your mother just from being here."

"Really?" Sophie turned to Brynna with misty eyes. "She did a beautiful job on it, didn't she? It always makes me feel closer to her when I come here. But I haven't been over for a while."

"Well, I feel very privileged to stay here. Even if it's just a short time."

Sophie's brow furrowed. "Why should it be a short time?"

"Oh, well, you never know. I'm just saying I think this cottage is really special."

Sophie's smile returned. "I do too. But not everyone appreciates it. Gina and Luna think it's too outdated. They want to make it all minimalist and modern, but I love it just like this."

"Oh, no, this cottage shouldn't be modern," Brynna said. "It's got such charm and personality."

"They say it's too much personality. But then they weren't as close to Mom as I was. Probably because I'm the oldest. And, well, Dad says I'm a lot like her."

"What was your mother's name?" Brynna asked. "I'm just curious. I mean, because I can sort of feel her here."

"Marcia, but she went by Marcie."

"Marcie." Brynna nodded, then pointed to the needlework by the door. "Did she make that?"

Sophie turned to see what she was pointing at. "Yes. That was one of her favorite verses. Dad said it was because she liked to spend money on frivolous things."

"Really?"

"Oh, he wasn't trying to be mean. But he's always been pretty frugal. And Mom, well, she wasn't exactly frugal."

"Well, I think she made good choices in here. It doesn't seem over-the-top, but very sweet and comforting."

"Yeah, she really wanted Grandma Jenson to come here. Grandma had emphysema from smoking, but then everyone in her generation smoked. At least, that's what she told me when I asked her about it once."

"And did she get to stay here?"

"No, unfortunately. After she moved down to San Diego, she got too sick to travel . . . and then she died."

"Now I remember. You mentioned how you lost your grandma and your mom pretty close together. I'm sorry."

"Yeah, that was pretty hard. On everyone."

"My parents died in a car wreck when I was in college, so I sort of understand."

"You lost both your parents?" Sophie's eyes grew wide. "That would be really terrible. I'm lucky to still have Dad."

"He must've done a good job raising you girls." Brynna felt like she was fishing for more information, but it wasn't really what she'd intended. "I mean, because you turned out so great, Sophie. I don't know about your sisters. Well, except that they don't like old-fashioned charm." She smiled.

"Oh, Gina and Luna are okay. Gina's the baby, but she's determined to help Dad with the vineyard. She even wants to quit college to do it. Of course, Dad's not so sure about that, but he gave her the summer to prove herself. And, man, is he working her hard. You'll probably meet her tomorrow."

"And your other sister, does she help out here too?"

"Maybe someday. Luna's in law school right now. Well, not right now. She took the summer off to intern with a law firm in San Francisco. But she'll probably pop in once in a while. Like for Grandma's birthday."

"Your grandma's birthday?"

"Dad's mom. Grandma Dorothy is turning eighty-five. My aunt Sherry was planning this ridiculously huge party for her. Then Dad got stuck hosting it here, so we'll be extra busy this summer." Sophie smiled hopefully. "Think you're up for helping?"

"Sure. However I can."

"Great. That's what I told Dad. Speaking of Dad, did you meet him yet?"

"No." Brynna glanced away.

Sophie cleared her throat. "Well, he sort of asked me to, uh . . . to make sure you understand you can't have any guests here in the guesthouse."

"Guests?" Brynna was confused. "Why would I have guests?"

"I don't know. But Dad saw that guy on the motorcycle, and he got all worried he might be your boyfriend and that you would want him to live here with you."

Brynna couldn't help but laugh. "That was *not* my boyfriend. He's just a friend. More like a friend of a friend. Just helping out."

"That's what I thought, but I promised to make sure." Sophie frowned. "So does that mean you don't have a car?"

131

"I have a car . . . back in Oregon." Brynna grimaced. "But I'm pretty much without wheels right now. I hope it's not a problem."

"Well, your commute's pretty short." She grinned. "And if you have errands, or if we need you to do something off the property, you can probably borrow a vehicle. We have some spares." Sophie went to the table and removed a jar from the basket. "This is raspberry jam I made last summer." She unpacked a loaf of bread, a wedge of cheese, a jar of homemade sauce, and even a bottle of wine. "I didn't know if you brought any food with you, but this is sort of your welcome to Sorrentino's gift."

"That's really sweet. Thank you. I did get some groceries yesterday, so I'll be fine for a while." Brynna picked up the jam. "You really made this? It looks lovely."

"Yeah. My raspberries really came in good last year. They look promising for this summer too. In fact, my whole garden looks great."

"That must be wonderful. I've always wanted a garden."

"You mean you've never had one? I would think you could grow lots of things in Oregon. Isn't it really wet up there?"

"Yes, but I live in a condo. As a kid, my mom had a small garden with tomatoes and squash and lots of flowers. I always enjoyed helping with that."

"Well, as much as I love my garden, it's a lot of work. Garth helps some and I'm trying to get the kids more involved, but it can be overwhelming at times."

"Do you need any help?" Brynna asked eagerly.

"Seriously?"

"Absolutely! I'd love to work in a garden. I mean after office hours, of course. But it would be nice to have something to fill my time. Do you live nearby? Could I walk there?"

"You could, but it's a bit of a hike. How about if I loan you my old bike? It's not like I'm using it these days." She patted her belly.

"A bike!" Brynna felt like clapping. "Perfect."

"I'll have Garth put it in his truck bed and bring it with him tomorrow." Sophie picked up the basket. "And if there's anything else you need, just let me know."

"I do have one concern." Brynna pointed down to her slightly rumpled and not-too-clean T-shirt and shorts. "The clothes I brought with me, well, I didn't bring a lot since I only expected to be camping, but most of what I have is dirty."

"Oh, you can do laundry in the house. Just go through the side door on the left. It goes straight to the laundry room."

"So I won't be disturbing anyone?" Brynna cringed at the idea of bumping into Leroy while sorting her whites.

"I doubt it. Gina does her laundry late at night, and believe me, Dad rarely does any at all. But that's because I do it for him."

"Okay, but it looked like there might be houseguests." Again, she felt like she was fishing. Sure she was curious, but more than that, she wanted to get her clothes washed without drawing attention to herself.

"Oh, that's right. Gina invited her friends here. I just met them. They're not really guests since they're supposed to be working. It's just Gina's college roommate, Mara, and Mara's sister and mom." Sophie rolled her eyes. "I think my baby sister might be playing matchmaker with Dad."

"Matchmaker?"

"Dad just told me that Judith—that's Mara's mom—is being awfully friendly."

Brynna nodded, trying to think of a neutral response. "Oh."

"But Dad's not really into dating. He's made it clear that he has no plans to remarry—ever."

"Because he still loves your mother?" When Brynna saw Sophie's brow crease, she wished she could retract those words. *Stop being so nosy!*

"Yeah, maybe that's part of it. I don't know. Dad would say it's because he's too busy—no time for a woman in his life. He used to say it was because of us girls. Now he just blames the vineyard."

"Well, I can understand that." Brynna was eager to change topics but came up blank.

"Although Judith might have figured out the way to get to him. Gina said she's a really good cook and Dad doesn't eat right most of the time. I have to admit, she does seem nice. And she's really pretty." She shrugged. "So, who knows, maybe Dad has finally met his match. To be honest, I'd be relieved if he found someone to look after him. Well, as long as she was the *right* someone."

Brynna felt her cheeks grow warm. This conversation was getting more and more uncomfortable. "Well, back to the laundry situation. Maybe I should wait until Gina's friends go before I try to do my laundry."

"But they might be here two weeks."

"Two weeks?" Brynna blinked.

"Yeah. It's supposed to be a working vacation. They're here to help spruce the place up. Right now Mara and her sister are painting trim on the barn and Judith is organizing the kitchen."

"That's nice."

Sophie nodded. "Gina has a long to-do list. You must've noticed how neglected and run-down this place is."

"I assumed it was part of its old-world charm." Brynna smiled.

"You sound like Dad."

"I'll take that as a compliment."

"Anyway, even though the house is full, you should be able to wash your clothes okay. Or else I can take your laundry with me and—"

"No way, Sophie. I won't have you doing my laundry." Brynna stuck out her chin. "I'll figure it out. But besides the laundry thing, like I said, I only have camp clothes. Really casual. Just jeans, T-shirts, and shorts. Nothing nice and maybe not too great for the office."

"Well, that's okay. We're pretty casual around here."

Brynna pointed to Sophie's floral-print dress. "That doesn't look too casual. And you wore something nice on Friday too."

"I've been wearing more dresses lately. But only because I'm so big and my maternity pants are too tight." She made a face. "Today, I dressed up a bit more for church. Not that anyone else does. But my mom always did."

"You do look very pretty." Brynna smiled.

"Thanks."

"Well, I don't want to offend anyone by appearing *too* casual in the office. I respect it's a business. And trust me, even teaching third graders, I dress with a bit more style. Maybe I should go shopping . . ."

"I know!" Sophie held up a finger. "Luna!"

"Luna?"

"Yeah. Luna cleaned out her closet during spring break. I've been meaning to take her cast-off clothes to Salvation Army, but I keep forgetting. The bags are still in my garage. You want them?"

"I, uh, I don't know." Brynna sighed. "I'm not exactly an average size."

"Don't worry. Luna's the shortest of us girls. She might be a little taller than you, but she's really petite." Sophie gave her a once-over. "I actually think a lot of her stuff might work for you. And she's the fashionista of the family, so there could be some pretty nice pieces in there. I'll drop them by in a little while, and you can go through and see if something works."

"Okay . . . thank you." Brynna forced a grateful smile, wondering how it would feel to wear Leroy's daughter's hand-me-downs.

"And, come to think of it, there are times when you should look more professional in the office," Sophie told her. "Sometimes a corporate wine buyer will drop by. Or an event planner. And Garth is hoping you'll be able to help in the tasting room occasionally. Anyway, I'm sure you'll find something appropriate in Luna's things."

"I'll do my best."

"Great. I'll meet you at the office at nine tomorrow to start training you. Garth promised to keep the kids until it's time to open the tasting room." She glanced at her phone, which was chiming. "That's him now. I'll explain more to you tomorrow. I'm glad you like the guesthouse."

"Like it? I *love* it!" Brynna thanked her again for the jam and goodies as she walked her to the door, but instead of following Sophie to the minivan, she waved from the porch. She just didn't want to see anyone . . . or have anyone see her. Not yet anyway. Perhaps by tomorrow.

Chapter 18

After Sophie left, Brynna decided to handwash some of her clothes in an effort to avoid having to use the main house laundry room. But for some reason, maybe it was the old-fashioned guesthouse, it turned into a surprisingly soothing chore. As she wrung out the last soggy T-shirt, she felt almost like a pioneer. She draped most of her garments outside on the porch banister to dry in the sunshine and was just hanging her wet underthings in the bathroom when she heard a loud knock on the front door. Certain it couldn't be Sophie again, Brynna froze. What if it really was Leroy this time? She was even less ready to see him now!

For a brief, horrifying moment, she stared at her image in the bathroom mirror. Had she ever looked worse? Besides her dirty hair that had been slicked back with a red bandana, she didn't have a speck of makeup on. She had a zit on her forehead, and her skimpy tank top—the only shirt she hadn't washed—was something she wore only as an undershirt. Her tattered shorts, really pajama shorts, weren't anything she'd ever wear in public either. Not on purpose anyway. But the knock came again.

She dashed through the bedroom then, crouching down low to avoid being spotted through the big front window, and crept over to peek through a side window next to the door. A white pickup was parked in the driveway. Could that belong to Leroy? If so, why would he drive here when he could so easily walk? The knocking came again, even louder this time.

"Bree?" a man's voice called.

She cowered lower. Had she locked the door? What would she do if Leroy suddenly burst in? Not that he would, but it was his property and he'd already been concerned about her harboring guests here. She felt sick.

"Hey, Bree!" the deep voice yelled again. "I'm Sophie's husband, and I brought you some things."

She crawled out from her hiding place, jerked open the door, and, using it to shield herself, peered at the young man she recognized from the tasting room. He had two large black bags in his arms. "Hello?" she muttered nervously.

"Sorry to intrude." He looked embarrassed. "I realize we haven't officially met, but Sophie insisted I bring you these." He held one of the bags toward her. "For you."

She gratefully grabbed the bag, clutching it close to conceal her strange attire. "Thanks."

"I'm Garth, Sophie's husband." He set down the other bag, then stuck out his hand.

"Nice to meet you, Garth. I'm Bree." Glad she remembered to use her alias, she smiled as they shook hands. "Sophie's told me so much about you. I feel like I already know you."

"Same here. Sophie's talked about you almost nonstop since Friday. She's so glad you took the job. She wanted me to bring you these bags today." Then he nodded over his shoulder. "Plus, I parked the bike by your porch. Sophie said you needed it."

She eagerly took in the sight of the retro-styled turquoise bicycle—complete with a wicker basket—that was sitting in the grass by the porch. "I didn't expect these things so soon, but I really do appreciate you taking the time today. Thanks so much!"

He nodded. "Well, Sophie is so thrilled you're here. She wanted you to have what you needed, and I was going to town anyway."

138

She thanked him again and was about to close the door when he spoke up. "I, uh, don't want to step over the line here, Bree, but I do want to say something. You see, Sophie has these really high standards, and I'm afraid they'll spill over onto you." He held his hands up in front of him. "It's not that I think you won't deliver, but I want you to understand she's a real perfectionist and sometimes she gets some unrealistic expectations. My mom says she's an overachiever. Anyway, Soph's gotten it into her head that you're like that too. She thinks you'll jump in right where she left off—after just one day of training. I told her that might not be possible and that she'll need to pace herself—and you will too. But she's convinced you're going to hit the ground sprinting tomorrow. And she's certain you'll have Sorrentino's running like clockwork by the end of the week."

"Oh?" Brynna tried to absorb this.

"I told her that's not realistic, but I'm not sure she was listening. So I just thought I'd give you a little heads-up. A warning, I guess."

"Okay. I appreciate that."

"Hopefully it wasn't TMI." He chuckled. "Sophie accuses me of overcommunicating sometimes."

"No, no. I appreciate it, Garth. And I'll keep it in mind with her tomorrow. Pacing ourselves is good advice. Especially since she needs to take care of herself and the baby."

"Absolutely. She always overdoes it. I want her to slow down." His brow creased. "By the way, she's even gotten this crazy notion that you're going to help in her garden."

"I want to help," Brynna insisted. "I can't wait to get my hands dirty. *Really!*"

He looked surprised. "Well, okay then. That's cool."

"And don't worry," she assured him. "I think I understand Sophie. Maybe better than you realize. We'll be fine. I promise."

He looked relieved. "Okay . . . great."

"Thanks again for bringing me the bike and clothes." She reached for the door.

"And, hey, you don't have to tell Soph I said anything."

She laughed. "Don't worry. Mum's the word."

"Thanks, Bree." He tipped his head. "You're all right."

As Garth got into his pickup, Brynna couldn't help but smile at his concern for his wife. She felt pretty sure Sophie had gotten herself a good man. It was reassuring to know good men really did exist. Not too long ago, although it seemed a lifetime now, Brynna had felt certain most men were jerks. Maybe she'd been wrong.

Still concerned that Leroy might unexpectedly show up, Brynna locked the door and decided it was time to do something about her neglected appearance and hygiene. She took a leisurely bath, vigorously shampooed and conditioned her hair, and after digging through one of Luna's bags, discovered a pale blue sundress that, to her amazement, fit almost perfectly. Then she went outside in her bare feet, hoping to dry her hair in the late-afternoon sun.

But as she sat there in the porch rocker, marveling at the gorgeous view stretched out before her, she noticed that the planting beds alongside the cottage were totally overgrown. On closer examination, she spied some little purple flowers struggling to grow amid the intrusive weeds.

And so, despite being all fresh and clean for the first time in days, Brynna got down on her hands and knees and started to tug out the pesky weeds. It didn't take long to accumulate an impressive pile. And her reward was discovering all sorts of growing treasures that lay hidden below. Feeling like a kid at Christmas, she unearthed lavender and verbena and delicate forget-me-nots, as well as some yellow blooms she didn't even recognize. The aroma was lovely! For a long moment, she just knelt there inhaling the sweet, earthy fragrance—heaven on earth.

But the sound of someone yelling interrupted her. "Dad!" a female voice called out, probably from the back of the main house. "Get yourself up here. It's time for dinner."

Although Brynna couldn't see who was yelling, she assumed it was Gina, the daughter who lived at home. But when she heard a male voice answer "Coming!" from down in the vineyard below her, she leaped to her feet and, with a racing heart, spun around in time to spot a lanky man coming directly toward her. Less than fifty yards away, she had no doubt it was Leroy striding between the grapevines, heading, it seemed, straight to the guesthouse. Of course, she knew he really had to be going up to his house, but seeing him like this was unnerving. And it seemed quite likely he'd seen her too. But did he recognize her? She still wasn't ready to find out.

Not wanting to draw his attention by bolting into the cottage, like she wanted to, she knelt down by the flower bed again. Focusing on a lavender plant that probably wanted to thank her for bringing back the sunshine, she picked a few sprigs and casually sniffed them and then, without looking in Leroy's direction, slowly turned around and leisurely strolled into the cottage. Like her heart wasn't pounding out of her chest.

Once inside, she locked the door and, trying to regain even breathing by inhaling the fragrance of lavender, leaned her back against it. Would Leroy follow her up here and knock on her door? And if he did, what would she say? She had yet to prepare a speech that would explain her presence in his world. But after several minutes of silence, Brynna realized he wasn't coming. He probably hadn't even noticed her. When she peeked out the bedroom window, discretely peering through the lace curtains, she could see he was already on the back terrace, which, similar to this morning, was set for the evening meal.

This time there was a long table, beautifully set with a tablecloth and flowers and several oil lanterns, although it was still light out. The smaller table, off to one side, was being filled with dishes of food by the younger women. Judith was talking to Leroy. Sophie and Garth and their two children, as well as an older woman, who was probably Leroy's mother, were gathering around the table as well. Before long, they were taking seats at the long table, all ten of them. She knew because she counted them. Judith lit the lanterns and sat down, then Leroy bowed his head and the others followed suit.

It was such a tender sight that Brynna couldn't help but stare. They all looked so congenial and connected and comfortable with each other, like one big happy family. Like something she'd always longed for, but never really experienced in her own life. With a deep-rooted longing, she watched them start to eat. Passing food, talking, pouring wine, laughing. As the sky became a dusky indigo-blue, the light from the lanterns glowed golden and warm. Brynna stared so intently at the picturesque scene that her eyes began to water. Finally she turned away, determined not to cry.

Refusing to feel sorry for herself, she decided to focus on putting the bedroom and bathroom in order. She started by stowing away her camp clothes, now clean and dry, as well as the numerous items she'd scavenged from Luna's castoffs. Surprisingly, most of them seemed to work. Why the girl wanted to get rid of such nice garments, some barely worn, was a mystery, but Brynna was grateful for them.

Almost done with her housekeeping, she was just putting her only two pairs of blue jeans in the bottom of the old dresser when she noticed a brown book in the back of the drawer. She removed a leather-bound Bible with the name MARCIA LOUISE JENSON embossed in gold letters. It seemed well worn. Brynna guessed that it must've been Marcie's before she married. But wouldn't one of her daughters want it? Brynna would have to remember to mention it to Sophie. But for now, Brynna opened it with reverence, flipping through the pages, many that had notes written in the margins.

Brynna paused on the decorative page between the Old and New Testaments that was designated for recording important dates. Marcie's birthdate was scribed in a childish hand, and unless there'd been some mistake, she would've been fifty by now, which made her two years older than Leroy. The next recorded event, their wedding date, had been twenty-eight years ago, which meant they'd been quite young when they married. It also meant that Leroy must've found Marcie shortly after Brynna had sent him that Dear John letter.

Well, it obviously hadn't taken Leroy very long to get over her. On one hand, that was a comfort because it suggested that seeing him now might not be nearly as awkward as she'd imagined. But on the other hand, it stung to realize he'd never cared that much. But hadn't she suspected as much back then? She'd never received a response to that final letter. At the time, she'd expected him to challenge her, perhaps even show up and beg her to rethink her decision. And maybe she would've . . .

Because if Leroy had been truly in love, wouldn't he have questioned her, or called, or insisted on a final conversation? But it seemed he'd simply taken it in stride. And then he'd gotten married.

Of course, she'd gotten married quite young too. Not that it had turned out as well for her as it had for Leroy. But studying these dates, trying to put the puzzle pieces together, she realized that she'd been completely forgotten long ago. Of course, that made her wonder, What was the point of her being here now? Except that she loved it here. And, really, wouldn't it be a blessing if he didn't remember her at all? If he saw her and simply shrugged? There would be no conflict, nothing for her to explain.

Leroy did his best to be congenial for the big dinner that Judith and the girls had worked so hard to prepare and serve. And it had been pleasant having Garth and Sophie and the kids there. And his mother too. But there were a few things that had troubled him. For starters, he didn't like how Judith allowed her daughters to have wine. Mara wasn't quite twenty-one and Cassie was still in high school! Oh, Judith claimed it was very acceptable in France, but this wasn't France, and he'd always been a stickler against underage drinking. Especially when it came to his daughters and their friends. Still, he didn't want to turn dinner into a big scene. Thankfully, Gina respected his rules.

And as far as the fancy cuisine went, he was tired after a long day and would've preferred burgers on the grill with just his own family. But he knew that Gina was happy having her friends here, and Judith seemed determined to wow everyone with her culinary skills. He had to admit that, even though it was meatless lasagna, it wasn't too bad. Although his mother's lasagna was better. But everyone else had seemed to enjoy it. And now they were all looking forward to dessert, some concoction he couldn't even pronounce that sounded like a bathtub—not something he cared to eat. He was hoping for an escape.

And when he noticed his mother was winding down, stifling a yawn, he decided this was his chance. He leaned over his mom and quietly asked how she was doing. "I know you're not a late-night person, Mom. Ready to call it a day?"

"I suppose I'm a little worn out," she admitted. "I got up rather early this morning to work on Sherry's herb garden. She neglects it so."

"How about I give you a ride home?" he offered.

She shrugged, but he could tell she was game so he stood. "Hey, if you'll all excuse us, I think I'll take Mom home now. She's had a long day, and she's not really a night person."

"What about dessert?" Gina asked. "Judith made clafoutis."

He was already helping his mom out of her chair. "Well, I have no idea what that claw-foot thing is, but I'm sure it's delicious." He gave them his brightest smile. "How about if I have some later?"

"Yes, of course." Judith beamed at him. "I'll save some for you and we'll send some home with Dorothy." She turned to Cassie. "Why don't you go get a piece ready, sweetie?"

"But we brought Grandma," Sophie told Leroy. "We should take her home."

"No," he insisted. "Stay and enjoy." He grinned at his grandkids. "You guys want dessert, don't you?"

Naturally, the kids didn't disagree, and so without further ado, Leroy got his mom and her foil-wrapped clafoutis out of there.

As they walked out to the Jeep, the golden light was just starting to meld into the edge of the western horizon, and the rest of the sky was turning a dusky shade of indigo. A nighthawk swooped by and Leroy had to admit to himself, this was one of his favorite times of day—and having a social gathering out on his back terrace was something he'd neglected for ages. But tonight, he'd remembered times gone by . . . as a boy with his family . . . with his girls and Marcie . . . happy family meals outside on a summer evening. From the soft jazz music that someone had put on to the glow of the kerosene lanterns, the conversations, and a good bottle of wine flowing—for adults only!—well, it was all pretty cool. All except for the present crowd sitting out there. Judith and her daughters weren't bad people, but they weren't his people. And he was relieved to be out of there!

Chapter 19

"I'm glad you were ready to head out," Leroy confided to his mom after they were safely in his Jeep. "I was just looking for an excuse to escape."

"Yes, well, I'm just not much for nighttime parties anymore." She sighed and leaned back against her seat. "Part of getting old."

"What did you think of Judith's meatless lasagna?" he asked as he pulled out of his driveway.

"You want my honest opinion, son?"

"Of course." He waited, knowing his mom wouldn't mince words with him.

"If you're going to make lasagna, make it like an Italian, not the French. Lasagna is supposed to be rich and spicy, with layer upon layer of goodness—sausage, mozzarella, ricotta, parmesan. Good grief, I wasn't even born into an Italian family like your father was, and I know that much."

Leroy laughed. "So, I take it you're not a fan."

She shrugged. "Well, I would never complain to the hostess." She turned to him. "She was certainly acting like the hostess, Leroy. Is there something I should know?"

"Like we told you, Judith and her daughters are Gina's guests. They're on a working vacation. And, believe me, Gina is really working them."

"Seems to me the mother is working on you."

He laughed again.

"I'm serious, Leroy. Women recognize these things in other women. That Judith has set her cap for you."

"Set her cap?" Leroy chuckled.

"You know what I mean. Casting her net, baiting her hook, setting her trap. That woman has set her sights on you."

"Well, I sort of suspected that myself. It's probably Gina's fault. I had a feeling she had something up her sleeve right from the start. And she keeps reminding me of Judith's fine qualities. I'll admit the woman is nice enough, and she's pretty and thoughtful and can carry on a good conversation."

"Oh?" She sounded interested.

"But she's not my type, Mom."

"Your type." She sighed. "What is your type?"

He didn't answer as he drove over the private back road that linked the two vineyards. Did he even have a type?

"You mean she's not like Marcie?" his mom tried.

"Well, that's for sure. Judith and Marcie are as different as night and day."

"Certainly, Judith has much more polish and poise than Marcie. But when it came to housekeeping, cooking, cleaning, and child-raising, you have to admit that Marcie was unbeatable."

He slowly nodded. "No complaints from me."

"So, I didn't do so badly, son?"

"What do you mean?" He felt a wave of uneasiness washing over him.

"Oh, you know that I worked hard to set you and Marcie up, Leroy. Her mother was my best friend. We both wanted you two kids to marry."

"Uh-huh." He was well aware of that.

"But you might not know that we coached Marcie. That we encouraged her to pursue you. We both thought you needed a good woman. You were so despondent after Dad got sick, having to quit school. And then Dad died."

"Yeah, we were all pretty sad, Mom."

"But you were extra sad, Leroy."

"Oh." He sighed. "I don't know."

"Well, I know. I'm your mother, and I saw it firsthand. I still remember when you came home from that high school church camp your grandma sent you to. You'd been so reluctant to go, but you came home like a new person. So happy and positive and full of life. At first I thought it was a spiritual experience."

"It was."

"Yes, but it was something more. I saw the letters you sent to that girl in Oregon, right before you headed off to college. You wrote two letters in one week, and I doubt you'd ever written a letter in your life before that."

"So?" Leroy stepped a little harder on the gas, more eager than ever to get his mom back to Damico's. He hoped a deer didn't jump across the road.

"So, something happened with that girl, didn't it?"

"Nothing *happened*, Mom." He turned on his high beams. "We just decided to call it a day, that's all."

"You *both* did?"

"Okay. No, she did. Okay? She decided to get back with her old boyfriend. End of story."

"So you really were interested in her? Were you in love?"

"Honestly, Mom, between you and my girls and their friends . . . sometimes I think I have way too many women in my life." He let out a groan. "Too many nosy women!"

"Oh, Leroy."

Relieved to see the lights of Damico's ahead, he slowed down. "I know you're not trying to be nosy, Mom, but some stones are better left unturned."

"I suppose."

"And I'm perfectly happy being a bachelor. I don't see why everyone is suddenly so intent on changing that."

"Well, your girls have grown up . . . We worry about you being alone."

"Alone?" He shook his head as he pulled into the round driveway in front of Tony and Sherry's sprawling home. "I wish I could be alone. My place is crawling with females right now."

She laughed, but as he pulled up to the house, her expression grew serious. "Take a bit of advice from a lonely old woman, Leroy. You're not getting any younger, so maybe you shouldn't be so picky about your companions."

"What are you saying? You think I should propose to Judith just because she's a good cook—and that's in the eyes of the beholder. You're suggesting I take her for my bride just because she's convenient and willing—like I did last time?" He instantly regretted those last words. "I take that back, Mom. Marcie doesn't deserve it."

"No, she doesn't. But I understand what you're saying, sweetheart. Judith just isn't your type."

He chuckled. "Isn't that what I was trying to tell you from the beginning?"

"Well, sometimes you have to drive around the block once to realize you're home." She reached for her handbag then paused. "But I'm still curious. What *is* your type? Do you even know?"

He honestly considered this and for some strange reason, the image of the young woman he'd seen in front of the guesthouse flashed through his mind. Wearing that simple blue dress, in her bare feet, her long dark hair blowing in the breeze as she worked on the flower beds. He knew she must be the new office manager—the one who'd arrived on the back of a Harley—but something about her had really stopped him. Still, he had no intention of admitting this to his mother, or anyone else for that matter.

He sighed. "I'm not sure what my type is. I just know that it's not Judith. She's too polished and stylish for me."

His mother laughed. "Well, that's a relief. I wasn't that impressed either. Good night, son."

He said good night, but as he drove back home, he couldn't shake the woman in the blue dress from his mind. Oh, he knew he was probably blowing it all out of proportion, but something about that image felt indelible.

———

Wearing the most businesslike outfit she could find in the bags of cast-off clothing—which was just a khaki skirt and a white blouse along with a blue bandanna she was using as a scarf—Brynna walked over to the winery office the next morning. Sophie had said to meet her there at nine, but Brynna went a few minutes early—just because she was eager. And nervous. What would she do if she crossed paths with Leroy? But to her relief, Sophie's van was parked nearby, and she was already in the office.

"Hey, Bree!" Sophie waved her inside.

As Brynna greeted her back, she wanted to tell Sophie that she actually went by Brynna, but that might require an explanation and she wasn't ready for that. Sophie was ready to show her around the office. She started with the front reception area that Brynna would primarily occupy, then they moved on to a windowless storage room for wine orders and file cabinets, and finally the back office that belonged to Leroy.

"But Dad hardly ever comes in here. Especially this time of year." Sophie ran her finger through the accumulated dust on his big oak desk.

"Well, I imagine he spends most of his time outside in the summer." Brynna took in the dark paneled walls and the floor-to-ceiling wine rack that was mostly full. Over an antique credenza hung a faded winery map of the world and a wall calendar still on February. She paused to study the photos by the big desk. Most seemed to be candid shots of Leroy's daughters at varying ages, taken, she imagined, by Leroy.

"It's a nice space." Brynna ran her hand over a worn leather chair.

"Nice and neglected. Anyway, you won't need to be in here much." Sophie pointed to a basket on the desk. "This is supposedly for important mail, not that he checks it much. So if anything is really important, I usually take it up to the house for him. There's an old mailbox by the front door specifically for this, and he's supposed to check it daily, but our real mailbox is down at the end of the drive and the mail is usually here by ten. I used to walk, but lately I've been driving."

"I wouldn't mind the exercise," Brynna said. "Or I could ride the bike."

"Great." Sophie continued going through the daily routine, explaining everything in detail while Brynna took fastidious notes. And, really, it didn't seem all that complicated. Even the computer program, almost exactly like the one Brynna used at home, was pretty simple.

Sophie explained how to take orders and how to check the inventory book. "We're still partly old-school here." She handed Brynna the black notebook. "I wanted to do it all on the computer, but Dad's been dragging his heels. Mostly because he wouldn't be able to access it himself since he's pretty technology-challenged."

"It's probably smart to do both." Brynna flipped through the pages where wines were listed on computer-printed pages and had handwritten tallies beside them. She pointed to an entry. "So this means you have twenty-three cases of 2010 Syrah?"

Sophie peered down at it. "To be honest, I'm sure we don't have that many. I'm afraid our inventory numbers are a little behind. And that's my fault." She patted her rounded belly. "And little Leroy's here."

"Little Leroy?"

Sophie laughed. "That's what I want to call him, after my dad. But Dad says no way. Anyway, when I should've been doing inventory last winter, I had really bad morning sickness. So the count is a little off now. I keep thinking I'll get around to inventorying, but—"

"Why can't I do it?" Brynna jumped in.

"Yes, of course! In fact, the sooner we get an accurate count, the better. I already filed an extension on our taxes, but we need to get caught up before that deadline."

Sophie continued taking Brynna through the paces then gave her a quick tour of the rest of the winery, including the "cellar" where barrels and cases were stored. It was actually an above-ground building on one side, but the other side was buried into the hill. Still, Sophie called it the wine cellar as she walked Brynna through, explaining the barrels and various wine sections and how they were arranged according to year.

"Hopefully you can get an accurate inventory before things get too crazy around here." Sophie struggled to pull the big wooden barn door closed, and Brynna jumped in to help.

"I'll start working on it as soon as I can." Brynna latched the door closed, watching as Sophie secured the lock then handed her the key.

"Keep it on the wall in the office like I showed you," Sophie reminded her then glanced at her watch. "It's already noon. That's when I usually take my lunch hour. Quitting time is four. Well, unless you're helping in the tasting room. That can run longer."

"But that probably doesn't feel like work."

"You're right. It's actually fun. But Garth told me I can't help him there anymore. He gets too many comments about pregnant women and wine. As if they think I'm imbibing." She rolled her eyes.

"And for your baby's sake, you should go home and have your lunch, Sophie." Brynna held up the notebook she'd been filling with tips and phone numbers and chores and suggestions. "I think I've got plenty to keep me busy until four. So you don't need to come back—"

"But I told Garth I'd spend the whole day with you."

"I know. But I feel like I've got this. And if I have any questions, I can just call you." She placed a hand on Sophie's shoulder. "It's okay for you to take it easy. Well, as easy as you can with two little ones to chase after. But really, you need to take care of yourself."

"Oh, Bree! You sound just like Dad."

Brynna smiled. "I guess we both care about you."

"You're sure you can do this without me?" Sophie frowned.

"I'll give it my best shot."

"And you promise to call if you need anything?"

"Of course. And if it's okay, I'd like to come by your house and work on your garden after work."

"Today?"

"Why not?"

"Well, if you really want. I guess it would be a chance for me to hear how your day went . . . in case you have questions."

"Perfect." Brynna smiled.

Sophie promised to text Brynna directions to her house and then, with a bit more encouragement from Brynna, she finally left. After a quick lunch "hour," Brynna returned to the office and went to work. It was fun to be busy, but every time she heard someone outside the door, she felt her heart rate increase. What if it was Leroy? What if he walked in and saw her? What would he do? What would she say?

To her relief, the afternoon passed without any sign of Leroy. Brynna knew he was busy helping a team of workers restore a burned section of the vineyard. She wouldn't mind if she didn't run into him for a few days. Long enough for her to get her feet under her and feel like a real part of this place. After that, well, she didn't really want to think about it. Fortunately, she had plenty to distract herself with.

At four o'clock, she locked the office like Sophie had told her, then hurried back to the cottage to change into gardening clothes. But, knowing it was possible she could run into Leroy, she made sure they were cute gardening clothes. Happy to be on a bicycle, pedaling through a beautiful field of grapes, she followed Sophie's directions by riding up the main vineyard road and over the hill, and finally, turning right at Quail Road, she soon found the manufactured home.

Sophie and the children came out to meet her. "How was your afternoon?" Sophie asked.

"Great." Brynna parked the bike, then waited as Sophie introduced her to her five-year-old daughter. Lucy had brown curls and brown eyes like her mother. And three-year-old towhead, Addison, peered curiously at Brynna with wide blue eyes.

"Bree is going to work in our garden," Sophie told the kids.

"Yes." Brynna rubbed her hands together. "I can hardly wait."

"You *want* to work in Mom's garden?" Lucy asked with furrowed brows.

"Of course." Brynna nodded eagerly. "I never get to work in gardens. I can't wait to see it."

"Right this way." Sophie led her around the side of the house and through a gate to a fenced-in area that was far bigger than Brynna had expected.

"Oh, this is absolutely beautiful." She looked over the raised beds and climbing berry vines and fruit trees and mounds filled with leafy plants.

"It's pretty weedy." Sophie bent down to pull a large dandelion from the path.

"It's heaven on earth." Brynna tugged on some crabgrass, then smiled at Lucy. "Do you know how lucky you are to have such a lovely garden?"

Lucy seemed to consider this. "Mom makes us work out here."

"I don't think of this as work." Brynna picked up a spade. "This is a treat."

Sophie laughed. "Well, hopefully you'll still think so later. If you'll excuse me, I need to get dinner started."

"No problem." Brynna was already weeding a raised bed filled with what looked like green beans and pea vines.

"Come on, kids," Sophie called over her shoulder. Addison trailed after her, but Lucy remained behind, curiously watching Brynna.

"You really like to do this kind of work?" Lucy asked.

"It doesn't feel like work to me." As she weeded, Brynna talked about the healthy plants growing there and how it wasn't fair for them to share the nutrients in their soil with weeds. "It'd be like if you and Addison were sitting down to a really good dinner and a bunch of hungry wolves walked in and sat down at your table. They'd gobble up all your food and you and your brother would go to bed hungry."

Lucy laughed. "My dad wouldn't let wolves in our house."

"I know." Brynna chuckled. "It's just a silly story." As she continued to pull out the weeds, she chatted with Lucy, and before long the little girl was pulling weeds too. They took turns making up a story about the Wicked Weed King and the Green Pea Queen and the battle they were fighting.

"My goodness!" Sophie said as she came over to Brynna and Lucy. "I can't believe how much you've gotten done. Or that Lucy is helping."

"We're making up stories," Lucy told her.

Brynna stood, smiling at Sophie. "Lucy is an excellent gardener. We're having fun."

"Well, it's dinnertime and I'm hoping you'll join us, Bree. We already set you a plate."

Before Brynna could protest, Lucy had grabbed her by the hand. Tugging her into the house, Lucy insisted she wanted to sit next to Brynna, and together they scrubbed their hands in the bathroom. Then Brynna, with Lucy by her side, sat down at their table, holding back happy tears as they bowed their heads and Garth said a blessing. It had been so long since she'd felt like part of a real family. Even if this were a onetime event, she knew she'd treasure the memory for a long time.

Chapter 20

Brynna hadn't participated in such an enjoyable meal like this since her own childhood. Sophie and Garth and their children were so easy and comfortable to be with. She felt like real family. Early in her marriage, she'd dreamed of this sort of thing but never got to experience it. But the meal was done now, and little Addison's head was drooping so low it looked like he was about to do a face-plant into the pasta.

"Looks like someone is sleepy," Brynna said.

"Two someones." Sophie nodded to Lucy. "Tell Bree good night, baby girl. Time for you to get ready for bed too."

To Brynna's surprise, as Garth scooped up his son, Lucy came over to hug her. "Good night, Bree. It was fun telling stories in the garden."

"It *was* fun." Brynna patted her head. "You're a very good gardener, Lucy."

"Will you come back tomorrow?" Lucy asked, rubbing the sleep from her eyes.

"If it's okay with your mom." Brynna stood and started to clear the table.

Sophie laughed as she led Addison down the hall. "No worries there, Bree."

Brynna carried a stack of dishes into the kitchen and had just started to rinse when Garth came in to help.

"You're a guest. You shouldn't be doing this," he told her.

"It's the least I can do after such a great dinner."

"Our pleasure. Sophie is definitely a great cook." He set a rinsed plate in the dishwasher. "And a great mom too."

"And a great gardener," Brynna added. "Probably like her mom."

"Well, I never met her mom, but I've heard Sophie's a lot like her. Although her mom was never into gardening. She didn't really like being outdoors too much." Garth shrugged. "I guess Sophie gets the green thumb from Dad's side. She's a lot like her grandma."

"Oh." Brynna wondered about that as she handed him a plate.

"So, do you feel like you can handle things at the office yet? Or do you still need Sophie's help?"

"I think I'm okay. It's pretty well set up. Seems like common sense to run it."

"Good to know." He smiled. "Maybe we can convince Sophie to spend more time at home and take it a little easier."

"Absolutely." She handed him the last plate.

"How would you feel about helping in the tasting room occasionally?" He closed the dishwasher and leaned against it. "Especially when we get busier, which has already been happening."

"Sounds like fun to me." She dried her hands on a dish towel.

"Great. Feel free to pop in and observe anytime. We have a group coming tomorrow at three."

"I'll be there, and I'll even take notes," she added.

He wiped down the sink then turned to her with a smile. "I'm really glad Sophie hired you, Bree. Not a moment too soon either. We needed you."

Brynna avoided his eyes as she nodded. It was nice to be needed and appreciated like this, but what would happen when Leroy figured things out? She didn't want to think about that now. So after

Sophie came back to the kitchen, Brynna told them both thank you and good night, then hopped on the bike and pedaled back toward her cottage. But as she crested the last hill, she couldn't help but pause for a moment to gape at the western sky. The sun was sinking into a bank of clouds, and the colors—layers of amber and purple and rose—were glorious. Still straddling the bicycle, she stared in awestruck wonder.

Somehow she knew that the God who'd created all this beauty was able to sort out the mess she feared she'd been making in her life. She couldn't even put into words how she knew this exactly—except that she just knew. It was like Motorcycle Mike had said. God was up to something. She suddenly felt a real sense of peace about it. At least for now.

—

Leroy paused from where he was restaking a slumping grapevine in the burn section to admire the sunset now painting the sky, a reminder it was getting late. He hadn't meant to linger in the burn area this long, but he'd stopped by after driving past Sophie and Garth's place earlier. His plan had been to "kill some time" then swing back by there to talk to Sophie.

Originally, Leroy had hoped to snag a good home-cooked dinner and see his grandkids. It would also be a good excuse to avoid another meatless meal at his female-packed house. But then he'd noticed the new manager was at Sophie's. He recognized Bree from a distance by her long brown hair and small stature. Today she wore blue jeans and a white T-shirt, and it appeared that she and Lucy were working in the garden together and having a pretty good time. Not wanting to interrupt the happy pair and realizing it would be difficult to inquire about the new employee while she was present, he'd simply driven on past.

He'd parked on the crest of the hill with a granola bar and lukewarm soda from the stash he kept in his Jeep, killing time and waiting for Bree to go on her merry way. When that didn't happen, he'd noticed the sagging section of vine and gone down to stake it up. Now, as he stood in the shadowy vale, looking up toward the colorful sky, he saw her again.

Bree had stopped her bike on the crest of the hill. With her back to him, she stared out at the same beautiful sunset that had caught his eye. He stood there, transfixed, unsure if he was watching the girl or the sunset, but his feet seemed to have taken root. For a moment, he considered calling out to her. Perhaps he could offer her a ride since it would be dusky soon. But he wasn't sure the bike would fit into the back of the Wrangler . . . or whether he was even ready to meet her yet.

He looked down at his stained T-shirt and dirt-encrusted hands. He'd neglected to use work gloves today. Plus, he suspected he smelled none-too-fresh at the moment. Maybe not the best moment to meet Bree. Something about her definitely intrigued him. It seemed the barefoot girl in the blue dress had many sides to her. She obviously liked gardening. He knew she'd been a schoolteacher, which suggested she liked children. She seemed to have already made friends with his granddaughter. And, watching her now, it seemed she appreciated the beauty of the great outdoors. All good things.

He watched as Bree got back on the bike and started to coast down the hill. Her silhouette against the sunset made a pretty picture. Then, to his surprise, she released the handlebars and, stretching her arms out, soared like a bird in flight. And unless he imagined it, or perhaps it was a nighthawk, she let out a shriek of delight. He couldn't help but chuckle. *What kind of woman is this?*

On her second day of work, Brynna got the office into decent order during the morning hours. Her plan for the afternoon was to sequester herself in the wine cellar and get a good start on inventorying. But first she'd set the timer on her watch to remind her to go help Garth in the tasting room at three. It was interesting seeing all the different kinds of wines. Far more than just whites and reds, there were names she'd never heard of before. Like Gewürztraminer. She couldn't even pronounce that one. And then there were the different years. All totaled, she guessed there were close to a hundred different types. By the time her alarm sounded, she'd made it through only the cabernet sauvignon section. Not being a wine aficionado herself, she wasn't sure if she'd ever even tasted cabernet sauvignon, but it did have an exotic sound to it.

Brynna arrived in the tasting room ten minutes early, but an older couple were already there visiting with Garth. He waved her over and after a quick introduction to the couple from Sacramento, he asked her to fetch some clean wineglasses from the house. "Gina was supposed to bring them out, but I haven't seen her around."

"Where in the house?" Bree asked, trying not to feel nervous over the idea of walking into Leroy's home.

"They should be in a basket either in the laundry room or in the butler's pantry, or maybe even in the dishwasher in the kitchen if Gina forgot."

"Okay . . ." She wanted to appear confident as she exited the barn, hoping she wouldn't bump into Leroy in his house. She went to the side of the house, using the door that Sophie said led to the laundry room. As she stepped inside, she reminded herself that Leroy would probably be out in the vineyard.

Brynna couldn't help but pause to admire the spacious laundry room. There were ample countertops, a stone sink, drying racks, cabinets for storage, and shiny modern appliances, but there was no basket of wineglasses. She quietly proceeded through the next door, which led into what she assumed was the kitchen, but then realized was probably just a very well-equipped butler's pantry, one that was far nicer than her kitchen at home. But again, there was no basket of glasses. She pushed open the swinging door to see that it led to the kitchen, but she could hear voices in there.

To her relief it was only female voices. So, standing straighter and wishing she were taller, she walked into the kitchen with what she hoped was an air of authority.

Two women were gathered at the table in conversation.

"Who are you?" a blond woman asked.

"I, uh, I'm Bree, the office manager." Her smile felt uneasy.

"Oh." The woman nodded. "I'm Judith, the houseguest."

"And I'm Cassie, Judith's daughter," a younger woman, who was also blond, said.

"I—uh—I'm looking for the glasses."

"Glasses?" Judith asked.

"Yes. Wineglasses."

"Wineglasses?" Judith's pale brows arched. "Why do you want wineglasses?"

"For the tasting room." Brynna picked up a large basket on the counter, but it was empty. "Garth said they were here."

Cassie slapped her forehead. "Oh, yeah, I totally forgot. Gina asked me to do that. I sure hope someone turned the dishwasher on." She hurried over to what looked like a drawer but turned out to be a dishwasher. She pulled out a glass and closely examined it. "Oh, good. Clean." She set it on the counter and, as she reached for more, Brynna set it in the basket.

"Cassie, you let Bree do that. *She's* the employee."

Cassie set two more glasses on the granite countertop. "But I can—"

"No, honey. That's Bree's job," Judith insisted. "That's what she gets paid for."

"Yes, of course. I can do this," Brynna assured them. She didn't care for the tone in Judith's voice, wondering why this woman was being so rude. As she carefully unloaded the glasses, neatly nesting them in the basket, Cassie left the kitchen. But Brynna could still feel Judith's eyes on her, making her uncomfortable.

After the dishwasher drawer was empty, the basket was only about half full. Brynna was about to leave when Judith spoke up.

"Don't you want to check the other drawer too? There might be more glasses in there."

"Oh, yeah." Brynna nodded as she slid open the lower drawer, which also had glasses. "You're right." She forced a smile as she began to unload it.

"Yes, well, I know this kitchen pretty well. In fact, I should be doing some prep work for dinner right now. So, in the future, please pick up the glasses earlier, Bree. When no one is using this kitchen. That will be much less intrusive and far more efficient for everyone."

Brynna just nodded, hurrying to fit the last of the glasses in the basket then draping a dish towel over the top. "I'll keep that in mind."

"Thank you." Judith's tone was crisp and superior.

As Brynna carried the loaded basket out, she felt a surge of resentment. She didn't like being regarded as the lowly servant. Although, wasn't that sort of true? Brynna was just an employee here. Not a houseguest. It was her job to unload the dishwasher. But couldn't Judith have been a bit more gracious about it?

Still, it wasn't just Judith's arrogance that was troubling. The truth was, Brynna felt plain old jealous! She resented Judith's occupation of Leroy's home, acting territorial, as if she owned the place. But maybe that was Judith's intention. And for all Brynna knew, it could be Leroy's as well.

Leroy was determined to meet up with his new office manager today. With that in mind, he'd taken more time with his morning routine and dressed with a bit more care. And instead of working with his field crew all morning, he played the role of supervisor. Then he'd taken an actual lunch break in the house, something he hadn't done since Gina's friends had taken over occupancy of his home. Of course, they'd been surprised to see him. Judith had insisted on making him a big salad. Not wanting to offend her, he hurriedly ate it, even though he'd prefer a tuna sandwich.

Afterward, Leroy went over to the office, casually strolling in with a ready introduction line, but the front part of the office and the manager's desk were unoccupied. He checked the store-room and even his office—which, to his relief, were both locked—something he'd taught Sophie to do when she stepped out. Apparently, Bree knew the drill too. But where was she?

He went over to the tasting room to find it was deserted as well. He glanced around the property, then realizing it wasn't yet one, he concluded she was on her lunch break in the cottage. He considered waiting by her driveway but didn't want to look like a stalker. Instead, he decided to return to his office and do some real office work for a change.

As soon as he entered the building, he noticed how tidy and orderly everything appeared. That was encouraging. Even his own private space appeared to have been dusted and straightened—and the calendar was on the correct month. Wanting to hear when Bree returned to work, he left his door open and surveyed his desk. His in-basket held several things that probably needed his attention. Nothing particularly urgent, but some items had been there awhile. As he sat down in his squeaky leather chair, he remembered that Sophie had been nagging him to get caught up. *No time like the present*, he thought as he reached for the first item.

By the time his in-basket was emptied, it was three o'clock, and the office manager still hadn't showed up. Curious as to where she could be, he went out to look around some more. He could see that the tasting room was open and Garth was handling about a dozen guests, but he didn't see Bree among them. Leroy even checked the wine cellar, which seemed an unlikely place for her to be. Although he did recall an employee, from several years back, who used to sneak in there to help himself to a bottle of wine. Leroy had quickly terminated him. Sophie had already assured him that their new office manager was practically a teetotaler, so there should be no worries there.

The cellar door was locked and when he went inside, it was dark and quiet and peaceful. Leroy breathed in the old smell of wood and wine and dust, an aroma that always took him back to his childhood when he would follow his dad and grandpa around the big oak barrels, watching as the men tested and sampled the wine, listening to them discuss the process—the trade he didn't realize would someday become his life. Did he resent that it had? No, not at all. He sighed as he slid the door closed and secured the lock. It was a good life. But where was that office manager?

Discouraged, he went into the house, hoping to find Gina to see if she knew anything. He discovered her in the kitchen with Judith, discussing the night's menu.

"*There* is our mystery man," Judith declared. "I just told Gina I'd forgotten to ask you if you would join us for dinner tonight. I was worried you planned to go AWOL again." She laughed.

"The truth is, I'm used to being pretty independent." He glanced at his daughter for backup. "Gina's used to that. I come and go, and sometimes I work late. Or I drop in on Sophie and—"

"Well," Judith interrupted him. "I hope you'll consider joining us tonight. Gina told me you love Italian cuisine, so I'm making pasta primavera." She pointed to a large basket of fruits and vegetables. "I found some lovely things at the farmers market this morning."

"I see." He nodded with pursed lips, then turned to Gina. "I was wondering if you'd seen our new office manager."

"You mean Bree?" Gina picked up an apple, taking a loud bite.

"Yes. Have you seen her today?"

She swallowed. "No, I haven't even met her yet."

"Really?" Leroy's concerns increased. Why was the new office manager so elusive?

"But I've been pretty busy, Dad." Gina took another bite.

"I met Bree," Judith declared with what seemed like a catty smile.

"You did?" He turned to her. "When was that?"

"Earlier today. She took me quite by surprise when she walked right into this kitchen without even knocking."

"Oh?"

"Yes. But I introduced myself, and she told me her name was Bree. Apparently she'd forgotten to get the wineglasses for Garth's wine tasting, so she was scrambling to catch up."

"I usually do that," Gina explained, "but I asked Cassie to handle it because Mara and I are working out behind the barn."

"Behind the barn?" Leroy asked her.

She nodded and took another bite of her apple. "We need to get all the grounds ready for the upcoming events. Besides wine-tasting parties, the vineyard open house, and Grandma's birthday, I've been thinking we might host some weddings. Anyway, we're all pretty busy. Sorry about the wineglass biz. I'll let Bree know about the dishwasher situation."

"Well, that Bree *seems* okay." Judith's tone sounded odd. "She's certainly pretty enough. But if you ask me, she's a bit of a scatterbrain."

"Scatterbrain?" Leroy felt surprisingly defensive. "I mean I haven't actually met her yet, but I've observed her a few times. She doesn't seem scatterbrained. In fact, she seems like a diligent, hard worker."

Judith shrugged. "Well, that was just my first impression." She laughed. "And you know what they say about first impressions."

"What do they say?" he asked in a flat tone.

"You only get one chance to make them."

He wanted to point out that his first impression of Bree had been positive but didn't really care to divulge that much to this woman. In fact, his first, second, and third impressions of Judith hadn't been nearly as nice as his impression of the new office manager—even from afar.

"I think Bree is helping Garth with the wine tasting," Gina told him, throwing her apple into the trash bin.

"I peeked in on the tasting and didn't see her." He reached for an apple. "But I guess I'll check again."

Leroy got caught up in fixing a loose board on the porch. So by the time he got back to the tasting room, the nearby parking lot was empty, and Garth was just closing the doors. "How'd it go?" Leroy asked him.

"Great. Nice crowd."

"Good." Leroy walked with Garth toward his pickup. "Have you seen Bree today?"

"Yeah, she helped with the tasting. It was her first time, and she was a perfect assistant. Very cordial with the guests and she didn't even get confused about the order of the wines. Apparently she studied the notes I gave her yesterday. Before long, I'll bet she could do the tasting herself."

"Well, that's good to know." Leroy smiled. "Do you know where she went?"

Garth checked his watch. "She left on her bike a little while ago. Headed up to the house to help Sophie with our garden. She's probably there by now."

"Oh, yeah." Leroy nodded like he knew this. "Seems like Sophie and Bree have really hit it off."

"For sure. Bree helped Sophie yesterday too. And now Lucy's in love with her. I think Sophie was spot-on with hiring her. Bree Philips, it seems, is a real treasure."

A hard-to-find treasure, Leroy thought to himself.

"Hey, you want to come up for dinner tonight?" Garth asked. "Sophie just texted me that she's making cannelloni."

"With meat sauce?"

"Is there any other way?" Garth grinned.

"Not where I'm concerned. Count me in."

"Oh, yeah, Bree might join us too. Soph plans to invite her. I hope you don't mind."

"Not at all."

Garth unlocked his truck and climbed in. "Sophie said seven. She got a late start."

Leroy assured him that seven sounded just fine, then, feeling a new spring in his step, he headed back to his house. Suspecting that Judith might still be in the kitchen, chopping up all those vegetables, he decided to use the front entrance and main stairway. Although he was much tidier than usual for this time of day, he wanted to spruce up a bit more. Part of him felt silly for even caring about making an impression on Bree. And part of him remembered Judith's words. You only get one chance to make a first impression.

Chapter 21

Brynna was happy to work in Sophie's garden again, but she was also a bit more tired than she'd been yesterday. Still, it was fun being with Lucy. And today Addison had joined them too. He wasn't as good at weeding as Lucy, but he was trying. Then, after Addison accidentally pulled out yet another immature carrot, Brynna set down her spade.

"I think we should take a break," she told them. "A story break."

Naturally, they both agreed. Similar to what she'd done with Lucy the day before, they took turns inventing garden characters and stories to go with them. And then she turned one of the stories into a silly song. They were singing and parading around the garden when Garth came out to join them.

"Time for you kids to clean up for dinner," he told his children. "Pappy is coming tonight."

Lucy and Addison began to jump around with glee, but Brynna felt a wave of trepidation wash over her. Was she ready for this? She looked down at the gardening clothes she'd pulled on after leaving the tasting room. They were the same ones from yesterday and were even dirtier now. Did she really want her first encounter with Leroy to be like this? And with Sophie, Garth, and the kids there to witness what could easily turn very awkward? Of course not.

As Garth herded his kids inside, Brynna went to find Sophie. "I know I said I'd stay for dinner," she began, "but I didn't realize how worn out I am. Can I take a rain check? Or maybe it's a tired check."

Sophie looked disappointed. "Are you sure?"

Brynna sighed wearily. "I really am tired. And I'm thinking about a nice, long soak in the claw-foot tub."

"I totally understand." Sophie patted her shoulder. "You've been working so hard these past couple of days. I appreciate you hanging with the kids while I got dinner going tonight."

"We had fun." Brynna glanced at the clock to see it was already six thirty. She worried that Leroy might already be on his way here. "Anyway, I better get going. Make my apologies to Garth and the kids."

"And Dad too? He should be here soon."

"Yeah, sure, of course." Brynna hugged Sophie, then hurried outside, hopped on her bike, and started pedaling as fast as her tired legs could pump. She did not want to meet Leroy here on the road. Even more so as she got closer to home. She was hot and sweaty and dirty.

She knew it didn't make sense when she considered how curious she'd felt about reconnecting with him, but the longer she delayed the inevitable meeting, the less she wanted it to happen. Maybe she'd be better off never meeting him. Although it seemed impossible to avoid it indefinitely. *But, please, God*, she prayed, *not now*.

⸻

Leroy didn't make it out of his house without being spotted by the women. It was bad enough being cornered by Judith and her two daughters, but when Gina joined in their inquisition, he felt personally betrayed.

"Like I told you earlier, I'm used to coming and going freely around here and—"

"But where are you going all dressed up?" Gina demanded.

"Dressed up?" He acted innocent. "A man puts on a clean shirt, and you call that dressed up?"

"Dad"—she crossed her arms—"you have on your good loafers and khakis and, unless I'm mistaken, you're wearing cologne."

"I took a shower." He moved closer to the front door. "That's probably just soap you smell."

"Looks to me like you're going on a date," Judith taunted him. "Who's the lucky lady?"

"I'm just having dinner at Sophie's," he said, raising his hands in defense.

"You never cleaned up to eat at Sophie's before," Gina argued. "Something's fishy. What's going on?"

"I think it's that new manager." Judith elbowed Gina with a sly wink. "She's sort of cute in a girl next door sort of way, and he was looking for her earlier, remember?"

"That's right." Gina nodded. "Is that it, Dad? Are you having dinner with Bree?"

"I told you, I'm going to Sophie's, and if I don't get out of here, I'm going to be late for dinner. I hate to keep my grandchildren up past their bedtime, so if you ladies will excuse me." He opened the door, then seeing that Babe was trying to follow, he told her to stay. "You can hang here with all the other females." He patted his disappointed dog's head. And before anyone could question him further, Leroy dashed out of there.

As he drove to Sophie's he wondered if he had overdone it. What if Sophie thought he looked "too nice" or Garth smelled his cologne, which really wasn't only soap, and got suspicious? This could get embarrassing. And really, why had he gone to so much trouble to impress a woman he had never even met? Maybe he could make up some excuse, like he had a wine-growers meeting later on tonight. Except that Garth would know that wasn't true . . . and Leroy hated lies. Fine. As he parked in front of their house, he decided he'd just tell them he cleaned up because he felt like cleaning up. No big deal!

The front door was open, so he walked right in and was immediately attacked by his grandkids. After the usual hugs, rocket rides, and general horseplay, they returned to the animated video playing on the TV, and he went into the kitchen fully expecting to find Sophie and Bree putting the finishing touches on dinner, maybe opening a bottle of Cabernet to go with the cannelloni.

"Hey, Dad." Sophie beamed at him as she set a huge pan of cannelloni on the counter. "You're just in time."

He took a whiff of the delectable concoction—*real* pasta, savory meat sauce, dripping with cheese. "Smells fabulous." He kissed his daughter's cheek. "I barely escaped dining on brown rice pasta smothered in vegetables. What is brown rice pasta anyway?"

"It's a poor excuse for pasta." Sophie laughed. "Seriously, doesn't that woman ever cook meat?"

"Nope." He glanced around. "Where's Garth?" Of course, that wasn't the foremost question on his mind, but it was the safest.

"Probably on the computer. Why don't you go tell him dinner's ready?"

Leroy walked back to Garth's office, glancing around as he did, hoping to spy Bree, but without success. He reached the den where his son-in-law was sitting behind a monitor. "Hey, Garth. Your wife says dinner's ready."

Garth turned off his computer screen. "I was just checking the sparkling wine market. We're pretty well stocked right now. I thought maybe we should do a price reduction and move some."

"We'll be using plenty at the anniversary celebration, and then more at Mom's birthday bash, so I wouldn't worry about it." As they walked back to the kitchen, Leroy casually inquired about Bree.

"Bree went home, Pappy," Lucy said, her lower lip extended into an impressive pout.

"Yeah, she was worn out," Garth added. "She's been so helpful—at work and here with the kids. She probably needed a break."

"Hey, Pappy, you smell just like Mommy on church day." Lucy grabbed his hand and peered curiously at him.

"Better than smelling stinky, don't you think?" He chuckled. And before anyone else could mention his cleaned-up appearance, he distracted them by bringing up his mother's upcoming birthday celebration, saying how everyone, even the kids, could help. Before long, Sophie was putting together a plan for her and the kids to make posters and banners and other decorative things. All in all, it was a good diversion from being questioned about his out-of-character spiffed-up appearance. Basically an exercise in futility . . . or stupidity.

It wasn't easy to conceal his disappointment over Bree's absence as they ate dinner, but the cannelloni was excellent—way better than what was being served at his house. Still, as he drove home afterward, he wondered what it would take to actually meet his mysterious office manager.

———

For the next couple of days, Brynna busied herself between working in the office, doing inventory, and assisting Garth in the tasting room. Her life seemed to have fallen into a comfortable routine of working until four then spending an hour or two with Sophie and the kids, then back to her little cottage to fix a simple meal, have a lovely bath, and prepare for the next day. One of the highlights of her day, almost a secret pleasure, was slipping outside just as the sun was going down. She'd started this after her bath Tuesday night, when her hair was still damp. She'd put on the little blue sundress that had become her favorite item of clothing. She loved walking through the shadowy vineyard barefoot. Something about the last ray of golden light and dusky blue sky, the warm fragrant air, and the soft cool soil beneath her feet—it was almost spiritual.

She was joined by who she'd discovered was Leroy's dog, Babe. The elderly yellow Labrador retriever was sweet-spirited and a welcome companion. Brynna hoped that she wasn't spoiling Babe by giving her occasional leftovers, but she did add doggy treats to her shopping list.

Brynna felt she was living a perfect sort of life. Except for the fact that she was an imposter and knew her visit here could be only temporary. Plus, there was the unnerving potential of meeting Leroy face-to-face constantly hanging over her head. She still wasn't sure how she planned to explain her presence to him. But my midday Thursday, she almost looked forward to it. In fact, on her way back to the office after her lunch break, she decided she wanted to just get it over with. So much so that she was actually on the lookout for him. She'd seen signs of him in the office the past two days, but nothing today. She had to chuckle at herself as she went into the office for the wine cellar key. Here she was, still *looking for Leroy.* Mike and Jan had checked on her a couple of times during the week, curious as to what was going on and almost in disbelief when she informed them "nothing." They were even more shocked that she and Leroy hadn't even met.

As Brynna continued with the wine inventory, which was about halfway done, she wondered if Leroy might be purposely avoiding her. She'd even left the door to the cellar open just in case he passed by and decided to pop in. But her only visitor was Babe, who simply plopped down to snooze on the cool, earthen floor.

By the time Brynna's alarm went off, reminding her it was time to go help Garth, she decided Leroy was simply too busy to bother about meeting his office manager. The bright side was that he must've been satisfied with her work so far. Perhaps she should just enjoy this time . . . except she felt on edge. Like the old adage, she was waiting for the other shoe to drop. But had the first one fallen?

After helping Garth with a fairly big and boisterous tasting group, Brynna suddenly felt very antsy, perhaps even eager, over the likelihood of bumping into Leroy. How much longer could it take for their paths to cross? As Garth chatted with a few lingering guests, Brynna wiped down counters and tables, gathering up the used wineglasses and attempting to bolster her courage. Finally, she felt like she was ready to do it. She would march the basket of dirty glasses over to Leroy's house, walk straight into the kitchen, and simply introduce herself. Except she felt sure he wouldn't be there this time of day.

And more than likely, she'd run into Judith again. Not an encounter she cared to initiate. Besides feeling snubbed by the somewhat patronizing woman, Brynna felt irritated. She hated to admit it, but whenever she noticed Judith and the girls up at the house—whether they were lounging out on the terrace or setting up an outdoor meal—Brynna felt a distinct jealous gnaw inside her. And it seemed perfectly ridiculous considering that Brynna hadn't so much as spoken to Leroy in almost thirty years. Seriously! Still, she wished that Judith and her daughters would just go home. Even more so after hearing what Sophie had to say about it the day before.

According to Sophie, Judith and her girls intended to remain for the full two weeks they'd originally agreed upon. "Although Gina is starting to have second thoughts," Sophie had confided. Brynna tried to appear uninterested as she helped Sophie and the kids work the garden, but she'd gently nudged out a bit more information. It seemed that Sophie was concerned for her dad and Gina. "Judith and her younger daughter, Cassie, have lost all enthusiasm for getting the property ready for the upcoming events. Apparently it's too much work."

Sophie rolled her eyes as she leaned on her hoe. "I guess when Gina offered them a working vacation, they figured they'd do a little work and then go into full-time vacation mode. She said Judith and Cassie are acting more like houseguests now."

Although it had given Brynna a tinge of hope that the houseguests weren't as welcome as she'd assumed, she still didn't care to bump into Judith. Seeing the last of the patrons leaving the tasting room, she called out to Garth. "Didn't you say Gina was going to pick up the glasses today?"

"She said just to leave them on the counter and she'd be by later." Garth came over to put the bottles back into the cabinet.

"Okay." Brynna lingered a moment. "I told Sophie I'd go up to the house again, but I haven't met Gina yet."

"Soph will understand if you stick around long enough to meet her baby sister." He nodded to the door. "Speak of the devil. Hey, Gina. Come meet our office manager, Bree Philips."

A pretty, slender girl with honey-colored braids and a straw cowboy hat came over to the counter to shake Brynna's hand. "Nice to meet you, Bree." She smiled brightly, then cocked her head to one side with a questioning look. "Have we met before?"

"No, I don't think so." Brynna shook her head.

Gina tipped her hat back, squinting as if to see her better. "Seriously? You seem really familiar to me."

Brynna smiled. "Well, you've probably seen me running around your property. It's such a gorgeous vineyard and winery. I really love it—and I'm so impressed with all you're doing to make it better. I hear you're the one behind a lot of the improvement ideas. I really like the way the brown paint looks on the barn doors and trim."

"Thanks. I'd love to do even more renovations if my dad would loosen his belt a little."

Garth laughed. "Dream on, Gina. You should be thankful Leroy is giving you as much freedom as he has."

"Well, hasn't it been paying off? I hear that sales are up."

"According to the books, they are," Brynna said. "I was just doing a comparison to your profits from last June. This year is much better, and the month is only half over."

Gina gave them both a high five. "Tell my dad that."

Brynna forced a smile. "I will . . . when I see him."

"Oh, yeah, he told me he hasn't even met you yet." Gina frowned. "What's up with that?"

Brynna shrugged, focusing on wiping an already clean portion of the counter.

"Well, I'll get these into the house." She peered curiously at Brynna again. "You sure do seem familiar though. Sure we haven't met?"

Brynna shrugged again, but a wave of nerves rushed over her. "Not that I can recall."

"Well, welcome to the team anyway. I'll nag my dad to come say hey to you. He's been super busy lately, but not so busy he should forget his manners."

After Gina left, Brynna turned back to Garth. "You really handled that big group well. I was impressed."

"Think you're ready to take on a group yourself yet?"

"Oh, I don't know . . . I mean, I'm willing, but I doubt I'd be as good as you. You're a natural."

"Thanks. It was fun having a young enthusiastic group." He closed the cabinet with a sigh. "But I have to admit, it made me kind of envious."

"Envious?"

"Those young couples just out having fun together. Soph and I never got too much of that. We were married so young and had kids so fast, you know."

"Oh, yeah, I get that." She frowned. "And another one will be here soon. Do you guys ever go out just the two of you?"

He laughed. "Sounds great. But it's not easy getting babysitters way out here. Sophie's grandma helps out in the day sometimes, but she's not really a night person."

"Well, I can watch the kids at night."

"Thanks." He nodded eagerly. "We'll take you up on that some-time."

"No time like the present," she told him.

"Seriously?" His eyes lit up. "You mean like tonight?"

"Why not?"

"It would be fun to go to town, get some dinner, see a movie . . ."

"Then just do it." She tapped his phone in his shirt pocket. "Call Sophie and tell her to get ready for a night out."

Within minutes, a plan was concocted. Brynna would spend the evening with Lucy and Addison while their parents enjoyed a much-deserved evening away.

Chapter 22

Leroy felt frustrated as he loaded a couple of wine cases into the back of his Jeep. Despite the current demands in the vineyard, he'd quit work earlier than usual today in the hopes of actually meeting Bree. But even though it wasn't quite four, the office door was already locked. Hearing the phone ringing, he'd gone inside to take the call. Good thing, too, since it was a large and urgent order for an impromptu wedding reception this weekend in the Bay Area. They wanted ten cases by the next day.

With the information about that order in his pocket, Leroy headed for the tasting room to find Garth. But seeing a large group inside, Leroy didn't want to interrupt. Still in his field clothes, and assuming Bree was inside helping Garth, he decided to use this time to make a fast dash to the house, where he quietly sneaked up the back staircase to take a quick shower. While he was putting on clean clothes, his cell phone rang. It was Jason Reed, an old friend from high school now living up in Bodega Bay. He'd called to place a special wine order.

"Sorry to be so last minute," Jason said, "and to call your personal number. Our tenth anniversary is coming up, and my wife just told me that she loves Sorrentino's chardonnay."

"Well, that's nice to hear." Leroy tugged on a button-up shirt.

"And, let me tell you, Laurie was quite impressed when I informed her that I personally know the owner of the winery." Jason chuckled. "I admitted we weren't best buddies, Leroy, but just the same, she thought it was pretty cool. Anyway, I'd love to drive down there and pick up a couple of cases of your best chardonnay, but I've got this big court case tomorrow and I wondered if you could do a fast shipment of—"

"Why don't I just bring it to you?"

"You'd do that?"

"Sure. It'd be a fun drive up 101."

Leroy ended the call with the promise to call back in an hour or so for more details, but by the time he reached the tasting room, it was closed and locked. Neither Garth nor Bree was anywhere to be seen. But determined to meet the new office manager, Leroy had actually marched up to the guest cottage and boldly knocked on the door. He noticed her bicycle parked in front, so he was surprised when no one answered. He even knocked louder and called out her name. Then, assuming she was out for a walk—like he'd seen her take just last evening when he was stuck out on his terrace with Gina and her friends—he decided to do a bit of walking himself. All for nothing. When he got back to the cottage, her bike was still there, but she still did not answer the door.

In frustration he called Jason back and agreed to deliver the order this evening. And now, with the Jeep loaded with his best chardonnay, he wished he hadn't agreed to this. Although it would get him out of his house for the night. That was worth something.

"Hey, Dad." Gina rolled a wheelbarrow full of gravel toward him. "What's up?"

"Just loading up some wine." He shut the hatch with a thud.

"Where're you taking it?"

"Just a delivery—out of town." He tried not to look as grim as he felt.

She frowned. "You're delivering it yourself?"

"It's for a friend." He sighed. "In Bodega Bay."

"Bodega Bay?" She cocked her head to one side. "That's a two-hour drive."

"Yeah, but like I said, it's for a buddy." He didn't want to deceive his daughter but didn't care to admit he was glad to take the delivery—just to escape the overload of females in his house. "And the coast highway will be pretty this time of day. I'll have a visit with my friend, spend the night, and drive back tomorrow."

"Oh?" She nodded. "Sounds like fun." She tweaked the rim of his hat. "And if anyone deserves some fun, I guess it's you, Dad. Enjoy!"

He frowned at her load of gravel. "You need help with that?"

"No, I'm a big girl, remember? Besides, I'm used to hard labor."

He grinned. "Well, that's what working a vineyard's all about, right? Hard labor."

She rolled her eyes. "Wish everyone in the vineyard agreed with that."

"Meaning?" He studied her. "Something I should know? An employee giving you a bad time? Not our new manager, I hope."

"No, she's fine. I actually met her today." She narrowed her eyes. "In fact, she reminds me of someone."

"Uh-huh?" He waited.

"Remember that girl you met at the high school camp? The one in all those photos?"

"Yeah, sure." He shoved his hands in his pockets, waiting.

"Bree reminds me of her."

He slowly nodded. "I kind of get that. I mean, I've seen her from a distance, and she seems kind of smallish with long brown hair. I guess that could resemble . . . that other girl." For some reason, he couldn't say her name. Brynna. Was that how deep the cut had been?

"So, you noticed it too?" Gina studied him closely.

"Well . . . from a distance, maybe. But Sophie said Bree's probably in her early thirties, and as you know, her name is Bree Philips. The girl I knew was my age, and her name was Brynna Meyers."

179

There, he said it. Maybe that would help inoculate him from any further pain. Why hadn't he burned those stupid photos by now?

"Yeah, I guess that sounds crazy. But she seemed familiar for some reason. Anyway, you really need to meet her, Dad."

"Believe me, I've been trying."

"Well, try harder." She lifted the wheelbarrow handles, tipped her head goodbye, then wobbled away.

The father in him wanted to run and help Gina with the heavy load, but he also wanted to remind her that she was biting off a lot this summer. Might be good if it bit her back. Maybe she'd be more apt to return to college in the fall. And, unless he misjudged her friends, Leroy didn't think the whole "working vacation" bit was going like she'd planned. *Live and learn*, he thought as he backed up his Jeep.

He was about halfway to Bodega Bay when he remembered he needed to talk to Garth. He dialed his number, but instead of Garth on the other end of his call, Sophie answered.

"Garth is driving," she told him. "We just had dinner and we're on our way to a movie."

"Oh? Family outing?" He adjusted the volume on the hands-free Bluetooth setup Gina had recently installed for him, talking while he drove.

"Nope. They're home." Sophie giggled.

"Home alone?"

"No, of course not. They're with Bree."

He shook his head, refraining from grumbling, *That figures.* If he hadn't agreed to deliver the wine, he could've popped in to meet Bree tonight.

"It was her idea to babysit so Garth and I could have a real date. Isn't that sweet of her?"

"Yes, very sweet."

"Bree *is* sweet. The kids absolutely adore her. And it's not like she lets them walk all over her either. She's firm but kind. And she's just so helpful and understanding and, well, I'm just so glad

I hired her. Garth agrees. He says she's doing a great job managing the office."

"Speaking of our office manager, I keep wondering why I never see her. Are you sure she's actually working? Or does she hire elves to get things done?"

"Of course she's working, Dad. If you ever stopped by the office, you'd see for yourself how much she's done in there. Have you even bothered to meet her?"

"I've tried, Sophie. And I do go by the office. More this week than in the last couple of months. In fact, I was there yesterday afternoon, and it was too early for the wine-tasting room, but—once again—she was gone."

"That's because she's been inventorying the wine for a couple of hours every afternoon. She thinks she'll complete that by next week. But seriously, Dad, you need to meet her. I know you're going to love her."

"It's not that I'm not trying, Sophie. I stopped by there again this afternoon. She was AWOL, and the phone was ringing off the hook."

"You know as well as anyone, we can't always be in the office. That's why we have that old answering machine."

"Uh-huh."

"Don't worry. Bree always checks the machine. She'll handle whoever it was."

"Well, I happened to handle this particular message. Can you pass it on to Garth for me?"

"Sure. Go for it."

"As it turns out, I took two orders today, and—"

"Why did you take them? That's Bree's job."

"One order is from a friend who called my cell phone. The other was the one in the office. That one is an urgent order from Monterey. Pretty big one too. They need it ASAP, so I promised to have it down there by tomorrow afternoon."

"So you want Garth to drive it?"

"Yeah. I'd go myself, except I already agreed to make this other delivery. I'm on my way right now."

"In the evening? Must be super urgent."

"Sort of . . . but fun too." He explained about Jason's wife. "It's a nice evening for a drive up 101. And between you and me, I could use a break from the women occupying my house. I'll spend the night at Jason's and return tomorrow."

"Sounds nice. Have fun, Dad."

"Thanks. You too, sweetheart."

"And promise me you'll make sure to meet Bree tomorrow. *Please?*"

"I'll try, Sophie, but I think your wonder woman might have vanishing powers."

She laughed and they said goodbye. As he drove along the scenic highway, instead of enjoying the gorgeous ocean view, he imagined Bree and his grandkids playing out in the yard or picking produce from the garden. Bree in her blue dress, chestnut hair blowing in the breeze, holding hands with Lucy and Addison. Naturally, he wished he was there for real. But at least his grandkids were in good hands. That meant a lot to him. And he liked that Garth and Sophie were out on a date. Hopefully, he could keep his promise to Sophie and meet this wonder woman tomorrow.

Brynna had two reasons to feel nervous on Friday. First of all, Garth was driving a big wine order down to Monterey, which placed her in charge of today's wine-tasting group—all by herself. Second, and far more disturbing, she felt certain today was the day she would meet Leroy Sorrentino . . . *for the second time.* She was convinced this was the day because last night, when Garth drove her home after she had watched the kids, he mentioned that Leroy had promised to introduce himself to her. "Sophie pushed him on it. They both think it's strange you two haven't crossed paths yet."

Brynna had agreed it was odd and reassured Garth that she

looked forward to meeting Leroy. And maybe she did look forward to it in a way. But only because she knew that it would finally put an end to her anxiety. As much as she loved being at Sorrentino's, she felt more and more certain she was living in a dream—one that could turn into a nightmare. And she would just as soon wake up before that happened.

But the day passed in the usual way, and by the time she was setting up for the wine tasting, she wondered if she might be able to escape one more day without having to confess to Leroy Sorrentino that she was an imposter—an intruder who'd deceived his daughter and invaded his space.

Because she was running the tasting on her own, she'd dressed up a bit more than usual that morning. At least, that's what she told herself, but she suspected it was more due to the imminent possibility of coming face-to-face with Leroy. Wearing a hand-me-down sundress with blue and white stripes, she'd tied a ribbon around her long ponytail and was even wearing her little silver hoop earrings. But the day had passed uneventfully so far. It wasn't until Sophie called that Brynna learned Leroy had delivered wine to a friend in Bodega Bay. "He might not be back until later today," Sophie informed her. "But I'm calling to invite you to join us for a barbecue. Dad's birthday is Sunday, and I'm hosting a get-together. It'll be at Dad's house, and I'd really like your help."

"Thank you, Sophie. I'd love to come, but I'm not sure."

"Oh? Do you have other plans?"

"Well, I, uh, yeah, I'm not sure. Can I get back to you on that?"

"Of course."

Brynna glanced around the tasting room. "I should go. I need to get the wineglasses from the house. No one brought them out yet."

"Gina and her helpful friends." Sophie made a growling sound. "I suppose I'll need to include them on Sunday too. I almost forgot about that."

"Then you'll have a small crowd." Brynna tried to sound bright as she promised to get back to her as soon as she knew what she was doing on Sunday. Somehow the idea of reuniting with Leroy for the first time at a family gathering didn't sit well with her. And on his birthday? That just seemed all wrong. But she didn't have time to think about it now. She had a tasting to set up.

To her relief, no one was in the kitchen when she walked in. She had almost finished unloading the first dishwasher drawer when she heard footsteps. Hoping it wasn't Leroy, she felt almost relieved to see Judith narrowing her eyes at her as if she were about to steal the silver. Brynna forced a smile as she said hello then continued unloading the glasses.

"Oh, I thought I heard someone in here." Judith gave her a condescending look.

"Sorry to intrude." Brynna set a glass in the basket.

"You're dressed up. Special occasion?"

"No. It's just that I'm running the wine tasting. Solo." Brynna forced another smile. "A first for me."

"Oh, well, I'm sure you'll do fine. It doesn't seem like it would take much." Judith took a glass from the dishwasher, inspecting it for spots. "I'm sure I could do it if I had to." She set it on the counter.

"Really?" Brynna wondered, transferring the glass into her basket. "Garth likes it done a certain way. But I suppose if he taught you, you could probably manage it just fine."

"Yes, I'm sure I could. In fact, I think I will volunteer my services to Leroy at dinner tonight." She opened the fridge. "We're planning a special meal to welcome him back from Bodega Bay. He should be home this evening, and I'm sure he'll enjoy a home-cooked meal."

"Right." Brynna opened the second dishwasher drawer only to discover that although the soap was in the tray, it hadn't been run yet. "Oh dear." She closed it and turned it on.

"Trouble?"

"Well, the glasses in this one are still dirty."

"And you don't have enough there?"

184

"I don't know. We're expecting quite a crowd today. Garth says a bus from a senior center is coming."

"Well, then, don't let me keep you," Judith said in a dismissive tone.

"Yes, I should get back out there. If you see Gina, can you ask her to bring the next load of glasses out when they're finished?" Brynna peered curiously at Judith. "Or maybe you'd like to lend a hand since you're interested in helping with wine tastings."

"Oh, no, not today. I don't do well with old people. Besides, I have too much to do to get ready for our dinner."

Brynna just nodded. Then, with the loaded basket in hand, she made a swift exit. Why did that woman always seem to rub her the wrong way? At least she now knew that Leroy wasn't even in the vineyard today. She felt a mixture of relief and regret as she set out the glasses. On one hand, she would be less stressed during the tasting. But on the other hand, it would've been nice to just get the unavoidable meeting over with.

As she set up the tasting room, even arranging some small bouquets of lavender, poppies, and a few other things in glass canning jars, which she set on tables, she tried to forget about Judith. Focusing instead on the guests who were about to arrive and thinking of ways to help them enjoy their visit, she was surprised to hear the hiss of the bus's brakes, followed by the cheerful chatter of people outside the barn. She went out to greet them, graciously ushering the guests into the barn. As she led them inside, she started out just the way Garth would, telling the story of how the Sorrentino family first came to this country by boat. "The clipper ship was called the *General Harrison*—" She was cut off by an elderly woman's exclamation that her ancestors arrived on that very same ship. "Perhaps they were friends with the Sorrentinos," Brynna told her. The woman laughed, and Brynna felt she was off to a good start.

Chapter 23

As anxious as Leroy was to get home, Jason had waylaid him by insisting he attend a brunch with some attorney associates. "We often bring in guests. It's a great way to connect. And an opportunity to promote your vineyard," Jason assured him. "Plus, you'll make me look good. My buddies will be impressed that I have a friend who owns a vineyard." Leroy wasn't too sure about that, but before the brunch ended, he handed out business cards and actually took two orders.

But it was after three by the time he got home and, judging by the bus parked near the barn, he knew the tasting room was occupied. He also knew that Garth was out making a delivery, so he surmised that Bree was probably playing host in there. This might be his chance to see the office manager in action and make her acquaintance.

"Hey, Dad." Gina came out of the house carrying a basket of wineglasses. "How was your trip?"

"Good. I even took orders for a few more cases while I was up there."

"Maybe you should hit the road more often." She nodded toward the barn. "I better get these in there. It's a big crowd today, and Bree might run short."

"Let me take them for you." He reached for the basket.

Gina's brows arched. "Have you met her yet?"

"Not yet." He grinned.

"Well, let me know what you think of her, okay?"

He cocked his head to the side. "Why?"

She shrugged. "I don't know. Just curious."

"Don't you like her?"

"Sure, I like her. She's great, but I'm—" Her words were cut off by Judith calling to her from the porch. "Oh, yeah," she said quickly. "Judith's planning a special welcome home dinner for you tonight. You better not miss it either."

He grimaced. "Yeah, well, I better get these glasses to Bree." As he headed for the barn, he wondered if there was any way to escape Judith's special dinner . . . and if there was any way for Gina to send her "working guests" packing. He had a feeling Gina was nearly as weary of them as he was. He pushed open the door with his elbow and stepped into the shadowy barn. It really was a good-sized crowd. It looked like a group of older folks, but judging by one of the guest's comments, which was followed by laughter, they were a cheerful crowd.

He paused behind the group clustered around the front counter, listening as a white-haired woman inquired about the volume of bottles produced annually. He was pleased to hear Bree answer correctly.

"I know this for a fact," she told them, "because I've just finished doing a complete inventory." She began to break the sales off into percentages of wine types, but something about her voice got his attention. It was as if he'd heard it before.

He circled around the edge of the crowd, hoping to get a glimpse of this mysterious woman. He stepped past a tall man and, about to set the basket on the corner of the counter, he saw her. Leroy stared then blinked then stared again. In disbelief he released the basket, which was not fully on the counter. It dropped to the floor in a loud crash of broken glass.

Everyone turned toward him—including *Brynna*. Although she looked as shocked as he felt, she seemed to recover quickly.

"Please, excuse the interruption," she calmly told the visitors. "But the man with the butterfingers is actually Leroy Sorrentino, the owner of Sorrentino's. It was his family, his ancestors, who created this lovely winery. In fact, he can tell you much more about the agricultural side of the vineyard. And so, I will turn you over to him while I clean up that little mess. I'm sure he'll be glad to field your questions." She looked hopefully at him.

"Yes, of course." He tried to keep the anger and indignation out of his voice, but he suspected it was futile. What on earth was she doing here? *Why?*

Brynna's smile looked artificial as she set a package of clear plastic cups on the countertop. "We might need these today." Then she moved to the other end of the counter and disappeared on the opposite side of the crowd.

The barn remained strangely quiet for a long moment, and Leroy had no choice but to take Brynna's place behind the counter. He attempted a smile, trying to focus his attention on the guests, but his head was spinning.

"Welcome to Sorrentino's," he said nervously. "I didn't expect to play host here today, but I'm happy to take any of your questions."

"I'm curious if last year's wildfires affected your vineyard," a bald man called out.

As Leroy described the fire damage and recent restoration effort, Brynna stooped nearby, cleaning up his mess and setting the few unbroken glasses on a back shelf. But before he finished his explanation, she was finished. He watched Brynna quietly exiting the barn with the basket of broken shards while a portly woman asked if they ever made champagne.

"No, we don't make champagne," he told the woman in a flat voice. "That's a little too festive for us."

———

As Brynna dumped the broken glass into the trash barrel outside the barn, her hands shook uncontrollably. She knew it was from shock. Not from seeing Leroy, as much as it was from witnessing his reaction to seeing her. He was not a bit pleased. In fact, he seemed seriously angered. Not that she blamed him. No one liked being tricked. And that was probably how it seemed to him.

She hurried over to the house with the empty basket, but not wanting to go inside and face Judith or the others, she set it on the porch and started to leave. Her plan was to get out of here as quickly and quietly as possible. But as she headed toward the guesthouse, she realized how she'd abandoned Leroy to the big crowd and that he wasn't used to hosting. Plus, he still needed to serve them wine and she knew that it was wrong to leave him like that.

As hard as it was to return to the barn, it was the right thing to do. So, composing herself, she held her head high and went back inside. Leroy was still taking questions, but she could tell the group was growing impatient. They'd paid to come here to sample wines, and it was up to her to handle it.

"I can take it from here," she told Leroy as she started to uncork a bottle of Chablis. "Unless you'd like to." She began to fill the plastic glasses, thinking it would be better to finish with the real glasses for the red wines.

"No thanks," he said stiffly. "I'll let you handle it." He stepped away.

"Sorrentino's is known for its variety of wines," she said as she continued to pour. "Unlike some vineyards that only produce one type, because this is an old family-owned vineyard, it has preserved many of the old ways." She continued to speak calmly and clearly, keeping her eyes on what she was doing, as well as the guests she was serving. She tried to imagine she was teaching a class of third graders. Somehow, all the while, as she worked from today's offerings of Chablis to chardonnay to pinot noir to merlot, she managed not to look up to see if Leroy was still there.

It wasn't until the tasting was over and the guests were being shuffled back toward the bus that she noticed Leroy sitting in a shadowy corner, just watching her. Not knowing what to do or what to say, she began to clean up. She put away the leftover wines, threw away plastic cups and napkins, filled a basket with used glasses, and wiped down the counter and tabletops.

Finally, she looked up from her work to see that Leroy was gone. Part of her felt relieved, but another part stung with the hurt of it. He had simply walked away without a single word. All that could mean was that he was very disturbed by her presence. He was angry. Who could blame him?

She stepped outside of the barn, and after glancing around to see that no one was nearby to see the tears now filling her eyes, she rushed to the guesthouse. Feeling ashamed and guilty and foolish, she started packing her things in a frenzy. It had been wrong to come here, wrong to take the office job, wrong to befriend Sophie. Wrong, wrong, wrong! And it was no surprise that Leroy was angered by it. She was a complete idiot to have done such a stupid thing and she deserved his wrath.

After her bag was packed, she straightened the guesthouse. Fortunately, it was already fairly clean, but she removed the sheets from the bed, gathered the towels from the bathroom, and gave everything a thorough wipe down. Then she removed all of the hand-me-down clothes from the closet and dresser, folded them, and left them on the bed. She didn't want anyone to think she'd taken anything with her that wasn't hers.

She neatly piled the used linens by the front door. As she stood, she reread the needlework Bible verse about filling the house with good things. But it was the same three words that grabbed on to her again. *Wisdom, understanding, knowledge.* More than ever, she longed for those elusive qualities—because she felt foolish, confused, and just plain stupid. She decided to ask God for help. She bowed her head and asked him to guide her.

After her prayer, she felt calmer. She didn't have all the answers, but she suddenly felt the urge to write a note to Sophie. She knew the girl would be hurt by her hasty departure, so she sat down to write. After that was done, she felt the need to write an explanation to Leroy as well. He deserved as much. She wanted it to be short like the note she'd written to Sophie, but once she started to write, it was as if she couldn't stop.

Dear Leroy,

I don't know where to begin or how to explain to you why I am here. I have asked myself that very question dozens of times during the past week. It's a very long story that started thirty years ago. But if you ever have the time, and if you truly want to hear it, I will be glad to tell you.

But for now, I just want to tell you I'm sorry. Very, very sorry. I'm sorry for so many things. Right now I'm mostly sorry for the way I've snuck into your world. Your beautiful world. How that happened is another part of the very long story. I'm sorry that you felt so blindsided by me being here. I was afraid that might happen, but it was like being on a train headed for disaster with no way to stop it. I just held on for the ride. And although some of the ride was scary, much of it was pure beauty. Almost too beautiful for words. Your beautiful daughters, your delightful grandchildren, your lovely vineyard and home. Your whole life, Leroy. It's amazing and wonderful. You are a very blessed man.

I even feel I've gotten to know Marcie by spending time in this sweet cottage. I know she was a special woman, and I can tell that Sophie is very much like her mother. Of everything I'll miss about this place, I think I will miss Sophie the most. And her sweet family. I hope I haven't hurt her too badly. But somehow, I know she will forgive me.

I also know that as much as I love your wonderful world, I do not belong here. I was an uninvited intruder who deceived you and your family—and I am so very sorry. I didn't mean to deceive. That was never my goal. But somehow it happened. I know that doesn't excuse it.

I realize you're very angry at me. You have every right to be. But I hope that, for your sake, you will forgive me. I hate to think of you going around in your beautiful world with unforgiveness in your heart. You don't deserve that. So, please, try to forgive me. I never meant to hurt you. It will probably take me a while to forgive myself, but I will work on it.

Finally, I thank you for your hospitality. You might laugh that I have the nerve to call it that, but your wonderful world welcomed me like no place I have ever been. Your adorable guest cottage was a haven like none I have known. And your sweet Sophie . . . well, I'll never forget her. Like I already said, you're a blessed man, Leroy. But I'm sure you know that. That's what makes me believe you will forgive me in time.

> *Sincere apologies,*
> *Brynna (aka Bree) Philips*

She set the two letters on the little table, anchoring them with a mason jar of lavender and poppies that she'd set out just yesterday. Next, she picked up her phone. She was tempted to call Jan and beg her to come and get her, but she knew that wasn't fair. Sure, Mike and Jan had pushed her to take on this fool's mission and promised to fetch her if it fell apart, but it wasn't their fault. She'd stayed on because she'd wanted to. Besides, even if Jan or Mike were willing to come, Yosemite was too far away, and it would take too long. She needed to depart tonight. She called a taxi service.

"We can't have anyone out there until seven," the dispatcher told her.

Brynna looked at her watch, dismayed that was nearly an hour from now. "That's the best you can do?"

"Sorry. It's Friday. I can try to get someone out there sooner, but I doubt it will be before six thirty."

"Thank you." She gave the address of the vineyard and, not wanting to chance a taxi pulling up to the big house, told the woman she'd be out on the road by the driveway.

During the next thirty minutes Brynna nervously paced back and forth on the little front porch. She didn't allow herself to look out over the vineyard but kept her gaze fixed to the floor planks. When it was almost six thirty, she gathered up her things and headed for the road. Her plan was to walk toward the main highway and hopefully meet the taxi far enough out that no one in the big house would notice her. But she was barely on her way when she heard him calling. She knew it was Leroy.

Brynna set her duffel next to the guesthouse and went over to where he was standing on the grassy mound that stretched between his house and the cottage. For a moment she thought perhaps she'd misjudged him. Maybe he wasn't angry at her for deceiving him like this. But as she got closer to him, she saw the steely look in his eyes, the hardened expression on his face. His hands were shoved into his jeans pockets, and his lips were tightly pursed, as if to contain his rage.

"Leroy," she began in a trembling voice. "I know you're upset, and I'd like to—"

"I don't know what your game is, but I'm not playing." His tone was terse.

"I'm not playing a game, I just—"

"You're not playing a game?" he shouted. "You come here and trick my daughter into hiring you? You pretend to be someone you're not? You deceive all of us? For what? Your own personal pleasure?"

"No, that's not how it is." She grappled for words. "I know it looks bad, but it's not what—"

He cut her off again. "What kind of a person does something like this?"

"I didn't want to hurt anyone."

"Wanting and doing are two different things." He pulled off his hat and ran his fingers through his hair. "I do not understand you, Brynna. I guess I never did. But I never, in all my days, expected you to pull a crazy stunt like this." He shook his head. "Do you get pleasure out of hurting people?"

"It's not like that." She felt tears coming now. "I'm sorry, Leroy. I was just getting ready to go. I assume that will make you happy."

"Happy?" He glared at her. "*Happy?*"

Just then someone called out his name from the back deck. Brynna turned to see that it was all set for another family dinner. Gina and her friends were standing up there, waving down to them and, like amused spectators, watching the show taking place down below. Judith left the others, coming down the slope toward them with a wide smile on her face.

"We've been looking for you, Leroy," Judith called out as she approached. She came over to stand next to him. "I made you something very special tonight, but it won't be any good if we serve it cold."

Leroy was still scowling.

"Come on, darling," Judith urged. "I know you must be starved."

He looked at Brynna with a slightly torn expression. "What about—"

"Don't worry about me," Brynna said. "I'm leaving." Then, without looking back, she turned away, grabbed her bag, and to her relief, spotted a small car rumbling down the road toward her. The taxi looked like a yellow blur as she hurried toward it, but it wasn't until she got inside that the tears poured freely. Fortunately, the taxi driver didn't seem to notice. She waited to speak until they reached the end of the long driveway.

"Having a hard day?" the woman asked in a kind tone.

"You could say that," Brynna mumbled.

"So, where can I take you?"

"I honestly don't know."

194

The woman turned around to look at her. "I see."

"I'd like to go to Yosemite."

The driver laughed. "That'd be quite a fare. I wouldn't mind, but I'd probably get canned."

"Just take me to the nearest town."

"Okay."

"Uh, is there a hotel there?"

"Not a hotel proper. But a friend of mine runs a nice B and B."

"Okay. Take me there."

"Will do."

As they drove toward town, Brynna tried to gather her thoughts and concoct a plan of some sort. But all she really wanted to do was go to bed. She felt so tired she thought she could probably sleep for several days. And maybe that was what she'd do. Just sleep it all off. Maybe when she woke up, life would look better.

Chapter 24

With Judith's arm entwined in his, Leroy watched the trail of dust behind the taxicab. He knew he should be relieved that she was gone, but instead he felt even angrier. Why had she done this? Why?

"Come on, Leroy," Judith cooed at him. "The girls are waiting."

He just nodded, allowing her to lead him up to the terrace. Once they got there, he excused himself to wash up, but instead of heading to the bathroom, he went out the front door, jumped into his Jeep, and took off. At first, he drove toward the highway, determined to catch up with the taxi and demand a full explanation from Brynna. But then he slowed down and, feeling totally confused, turned the Jeep around and headed over to Sophie's. Maybe she could give him an explanation.

He parked in front of his daughter's house and waved as he got out. Sophie was seated in a camping chair, and the kids were kicking a soccer ball back and forth across the front lawn.

"Dad!" she exclaimed happily as he came into the yard. "What're you doing here? The kids and I already had dinner, but I've got leftovers warming for when Garth gets home. There's plenty if you want—"

"I'm not hungry."

"Oh?" She frowned. "What's up?"

"Just stopped by to say hi." He took the chair next to her, blowing out a loud breath of air as he sat down.

"Are you okay?"

Before he could answer, the kids were tugging on him, each pulling one arm and begging him to play ball with them.

"You two leave your pappy alone," Sophie scolded. "He doesn't always have to play with you."

"Oh, it's okay." He started to stand, but Sophie stopped him.

"Why don't you show Pappy your gymnastic skills, Lucy?" she said quickly. "Show him your cartwheels and somersaults. You were doing them beautifully earlier."

"I can somersault," Addison declared. Suddenly both children were doing tricks on the lawn, competing for Leroy's attention.

"So, what's up, Dad?" Sophie asked under her breath. "I can tell something's bugging you."

"When's Garth going to be home?" He peered down toward the road.

"He just called a few minutes ago, said he was almost home." Sophie leaned back, rubbing her belly. "And not a moment too soon."

Leroy grew nauseous. Her due date was more than a month off, but you never knew. "Are you okay, honey?"

"Yes, Dad." She rolled her eyes. "Just worn out is all." She sighed. "I don't have the same energy I had when I was pregnant with Addison. I'm so glad that I hired Bree. I can't imagine what I'd have done without her."

Leroy cringed inwardly.

"There's Garth's pickup now." She pointed to the road.

"Is it okay if I talk to you privately?" Leroy quietly asked her. "After Garth gets here?"

She looked alarmed now. "Yes, of course. What's wrong?"

"Later," he said as Addison yelled for them to watch his cartwheel. They both clapped as he made a sloppy attempt, followed by Lucy's much better one. Soon Garth was there and both children happily mobbed him. He let out a dramatic yelp and tumbled into the grass, pretending like they'd successfully tackled him. Suddenly the three of them were yelling and rolling and laughing.

"Garth," Sophie called out over their racket. "I need to talk to Dad. Your dinner's on the stove."

"Huh?" He looked up with a confused expression.

"Dad's taking me for a ride," she said as she tugged Leroy toward his Jeep. "We'll be back soon. Okay?"

"Yeah, sure." Garth nodded. "Everything okay?"

"Just need some daddy time with my daughter. No big deal," Leroy reassured him as he helped Sophie into the Jeep. "We'll be back soon."

"Feel free to get the kids ready for bed," Sophie called out.

After they were on the vineyard road, Leroy took in a deep breath, trying to think of a way to begin this conversation. "Sophie, how much do you really know about Brynna—I mean, Bree?"

She grabbed his arm in a viselike grip. "What's wrong? Did she do something bad?"

Leroy pulled the Jeep over on top of the hill and turned off the motor. "Not exactly."

"Not exactly?" Sophie released his arm. "What did she do, Dad? Please tell me she didn't embezzle or something."

"No, no, it's nothing like that." He shifted in his seat so he faced her. "Did she tell you anything about me?"

"What do you mean?"

"Did she ever mention that she knew me? I mean . . . before."

"Before *what*?"

He pulled off his hat, then tossed it in back. "It was a long time ago. Did she tell you that she and I were, uh, involved? Back before I married your mother?"

Sophie's eyes grew huge. "Are you kidding?"

"I'm dead serious. Did you know about it?"

"No way. She never said a word."

He ran his fingers through his hair. "I just don't understand why she did it."

"Did what?"

"Came here. Started to work for us. Why?"

"I don't know . . ." Sophie looked even more confused than he felt, so he explained about the long-ago romance and how Brynna Meyers broke his heart.

"Bree Philips is Brynna Meyers," she said slowly. "And she's been here all this time—and you didn't even know it?"

"I never really met her. Until today, I only saw her from a distance. She reminded me of Brynna, but I never would've guessed. Not in a million years."

"You met her today?" she asked. "What happened?"

He told her about the awkward tasting room debacle. "I was totally blindsided."

"That's how I feel now. *Blindsided*." She shook her head. "I really liked Bree—I mean Brynna. I trusted her completely. I thought she was the real deal. I can't believe she'd do this to us, Dad. Why *would* she?"

"I don't know, but the more I think about it, the more it seems very cold and calculated to me. Like she planned it all out. As if she thought she had something to gain by it. Something like this doesn't happen by accident. It's not a coincidence. She knew who she was, and she knew who I was, but she kept it from us. She tricked you, Sophie. She manipulated you."

"I get that. But she never seemed conniving to me. She worked so hard. She seemed so sincere." Sophie was crying now. "I thought— I thought she really liked me."

He hugged her. "I'm sorry, Soph. I feel like this is my fault."

"No, it's my fault. I'm the one who hired her."

"Well, she's gone now anyway. I just wanted you to know."

Tears streamed down Sophie's flushed cheeks, and her shoulders heaved up and down with her sobs, reminding him of when she was little. It broke his heart.

"I don't want you to blame yourself or feel bad, sweetie. Brynna was obviously playing some sort of weird game with us. It's good that she's gone now." He stroked her hair. "We'll be fine. We'll find someone to replace her. Don't worry about it, okay?"

They talked a while longer, trying to make sense of what seemed senseless, and then he took her home. He made her promise to let it go and not worry about it, but he knew she would. He knew he would too. As he took his time going home, he remembered the woman with the brown ponytail, sailing down this very hill, arms extended, whooping in delight. *Why?* He couldn't stop thinking *why?* Why would someone do something like this? *Why?*

When he got home, all he wanted was to slip up the back stairs and go to his room. He knew the women would be mad at him for skipping out on their welcome home dinner, but the last thing he wanted was to have to explain this mess to them.

He tiptoed through the back door and was just heading up the stairs when Gina called out to him. "Not so fast, Dad."

"What is it?" he growled back at her.

"You owe me an explanation." She stood at the foot of the stairs, hands on hips, glaring up at him.

"Is anyone else around?" he asked quietly.

"They're watching a movie downstairs."

She was right. Leroy knew Gina deserved some kind of explanation. Best to get it over with. "Okay," he said, coming down the stairs. "I'll tell you what happened."

She led him into the kitchen. "I know it has to do with Bree."

"That's true. But her name's not Bree."

Gina's eyes lit up. "So I was right? She really is that girl in the old photos! Your old girlfriend!" She pulled out a barstool, eagerly watching him. "I just knew it!"

"Good work, Nancy Drew." He opened the fridge.

"Are you hungry? Judith saved a plate for you."

"No thanks. I'll fix myself something." He removed some lunch meat and cheese.

"I kept imagining it was Brynna, but I didn't actually believe it. I mean, for one thing, she doesn't seem that old."

"Well, she is."

"And you didn't figure it out until today?"

He shook his head as he constructed a sandwich, explaining about his shock when he made his discovery. "I had no idea, Gina. Anyway, she's gone. End of story."

"That's so bizarre!" Gina slapped the countertop. "But why'd she do it? Why'd she come here? What was the point?"

"Good question."

"I mean the obvious answer is that she still likes you. But why take a job? Why this whole charade, calling herself Bree Philips? What's her real name?"

"It used to be Brynna Meyers. But she did get married, so her name would've changed." He took a bite of his sandwich, slowly chewing. "Not that it matters. She's gone now."

"Are you glad she's gone?" Gina locked eyes with him.

"Mostly I'm just tired." He held up his sandwich. "Mind if I finish this in my room? I'd like to escape before your houseguests pounce on us. I want to hit the hay early tonight."

She nodded. "Thanks for telling me what was up, Dad." She hugged him. "I hope you're not too hurt by this whole thing."

He forced a smile. "Mostly bamboozled."

She patted his back. "I bet. Sleep well, okay?"

He said he would, but as he trudged upstairs, he suspected that was a lie. Despite his anger at the way Brynna had connived and tricked them, all he could think of was the hurt in her eyes before she left. And that just made him mad. She was the one who created this mess—why should he feel guilty about it?

⁓

After a mostly sleepless night, Leroy got up early the next morning. He made a pot of coffee and took a steaming mug out to the back terrace. Sitting in a chair with Babe lying nearby, he stared out over the little guesthouse where Brynna had been living—right under his nose—all this time. And he'd been oblivious. Or had he? He remembered the times he'd spied her . . . walking barefoot through the vineyard at dusk, playing with his grandkids in Sophie's garden, watching the sunset on the bicycle. And each time, what had he thought of? Brynna Meyers. Was it possible that somewhere in his psyche he'd really known it was her but had been afraid to admit it? No, that was ridiculous!

"Hello there, stranger." Judith came out with her own mug of coffee. "Mind if I join you?"

He wanted to say "I do mind," but knew that was rude, so he just shrugged. "Suit yourself."

"Thank you." She scooted a chair next to him, disturbing Babe from her place. The old dog gave Judith a questioning look, then moved to his other side. For some reason he thought Babe was making a statement about Judith. She didn't like this intrusive woman any more than he did.

"I know you're feeling out of sorts," Judith said quietly. "Gina told us the story, and I must admit it's a strange one."

"Uh-huh." He'd "thank" his bigmouthed daughter for that later.

"I thought there was something suspicious about Bree, or Brynna, or whatever she goes by. But I never dreamed the woman was a stalker."

He turned to stare at her. "A stalker?"

"That's what it seems like. I mean, showing up like she did. Pretending to be someone else. Seriously, it reminds me of that creepy *Fatal Attraction* movie." She shuddered. "Next thing you know, she'll be boiling a rabbit."

He suppressed the urge to tell Judith to shut up and leave him alone.

"Clearly that woman was out to get her claws into you, Leroy. You must know that by now. She probably saw you as a nice prize." She waved a hand toward the fields. "With all your vineyards, the owner of Sorrentino's."

"She'd been working in the office, Judith. She saw the books. She obviously knew the winery was barely scraping by." He narrowed his eyes at her. "Not exactly a gold digger."

"Maybe not." Judith smiled coyly. "Maybe she just likes you for your looks. Can't blame a woman for that."

He rolled his eyes but kept his thoughts to himself.

"Oh, really, Leroy, I think you're taking this whole thing much too seriously." She leaned forward to look directly at him. "That is, unless you still have feelings for this woman. *Do you?*"

He blew out an exasperated sigh. "I don't know *how* I feel, but I know this—I've got work to do." He stood and excused himself. But as he stormed off toward his Jeep, with Babe right at his heels, he bristled at Judith's suggestion that Brynna was the kind of woman to stalk anyone. Or that she'd boil a rabbit! *Seriously?*

Chapter 25

Brynna had broken down and called Jan last night, pouring out the whole sad story. "But don't worry. You don't need to do anything," Brynna had finally said. "I'm going to stay at this sweet little B and B for a few days. Just until I can get a flight out of San Francisco, and then I'll go home."

"I'm sorry it fell apart," Jan told her.

"Yeah. Me too. But it was a dumb thing to do."

"We shouldn't have encouraged you, Brynna. It sort of occurred to us later that we shouldn't have pushed you so hard. But at the time, it seemed right. I'm sorry."

"Don't be. I'm glad I did it. I mean, sure, it hurts a little. But it's good to know that Leroy has no interest in me. I think it was actually kind of therapeutic." She sighed. "What I'll miss most of all is his daughter Sophie and her family . . . and the land." She wanted to add "and the dream of a life like that" but knew that sounded pathetic.

"Well, Mike and I are coming to get you," Jan had said. "We've had enough of Yosemite. We'll leave tomorrow around noon. We should be there by dinnertime."

"You really don't need to—"

"We want to." She paused. "Mike says we're definitely coming, Brynna. No arguments."

It was settled. But as Brynna went to bed, she almost regretted agreeing. She'd been looking forward to some rest and a few calm days in the B and B.

But by morning, after a sleepless night in a bed that wasn't as comfortable as the one back in the guest cottage, she was glad to know she'd be leaving that evening. As she repacked her bag, she realized her cell phone was dead, but she couldn't find her charging cord anywhere. Maybe it didn't matter. It wasn't like she had anyone to talk to anyway.

She checked out just before ten and, after leaving her duffel in the lobby and her phone charging behind the counter with a borrowed cord, she set out to explore the small town and find something to occupy her mind. But as she wandered from shop to shop, with no real reason to look at anything, she felt lost . . . displaced . . . almost like an alien from another planet. As if she didn't belong here. But did she belong anywhere? Finally, she sat down on a park bench in the center of town.

She felt lonelier than ever as she watched parents and children come and play and then go on their merry way. Or sometimes not so merry. One toddler threw a tantrum when his mother told him it was time to leave the sandbox. But even the child's noisy fit looked preferable to being alone. It felt like everyone in the world had someone. Everyone except her. Brynna had never liked feeling sorry for herself, but if she were being honest, she had to admit that's what she was doing right now. Having a pity party . . . for a party of one.

So once again, she prayed. She asked God for the strength to bear this heartache and for him to help her find her way. And for something else too. She asked God for a place to go home to and a family to love and be loved by. Oh, she knew that was a lot to ask. Too much to expect. But she also remembered her mother telling her that prayers were about faith and believing that God really wanted to do good things for his children. She wanted to believe that she was still God's child. Hadn't she given her heart to him once? Certainly, he hadn't cast it aside. Even if it felt like that sometimes.

As Brynna watched a group of children playing, she remembered how teaching her third graders used to fill that lonely place in her heart. Her school often felt like a home, the children like a family. Maybe that was enough.

———

Leroy was too distracted to be much use in the vineyard that morning, but at least his crew was on task. Finally, he realized part of his issue was just plain hunger. Thanks to Gina's working guests, he'd been avoiding his kitchen, and as a result, he hadn't eaten anything since his sandwich the night before. *Women!*

Determined to take back his kitchen, regardless of the females occupying it, he parked his Jeep in front of his house and was about to go inside, but he spotted Sophie's van pulling up to the guesthouse and it fueled his curiosity. Instead of storming the kitchen, he went over to see what his eldest daughter was up to.

She was standing on the porch when he got there. "Whatcha doing, Soph?" As he got closer, he could see her eyes were red-rimmed and puffy. "Everything okay, honey?"

"No." She shook her head. "Nothing is okay."

"What's up?"

"I'm worried about Bree—I mean Brynna. I've been calling her phone all morning, but it's turned off. That's not like her. So I, uh, I wondered . . . I thought maybe she'd come back here. I hoped and prayed she had."

"Did she?"

"No. She's gone. But I wanted to know for sure. I can't imagine how she must feel right now. You must've hurt her feelings pretty badly yesterday, Dad. She wouldn't have left like that unless you did."

"I hurt *her* feelings?" He scowled. "What about mine? She comes here and pretends to be—"

"That was *my* fault. I thought it all through in the middle of the night last night when I couldn't sleep. I practically forced her to take the job."

"Forced her?" He shook his head. "Hard to believe."

"It's true. She showed up and I assumed she was the applicant you were supposed to interview. Remember? You had to go meet with Aunt Sherry, so I took over. Anyway, I found Bree standing outside the office, and when she started to ask about you and the vineyard, I just assumed she was there for the job, so I jumped right in. I made her come into the office and started the interview. In hindsight, I can see she was caught off guard by my questions, but she answered me. And instantly I liked her. She seemed like a genuinely good person."

"A good person who tricked all of us?"

"I don't think she meant to, Dad. I think she just wanted to be here. She *loved* it here. I know she did. And I know she never meant to hurt anyone. I *know* she is a good person."

"You sound pretty sure of yourself." He folded his arms against his chest. "Tell me, Sophie, how well do you think you *really* knew her?"

"We spent a lot of time together. I considered her my friend, and she was very transparent about her life."

"Really?" He didn't like being so skeptical, but he couldn't seem to help it.

"She told me about losing both her parents when she was young."

"Her parents died?"

"Yeah. In a car wreck during her first year of college."

"Oh."

"And she told me about Dirk. *Dirk the jerk.*"

"Dirk the jerk?"

"Her high school boyfriend then husband. I guess he was sort of a jock and popular with the girls. Anyway, he kind of took over her life after her parents died. She said it might've been because she had a small inheritance and he'd lost his athletic scholarship because of an injury. So they got married in college and she used all her money to put them both through school and to buy a condo. She wanted to buy a house with a yard because she loves to garden, but Dirk the jerk wouldn't let her."

"Huh?" Leroy remembered how blue Brynna had been when they first met, moping over her boyfriend—that must've been Dirk the jerk. He pointed Sophie toward a rocker. "Maybe you should sit down, honey."

"Thanks." She sat, and he lowered himself onto the steps in front of her. "So I'm saying I do know her, Dad. She also told me about how Dirk never wanted kids and she did. She loves kids— that's why she became a teacher. I can tell by the way she is with Lucy and Addison, she really does love kids."

"Uh-huh." Leroy remembered seeing her playing with his grandkids. It was one of the things that had attracted him to her . . . from a distance.

"Anyway, Dirk cheated on her. He had an affair with a girl who's younger than me. They're married now, and guess what?"

"What?" He rubbed his chin, not sure if he wanted to hear any more.

"Dirk the jerk and his new bride are about to have a baby. Can you believe that? Bree, I mean Brynna, ran into them just a few weeks ago. That was one reason she went on this crazy camping trip with her teacher friend. Just to get away and not think about stupid Dirk and all that. She's had a rough go, Dad. I don't know what all you said to her yesterday, but I bet it broke her heart."

Leroy felt kind of sick now. "I didn't mean to hurt her."

"Well, think about it. She's had so much hurt in her life. And she was so happy here. Why do you think she took the job? Why do you think she stayed on?"

He shrugged.

"Because she obviously still has feelings for you!" Sophie put a hand under her stomach and raised herself to her feet. "Why on earth would she have done such a crazy thing if she didn't? Yeah, I'll admit that it was crazy. But I get it, Dad. And I feel sorry for her." Her eyes looked glassy. "And I feel sorry for me too. I lost a good friend." She pulled out a key as she started to cry, then unlocked the front door and went inside.

Leroy felt like a total heel. And, like Sophie, he was now concerned for Brynna. Where had she gone in the taxi? Was she really brokenhearted? And why was her phone turned off?

"Dad!"

He jumped to his feet and rushed into the guest cottage. "What is it?"

"Bree left us letters. One for you and one for me." Sophie sat down in one of the kitchen chairs, opening an envelope. He took the other and followed suit, reading what seemed like a sincere and heartfelt letter of apology from Brynna. Now he felt like even more of a heel.

"Poor Bree." Sophie slid her note back into the envelope. "She even wrote in here that Bree wasn't a fake name. It was her dad's nickname for her." She pointed to his letter. "What did she write to you?"

"Mostly an apology and explanation. It pretty much lines up with what you told me." He blinked to hold back the tears trying to break free. He didn't want to break down in front of his daughter.

"So, you see, she really wasn't out to trick us. That wasn't her intent, anyway."

"Yeah, I guess not." He remembered how Judith had tried to portray Brynna as a crazed stalker who boiled bunnies. "But what do we do about it now?"

"Go find her, Dad." She grabbed his hand. "Bring her back. She belongs here. With us."

"Oh, honey, even if I could find her, and I'm not sure where to look, what would I tell her? It's not like I'm ready to rekindle a romance."

"But you could get to know her. You could give her a chance and just see what happens."

"I doubt she'd want to come back." He waved his letter. "This sounded final to me, Sophie. Pretty cut and dry. She admitted she'd made a mistake and was sorry for it. She seemed determined to leave."

"Who could blame her after you raked her over the coals?"

He wanted to defend himself, but figured his daughter was right. He had been hard on Brynna. Pretty coldhearted. He slowly stood, then, realizing he still was hungry, he went over to the old-fashioned fridge—just one of the many expensive toys Marcie had insisted were necessary for the guest cottage. He opened it and stared at the neatly stocked shelves. "Hard-boiled eggs?" He took one from the bowl, spinning it on the countertop to see if it really was boiled.

"Dad? You're raiding her fridge?"

"It's our fridge, honey." He started to peel the egg. "And I never had breakfast."

"Hey, there's her phone charger." Sophie pointed to a cord plugged in by the little coffee maker.

"Maybe that's why she wasn't answering," he suggested. "Her phone is probably dead."

"I hope that's why."

He helped himself to some orange juice and popped two slices of whole grain bread into the toaster. "I like Brynna's taste in food." He attempted a smile. "Simple but good."

"You'd like *everything* about her, Dad." Sophie sounded exasperated. "If you'd only get to know her."

He sighed. "She's gone, Soph. The sooner you accept this, the better you'll feel."

"Fine." Sophie stood. "If you won't go get her back, I will. I told Garth to drop the kids with Grandma if I didn't come back within an hour. I'm going to drive over to—"

"No, honey." Leroy put a hand on her shoulder. "If anyone is going to look for her, it should be me."

"You will?" Her eyes brightened.

"I'll give it a shot."

"You're not just saying that? Not just trying to pacify me? You'll really look for her and try to bring her back?"

"I'll try." He took a bite of toast, slowly chewing, wondering if it was possible to find her, and what he'd do if he did.

"Give me your phone." Sophie stuck out her hand. "I'll put Bree's number in your contacts. I just tried calling again, and it's still off. But you'll have to keep trying."

"Right." He finished the last of his make-do meal then hugged Sophie. "I'll do my best, but I can't promise you it'll work out. Even if I find her, she might refuse to come back."

Sophie slowly nodded. "I can accept that. Just give her a chance. If she says no, I'll understand."

"And you won't blame me?"

She shrugged. "Well, maybe a little. But I'll forgive you." She smiled.

He hugged her again and, promising to stay in touch with her during his search, he headed out. But as he turned onto the highway and drove toward town, he had no idea where to begin. For all he knew, Brynna could've taken the taxi straight to the municipal airport, gotten a flight to San Francisco International Airport, and flown standby back to Oregon. She could be home by now. But he hoped she wasn't. As he drove, he actually prayed, asking God to help him find her. He told himself it was for Sophie's sake, but he had a feeling it was more than that.

Chapter 26

As the afternoon grew hotter, Brynna grew weary of town and, after purchasing a book to distract her from her unsettling thoughts, she returned to the B and B. She asked for her phone, explaining to the owner that she was still waiting for friends to pick her up.

"Just make yourself at home in our sitting room." The woman handed Brynna her phone. "It's all charged. Sounded like you missed some phone calls."

Brynna thanked her and took the phone to the other room to see the missed calls were from Sophie, as well as several from an unknown number. Probably a telemarketer or scammer. Seeing that Sophie had just left a message, Brynna listened. To her surprise it sounded as if Leroy was out looking for her. "Please, call him if you get this message," Sophie pleaded. "Tell him you're okay. We're very worried about you." And then Sophie left the number. It matched the unknown number.

Brynna was tempted to ignore it. Really, what good would it do to talk to him now? He'd made his feelings crystal clear yesterday. Her intrusion had rocked his world, but not in a good way. Despite her resolve to be strong and resilient about it, she wasn't sure she could handle more humiliation from him. Not that she didn't deserve it—she knew she did. But why not let sleeping dogs lie? She set her phone down and picked up her book, but before she'd read one page, her phone was chiming. The unknown number again. Knowing it must be Leroy, she let it ring a few times then thought she might as well get this over with. She answered, her tone stony.

"Brynna?" His voice sounded worried. "Are you okay?"

"Yes. I'm fine." She tried to insert some warmth, but knew it sounded phony.

"Oh . . . that's good." There was a long pause. "Well, this is Leroy."

She didn't respond. She couldn't think of anything to say.

"Sophie asked me to find you, Brynna. She's sick with worry."

"I'm sorry." She felt bad imagining Sophie suffering. "I didn't want to cause any more hurt, but I left her a note."

"Yes, she got your note." Another long pause. "We both did."

Again, she could think of no response. Really, what more was there to say?

"Your note to me, well, it said you had more to tell me, if I was inclined to listen. And I guess I'm calling to say that I'm inclined."

Her heart lurched slightly. "Oh?"

"Yes, and I want to apologize to you, Brynna. I know I over-reacted yesterday. It's just that I was so blindsided by—by every-thing. But I'm afraid I was pretty hard on you. I really am sorry."

"I'm the one who should apologize. I tried to, but—"

"Yes, I know. Apology accepted. Now, unless you're already back home in Oregon, can we arrange to get together and talk?"

"Talk?" A tiny ripple of hope surged through her.

"Yeah, I promised Sophie I would—"

"So, is this about Sophie? Or you?" She felt uneasy being so bold, but she needed to know his motives. If he was just reaching out for Sophie's sake . . . well, that was nice, but it didn't make her want to risk more pain. A heart could only take so much.

There was another long pause. "To be honest, Sophie did hold my feet to the fire over this, but she's not the only reason I want to talk. Truth is, I'd like to hear the rest of your story. Your letter said if I was willing to listen . . ."

"Right." She told him where she was, and he said to expect him in the next two minutes. She blinked. *"Two minutes?"*

"Yeah. I'm just down the street."

"Oh, well, okay. I'll meet you outside of the inn."

He was there in less than two minutes and, since a young couple was already occupying the front porch, he suggested a ride in his Jeep. She wasn't sure she wanted to be "trapped" with him, but there didn't seem to be much choice. At least he didn't try to get her to spill out the "rest of her story" immediately. She knew it would take a few minutes to gather her thoughts and calm her pounding heart.

"Where were you planning on going after your stay at the B and B?" he asked as he leisurely cruised through town.

She explained about her camping friends, and how Jan and Mike planned to pick her up this evening. "They've been camping at Yosemite. I was supposed to camp there with them, but . . . well, our plans took an unexpected detour . . . for me, anyway."

"Because you came to work for us? By the way, Sophie explained that all to me. She assumed you were there for an interview. And she claims she sort of twisted your arm to accept the job."

"She was very friendly and encouraging. To be fair, Jan and Mike were a bit pushy too. But I'm the one who agreed. I take the blame for that."

"Sophie told me a little about your past too. I was real sorry to hear about your parents, Brynna. I'm sure that was hard on you. She also told me about your marriage to Dirk. She calls him *Dirk the jerk.*"

Brynna couldn't help but laugh. "That sounds about right."

He glanced at her. "I'm sorry about that too."

There was another long pause as he drove past a large vineyard and up a hill.

"I heard most of your story too," she confessed, breaking the

214

silence. "I know how you lost your dad and quit college in order to run the vineyard. I know you, like me, got married fairly young. And then you lost your wife. I'm sorry."

"Yeah, we've both had our losses."

He turned into a pull-out vista area and shut off his engine. "I like this view. You can see about seven different vineyards from here if you know where to look."

She gazed out over the rolling green hills. "It's beautiful." She sighed. "The beauty of Sorrentino's was one of the big reasons I took the job. It is such a comforting place. And that darling guest cottage . . . and Sophie and her sweet family. It was all perfectly charming. I think I was charmed."

"So, maybe I flattered myself imagining it had something to do with me." He laughed, but it sounded a bit hollow.

"Oh, it had something to do with you originally. I can't deny that." She told him about camping at the same campground where they'd first met. "I was flooded with memories, and I told Jan and Mike about it, and they decided that we should look you up." She explained about not recalling his last name. "So Jan and Mike invented this game called *Looking for Leroy*. They kept taking me to vineyards, hoping to find you. I played along, never dreaming we really would locate you. Do you know how many vineyards there are in Sonoma?"

"A lot."

"So when we found Sorrentino's and I bumped into Sophie and she offered me the job, Mike was convinced it was a God thing. I told Sophie I'd think about it but never intended to accept. Then Jan and Mike really pressured me. Maybe they just wanted to be rid of me. I suspect they have a budding romance going on."

He laughed again, but this time it sounded a little more genuine. "So you went looking for Leroy, but when you found him"—he turned to look at her—"instead of meeting him face-to-face, you avoided him altogether?"

"Do you often refer to yourself in third person?" She wanted to sound lighthearted as she returned his gaze—but only to cover her racing heart. She'd forgotten those kind eyes that seemed to see deep inside of her. And was it her imagination or had he gotten even better looking the past thirty years? With his shaggy brown hair and tanned face, he was truly ruggedly handsome. She swallowed hard, trying to remember what they were talking about.

"So why were you hiding out from me, Brynna?"

"I wasn't exactly hiding," she said. "In fact, when I really wanted to cross paths, you never seemed to be around. A couple of days ago, I looked everywhere, but couldn't find you."

"So the Looking for Leroy game continued?" His brown eyes twinkled.

"I guess so. But a lot of the time, I was intimidated at the idea of bumping into you. I probably did want to avoid it. Or at least postpone it. I had fun getting to know Sophie and Garth and the kids. I loved my work and the vineyard, and I didn't want it to end. I was afraid that meeting you could ruin everything. Plus, you had all your guests, a houseful of women. Seemed to me you had your hands full."

He put his hands up in front of him. "Not of my own choosing. Believe me."

"Really?" She studied him. "Judith seems to think differently."

"Differently. That pretty much describes it."

For a long moment neither of them spoke. They both just gazed out over the rolling vineyard hills. But it didn't feel like such an awkward silence now. Still, Brynna had no idea where they would go with all this. What did it really mean to Leroy? Two old friends just catching up? Or did he feel like she did, like it was something more?

"So I know more about you now than I did yesterday, Brynna, but there are still some missing pieces." He blew out a puff of air. "I'm curious about what happened a few months after, you know, after we parted ways at camp and up until early December."

"Well, I wrote you plenty of letters then," she reminded him.

"I think I wrote at least two a week. Sometimes more. But I only got two from you."

"I was never good at writing. And school was demanding. You're the one who was a writer. You wanted to be a journalist." He tilted his head to one side. "What happened to that dream?"

"Life." She sighed. "A lot of dreams fell by the wayside. How about you? You were going to be a photographer."

"Yeah . . . I still take photos sometimes. Mostly on my phone. Like you, I guess, life got in the way." He gripped the steering wheel with both hands, leaning back and extending his arms as if to brace himself. "So then you sent me that last letter. I got it right before winter break began. You told me not to write to you anymore."

"Is that what I said?"

"Yep. You explicitly told me no more letters, that you were back with your old boyfriend and he'd given you a promise ring and that was that."

"Right. Well, that was true. Dirk made me write that letter. He got jealous when he discovered I was writing to you." She paused, trying to decide how much to say, then realized she had nothing to lose. "The truth is, I was hoping you'd write again anyway."

"Really?" He sounded skeptical.

"Yes. And I know that probably sounds flaky. Let's just blame that on youth. But I do think part of me knew that Dirk wasn't right for me. Still, it was confusing. I mean I'd had a crush on him throughout most of high school. And then he was so persuasive. Really, Dirk Philips was a force to be reckoned with back then. He was so full of himself and so used to getting his way. He was a very persuasive guy. I used to think he'd have been a good politician."

"Sounds like a real charmer."

She didn't miss the sarcasm in his voice. "Yeah, believe me, I know. Anyway, that winter was like a bad dream. Everything seemed to happen at once. My parents died, then Dirk got injured and lost his athletic scholarship. For the first time ever, school felt hard for me. Now I know it was because I was still grieving my parents." She took a deep breath. "I felt lost and alone. Then, out of the blue, Dirk declared we should get married. I still felt confused, but I went along with him. Anyway, those aren't excuses as much as an explanation. No one forced me to marry Dirk. It is what it is . . . or was."

Leroy released his grip on the steering wheel and slowly shook his head. "I guess I sort of understand that." He looked like he was about say something more, but his phone interrupted the moment. She could tell by his answer that it was Sophie.

"Yes, I found her . . . Sorry, I forgot to call and tell you . . . Yes, she's with me now . . . No, I don't know. Maybe you should talk to her." He held his phone toward Brynna. "It's Sophie."

Brynna took the phone. "Hello?"

"Oh, Bree! I'm so happy to hear your voice. I'm so relieved you're okay. I was seriously worried. Is Dad bringing you back now?"

"Bringing me back?" Brynna frowned.

"Yes, that's why he went for you. He's going to bring you back here. You do want to come back, don't you?"

"Well, yes, but I—"

"I knew you would. I told Dad that, but he wasn't so sure. I told him how much I need you, Bree. We all do. I'm so glad you're coming back. You really did like it here, didn't you? You seemed so happy."

"Yes. But I don't—"

"Please, say you're coming home," Sophie pleaded. "If nothing else, just come back so we can have a proper goodbye. But really, I hope you'll stay longer. Even if it's just for summer like you said when I hired you. We really do need you right now. There's so much going on at the winery. And I could use your help with the birthday barbecue tomorrow. Please, say you'll come home."

"Let me talk to your dad about it. Okay?"

Sophie said a reluctant "okay," then they hung up. "Sophie is pretty insistent that I need to go back with you, Leroy. Even if it's just to say goodbye. But I think it should be your choice. I don't want to intrude on your life . . . again."

He pursed his lips as if carefully thinking this over. "If you want to come back, you're welcome. It's up to you."

Something about that didn't feel exactly inviting. She'd been glad to sort of clear the air with him just now, and the attraction she felt was promising, but she had no idea what was going on with him. For all she knew, he just wanted her to be on her merry way.

She took in a deep breath. "You know, Leroy, I think it might be best for everyone if I didn't go back. I'm sure Sophie will understand. Maybe I can write her a letter from Oregon."

There was another long silence, but it wasn't a comfortable one this time. "Well," he began, drawing the word out, "maybe I didn't put that quite right. The fact is I did promise Sophie I would do all I could to bring you back. But maybe I should've made my invitation a bit more *inviting*."

She shrugged. "Hey, I don't blame you for wanting me out of your hair. I know you've got a lot going on, and I caused you some serious stress yesterday."

"That was yesterday. Here's the deal, Brynna. This whole thing is awkward. I'll be the first to admit that. And I guess I'm not eager to sound like I'm begging you to come back—I don't want to give you the wrong idea."

"Right." She nodded firmly, trying to appear stronger than she felt. "And I wouldn't agree to return if that gave *you* the wrong idea. I wouldn't want you to misread my motivation. If I came back, it would simply be to see Sophie and Garth and the kids again. Just to say a proper goodbye."

"Okay then. It's settled. I'll take you back. Let's swing by the B and B and pick up your things."

She agreed, but as he drove back toward town, she remembered Mike and Jan. "I nearly forgot that my friends are on their way to pick me up. They'll be here in a few hours."

"Why not just have them come out to the vineyard? They can camp overnight there if they want."

"Really? Mike will love that."

"I don't see why not. Unless they'd prefer a real campground."

"No, I'm sure they'd love to camp one night at Sorrentino's. Thanks. I'll text Jan." Glad for a distraction, she messaged Jan about meeting up at Sorrentino's and the offer of a free night of camping. But after she sent it, she instantly regretted agreeing to Leroy's offer. It would be painful to return to Sorrentino's . . . to see the place she'd so grown to love . . . to spend one night then tell it all goodbye.

Chapter 27

Brynna did her best to make small talk with Leroy on the way back to Sorrentino's. They chatted about his grandkids and the baby Sophie seemed determined to name Leroy.

"I keep telling her she doesn't have to name him that," Leroy said, "but she's determined."

"It's because she loves you. And," Brynna added, "she thinks you always wanted a son. She hopes her little Leroy will be extra close to you."

"You never can tell."

"I think Gina tries to be like your son," Brynna said.

"That's true. Sometimes she acts like she can run the whole vineyard and winery single-handedly."

"I've noticed she's a real go-getter. Gotta admire that. And she has some really good ideas."

"Maybe. But she needs to be reined in sometimes too."

"I really admire how you've kept Sorrentino's a genuine family business." Brynna gazed out the side window, watching as they passed a huge winery with a Mediterranean-style mansion atop a small knoll. "It makes your place feel truly unique and special."

"It's not easy. A lot of family-owned wineries sold out for big money in the late nineties. I've been tempted a time or two. Especially after the wildfires."

"Does your other daughter Luna have any desire to work for you?"

"Hard to say. Sometimes she seems interested—like when she first comes home for a college break—but after a few days she gets bored. Her dream's always been to be a big-city attorney. And I try to support that, but I have a tough time imagining her being happy with it indefinitely."

"I heard she's interning for a law firm in San Francisco. Maybe that'll give her a good taste of what it's like." Brynna didn't understand how anyone would pass up the opportunity to be part of a place like Sorrentino's, but she hadn't grown up there and she understood how familiarity could lead to complacency.

"She called the other day, and it sounds like she loves San Francisco and working for the firm. And I can understand that feeling, being young and wanting to go out into the big wide world." He laughed lightly. "I was like that, too, a long time ago. I believed the grass was greener elsewhere. But life pulled me back to reality. And, honestly, I don't regret it. Working the land seems to be in my blood. I just didn't realize it as a kid."

"Having spent what little time I did at your place, I think you and your family are hugely blessed to have the land and your work and most of all each other. Not many people get to live like that." She instantly wished she hadn't said that last bit. Besides sounding sort of pathetic, it probably came across as a plea to be invited back into his fold. "Of course, I realize it's a whole lot of work too. I'm well aware you guys don't live in la-la land. The reason Sorrentino's is such a great place is because you invest yourself." She felt like she was rambling now. "Anyway, I respect you for that."

"Thanks."

Neither of them spoke for a while, so when Brynna's phone chimed with a text, she was grateful for the distraction. She read the message then texted back. "That was Jan," she told Leroy. "She and Mike are grateful for your offer to camp for the night. She said they'll have dinner on the road and hopefully arrive before sundown."

"Sounds like a good plan."

Brynna had mixed feelings as they turned onto the road to Sorrentino's. On one hand, she was relieved to be done with this awkward drive and suspected Leroy felt the same. On the other hand, it hurt to witness the green and gold beauty of the vineyard again, knowing she was here only to say goodbye. The lump in her throat grew harder as the barn, house, and guest cottage came into view. She wanted to comment on what a lovely setting it all made but was afraid she'd break into tears. Seeing she had another text, she focused her attention on it. "This is from Sophie," she told him. "She says the guest cottage is unlocked."

"I'll drop you there then," he said a bit gruffly. "I've got some business to attend to."

She thanked him and, refusing his effort to help with her bag, jumped out of the Jeep and hurried to the cottage. She had no idea how she planned to spend the next few hours. Would she just hole up here and lick her wounds? Or would it be better to go out and thoroughly enjoy her last hours in this magical place?

She paused at the cottage door to admire the flower beds she'd carefully weeded and tended and watered. They looked healthy and pretty now, but would anyone keep them up after she was gone? Perhaps it didn't matter. As she went inside, she felt that familiar feeling of sweet hominess. She set her bag on the floor, then noticed that the bed was now neatly made and fresh linens were in the bathroom. Probably Sophie's way of welcoming her back.

After getting settled and freshening up a bit, she texted a thank you to Sophie. She'd barely hit send when her phone rang.

"Oh, Bree, I'm so glad you're back," Sophie gushed. "If you're not worn out, I could really use your help this afternoon."

"Of course." Brynna felt a wave of relief to have something to distract herself with. "Anything you need. Just ask."

"Garth is working the tasting room today, and I'm trying to finish baking and decorating a cake. Plus, I've got some other things to do before the birthday party tomorrow, but the kids are driving me nuts."

"Why don't I come lend a hand?" she offered. "I noticed your bike's still here. I could be at your place in about fifteen minutes if I pedal fast."

"Thank you!"

Brynna hurriedly changed into faded jeans and a white T-shirt then hopped on the bike. Even though the sun was beating down hard, she pedaled as fast as she could over to Sophie's house. As she coasted down a rolling hill, bracing herself for going up the next one, she mentally debated whether to let Sophie know she was here only until tomorrow. It seemed kinder to say nothing . . . and yet Sophie had asked for a "proper goodbye." As she pedaled up the next hill, she silently prayed, asking God to lead her. It was the third time she'd prayed today. Was this getting to be a habit? If so, she liked it.

———

So far no one had mentioned anything about Leroy's birthday tomorrow, and he felt fairly certain the date had fallen below their radar. That worked for him. He'd never enjoyed that kind of attention. Considering how busy everyone was—with the winery improvements, Gina with her houseguests, Luna with her internship, Sophie with her family and pregnancy, plus the birthday celebration being planned for his mother—he was relieved to be forgotten.

When he'd told Brynna he had work to do it wasn't completely untrue. There was always work to do around here. However, he didn't have anything specific in mind as he drove over to the burn area. Even as he busied himself with digging and staking and cleaning where the crew had left off, his labors felt mechanical. As if he weren't really there. As if his mind and his heart were somewhere else . . . somewhere far away.

As he toiled in the hot sun, the information he'd learned about Brynna continuously looped through his head. Round and round, as if replaying it over and over could make him grasp it better. He thought about what Sophie had told him, and what Brynna had written in her letter, and most of all, what he'd gleaned from their conversation in the Jeep. Finally, hot and tired and dirty, he climbed into his rig, ready to call it a day. But first he wanted to talk to Sophie. He knew she assumed that he'd brought Brynna back to stay here and he wanted her to understand it was just for the night—to say goodbye.

But as he pulled into the driveway, he noticed the turquoise bike parked by the house. Had Garth brought it back here or was Brynna visiting? It wasn't that he wanted to avoid Brynna exactly . . . well, maybe he did. But as he saw his grandkids tearing around the side of the house with Brynna right behind them, he knew it was too late. *Just man up and get out*, he silently chastised himself.

As he waved to the kids, noticing his ash-blackened hands and clothes, he realized he looked like a bum. But that was life on a vineyard. He called out to his grandkids, cautioning them that he was filthy as they redirected their path toward him. Oblivious to the dirt, Addison grabbed onto Leroy's leg, but Lucy folded her arms in front of her with a scowl of disapproval.

"Pappy, you should go wash up," she sternly advised him. "Just don't wipe your dirty hands on Mama's nice white towels or she'll yell at you."

Leroy chuckled. "Thanks for the warning." He looked at Brynna. Her face was flushed and her brow glistened, but she looked as pretty as ever—and could've passed for a young baby-sitter in her blue jeans, T-shirt, and long brown ponytail. "Hello there," he said, suddenly feeling a bit like an awkward teenager.

"Hello." She shoved her hands into her pockets with what looked like a forced smile. "Looks like you've been busy."

"Yeah." He nodded. "Working on the burn area."

"Thirsty?" she asked. "I made a pitcher of sweet tea. I could bring you out a glass if you like."

"That sounds great." With Addison still clinging to his leg, he limp-dragged the youngster over to a lawn chair that was in the shade and sat down, then he proceeded to tickle his grandson until he had to let go. "What are you kids up to?" he asked Lucy, who was still keeping a safe distance. "Where's your mom?"

"She's inside," Lucy informed him. "Cooking something."

Leroy felt his stomach growling. "What's she cooking?"

"I dunno." Lucy shrugged with a funny expression on her face. "But she told us to stay out of the kitchen."

"Right." He looked up to see Brynna coming out with some paper cups and an oversized mason jar filled with tea.

She sat down on the other lawn chair, then filled four paper cups, handing them out. "I don't usually add sweetening to iced tea," she said, "but that's how Sophie likes it."

"That's how we like it too," Lucy said.

"It's how Sophie's mom used to make it." He took a long swig. "And today it hits the spot." He downed his tea then, smiling, held it out for more. He studied Brynna as she refilled it, noticing how blue her eyes looked in this light. Kind of a periwinkle blue.

"I was wondering where you'd like Jan and Mike to set up their camp tonight," Brynna said. "They don't need much room. Jan's trailer is pretty small, and Mike has a tent that's even smaller. I wondered about the parking area behind the barn. Sophie told me there's no tasting scheduled for tomorrow."

"I suppose that'd be okay," he told her.

She frowned. "Or maybe you've changed your mind about them camping here."

"No, no, that's not it. I was just thinking there might be prettier spots to camp than back behind the barn."

"Oh?" She tilted her head to one side. "I suppose that's true, but I don't think there are any unattractive spots around here. Even behind the barn, you get a decent view of the vineyard. And Gina and her friends have done a nice job of cleaning things up for your mother's party. Their flower barrels are looking really good."

He nodded. "Yes, I'm sure it's just fine. Go ahead and help them get set up there." He crumpled his empty cup and stood. "I think I'll go say hello to Sophie now."

"No, Pappy." Lucy stepped in front of him. "Mama said *no one* in the kitchen."

"Even me?" He acted hurt.

"Yeah. You're too dirty to go into the kitchen." Lucy stood her ground, blocking his path to the front door.

He shook his head. "Banned from my daughter's house. What is the world coming to?"

"Want me to go see if Sophie can come out here to talk to you?" Brynna asked.

He considered this. "Nah, it's not important."

"I'll get Mama for you!" Lucy took off like a shot. Addison started to follow, but Brynna stopped him.

"Hey, why don't you go find the soccer ball so you can show your pappy how good you're getting at kicking a goal," she suggested. As he took off, she pointed to a couple of boxes set up in the front yard. "That's our makeshift goal."

Addison had just demonstrated his kicking skills by knocking into a box when Sophie came out. "You wanted to see me, Dad?"

"Well, it wasn't that important." He felt conspicuous since this didn't seem like the right time for a conversation about Brynna. "Anyway, thanks for the tea." He held out his filthy hands. "I better get home and get cleaned up."

She nodded. "Yeah, you're a mess, Dad. Why don't you give Bree a ride back? It's so hot out and—"

"That's okay," Brynna said. "I have the bike and—"

"I can give you a lift," he told her. "If you don't mind riding with a dirty bum."

"You're not a dirty bum," Lucy told him, coming out the front door. "You just need a bath, Pappy."

"You can take a bath here." Addison pointed to their nearby wading pool. "That's what I do."

They all laughed. Then Leroy thanked his grandson for the offer and he and Brynna got back into the Jeep. It wasn't exactly what he had planned when he'd stopped, but he didn't exactly mind either.

"I'll show Jan and Mike where to camp when they arrive," Brynna told him as he drove. "And if it's okay, I'll help them get set up with water and electricity from the barn."

"Sure, that's fine."

"I don't want their visit to be any trouble for you," she said. "And we'll be out of your hair sometime tomorrow."

"Look, Brynna, I may have given you the wrong idea. It's not as if I want you off the place ASAP. That's not it at all."

"Well, I don't really see the point of prolonging my goodbye. I was going to tell Sophie about me leaving, but she seemed kind of stressed and I was there to give her a break from the kids. Didn't seem like good timing."

"I understand." He tried to think of a way to say this. "What I meant is that you don't really have to leave, Brynna. Not if you don't want to."

"What does that mean?"

"I mean, I realize you've enjoyed working here, I get how much you like this place, and well, I was thinking about everything while I was working on the burn area. I decided that if you really wanted to remain on throughout the summer, well, I don't mind."

"You don't mind?" She sounded a little hurt.

"I guess that didn't come out right." He grimaced. "I would like it if you stayed on, Brynna. I know it didn't sound like that earlier, but I think I'd like the chance to get to know you better. And since you seemed to like it here and you had the whole summer to work for us—and as you know, we need the help—well, I'd like you to stay."

She didn't answer, which worried him. Had he said too much, not enough, or was she just trying to think of a graceful way to escape this whole crazy mess?

"I'll understand if you don't want to stay," he continued nervously. "I know I haven't exactly made you feel welcome. I guess

I'm not much good at that. I leave hospitality matters to my daughters. They've all made it clear that I'm about as friendly as an old bear sometimes."

She chuckled, which made him feel a tiny bit better.

"So, anyway, if you'd like time to consider the offer—you know, maybe sleep on it—I will understand."

"Thank you."

He drove up the guest cottage driveway then turned to look at her. "I'm not good at this kind of thing, Brynna." He looked down at his grimy hands and clothes. "As you can see, I'm not exactly Prince Charming. But I'll state it more plainly—I would like to get to know you better . . . again. And I don't see how we can do that if you go back to Oregon. As you know, I'm not much of a letter writer."

She smiled now. "I'd like to get to know you better too, Leroy."

A wave of relief washed over him.

"I have an idea," she said. "Do you have dinner plans?"

He glanced up toward the house. "I don't, but they might."

"Oh, well, I wouldn't want to interfere with—"

"What did you have in mind?" He didn't even care *what* she had in mind as long as it included more time with her.

"How would you like to come here for dinner tonight? I'm not a fancy cook like Judith, but I think I could throw something simple together."

"I like simple." He stopped himself from confessing he'd helped himself to her groceries just this morning.

"Around seven okay?" she asked.

"Perfect. Plenty of time to clean up my act." He smiled as she got out, watching her as she went into the cottage. Even if tonight's dinner was nothing more than egg salad sandwiches and carrot sticks, he would not complain. In fact, that menu sounded pretty good compared to what he could imagine Judith was cooking up right now. The question was how to get out of another one of Judith's "fine cuisine" meals graciously. Or maybe he didn't care.

Chapter 28

Brynna did a quick inventory of her fridge and cupboards. Since borrowing a rig and dashing off to the grocery store wasn't an option at the moment, she decided to thaw some frozen chicken she'd brought last week. She also had enough veggies from Sophie's garden to throw together a simple green salad, as well as some fresh asparagus she could cook, also from the garden. To make their dinner feel more complete, she'd make some pasta and use some of the home-canned marinara sauce Sophie had given her. It wouldn't be fancy by any means, but perhaps the bottle of sauvignon blanc that Sophie had given her last week might make the evening feel more special. For dessert she would serve decaf coffee and what was left of her vanilla bean ice cream topped with fresh peaches. Not bad for a last-minute meal.

After getting the chicken thawed and seasoned for broiling, Brynna took a quick bath and washed her hair. But seeing that time was against her, she threw on her favorite garment, the little blue hand-me-down sundress. Hopefully she'd have time to change into something more festive later.

With damp hair and bare feet, she set out to make dinner. She got the chicken broiling and pasta boiling. She made the salad, then got the asparagus ready to steam. She started to set the table, but the cottage felt hot and stuffy and she thought it would be lovely to eat on the front porch. With a little finagling, she managed to move the table and two chairs outside.

She carefully set the table with the pretty dishes, silverware, and cloth napkins from the cottage. She even added a hurricane candle that she surrounded with a wreathlike ring of lavender, daisies, and poppies. She stepped back to admire the scene. Pretty as a picture, but was it too romantic? Maybe she didn't care.

She set out the salad and the asparagus, which was wrapped in a tea towel to keep it hot. And then she lit the candle, once again stepping back to admire her spur-of-the-moment setup. Not bad. Just then she heard the sound of footsteps on the porch. Thinking it might be Leroy, she was surprised to see Babe.

"Well, hello." She bent down to pat the dog. Babe's thick tail thumped happily against the porch railing. "Are you here for dinner too?" She glanced down the drive to see that Leroy was approaching. Noticing he looked clean and handsome, Brynna realized she was still in her plain blue dress and bare feet, and her hair was still damp. "You're here too," she said awkwardly as she stood.

"Too early?" He paused to look at Babe with a curious expression. "And with my dog. I didn't invite her along, but she seemed to know where I was headed. Seems like she knows you too."

"Yes. Babe and I are old friends. And no, you're not too early." Brynna smiled apologetically. "It's me. I'm not quite ready."

He stepped onto the porch then looked at the pretty table. "Doesn't seem that way. This all looks great to me."

She thanked him. "I meant *me*." She waved down to her simple dress and shoeless feet.

"You look great too." He smiled, seeming nervous.

"Well, thanks."

He sniffed toward the still-open doorway. "And something in there smells pretty good."

"I'm sure everything is almost done. Why don't you sit down?" She pointed to the farthest chair.

He picked up the bottle of white wine. "Should I open this?"

"Yes. If you think I chilled it enough."

"Feels just right."

"Great. I'll be right back." Brynna felt her heart fluttering as she went back inside, followed by Babe. She couldn't ever remember having been so excited over serving a meal. And she'd never served one in such a beautiful location. Worried that Mike and Jan might arrive too early and disrupt everything, she'd even shot off a quick text asking them to wait until at least eight thirty before showing up.

"Need a hand in there?" he called out.

"No thanks. Babe is helping." She tossed Babe a little piece of chicken, then, with a bowl of pasta in one hand and the small platter of chicken in the other, she went back out. "Like I warned you, it's pretty simple." She set the dishes down.

"Simply perfect." His eyes lit up like he meant it. "I like simple food, Brynna. Fancy food doesn't agree with me."

She sat down with a smile. "I like simple food too. Simple but good."

Leroy looked at her over the table. "Can I ask a blessing?"

"Yes." She nodded eagerly. "Please do!"

After a sweet but short blessing, Brynna passed the chicken to him. "I hope it's not tough. It was frozen."

"Looks good to me." He forked into the biggest piece with enthusiasm, setting it onto his plate.

"And the pasta sauce was made by your own Sophie, so I'm sure you'll like it."

"Everything looks delicious." He grinned. "I'm starved."

"Well, dig in!"

As they started to eat, with Babe nestled beneath the table, Brynna realized she was quite hungry too. She'd hardly eaten anything all day—hadn't wanted to—but now she felt relaxed and happy and hopeful. And to her relief, everything—even the chicken—was just fine.

"I've never been much of a wine drinker," she said as she took a sip, "but this is really good. Sophie kept telling me I needed to try it. She said this year's sauvignon blanc was one of the best you've ever had. I'm not sure what that means, but I do think it's good."

"Thank you." He held up his glass, examining the clarity in the fading sunlight. "To be honest, I'm not much of a wine drinker myself. Not that you need to go public with that. Not exactly the image one expects of a vineyard owner."

She chuckled. "Mum's the word."

It didn't take long for Leroy to clean his plate. "Mind if I have seconds?"

"Of course not." She eagerly passed the chicken platter to him.

"Everything tastes really good, Brynna. Thanks for doing this."

"It was fun." She looked out over the vineyard rows. "And it's fun to eat out here. It was so warm and stuffy inside, I thought it'd be nice to get some fresh air."

He glanced over his shoulder in the direction of his house. "And it's nice that this porch can't be seen from up there."

"Meaning you don't want them to know you're down here?" she teased. "Eating in the servant's quarters?"

"You're not the servant."

She shrugged. "It's okay. I don't mind."

"Well, you're not," he protested.

"I'm not sure everyone up there would agree with you. But honestly, I love it down here so much, I don't really care what they think."

He held up his glass. "Here's to not caring."

She held hers up, clinking it with his. "To not caring."

For a while they both ate quietly, but then Brynna started wondering what the women up in that house really were thinking. "Did you tell Gina and her friends you were dining down here with me?"

He looked sheepish.

"You didn't, did you?"

233

"Truth be told, I sneaked out the back door without saying a word to anyone."

She couldn't help but laugh.

"It's terrible having to sneak around in your own house," he continued. "But it feels like they're everywhere. If it's not Judith, it's one of her daughters or Gina. It's like I'm surrounded by females these days."

"How long are Judith and her girls supposed to be here?"

"I have no idea. It seems like they don't either."

"They must be enjoying themselves."

He shrugged. "I guess. Gina seems to run hot and cold on them. Sometimes she sounds fed up with her friends, and the next thing I know, she's singing their praises. I thought they'd be gone by now, but for all I know they could be here all summer." He chuckled. "Maybe me ducking out of their dinner again will send them packing. Ya think?"

"I don't know . . ." Brynna remembered that Sophie had invited Gina's guests to the birthday barbecue and doubted they'd leave before that. Not that she planned to mention tomorrow's surprise. Instead, she asked him about the preparations for his mother's big birthday party.

"Hopefully the pieces are falling into place," he said.

"Well, let me know if there's anything I can do." She smiled. "I know it's not in my job description, but I'd be happy to help."

"I appreciate that. I'll keep it in mind." He pushed his empty plate aside. "That was really good. Thanks again."

"Any room for dessert?"

He sighed and leaned back. "I'm not a big dessert eater."

"Me neither. But I have some vanilla ice cream and fresh peaches if you're interested."

"Fresh peaches?" He rubbed his chin. "That actually sounds pretty good. Maybe just a small serving, but not until we finish the last of this." He refilled her wineglass. "And if you've no objections, I'd like to relax and enjoy the view first." He gazed down toward the sloping rows of grapevines. "I love this section of vineyard. It's why I put that big terrace out behind my house. I've missed sitting out there lately."

She suspected that was due to his houseguests. "I noticed you had some festive-looking dinners on the terrace this week. It seems like the perfect place for gathering."

"I always thought so. I remember when I put in the outdoor kitchen and Marcie thought I'd lost my mind."

"Why was that?" Was she rude to question this?

"Because it was an expense, and she'd been wanting to remodel the kitchen in the house." He shook his head. "Naturally, I had to give in to her after that. But her kitchen remodel cost about ten times more than the outdoor one."

"It is a beautiful kitchen. I mean the indoor one. I've never seen the outdoor one. Not up close, anyway." She wasn't about to admit she'd studied it from a distance, or that she'd spied on their social gatherings a couple of times. "Anyway, I think Marcie did a wonderful job with it. And I know she put this cottage together too. She had very good taste."

"Very expensive taste."

Brynna didn't know what to say. She certainly didn't want to bad-mouth his deceased wife.

"But it's nice that this cottage enjoys the same view." He took a sip of his wine. "I'd forgotten."

"I love sitting out here this time of evening." She leaned back as well. "The way the long rays of golden sunlight filter through the dark-green grape leaves. It's just so rich and beautiful. And when there's a backdrop of dark clouds, like we had a few evenings ago, it's truly magical. I love how the vines seem spotlighted, and the colors become so vivid and clear."

"That's what they call God light. A great time to take photos."

They visited together in a way that felt like they were old friends for a while, then Brynna served the dessert alongside some decaf. They were just finishing up when Leroy spied headlights on the road. "Looks like your camping buddies are coming. Maybe we should go out and meet them."

"Let me get some shoes on," she said.

"Good idea. I'll head down to point them in the right direction."

As Brynna put on her shoes, she wished that Mike and Jan had tarried a bit longer. She and Leroy had seemed to have made such headway tonight. She hated to see it end . . . ever.

Chapter 29

It was getting dusky as Brynna hurried down to the barn to check on her friends. Despite wanting to extend her evening with Leroy, she looked forward to seeing Jan and Mike again. When she got there, Mike was parking his motorcycle and Leroy was directing Jan to an appropriate spot for her trailer. With the vehicles in place, Brynna took the initiative to properly introduce everyone, and Jan and Mike thanked Leroy for his hospitality.

"Camping at a vineyard." Mike grinned. "Doesn't get any better than this."

"Better than Yosemite?" Brynna asked.

"Well, that's kinda like apples and oranges," he said.

"Anyway, we do appreciate it," Jan told Leroy.

"Well, I'll let you guys get set up before it gets really dark," Leroy said. After he left, Brynna helped Jan connect to the utilities and set out the camp chairs. Then they watched as Mike pitched his tent by lantern light. Before long, the three of them were seated outside of Jan's trailer and started to catch up. Jan and Mike described the wonders of Yosemite, then Brynna gave a brief explanation of how it had all gone sideways with Leroy yesterday afternoon but turned back around today.

"So I've sort of agreed to stay on. But to be honest"—she shifted in her seat—"I'm not convinced it's the smartest thing to do."

"Why's that?" Jan asked.

"I don't know . . ." Brynna wondered just how transparent to be. "It's hard to explain, but I think I could be setting myself up for, well, some serious pain."

"Oh?" Jan nodded. "I guess I get that."

"I don't," Mike declared. "You know what they say, girls. No pain, no gain."

Brynna grimaced. "Thanks a lot."

"I didn't mean to sound trite." His tone turned apologetic. "But the older I get, the more I realize the only way to live life is to *really* live it. I don't wanna be on my deathbed thinking about the things I never did because I was too scared. Ya know?"

"He's right." Jan turned back to Brynna. "That's why I got my trailer and took this trip. Some people thought I was nuts, but I have no regrets."

"And I can respect that . . . for you." Brynna sighed. "I'd like to be that brave, but this is a little different than taking a big camping trip, Jan. This involves my heart."

"I know." Jan patted her arm. "But shouldn't you give it your best shot? Even if you do get hurt? You can't just give up."

"I don't know."

"Nothing ventured, nothing gained," Mike said.

Brynna playfully socked him in the shoulder. "I forgot you're the cliché king."

He just laughed. "Make fun of me, but I speak from experience."

"Me too." Jan turned to Mike with a look of tenderness. "I've taken some risks lately, and I'm not complaining."

Brynna stared at both of them in the flickering kerosene lantern light. "I had a feeling you two were starting up something."

"A little road romance," Mike said gently, "which I hope will continue to grow."

"Anyway, we're giving it a chance." Jan turned back to Brynna. "But if you want to chicken out with Leroy, well, we could always take you with us tomorrow."

Brynna slowly shook her head. Even if things deteriorated with Leroy, she didn't want to become a third wheel in Jan and Mike's "road romance." Not that she planned to admit her motives for this new resolution. "You're both right. I do need to give it my best shot. Let it play out."

"Good girl." Jan slapped her on the back.

"Hello, campers," Leroy called out as he approached with Babe by his side. "I brought you folks something." He set down a portable firepit. "I know campers like a campfire, but we have to be extra careful around here." He held up the screen top. "You have to really keep an eye on things when you use this."

"Yes," Brynna said, backing him up. "They've had trouble with wildfires."

"Not usually this time of year." Leroy bent over to rearrange the firewood and twist some newspaper. "But you can never be too careful."

"We saw some of the blackened vineyards," Mike said as he went to get another camp chair. "Too bad."

Leroy pulled a lighter from his pocket and quickly got the fire going. "How's that?"

"Perfect." Jan pointed to the extra camp chair. "Have time to sit and enjoy it with us?"

"Thanks." Leroy sat down next to Brynna. "I haven't been around a campfire for some time."

"I noticed a firepit out on your back deck." Brynna didn't want to admit she'd seen the fire going one evening when she'd been spying on one of the dinner parties.

"Yeah, but that runs on propane. You know, to be safe. This is different." He pointed to the trailer and Mike's tent. "It's more like real camping."

For the next hour or so, the four of them visited congenially.

Brynna was impressed with how easily Leroy got along with Jan and Mike. She was equally impressed with how Jan and Mike so easily extracted more information about Leroy's life and the vineyard's history. For instance, she hadn't known that Leroy's mother was his father's second wife or that his father had been old enough to be Leroy's grandfather.

Finally, the campfire had burned down to embers and Brynna suspected it was pretty late. Despite how much she'd enjoyed spending time with Leroy this afternoon and evening, she was exhausted. She stood and stretched. "I'm afraid I'll fall asleep right in this chair if I don't call it a night," she told them.

"Me too." Leroy stood as well. "We'll bid you good night."

"Rest well," Brynna told the campers. Then, as she walked away from their little campsite, she stumbled on something in the dark, and Leroy caught her.

"Careful there." He wrapped his arm around her waist. "Babe and I will escort you back to the cottage."

She wanted to protest that it wasn't necessary but stopped herself. Why not enjoy this sweet moment of intimacy? As they walked through the darkness, he pointed out stars and constellations. "My dad taught those to me," Leroy told her. "He said he'd wanted to be a sailor as a boy but never had any choice since he was expected to take over the vineyard."

"I'd rather run a vineyard than be a sailor."

"Yeah, me too." Leroy sighed. "But Dad had planned to take my mother on some cruises after he retired . . . course, he never got the chance."

"I guess that's a good reminder to all of us."

"What's that?" he asked.

"Oh, you know, don't wait too long to pursue your dreams." They were up to the cottage now. The remnants of dinner remained on the table. "Thanks for a lovely evening," she told him.

"I'm the one who should thank you." He gazed down at her for a long moment, and she wondered if he was about to kiss her—but the sound of someone calling out "Dad" sliced through the moment.

"Sounds like Gina," he said. "Better go before she calls out the cavalry."

"She's probably worried." Grateful that the darkness concealed her disappointment, Brynna stepped away from him.

"Yeah, I've been pretty much AWOL all day. She'll probably give me hecky pecky too."

Brynna smiled at the old-fashioned terminology. "Good night, Leroy."

"Good night." He nodded to her, then gave Babe the command to go. They both jogged up the slope toward the house.

After he was gone, she went back into the cottage and leaned against the closed door to steady herself. She'd really hoped that he was going to kiss her. So wanted him to kiss her! Was he really about to? Or had she imagined it? She didn't want to hold the interruption against Gina. She probably really was worried about her dad. But besides that, Brynna suspected Gina didn't like her. Whether it was because of Judith or something else was a mystery, but Brynna got the distinct feeling that Gina would be happier if Brynna wasn't around. Did she even know that Brynna had returned?

Brynna jumped at the sound of someone trying to open the door. Was Leroy back? She flung it open with a smile on her face, but instead of Leroy, it was a young woman with a suitcase.

"Who are you?" the woman asked with wide eyes.

"I, uh, I'm Brynna."

"What are you doing here?"

"I'm the office manager. I've been living here."

"Gina said you were gone. She told me I could stay overnight in the cottage."

"Who are you?" Brynna asked.

"I'm Luna Sorrentino." The petite woman straightened her posture.

"Oh." Brynna nodded. "Leroy's middle daughter."

"That's right." Luna frowned at the table still on the porch. "What's going on here?"

"Oh, that was just dinner. I was about to clean it up." Brynna slipped past Luna and started to stack the plates from their dessert, trying to think of what to do about Luna. "So, I assume you need a place to stay?" Brynna stood, looking directly at her.

"That's the main objective. All the rooms in the house are occupied with Gina's friends." She scowled. "But I suppose I could bunk with Gina."

"Why don't you stay here? You can have the bed. The sheets are fresh. And I'll sleep on the sofa."

Luna tilted her head to one side. "I don't want to put you out."

"It's okay." Still holding the dirty dishes, Brynna led the way inside.

Luna stopped to stare at the kitchen. "Looks like you had quite a dinner party."

"Not really. I just haven't had time to clean up yet." She set the dishes by the sink.

"Well, I'm exhausted. It's been a long week. I want to take a nice soak in that old claw-foot tub and then I'm going to bed."

"Right. Just let me get some of my things out of the bedroom first." Brynna hurried in to grab a few necessities.

Luna leaned against the doorframe as Brynna packed. "Excuse me for asking, but where did you get that dress?" She stared intently at Brynna's outfit.

Brynna felt her cheeks grow warm from embarrassment. "Uh, your sister Sophie gave me some used clothes. I think they belonged to you."

Luna laughed. "I thought it looked familiar."

"I hope you don't mind."

"No, of course not." She came in and sat on the bed, crossing one leg over the other and looking quite stylish in a nicely tailored gray pantsuit. "I never did like that dress. Too juvenile."

Despite being old enough to be Luna's mother, Brynna felt "too juvenile" too. "Well, I do appreciate the recycled clothing," she said quickly. "I'd left most of my things back home in Oregon." She headed for the bedroom door, eager to escape more criticism. "I hope you get a good night's sleep, Luna."

"You too."

Brynna closed the door and instantly longed to be somewhere else. Anywhere else! If it wasn't so late, she'd sneak over to Jan's trailer and beg for her old bed back. But seeing the messy kitchen and some things still out on the porch, she decided to do the adult thing and clean everything up. Quietly. Hopefully by the time she finished, she'd be so worn out she'd sleep soundly tonight.

It was nearly midnight by the time she crawled into her make-shift bed in the living room. Despite her fatigue, the sofa was not comfortable. But it was her overly active mind that kept her tossing and turning for what felt like hours. Her encounter with Leroy's middle daughter was more than unsettling. Luna clearly did not want Brynna to be here.

———

Leroy couldn't remember the last time he'd woken up happy on his birthday. But today was different and he knew why. He wasn't completely sure where this thing with Brynna was actually headed—and he was determined not to get his heart broken—but something about the whole thing just felt right to him. Still, as he showered and dressed—and considered everything—he knew that only time would tell. Life had taught him to be a realist, to take what was dealt him and make the best of it.

As he went downstairs, he prepared himself for some sort of recognition of his birthday, but for a pleasant change, his house was very calm and quiet. Of course, it was still early for a Sunday. They might all be sleeping late. He made a pot of coffee, wondering how much longer Gina's "working" houseguests planned to stay on. Clearly Gina's attempt at matchmaking, if that's what it had been, was a flop. It seemed like Judith would take the hint and move on. Unless . . . maybe she thought he was playing hard to get.

He filled his coffee mug and, worried the women might suddenly pop in and start cackling like a flock of agitated hens, he quietly whistled for Babe, and the two of them slipped out to his back terrace to sit in the sun. With his coffee in hand, he gazed out toward the guest cottage and briefly toyed with the idea of a surprise visit. Maybe he could invite Brynna to go to town with him and have breakfast. His stomach was growling.

He was about to go over and knock on her door when his cell phone rang. Of course, it was Mom. Just like every year, she'd called to sing "Happy Birthday" to him. He listened, then thanked her, and when she asked him to come over for breakfast, he reluctantly agreed. He would have preferred more time with Brynna, but having breakfast with his mother was preferable to getting stuck here with Gina and her friends.

He hopped in his Jeep and headed over to Damico's. As he drove, he remembered how it had hurt his feelings when his mother chose to live at his sister's place instead of here, but in the long run, he knew it was for the best. As much as he loved his mom, they didn't always see eye to eye on things. It hadn't helped matters when she'd started picking fights with Marcie. Usually over finances and the vineyard and household chores. And when Marcie got sick, Leroy had known it was time for his mom to move on. Fortunately, she had understood. Sherry's boys were little at the time, and having their grandmother nearby had been welcome all around.

His mother had a nice little breakfast all set up on the back terrace. After they sat down, she explained that she'd begged out of going to church with Sherry and Tony and the boys. "That loud music plays havoc with my hearing aids." She filled his coffee cup. "I told Sherry I'd rather have breakfast with my firstborn on his birthday." She chuckled. "Of course, that made her jealous. But what's new about that?"

He shrugged. "I think it's just youngest child syndrome. Gina always thinks Luna and Sophie have had it better than her."

"So, any big plans for today?" She had a mischievous twinkle in her eye, almost as if she knew something. Had she heard about Brynna . . . or had she put two and two together?

"I don't know." He studied her closely. "Did Sophie tell you about our office manager?"

Her pale brows arched. "Your office manager?"

He decided to just get it out in the open. "Yeah. She was going by Bree, but her name's actually Brynna. Did Sophie mention she's the same girl I met thirty years ago at summer camp?"

"Your first love?" She set down her orange juice glass with a loud clunk. "The office manager is the *same girl*?"

He nodded.

Her jaw dropped.

"Yeah, I was pretty shocked too."

"You had mentioned to me that Bree—or Brynna—that the new office manager had reminded you of that other girl."

"Well, she *is* that other girl."

"I hardly know what to say."

He explained the situation in a bit more detail, trying to make her understand that Brynna's motives hadn't been to trick anyone. "Still, I felt pretty blindsided. It was a lot to take in."

"And how do you feel about it now?" she asked.

He smiled. "I guess I'm open to the possibilities."

"Really?" She blinked.

"Yeah. I mean, I'm not stupid, Mom. I know it could blow up in my face . . . again. But I guess it's a risk I'm willing to take."

"Well, I'll be." She shook her head with a stunned expression. "That's interesting to hear, son. Very interesting."

"Anyway, I'm glad you know. Because, well, I plan to spend time with her." He explained how he'd talked Brynna into coming back to work after she'd taken off yesterday. "It was sort of touch-and-go. I was pretty mad about the whole thing at first. But

245

I spent a lot of time with her yesterday, getting reacquainted. She's been through a lot of hard stuff." He went into more detail and, to his relief, his mother seemed sympathetic.

"So does the rest of the family know about this?" she asked.

"Sophie does. And she told Gina."

"Can I tell your sister?"

He shrugged. "Doesn't matter to me. It is what it is." Still, he wondered how his sister would respond to this tasty tidbit of gossip. Would she and the others misjudge Brynna and treat her like an interloper? What if they assumed his relationship with Brynna was more evolved than it was? Would they be supportive, or suspicious and overprotective? One thing he knew about his family was that they were opinionated. And they could be unpredictable. Hopefully they'd treat Brynna with respect.

Chapter 30

By the time Brynna woke up, the sun was pouring brightly in through the kitchen window and, according to the wall clock, it was half past nine. Very late for her. But since it was Sunday, no one would care. Seeing the bedroom door open, she peeked inside to find the bed was unoccupied and unmade. But the way Luna's bags and clothes were spread across the room suggested she planned to stay awhile.

Brynna was relieved to discover the bathroom unoccupied too. Although, as in the bedroom, Luna had clearly made herself at home in there. Picking her way through Luna's jumble of hair products, cosmetics, and skin care stuff, Brynna freshened up then dressed. She was just about to make coffee when her phone chimed. Glad to see it was Jan, she answered.

"Hey, you. Mike and I are having a late start day." Jan's tone was chipper. "But we've got this huge breakfast going on. Want to join us?"

"I'd love to!" Brynna set the coffee canister down. "I'm on my way."

When she got to their temporary campground behind the barn, Jan handed her a plate of hotcakes, hash browns, bacon, and eggs. And Mike gave her a hot mug of coffee.

Brynna thanked them and sat down. "This is a lot better than the yogurt I planned to have this morning."

"Well, Mike was making hotcakes on his little cookstove and I'd already started the other things." Jan grinned. "Glad you could join us."

Brynna stretched her neck with a little groan. "This is a morning when a little TLC goes a long way with me."

"Why's that?" Mike asked. "Something wrong?"

She explained about her unexpected houseguest last night. "I gave Luna the bedroom, but the sofa's not so comfy."

"How long does Miss Luna plan to stay?" Jan asked.

"I don't know. I, uh, I think I'd like to leave with you guys after all."

Jan frowned. "Just because of Luna?"

"I'm in over my head." She spoke quickly, not giving them a chance to interject anything. "I know that Leroy's daughters are central to his life and I totally respect that. I feel certain there's not room for me in his world. Luna clearly resents me, and I'm pretty sure Leroy's youngest girl, Gina, feels the same. They don't even know about my relationship with Leroy yet. At least, I don't think they do. But if I get more involved with their dad, I know it'll cause problems."

"Naturally, there'd be an adjustment period," Jan said pragmatically. "But that's normal. I think you're giving up too easily."

"And too soon." Mike pointed his fork at her.

"Leroy is extremely close with his daughters. They were all he had after his wife passed. I have a feeling that's the way it's always going to be. The way it should be. I just don't see how I can possibly fit in here. Well, other than as an employee. And, as much as I've loved working here, I can't keep doing it. Not under these conditions. I'd be like the odd girl out. The fifth wheel. The kid with her nose pressed up against the toy store window."

"Wow." Jan sipped her coffee. "Sounds like you've given this some thought."

"I was up half the night stewing over it."

"Well, maybe leaving really would be for the best," Mike told Brynna. "Might give Leroy the chance to decide if he wants to chase you down."

"Chase me down?"

"Yeah, if he loves you, he'd probably go after you." He winked at her.

Brynna wasn't so sure about that. If Leroy hadn't bothered to chase her down thirty years ago, why would he now? Maybe it didn't matter. She was probably just tired.

"So you'll be ready to leave with us today?" Jan asked as she refilled Brynna's coffee mug.

"I guess so. But I only want a ride to the nearest town. I'll find my own way home after that."

"And since it's a woman's prerogative to change her mind, we won't hold you to it," Mike teased.

"We could stick around a few more days," Jan added, "give you time to figure things out."

"It's not a bad spot to camp." Mike gestured toward the rows of grapevines.

"Well, maybe you should at least stay one more night," Brynna told them. "I almost forgot to tell you that it's Leroy's birthday today. They're having a barbecue this afternoon. His daughter Sophie is in charge, and she told me to bring you guys. It's supposed to be a surprise, and I promised to help her. She's got two kids under five and another on the way, so she could use another hand."

"I remember Sophie from when we dropped you here," Jan said. "She seemed like a sweet girl."

"She really is." Brynna took a last bite of bacon. "That's just one more reason I think I should leave. Sophie would be caught in the middle of everything with her sisters and her dad. I don't want to do that to her." Brynna checked her watch. "Speaking of Sophie, I should probably give her a call and see if she needs help yet."

She thanked them for breakfast and told them when to come

over to the barbecue. Then, trying to convince herself this was no big deal, Brynna headed back to the cottage. She felt certain that leaving with Jan and Mike was the right decision. It might not be easy, but it was for the best . . . for everyone. A widower with three grown daughters didn't need another woman in his life.

———

Leroy hadn't expected to spend so much time with his mother, but for some reason she seemed insistent on keeping him around. First she wanted help in her garden, and then she had some fencing that needed to be moved. Finally, around two, she announced she was in need of some things in town. "You don't mind taking me, do you?" she asked as she reached for her handbag. "It won't take long."

He shrugged. "Okay."

But as they were driving the road that linked Damico's to Sorrentino's she seemed to change her mind. "You know, I could probably get the things on my list from your house. Sophie always keeps your pantry so well stocked. Let's just stop there and grab a few things. Then you can take me back home. I'm ready for my afternoon nap now anyway."

Glad to cut this trip short, he pulled up to his own house. They were barely in the front door when he heard choruses of "Surprise!"

"What?" He looked to see all three of his daughters and Sophie's family, as well as Gina's guests and several other friends from neighboring vineyards. And standing by herself, near the dining room, was Brynna. She had on an apron and a slightly impish smile.

Leroy laughed loudly. "You guys really got me." Although he'd never been a big fan of surprise parties, he went around greeting everyone and thanking them for coming.

"Were you really surprised?" Sophie asked him.

"Blown away."

"I've been planning this for days, and I asked Grandma to keep you until two." Sophie patted her grandmother's back. "Good work, Grams."

"Well, this is really nice." Leroy hugged Sophie. "Thanks, honey. I'm sure it was a lot of work."

"Bree's been helping me a lot." Sophie nodded to where Brynna was just ducking into the kitchen. "And I kept everything the way you like it, Dad. Hamburgers on the grill, potato salad—just simple food."

"A girl after my own heart." He grinned at Luna and Gina as they made it over to him, hugging him and wishing him a happy birthday.

"I never expected to see you today, Luna." He kissed her cheek. "I thought the lawyer lady would be too busy to tell her old man happy birthday."

"I took a couple of days off this upcoming week. I got here late last night." She lowered her voice. "I'm staying in the guest cottage with that new manager you fired. Gina told me she'd left, but she's back, Dad. Maybe you should—"

"I know she's back," he told her. His pulse quickened. "Her name is Brynna, and she's here because I asked her—"

"You mean you *want* her here?" Luna frowned.

Before he could answer, other friends came over to greet him, including Mike and Jan. Leroy patted Luna on the back, hoping she'd understand this was a conversation for later. As more guests came up to share their well-wishes, he tried to catch another glimpse of Brynna, but she had vanished into the kitchen with Sophie.

"Well, birthday boy." Judith linked her arm in his. "It's time for you to come outside so that we can treat you like king for a day." She laughed as she led him to the back deck. Other guests were already settled in deck chairs. A few children were playing on the lawn below. Feeling conspicuous and a bit irritated by Judith's proprietary airs, Leroy forced a smile as he greeted Sherry and Tony, then waved to his nephews, who were starting to play horseshoes.

"Here you go." Judith pointed to a chair that had been decorated specially for him. To make matters worse, she put a birthday hat on his head. Not the kind of attention he enjoyed, but realizing he would offend her by objecting, he sat down.

Judith sat next to him with Luna on the other side. Meanwhile, Gina brought over a tray of appetizers and took drink orders. The whole while, Judith congenially chatted with him and others—playing the part of hostess. She was so comfortable in the role, it was clearly not her first rodeo. Before long, food was being served, so when no one was watching, Leroy removed the silly hat.

As they ate, Judith, Gina, and Luna engaged him in conversation. And then some old friends from a neighboring vineyard took over. His time was so occupied that he couldn't get an opportunity to seek out Brynna like he'd wanted. He'd been hoping for the chance to invite her to join them, as a way to introduce her to family and friends, but perhaps it was for the best. Maybe she wasn't ready to meet all these folks. Still, he would've preferred spending his time with her.

"Time for gifts," Judith announced as people were finishing up their meals.

"Oh, no," he said. "Please, no gifts. I don't—"

"You can't refuse our gifts." Judith shook her finger. "After that we'll have cake." Judith summoned Cassie to gather up a small pile of wrapped packages and present them to Leroy. As she set them down, Leroy noticed Brynna lurking just inside the doorway, watching with interest. He gave her what probably looked like a wimpy smile. But what could he do?

Uncomfortable with this fuss, Leroy knew it was best to just get it over with, so he tore into the gifts. Fortunately the ones from his friends tended to be silly gag gifts, providing some levity. His family's gifts were a bit more personal, but there was nothing he particularly needed or wanted. Even so, he feigned proper appreciation. Judith's gift, the largest package, was expertly wrapped and looked a bit more daunting. He opened it to find an expensive-looking crystal wine decanter and a set of goblets. He felt more aggravated than grateful. Why was she going to all this trouble for him? He tried to look congenial as he thanked her, but he mostly wanted this whole thing to end.

"Well, that's my way of thanking you for our lovely visit here. You've made us feel so at home, Leroy. Almost like family." Judith smiled brightly.

"Oh, here's another one. I didn't see it before." Cassie held up a small package wrapped in brown paper. She handed it to him. Leroy examined the delicate bouquet of wildflowers tied on the front with a twine bow.

"No card?" Leroy slowly unwrapped the package. Inside was a little wooden bear with the words SURFSIDE SHORES CAMPGROUNDS at the bottom.

"Who's this from?" Judith asked. "Looks like a tourist trinket."

Leroy recognized the name of the camp. It was where he and Brynna had first met. A miniature of the big carved bear on the dining hall porch. He glanced over to see Brynna watching him and had no doubt it was from her. He held it up with an appreciative nod, then slipped the bear into his shirt pocket. He would thank her later.

After the cake was presented and everyone sang to him, Leroy finally managed to extract himself from the "birthday boy" chair. His hope was to get a moment alone with Brynna, but instead he found himself trapped once again. In the living room, he was forced to engage in more small talk with his guests who were just leaving.

It didn't escape his observation when Judith handed Brynna a stack of dirty dishes, treating her as if she were hired help. Shortly after that, he noticed Gina and Luna doing the same by heaping more dishes onto a tray Brynna carried. And although Brynna seemed to take it in stride, it made him feel ashamed. And angry.

He was tempted to march into the kitchen, take Brynna by the hand, lead her out here, and proudly introduce her to the remaining guests. After all, it was his birthday! Didn't he have the right to her companionship if he wanted it? But he knew that if he made a scene like that, Brynna would probably be embarrassed.

Seeing his mother sitting in an easy chair by herself, apart from the other guests, Leroy felt concerned. Was she feeling unwell? He bade his friends goodbye then went over to check on her.

"I'm just a bit worn out," she admitted. "Waiting for Sherry and—"

"I'll take you home." He offered his arm to help her up.

"But it's your party, Leroy. You should—"

"It's okay." He helped her to her feet, speaking quietly as he led her to the door. "It's more like Judith and the girls' party now. I'm just as glad to get out of here. Most of my friends are gone anyway." He called out to Gina, who was nearby. "I'm taxiing Grandma home. I'll be back." Before she could respond, he was out the door. Although he'd promised to "be back," he hadn't said when. And he intended to take his time!

⁓

Brynna didn't mind helping in the kitchen. Really, it was preferable to being out there with all those people she didn't know and, even more so, the ones she did. She had no doubts that Judith, Luna, and Gina, as well as Judith's girls, resented her presence there today. She'd tried to make it clear that she was only there to help Sophie, but she hadn't expected them to treat her like she'd been assigned to KP duty.

Then, as the party wound down and Sophie looked close to exhaustion, Brynna had insisted she go lie down for a bit. Now she had the kitchen to herself. The quiet was most welcome. She knew that Leroy had departed to take his mother home. Gina, Luna, Judith, and her girls were visiting in the dining room. It sounded as if they'd just uncorked another bottle of wine.

"Well, done, ladies," Judith said, her voice loud enough to carry into the kitchen. "You all helped to make this a successful celebration."

Brynna was tempted to call out that it had been Sophie who'd done all the organizing and most of the work. But not wanting to create more disparity, she continued to quietly rinse plates.

"Well, Dad was sure surprised," Luna said. "That was something."

"And he seemed to enjoy it," Gina added. "I wasn't so sure he would."

"It was fun meeting some of your neighbors," Judith said. "But that one couple, I can't remember their names, they told me they were friends of Bree."

"Yeah, they're the ones camping out by the barn," Gina said. "I'm not a big fan either. Especially after we worked so hard to make that area attractive."

Brynna stopped rinsing to listen closer.

"Well, those two seemed like misfits to me," Judith said. "And they didn't appear to know a soul here. I wasn't surprised to see them leaving early."

"Why are they camping here?" one of the girls asked. "Is your dad going to turn this place into an RV park?"

"No, of course not." Luna sounded exasperated. "I told him it makes the winery look trashy. Hopefully they won't stay long."

"Dad said they came to take Bree home," Gina said. "I think they'll all leave today."

"Good riddance," Luna declared.

"So, our little office manager is leaving for real this time?" Judith sounded pleased. "Well, I'm sure that's best for everyone."

"The sooner, the better," Luna said. "I don't like sharing the guest cottage with her. And I think she's lazy. She was still asleep when I got out of there around nine."

"What're you guys talking about?"

Brynna caught her breath. That was Sophie's voice, and she sounded angry. How much had she overheard?

"Oh, there you are," Luna said in a cheerful tone. "We thought you'd gone home, big sister."

"Garth took the kids home," Sophie snapped back. "I was having a nap. But I want to know what you guys are talking about. Bree is *not* going home."

"Yes, she is," Gina insisted. "I'm going to place an ad for a new office manager tomorrow."

"Did Dad tell you to do that?" Sophie demanded.

There were a few seconds of silence before she replied. "No. But you can't go back to work, Soph—"

"I'm not talking about *me*, Gina. I'm saying that *Bree is not leaving.*"

"But she already left once. She blew out of here yesterday," Gina protested. "Supposedly for good. Dad told me yesterday that she was only coming back to tell you goodbye."

"That's what I heard too," Judith said, backing her.

"Well, that is wrong! All wrong. And I can't believe you're all in here gossiping about Bree like this. It's so rude and—"

"You're the one being rude, Sophie. We're just having a calm discussion and you come in here like a wild woman. Just because you're pregnant doesn't give you the right to go nuts on us."

Suddenly they were all yelling at once—choosing to express themselves by volume rather than intelligible words. Brynna had always hated arguments and couldn't stand to hear another harsh word. Especially the ones aimed at Sophie. Didn't they care that she was pregnant? She was halfway tempted to go in there and demand they stop at once but suspected that would only make matters worse.

So, while the sisters shouted mean words at each other, Brynna slipped through the laundry room and out the side door. As hard as it was to face it, her premonition had been right. Her presence had already created serious contention between Leroy's daughters. How much worse would it become if and when they discovered how Brynna felt about their father? And what about poor Leroy? Would he be torn between her and his daughters? She knew what she had to do—the sooner, the better!

Chapter 31

No longer at home in the guest cottage, Brynna went over to Jan and Mike's campsite. Knowing they were about as welcome here as she was, she hoped they'd be willing to make their departure today instead of tomorrow—and to take her with them. Although their camp was still in place, it was unoccupied. Noticing Mike's motorcycle gone, she guessed they'd gone for a ride. It was such a pretty afternoon, she didn't blame them. And since it was late in the day, she suspected they wouldn't want to break camp and leave now anyway.

As she walked back to the guest cottage, she decided to just make the best of what she knew would be her last night here. She would absorb the beauty of the vineyard one last time. She would take the time to tell both Leroy and Sophie goodbye, either this evening or tomorrow, and then she would leave with Jan and Mike.

Praying that Luna would remain in the house for a while longer, hopefully not still feuding with her sisters, Brynna decided to take advantage of the alone time by taking one last bath in the claw-foot tub. After her long day of kitchen duty, a good soak was most welcome. She was just finishing up when she heard Luna coming into the house. She hurriedly dressed, pulling on the same little blue sundress from yesterday, since it was hanging on the hook, and emerging with damp hair.

"Oh, you're still here?" Luna frowned. "I thought you and your friends had left."

"No, not yet." Brynna tried to keep her voice light. "Tomorrow, I think."

"Oh, well, good." Luna pursed her lips with what seemed like a thoughtful expression. "I don't mean good that you're leaving. I realize now that you worked hard while you were here. Sophie just told us about all that. But I guess, considering your history with our dad, well, it's probably for the best. *Right?*"

Brynna was taken aback by what almost seemed like concern. "It's, uh, complicated."

"Well, anyway. I'm sure you're doing what you think is right." Luna straightened, standing just an inch or two over Brynna, with a determined expression on her face. "Because my sisters and I do not want to see our dad get hurt. I don't mean to be coldhearted, but I think you must realize he's vulnerable. According to Gina, you were his first love. The girl who broke his heart, *right?*"

Brynna didn't know what to say.

"And then you sort of snuck in here, taking that job with Sophie, and hiding your true identity. *Right?*"

Brynna remembered that Luna was studying law. Was this her attempt at an interrogation? "Well, you are *partially* right."

"The point is we don't want Dad getting hurt," she said again. "And the truth is, we don't trust you. Sophie might, but the rest of us, well, not so much."

"It's hard to trust someone you don't know," Brynna said calmly. "You don't know me."

"Precisely. We don't know you. You're an outsider, and in my opinion, that's just one more reason you don't fit in here."

"You don't need to worry," Brynna stiffly reassured her. "I'll be gone soon."

"Well, that's a relief."

Brynna studied Luna for a moment. Part of her understood and even felt sympathy for this girl. Luna thought she was protecting her beloved father. And maybe she was. But another part of Brynna wanted to just shake some sense into her. Instead, she took in a deep breath. "In fact, I think I'll tell you goodbye right now. I can bunk with my friend Jan tonight. We were camping together in the first place, and my bed in her trailer is a lot more comfortable than the sofa."

"Oh, well, I don't want to drive you out of here, but if you'll be more comfortable." Despite her words, Luna seemed pleased.

As Brynna gathered her things, she wanted to tell Luna she'd be more comfortable sleeping on the dirt in the vineyard than in a house where she was unwanted, but she kept her peace. It didn't take long to pack since she'd barely unpacked yesterday. Since Luna had retreated to the bedroom, Brynna quietly took her leave.

To her dismay, Jan and Mike were still gone. But the camp chairs and firepit were out there, so Brynna sat down and tried to make herself at home. She felt restless and anxious and uncertain. After a while, she wondered how long Jan and Mike would be out joyriding. She pulled out her phone, thinking she'd send them a text and then call Sophie with her departure news, but her phone was dead.

She stood up and began pacing. She wondered about walking over to Sophie's, which would probably take an hour, but she was not eager to break the bad news face-to-face. And knowing it would upset Sophie, she decided to simply stroll through the vineyard instead. She wanted to absorb the sweet, pungent smell of the earth and the vines, the rich shades of green and gold, the warmth of late-afternoon sun on her head. She just wanted to soak it all in. Perhaps it would keep her warm on some cold rainy winter night up in Oregon.

———

After about an hour, Brynna realized the sun had dipped low in the western sky, and she wondered if Mike and Jan might be back by now. Plus, not having taken time to eat at the birthday party, her stomach was loudly rumbling. Not that she thought she could eat much. But when she got back to the camp, all was quiet, and the motorcycle was still missing.

"There you are!"

She turned to see Leroy striding toward her with a furrowed brow. She forced what she hoped was a believable smile onto her face and cheerfully greeted him. Feeling uneasy, she knelt to pet Babe, rubbing behind her ears. Anything to avoid looking into Leroy's eyes. She suspected he knew about her recent change of plans.

"I've been calling your phone and searching all over for you." He sounded aggravated.

"I'm sorry. My phone was dead. I was out walking. And I came here because I thought I'd spend the night with Jan tonight. More comfortable than the guest cottage sofa." She slowly stood, daring to look at his face. It seemed hard as stone.

"Luna told me you were leaving. Is that true?"

Brynna glanced around. "We're not leaving tonight. Mike and Jan aren't even here and—"

"Does that mean you're leaving tomorrow?" he demanded. "Leaving for good?"

"Yes, I think it's for the best." She folded her arms across her front, trying to bolster her resolve, or maybe to protect her heart.

"For the best?" He frowned. "Whose best?"

"Everyone's."

He shook his head. "I don't get you, Brynna. Is this some kind of emotional cat-and-mouse game with you? You're like a human ping-pong ball. First you say you're leaving, then you're staying, now you're leaving again. What is going on with you? Are you some kind of psychotic nut like Judith keeps suggesting?"

She tried to ignore the sting of those words. "I know it must seem confusing. I'll admit I'm confused too."

"Is it because I couldn't spend time with you at that silly birthday party?"

"No, I understood that. Those were your friends and family and—"

"Is it because of the way Judith—"

"No, that has nothing to do with my decision. It's just that—"

"So you were going to leave anyway? Just flit away? Were you even going to tell me? What about Sophie? She still believes you're staying on. Just like you told her, she assumes you'll be here throughout the summer. Until her baby comes."

"I wish I could." She felt a lump in her throat.

"I don't get it. Why do you keep jerking us around like this?"

"It's complicated, Leroy." Tears gathered in her eyes as she gauged her words. She didn't want to speak badly of his daughters. Didn't want to blame Luna and Gina and just make things worse. Before she could think of a reasonable explanation, she heard the deep rumble of the motorcycle. She glanced down the road to see Mike and Jan coming this way on the Harley. She had to get the words out fast, even if they didn't make sense.

"As much as I would love to stay here, I honestly think I need to go home. It's for the best. And don't worry, I'll explain it all to Sophie tomorrow. I'll make sure she understands. And then we'll break camp and get out of here."

Leroy peered into her eyes as if trying to see what was hidden deeper inside. It took all her strength to keep from crying and grabbing onto him and just holding on tightly—like she wanted to. But the motorcycle, sluggishly turning in behind the barn, seemed to empower her to make this break swiftly.

"I'm really sorry, Leroy, but I think it's for the best—" Her voice cracked with emotion. "The best. For everyone. I'm sorry."

He slowly shook his head and, without even acknowledging Mike and Jan, stormed off. She had no doubt she'd hurt him. Probably deeply. Maybe unforgivably. But wasn't it better to nip this thing now? Better than to divide and tear up his family later?

Choking back tears, she explained to Jan and Mike that she wanted to leave as soon as possible tomorrow. To her relief, they didn't even question her this time. Maybe they'd decided that she was just plain flaky . . . or perhaps they finally understood that leaving truly was her best option. But why did best have to hurt so much?

———

Leroy was fed up. *Women!* Who needed them? Oh, he couldn't get along without his three daughters—even if they drove him nuts sometimes—but the rest of the females in this world? He wanted nothing to do with them. Ever again! As he stormed into his house, he had one agenda on his mind. It was time for Judith and her girls to go home. Gina's working guests had worn out their welcome.

The house was quiet and, not surprisingly, the women were all loitering out on the deck, acting like this was some sort of vineyard resort and they were simply enjoying an extended vacation. Leroy took in a deep breath before going outside. As angry as he felt toward the feminine persuasion, he didn't really want to be rude. Just firm.

"Excuse me, ladies," he said loudly. "I don't mean to interrupt you, but I have an announcement."

"Oh, Dad," Luna called out. "We were hoping you'd join us. Judith fixed us a—"

"I'm not here to eat," he interrupted.

"Then have a glass of wine." Judith held up a bottle of one of his best cabernets. "We want to continue celebrating your birthday."

"I do *not* want a glass of wine," he said, keeping his tone firm. "I am here to say that, although we have appreciated your help here, Judith and Mara and Cassie, it's time to call it a day."

"Dad!" Gina looked shocked.

"I'm sorry," he continued, ignoring his daughter's incredulity, "but it's time for this party to end. I hope you enjoyed your visit. But it is officially over tomorrow morning." He locked eyes with Gina. "It's time to get focused on the vineyard and the work here.

There's no room for guests. Not even working ones." Without giving them a chance to respond, he turned on his heel and marched off. He had no doubts they'd think him an old ogre. A rude and ungrateful beast. That was fine. As long as his houseguests left.

As he walked through his quiet house, he wondered what it would be like to have it all back to himself again. Well, himself and Gina. Although she probably wouldn't be speaking to him for a while after this, but that was okay. He didn't want to speak to anyone right now. Maybe he could just give up speaking altogether.

He went out the front door and headed down the porch. Without inviting Babe to join him, even though she peered up with sad brown eyes, he got inside his Jeep and started the engine. As he sped off, he planned to drive to the top of the vineyard, where he'd get out and walk and walk and walk. It would be too much for his old dog to keep up. He would allow the earth and the vines to calm him, like they always did. The problem was that after almost an hour of walking up and down the rows, he felt no better. And as the sun dipped below the western hills, he wondered if he'd ever feel better.

How could he have been so stupid? Didn't someone say the best way to predict the future was to pay attention to the past? Brynna had hurt him once, and now she'd done it again. And he'd stupidly allowed it. Practically invited it! Why hadn't he known better? Gina had tried to warn him. But he didn't even listen to his own daughter. Well, he'd gotten exactly what he deserved.

He wanted to pray, to beg God to help him through this pain, but the words refused to come. Instead, he looked up at the sunset colors streaking across the dusky sky and let out the loud howl of a wounded lone wolf. Then, feeling foolish, he just shook his head and slowly walked back to the Jeep. Happy birthday, Leroy.

Chapter 32

In the morning, Brynna borrowed Jan's SUV to drive over to Sophie's, but halfway there, her cell phone rang. Not recognizing the number, but seeing it was local, she pulled over to answer. To her surprise it was Leroy's mother, Dorothy Sorrentino.

"I realize we haven't had a chance to get acquainted," the older woman began, "but I would very much like to speak to you."

Brynna braced herself. Was Leroy's mother about to read her the riot act for hurting her son? It wouldn't be surprising, but how could Dorothy possibly know?

"I don't like talking on the phone," she continued, "so I'm hoping you can come over here and have coffee with me."

"I, uh, I guess I could do that." Everything in Brynna wanted to decline this strange invitation, but out of respect for Dorothy's age, and the fact that she was Leroy's mother, she agreed. Dorothy gave Brynna directions to the neighboring vineyard, where she said she lived with her daughter, Sherry, and before long Brynna was sitting out on the terrace with her, pretending to sip her espresso while imagining how to make a graceful exit.

"I've heard through the grapevine"—Dorothy's blue eyes twinkled with amusement—"Isn't that an appropriate saying here in vineyard country? But it's true. I did hear something by way of others. My daughter, Sherry, heard it through Gina that you are leaving us."

Brynna set down her coffee cup. "That's right."

"May I ask why?"

Brynna wanted to ask her why she wanted to know but suspected that would sound rude. "Because it's for the best, Mrs. Sorrentino. For everyone."

"Please, call me Dorothy."

Brynna nodded.

"Why do you say it's for the best, Brynna? That is your real name, is it not? Although I've heard Sophie call you Bree."

Brynna explained that both were right. "My dad used to call me Bree."

"Oh. So back to my question. Why do you believe that leaving is for the best?"

Brynna frowned. "How much do you know about me?"

Dorothy's pale brows arched. "More than you'd expect." She quickly delivered a fairly detailed but condensed bio of Brynna. "My son and I talk. Did I get it mostly right?"

"Yes." Brynna sighed.

"Let me cut to the chase. Do you love my son?"

Brynna blinked.

"Please, answer my question."

"Can we keep this between you and me?"

"I think so." Dorothy tipped her head slightly.

"Okay, yes, I do love Leroy." Brynna took in a quick breath. "It's hard to admit it, but it's true." For some reason it was comforting to say it aloud.

"So back to my original question. Why are you leaving? And why do you say it's for the best?"

"Can you also keep this between us?" Brynna asked.

Dorothy nodded, and Brynna tried to explain. "It's fairly obvious that Luna and Gina aren't overly fond of me. And I understand them feeling protective of their father, but I don't like how my presence here pits them against poor Sophie." She sighed, wondering if this even made sense to the older woman. "And then there's Judith and the way Gina wanted to play matchmaker. It's hard to admit, but I can see how someone like her fits better in Leroy's world."

"Leroy can barely tolerate that woman. In fact, I hear he's sent Judith and her daughters packing."

Brynna had seen Judith's fancy SUV parked in Leroy's driveway earlier that morning. "Really?" she asked skeptically. "You think they've gone?"

"According to my grapevine sources, they're to be out this morning."

"Well, Judith really wasn't a major factor in my decision," Brynna admitted. "It had more to do with Leroy's girls." She explained about the feisty sisterly feud she'd overheard yesterday. "And poor Sophie was trying to defend me. It just felt so wrong. All that fighting because of me."

Dorothy threw her head back and laughed. "Oh my goodness. You never had sisters, did you?"

"No."

"Well, those girls fight like cats and dogs sometimes. And Gina and Luna are often at odds with Sophie. There's sibling rivalry and competition over all sorts of silly things. But trust me, those girls love each other. And if anyone outside the family goes against one of them, the other two will fight tooth and nail to protect their sister."

Brynna considered this. "I understand what you're saying, but I would still be the outsider. And even with Sophie's support, Gina and Luna would be in opposition. The battle line's been drawn."

Dorothy waved a hand in the air dismissively. "Oh, they would get over it in time. They're all intelligent girls with good hearts, though a little stubborn and spoiled perhaps. Leroy's partly to blame for that. After Marcie died, he indulged them a bit too much." She leaned across the little bistro table, looking intently into Brynna's eyes. "Tell me true, do you really love my son?"

Brynna mutely nodded. Hadn't she said as much already?

"Well, then I don't see why you're running away."

"I know how much Leroy loves his girls . . . how devoted they are to him," she said slowly. "It's really a sweet and lovely thing. I don't want to be the outsider who steps in and messes that all up. In time I think they'd all hate me."

"Oh, you might shake them up for a bit. At first, anyway. But Leroy needs you, Brynna."

"I don't know . . . I get the impression he's a very self-sufficient sort of guy." She remembered the hard glint in his eyes when he'd turned away yesterday. After she'd hurt him. "It seems like he doesn't really need anyone. I mean, outside of who he has already."

"You're wrong." Dorothy reached across the table to grasp Brynna's hand. "Leroy does need you."

This act of kindness cut right through Brynna. Suddenly her eyes filled with tears and she was pouring out how badly she'd hurt him the day before and how worried she was that he could never trust her again. "And I don't blame him. I'm sure he must think I'm indecisive . . . untrustworthy . . . undependable . . . disloyal." All the words that had been rolling around in her head throughout last night's sleeplessness. "He called me a human ping-pong ball. I'm sure he thinks I've done all of this intentionally. Like I'm playing some nefarious heartbreak game. But I'm not. I never wanted to hurt him, but I did."

"I'm sure you did." Dorothy leaned back in her chair. "But you couldn't have hurt him like that if he didn't love you. And I'm fairly certain that he does love you, Brynna. Love isn't something you can turn off and on. At least I know Leroy can't." She studied Brynna. "Can you?"

"No. I think after this summer, I will love Leroy for the rest of my life." She went on to admit how she wished she'd never given up on him thirty years ago. "I was young and foolish."

"Well, hopefully you're not old and foolish now."

Brynna felt like she was.

"I don't like to interfere in my children's lives." She smiled. "Though they probably don't agree with me on that. The only time I step in is when I think I see something they're missing. And that's how I feel about Leroy right now. Yes, I know he *thinks* he's washed his hands of you. Sherry said he made some speech to Gina and Luna early this morning, saying how he was finished with women and planned to be a bachelor for the rest of his days. But I know underneath all that bravado, he's lonely. Gina and Luna will eventually marry and move on, Sophie will get even busier with her growing brood, and God knows I won't be around forever. Someday Leroy will be all alone."

Brynna felt torn and confused. "I feel badly, but I also feel like it's too late," she confessed. "I've burned the bridge between us. I seriously doubt that he'll ever give me the time of day again." She threw her hands in the air. "Who could blame him?"

Dorothy nodded with a faraway look. "Have you ever heard the Bible story about Ruth and Boaz?"

"I think so. Wasn't Ruth the poor desperate woman who laid herself down at the rich landowner's feet in the hopes he would take her in, or something to that effect?"

"Yes. But I never think of her as poor and desperate. I think she was wise, and I think she knew that Boaz was lonely and needed her. I think it was as much about him as it was about her. But Ruth was the one who had to humble herself and make the first move."

"Oh." Brynna tried to wrap her head around what Dorothy was saying. "Are you suggesting I go lie down at Leroy's feet?"

"Not exactly. But I do know a little something about the Ruth and Boaz story from personal experience."

"How's that?" Brynna asked, curious.

"Well, I'm not sure how much you know about Leroy's father, but I'm his second wife. Sergio married the love of his life as a young man. She died in childbirth just a few years later. Sergio was certain he'd never get over her. He was determined to never marry again, but he was a lonely man. I met him through friends when I was in my midtwenties. He was older than me, but I was smitten and determined to get him down on one knee. I did what I could to get him interested, but it wasn't working. Finally, I realized I had a choice to make. I could go my own way with my head held high, or I could toss my pride aside and tell Sergio he needed me in his life."

"And?"

"Obviously, it worked. I know I wasn't the love of Sergio's life, but I did eventually win his love." Dorothy pointed at Brynna. "You have an advantage there since you really were Leroy's first love. But it seems to me you might have to do like Ruth and I did, Brynna. You might have to humble yourself. You might have to take a risk. No more bouncing back and forth like a human ping-pong ball." She refilled her coffee cup from the carafe on the table.

The meaning gradually sank in and Brynna nodded. "That does make sense. I can see how I might need to humble myself. Especially since I'm the one who's waffled back and forth. And that does sound a little risky. Especially since I know Leroy's fed up with me."

"Fed up perhaps. But that doesn't mean he's quit loving you. Remember that." Dorothy paused at the sound of Sherry calling out to her, then checked her watch. "Oh dear, I nearly forgot that I have a dentist appointment. We will have to finish this conversation later." She stood, then reached for Brynna's hand. "At least, I hope so."

Brynna thanked her, promising to give the Ruth story more thought. But as she drove back toward Sorrentino's, she had no idea how to fix the mess she seemed to be perennially stuck in. Going, staying, going, staying, going . . . Leroy was right, she *was* a human ping-pong ball. It was more than humbling. It was humiliating. And she was done with it.

Instead of stopping by Sophie's, she drove straight back to the barn, where Jan and Mike were all packed up and waiting. While they hitched Jan's trailer to her Yukon, Brynna relayed her conversation with Leroy's mother.

"I want you guys to just go like you'd planned," Brynna said as she removed her bag from the trailer. "I'm going to stay on a while longer."

Jan gave her a thin smile. "Do you want us to come back and check on—"

"No. I want you to just go on your way. Don't worry about me. If it doesn't work out, I'll get a taxi then catch a flight back home—and Leroy will never see me again."

"And if it works?" Jan asked.

Brynna shrugged. "Then I'll give my resignation at the school."

"So, this is it?" Jan looked dubious. "All or nothing?"

"Yep." Brynna slung a strap of her duffel bag over one shoulder.

"I like that plan." Mike winked at her. "You don't need any easy outs."

"Leroy is a good guy," Jan reassured her. "I could see that the other night when we visited around the campfire together. Please, tell him goodbye for us and thank him for letting us stay here."

"And promise you'll invite us to the wedding." Mike nudged her with his elbow.

Brynna rolled her eyes. "Don't hold your breath."

Judith jerked her thumb toward the main house. "And here's some good news. Shortly after you left, I saw Judith and her girls load up their SUV and head out," she said. "Judging by their faces, they weren't too happy either."

"That reminds me," Mike added. "I was taking the firepit over to the house when I noticed Leroy's daughter—can't remember her name. The fancy lawyer girl. Anyway, she was putting luggage into a small car. Looked to me like she was leaving too."

"Really?" Brynna felt hopeful. Did this mean the guest cottage was free again?

"Well, good luck." Jan hugged her.

"Hang in there." Mike patted her back.

"Keep me posted," Jan said as she got into the SUV.

Brynna waved and promised to do so. Then, loaded down with her duffel, she walked over to the guest cottage. Relieved that no one seemed to have observed her, and even more relieved that the front door was left unlocked, she let herself inside. Feeling a bit like a squatter—or maybe like Ruth in the Bible—she made herself at home by taking a much-needed nap.

———

Leroy was driving down from the burn area after giving his crew instructions when he noticed the camping trailer, followed by the motorcycle, making its way toward the main road. He told himself he should feel relieved, but all he felt was empty and sad. Brynna was gone. This time for good.

Luna had decided to leave today as well. She claimed they needed her back in the law office, but he suspected she was simply getting bored. Whatever the case, they'd said their farewell over mugs of coffee earlier this morning. But when she'd kissed him goodbye, he sensed something different in her. It was as if she was apologetic about something. He wasn't sure, but he suspected it had to do with Brynna. Or maybe she was just sorry for him. Not that he needed her sympathy—or anyone's, for that matter. A lone wolf didn't need pity.

He'd been relieved to hear from Gina that Judith and her girls were gone as well. Oddly enough, Gina seemed slightly apologetic too, as if she were somehow responsible for his somber state. Or maybe she regretted the way she'd forced her female friends onto him these past few weeks. But like he'd told her, at least it would be quiet around here for a while. Give them more time to catch their collective breaths and prepare for the upcoming vineyard events that Gina had scheduled. Not that he looked forward to any of it. He would leave the celebration business to Gina. So far she'd managed to prove herself by getting the place fixed up. Just this morning, he'd expressed his pride, thanking her for how well she'd been handling things. And she'd promised to initiate an earnest search for an office manager starting today.

So, really, he should be feeling pretty good about life. Except that he wasn't. Even as he walked through his empty house, which should've felt peaceful, all he felt was strangely out of place. Or maybe just out of sorts. He fixed himself a late breakfast, or maybe an early lunch, but he didn't care to stay inside to eat. Something about sitting down and leisurely eating felt odd. As he carried his sandwich and banana out to his Jeep, he felt like an antisocial hermit. Gobbling down his food and slopping mustard on his shirt as he drove to the south section of the vineyard, he thought perhaps he really was a lone wolf. Maybe it was for the best.

———

Brynna woke up surprisingly refreshed. Okay, she felt a little strange being here in the cottage that everyone assumed was vacant. Kind of like Goldilocks waiting for the three bears. She decided to venture outside. Her plan was to go to the office and, since it was Monday, she'd simply go back to work. Part of her felt silly, but she didn't know what else to do. As she strolled over to the office, she prayed, once again, that God would help her through this. She prayed he would help her to be humble like Ruth. And then she put the whole thing, including however it turned out, in God's hands. Really, what more could she do?

As she neared the office, she remembered she'd left her keys inside. But when she reached the door, she was surprised to discover it was open. She was even more surprised to see that Gina was sitting at the front desk. "Hello?" she called out in a voice that sounded much more confident than she felt.

"What?" Gina looked up with wide eyes. "What on earth are you doing here?"

"I'm like that proverbial bad penny." Brynna shrugged. "I keep coming back."

"But I thought you and your friends left. I saw the caravan drive off about an hour ago."

"Well, your grandmother gave me a little pep talk this morning." Brynna sat down in the chair across from Gina. "She has strongly encouraged me to stick it out longer."

"Oh?" Gina leaned back with a hard-to-read expression on her face. "Does my dad know about this?"

Brynna shook her head. "Not yet."

"Oh?" Gina's brow creased as she laid down a folder. "I was just going through some applications from people who actually applied for the office manager job. You know, before Sophie hired you."

"Right." Brynna studied her for a long moment. "I realize you don't like me, Gina. And I get that. I'm sure you felt tricked by me, but I never meant—"

"Sophie already told us about that." Gina waved a dismissive hand through the air, but her tone was sharp. "You don't need to explain anything to me."

"I appreciate that, but I still feel I owe you an apology. I never meant to deceive anyone. I just got off on the wrong foot, and after that, it got really awkward. I took the job because it seemed like an interesting opportunity. It didn't take long to realize it was a mess just waiting to happen. By then I was torn. I knew I should get out of here, but I couldn't force myself to leave this place. The truth is, I love being here, Gina. I love the work. Love the vineyard . . ."

"Love my dad?" Her eyes narrowed.

Brynna nodded somberly.

"But you dumped him once, Bree. Then all these years later, you show up here and play your games and then leave abruptly. Then you come back, acting like you're going to stay. But the next thing we know you are leaving again. Even though Dad says he's done with women, I know he's hurting. Seriously, I don't get it. I really, really don't get you."

"I'm sure I look flaky. But the truth is, it seemed best for everyone if I left. For good." She pursed her lips. "I realized that when I overheard the argument yesterday. I heard you and your sisters and your friends after the birthday party. I could see I'd come between you and Sophie. And Luna was upset too. I hated to hear you girls arguing like that because of me. I hated seeing Sophie hurt by—"

"Oh, we go on like that all the time," Gina interrupted. "It's who we are. Blame it on our Italian roots. It's part of being a Sorrentino. We don't take our fights seriously."

"Oh?" Brynna wasn't fully convinced. "It sounded serious to me. At least as far as I was concerned. You girls got awfully loud."

"Yeah. We flare up and shout a lot, but then we cool off. We forgive and forget."

"Your grandmother mentioned something to that effect, but I'm not used to it."

For a long moment neither of them spoke, but Brynna could feel Gina looking intently at her.

Finally, Brynna decided to lay her cards on the table. "Anyway, the reason I decided to stay on was because of what your grandmother told me. She felt that . . . well, that your dad might want me to stay."

Gina leaned back with a relieved sigh. "I suppose Grandma could be right. Although that's not what Dad said this morning. And he wouldn't want you around if you're just going to hurt him again."

"I don't intend to hurt him. It's hard to admit this out loud, but I really do love him. I think I've loved him for a very long time."

"Okay, that's fine. You say you love him, but then you take off like a scared rabbit just because we girls have a little squabble." Gina tipped her head to one side. "How's that supposed to work?"

"I don't know. All I know is that I don't want to ruin what your family has here. I can see it's something special. Your dad loves you three girls more than anything in this world. I don't want to mess any of that up. That's why I decided to leave."

"What would keep you from doing it again?"

"Humility." Brynna bit her lip, trying to think of a way to explain this. "I'm determined to see this through all the way this time. I plan to plead my case with your dad. And if he rejects me, I'll go and never come back."

Gina leaned forward, placing her palms on the desk. "Okay, I guess I have a confession, Bree. Or Brynna. Or whatever. Anyway, I can admit I never gave you a chance. The truth is, I disliked you from the start."

"Oh." Brynna nodded, trying not to show how much her words stung.

"Call it women's intuition or Judith's influence or whatever, but I felt something was off with you. And then when we found out who you were, I got really enraged. I already knew all about you and Dad at that camp. I knew how badly you'd hurt him when you guys were in college. I didn't want you to ever hurt him again."

"I don't want to ever hurt him again either." Brynna took in a deep breath. "I would rather he hurt me this time. I'm putting myself at his mercy. He might throw me out when he finds out I'm still here."

"He might." Gina stood abruptly, but her expression seemed softer.

"I wouldn't blame him."

"So . . . I guess I could postpone hiring a new manager for now." She moved toward the door. "To be honest, I wasn't looking forward to interviewing people this week."

"You could interview me." Brynna attempted a smile.

"Thought I just did." Gina's eyes twinkled.

"So, you're okay if I keep working here today?"

"Fine by me." Gina opened the door. "But Dad gets the final say. As long as you're here, there are some phone messages that need attention, and I haven't even gone through the mail. Plus, I noticed some new orders on the website."

"I'll handle it. Thanks, Gina." Brynna felt a ripple of hope "And I'd appreciate it if you didn't tell your dad that I'm here? I'd like to do that myself."

Gina shrugged. "Sure. Whatever."

After Gina left, Brynna sorted through the stack of mail on the desk. It felt good to be back in here, doing a job that needed doing, passing the time with the simple office chores. It was peaceful and comforting. But she knew it could simply be the calm before the storm. Everything could blow up in her face when she crossed paths with Leroy. But she'd already put that in God's hands. Like Ruth, Brynna felt powerless in this situation. If it was meant to be, it would be.

Chapter 33

Two Days Later

Leroy's therapy was to immerse himself in hard work. Because of Sorrentino's budget concerns, he'd dismissed the temporary crew that had been salvaging the burn area. He knew several other growers in need of burn restoration, so he sent the workers their way. Then, without speaking to Gina or anyone, he'd take off early in the morning and work the remaining burn area until it was too dark to see. He didn't take Babe with him anymore because the long days were too much for the old girl. Maybe it was too much for him. But he didn't care.

Despite the clear warm weather, his world felt bleak and gray and dreary, kind of like the soot and ashes that covered him at the end of the day. His life was work: digging out dead vines, pruning, and staking up the survivors. He did it all until he felt like the vineyard zombie, trudging up and down the rows of blackened soil. The most troubling part was his attitude.

Although he put in the effort, he no longer cared if these vines ever grew strong enough to support grapes again. Did it even matter? Would he even care if another wildfire raged through here and destroyed the rest of his vineyard? Maybe it'd be for the best. He hated those three words. *For the best.* Who knew what was best? Maybe God did, but it didn't seem like many humans did. He sure didn't.

His payoff at the end of each long day was being so fatigued that he fell into bed exhausted enough to actually sleep. It wasn't a restful or restorative sleep, but at least he was too tired to lie awake thinking. He knew this was a miserable way to live, but again, it was probably for the best, especially if he was destined to be a lone wolf.

By the end of his third day of self-inflicted, punitive isolation he realized this crazy masochistic pace was going to kill him. Was that why his dad's life had ended early? That's what Gina said as he trudged into the house well after 9:00 p.m., kicking off his ashen boots in the laundry room. Thinking she could be right, he promised Gina that he'd take tomorrow morning off. Then he grabbed some food to take upstairs—to the wolf den.

But before he could escape, Gina yelled up at him. "Maybe you can pay some attention to what's going on in your winery!" She sounded angry. Not that he cared.

Just the same, he paused to scowl down at her. "I thought you had everything under control. Are you saying something's wrong?"

"Not exactly." She growled back at him. "But might be nice if you weren't so checked out, Dad. Might be nice if you were still around. You're like a dead man walking."

"That's right," he mumbled as he headed for his room. He felt like a dead man as he closed the door behind him. The wolf den was exactly as he'd left it that morning, a sorry mess. Filthy work clothes strewn everywhere. Smelly leftover food and dirty dishes and glasses on the floor. Even a banana peel that had adhered to the bathroom floor. It was like something you'd expect from an adolescent, not a middle-aged man. His bedding looked twisted and knotted and dirty from the nights he'd fallen into bed without even showering. He should be ashamed. Except he wasn't. Because he didn't care.

But as he peeled off his dirty clothes, he felt a twinge of guilt.

Sophie usually came on Thursdays to lend a hand with his house-work. That was tomorrow. He didn't like the idea of her cleaning up his messes. Hopefully he'd remember to pick up some in the morning. If not, he might have some explaining to do.

———

Brynna didn't know what to think after three unsettling days had passed without a single glimpse of Leroy. By Thursday morning, she was so on edge that she broached the subject with Gina. But the girl seemed unconcerned as she dropped some mail on the desk, simply claiming that her dad had been obsessed with getting the burn area all cleaned up.

"By himself," Gina said with nonchalance. "Seems kind of crazy to me, but it's what he wants and he's the boss. So what can you do?"

"Oh." Brynna nodded. "I just wondered."

"At least he's sleeping in this morning." Gina glanced at the clock. "But he'll probably be back at it before long."

Brynna pointed to the dog snoozing on the office floor. "I hope it's okay that Babe's been hanging out with me every day. I know she sometimes goes to work with your dad. Do you suppose he misses her?"

"Dad says it's too long of days for her. She's getting old, poor girl." Gina bent down to stroke Babe's haunch. "You know, she's been around since I was in second grade."

"Wow, that old?"

"She'll be thirteen this fall. Mom got her for dad for a Christmas present. She was just this fluffy blond ball of fur. So cute. Dad used to cradle her in his arms and rock and sing to her like a baby. It cracked us up. That's how she got her name."

"That's a sweet image." Brynna looked down at Babe, who had her orange rubber ball in her mouth and was wagging her tail hopefully. "I love having her in here with me. She's good company and such a happy girl."

"I wish Dad could be happy too." Gina bent down to get Babe's ball. "Come on, old lady. I'll throw that ball for you."

Brynna watched as Babe eagerly followed Gina out into the sunshine, barking at her to "throw the ball." She really was a happy dog. And like Gina, Brynna really wished Leroy could be happy too, but she'd been unable to say those words to Gina. Because of guilt. Brynna felt certain Leroy's insanely long workdays were because of her. But she still didn't know what to do about it.

At first she'd imagined cooking a special dinner for him, similar to the other night when they'd eaten on the front porch of the cottage. But what if it turned into a dramatic showdown? Who would feel like eating then? She played with other scenarios, but nothing felt right. Plus, the opportunities just didn't come. Perhaps she should go up to the burn area, chase him down, tackle him right there in the vineyard, and declare her undying love for him. Or maybe not.

She'd even imagined sneaking into his house and waiting up in his room where she, like Ruth, would throw herself at his feet and beg for mercy. But somehow that didn't feel right. Or proper. She just couldn't quite imagine a scene that could work. Or maybe it was like Dorothy had said, she just needed to remain patient. But every day, she'd asked God to direct her . . . to show her what to do.

During this waiting time, she'd been content to do the office work. It was demanding enough to keep her occupied, but it had a peaceful, calming effect too. After work, she'd spent the past two afternoons with Sophie, helping with the kids or in the garden, which was really producing now. Sophie hadn't seemed the least bit surprised that Brynna hadn't left like her sisters had claimed she would. Brynna was relieved and felt that what Sophie didn't know couldn't hurt her.

Whenever she was at Sophie's, Brynna would stay on the look-out for Leroy to pop in to play with his grandkids like he often did. Sure, it would be awkward to see him, but at least she'd get her chance to explain herself. But he hadn't shown up. When Brynna had asked Sophie if she'd seen him, Sophie acknowledged that he was working hard in the burn area, but she seemed unconcerned, or maybe just oblivious.

Brynna had received a phone call from Leroy's mother yesterday afternoon. Brynna had reassured Dorothy that she'd taken her advice to heart but was now waiting for the opportunity to speak to Leroy. Dorothy sounded happy to hear it, reminding Brynna that timing was everything and to be patient. Easier said than done.

Brynna was trying to be patient. As much as she enjoyed extending her stay at the vineyard, by noon on Thursday, she wondered if she'd ever see Leroy. Every evening she'd sat outside to enjoy the sunset, watching for his Jeep to show up, hoping for an impromptu encounter. But then it'd get dark and she'd finally give up and go inside. She got the feeling she was living on borrowed time. The more time that passed without an encounter with Leroy, the more she questioned how this would all play out.

Yet, at the same time, she was determined to take Dorothy's advice. Like Ruth, Brynna planned to humble herself . . . to confess her true feelings and accept the outcome, whatever it turned out to be. It felt risky and went against her old stereotypical expectations of being pursued by a knight in shining armor, but she was willing to sacrifice her pride and do it.

Brynna was just leaving the office for her lunch break when Gina came over to talk to her. "Dad is still home," she said quietly. "He slept in really late. I'm hoping he'll skip work altogether today. He's so worn out. But this could be your chance to see him."

"Oh, well, okay." Brynna smiled nervously. "Thanks for the heads-up."

"I thought you should know." Gina glanced over her shoulder toward the house. "Good luck."

Brynna blinked. "Really? *Good luck?*"

Gina shrugged. "Hey, if you can bring Dad out of his deep, dark depression, I'd be grateful."

"Right." Brynna grimaced. She wished she could help Leroy

feel happy again. But at the same time, she knew it could go in the complete opposite direction. She suddenly remembered how angry he'd been the last time they'd talked. Even when she'd tried to explain, he refused to listen. That could easily happen again.

———

Leroy couldn't remember the last time he'd slept in so late. But as he got out of bed, he still felt tired. And achy. As tempting as it would be to just sleep all day, he didn't relish the idea of Sophie showing up to do housework and finding him here. She'd be shocked and upset, and he'd never be able to convince her he wasn't sick or dying.

After a long hot shower and shaving for the first time since Sunday, he picked up some of the messes he'd strewn throughout the master bedroom. He didn't make it look too clean since that would make Sophie equally suspicious. Besides, she liked the excuse of having his housework and laundry to do—her break from the kids. He wouldn't deprive her of that.

To his relief, Gina wasn't around downstairs. He had the house to himself. She'd left half a pot of coffee but turned off the burner. As he filled a cup, Babe wandered out from the laundry room, where she'd probably been sleeping. Her tail wagged happily as he filled a bowl with cereal. She sat and watched as he ate it, along with a banana. Then as he drank orange juice straight from the container, something he'd never let his kids do, his dog looked on with what seemed like canine amusement.

Not sure what to do, and not ready to return to hard labor, he began to wander from room to room, reacquainting himself with his house. All the while, Babe followed him as if to show how much she'd missed him. Then he headed back to the kitchen to refill his coffee mug with the lukewarm brew.

"Poor old girl," he said to Babe. "Have you felt abandoned too?"

Her tail swung happily as she followed him out to the back deck. As he sank into an Adirondack chair, he tried to remember the contentment he used to feel just sitting out here. How he used to enjoy looking over this stretch of vineyards, soaking in the rich colors and absorbing the sweet, pungent smells. But today felt just like the past three days. Bleak and colorless. Scentless and silent, as if the whole world, like him, had gone dead and dormant. When would it get better? Or was he destined to live like this always?

He checked his watch, surprised to see it was a bit past noon and he hadn't even put on his work clothes yet. He really was a lazy bum today. But what did it matter? He sipped the cool coffee and stared down at the little guest cottage. He didn't want to remember the last time he'd been down there . . . that dinner on the porch with her . . . when everything had felt so magically perfect. He needed to wipe the torturous memories from his brain. Needed to move on.

Leroy let out a long, weary sigh, leaned back in his chair, and tightly shut his eyes. The old saying "time heals all wounds" flashed through his head. Something his mother liked to say, but was it true? He doubted it. Thirty years had never healed that brokenhearted boy. Although he had to admit, it did eventually get better.

He heard Babe get to her feet and trot across the deck as if she had a destination in mind. Leroy opened his eyes, blinked against the bright light, then closed them again. Was he hallucinating? Had he really just seen the brown-haired girl in the blue dress strolling toward the guest cottage?

He opened his eyes again, but now there was no girl. Only Babe, who was cautiously making her way down the deck stairs. Due to her age and arthritis, she didn't much like stairs, but probably needed to take care of business. Instead of her usual, leisurely stride, she was running. With a wagging tail, she made a beeline for the guest cottage. Had she seen a rabbit?

Leroy stood and called out to his dog, but she ignored him. He watched as she disappeared about the corner of the cottage. Curious, he followed her trail, approaching the cottage then turning the corner, where he saw Babe on the front porch. And it wasn't his imagination. Brynna, wearing the simple blue dress, was kneeling down and rubbing Babe's ears.

"*Brynna?*" He felt his eyes widen as he slowly approached the porch steps.

She stood with a surprised expression. "Leroy." She brushed dog hair and dust from her hands, smiling shyly. "Hello."

Feeling slightly delusional, he ran his fingers through his un-combed, shaggy hair. "Wh-what're you doing here?"

She waved to the pair of rockers. "You have time to sit? And talk?"

"Sure, I guess so." He slowly ascended the steps as she sat down in a rocker.

She watched him as he sat beside her and for a moment no one spoke.

"I'm sorry to take you by surprise," she began in a calm voice. "I was hoping to see you before this, but Gina tells me you've been working like crazy over in the burn area. Apparently no one has seen you. Not your mother or Sophie or—"

"You've spoken with my mother?" He tried to imagine this.

"Yes, she's a big part of the reason I'm still here." She told him about having coffee with his mother on the day she'd planned to leave. "She challenged me to stay."

"*My* mother?"

She nodded. "The reason I couldn't go was that I need to tell you that I realize what a mess I made of everything, Leroy. Like Gina said, I ran like a scared rabbit instead of telling you the truth."

"Gina said that?"

"Yes. Gina and I have had some good conversations. She's ex-plained several things to me."

"What did she mean about telling me the truth? What truth?"

"Okay . . . I know you could toss this back in my face," she spoke slowly, "but the truth is . . . I love you, Leroy." She paused to take a breath. And he did too. Then she continued. "There, I've said it. And I have to admit it feels very risky to speak to you like this. I know how angry you've been at me for being such a flake. And you have every right to be. I wouldn't be surprised if you threw me off of your property."

Leroy felt his head spinning as he tried to absorb all this. Had she really just said she loved him? Was this real?

"But before you throw me out, you need to know that I think I've loved you for a very long time. I couldn't admit it when I was young. I was scared and naive, and Dirk took advantage of my confusion. But when I got here and when I saw you and realized who you really are, well, I knew that old love had never died. I'm pretty sure it never will." Her eyes glistened with tears.

Leroy was speechless. How could he respond when he couldn't even think?

"So, even if you tell me that you don't love me and that you'll never love me and that I should go home, I still needed to say it." She barely smiled, and her eyes were sad. "I'm glad I said it. It's like a weight's been lifted off my shoulders. This is why I didn't go home with Jan and Mike—so that I could say these words to you." She peered curiously at him, probably hurt by his stony silence. "And, really, I don't want you to feel bad if you need to send me packing. I just want you to be honest with me. I promise I'll understand. But I'll still love you." She sighed, a nervous expression crossing her face. "And so there you have it."

He scrambled for words, but it felt like his brain had been through the grape-crushing machine. Another part of him started to question what she'd said. What if this was just another game? What if she was just waiting for him to fold so she could get up and run?

"I don't blame you for not trusting me," she continued as if she'd read his scrambled thoughts. "You called me a human ping-pong ball once, and I think that described me pretty well. But there was a lot going on. I have my own past issues and insecurities. But even more than that, I was really worried about your girls. I didn't want to start a war in your lovely family. But your mother and Gina both assured me that sisters fight a lot, about lots of things. It's just their Italian Sorrentino heritage."

"That's true," he managed to mumble.

She peered intently into his eyes. "So I assume you don't feel the same. That's why you're not saying anything. But it's okay, Leroy. I understand. As badly as it hurts, it's kind of a good hurt, and I'm determined to accept it." She stood and, biting her lower lip, looked at him with tear-filled eyes. "Maybe this helps make us even for how I've hurt you. Maybe it will help you to move on with your life. You can now be assured that you've hurt me. Probably worse than I've hurt you." She turned to go in the house. "I'll be out of here within the hour."

"Wait," he yelled.

She paused by the door, looking at him with tears rolling down her cheeks.

"I-I just don't know what to say." He stood. "I think I'm kind of in shock here. I mean I wasn't expecting anything like this. I didn't even know you were here. I thought you were back in Oregon by now."

She wiped her tears with her palms. "I know it's a lot for you to take in, Leroy. I'm so sorry. But I honestly didn't know how else to do it. I kept waiting. And your mother told me I should—"

"No, that's not it." He rushed over and swept her into his arms. "I'm glad you said what you did, Brynna."

"You are?" She blinked. "You really are?"

He looked down into her surprised face. "And you're right, it does feel risky. To me too. But did you really mean it? What you said? Do you *really* love me?"

"Yes." She firmly nodded. "I meant it. I love you, Leroy Sorrentino. And I don't care who knows it or what happens next. But yes, I do love you."

He felt a rush of emotion. "Okay then, I'm going to say it too. I love you, Brynna. I've loved you since the first day I met you at camp. You were sitting on the bench and looking so blue, and I asked to take your picture as an excuse to talk to you."

"Really?" Her eyes grew wider. "You really still love me? After all my crazy waffling? The human ping-pong ball?"

He kissed her and suddenly all the light and color flooded back into the world—only brighter and clearer than ever before. He kissed her again, and it was like sweet music and the scent of grape blooms and—and fireworks! "I love you, Brynna," he said quietly. "I really do."

"And you aren't going to send me away?" she asked with shining eyes.

"Never. You're staying here with me. Welcome home." He wrapped his arms around her and, holding her close, he listened to the happy thump-thump-thump of Babe's tail against the wooden porch. His dog approved.

Two Weeks Later

The dinner set out on Leroy's back deck looked more festive than any that Brynna had secretly observed through the lace curtain spy-hole in the cottage's bedroom. Although she could recall how lonely and left out she'd felt back then, after the past two weeks with Leroy, that old memory felt like another lifetime.

Tonight, the long dining table was set with a potluck of foods brought here by Leroy's family. His mother, Gina, Luna, Sophie and Garth and the kids, and even Sherry and her husband and boys—fourteen of them all together—were taking their chairs and congenially lining up on both sides of the table. Despite the hot family discussion just yesterday when Luna had arrived, no one was fighting now.

Brynna smiled when she saw Leroy take his seat at the head of the table. His eyes twinkled, and he grinned like a little boy with a big secret. Oh, she suspected some at the table might have an inkling as to what was up his sleeve, but she was the only one who knew for sure what their host was up to. And what a lovely summer evening for this joyous celebration. The sky was cooperating with a canvas of coral, amber, and periwinkle and, as the sun sank low into the golden horizon, the warm summer air felt like velvet against Brynna's bare arms. Had there ever been a more perfect day?

Everyone now seated at the table appeared to be in good spirits, but none happier than Brynna. Well, except for Leroy. He claimed he was happier. That's what he'd been telling her these past two weeks of what felt like the sweetest courtship of all time.

And it was Leroy who'd actually planned tonight's gathering. He'd invited his family, and since he wasn't much of a cook, he'd also invited them to bring their favorite dishes. Brynna suspected Sophie might've helped orchestrate the food since all the dishes seemed to complement each other. Leroy had put Luna and Gina in charge of the table, which looked splendid with fine table linens, fresh flowers, and golden glowing lanterns. It was truly magical!

Leroy bowed his head to ask a blessing on the meal. It was the usual prayer of gratitude, but after he said amen, he encouraged everyone to lift the glasses that Garth had just filled with sparkling wine from the Sorrentino collection.

"I want to make an announcement." He stood and went over to take Brynna's hand, helping her to stand beside him. "I have asked Brynna to be my wife, and she has agreed. I wanted to share our happy news with our loved ones. I hope you all will wish us well." As he turned to kiss her cheek, there was a brief silence, followed by a couple of childish twitters and nervous giggles . . . and finally the whole table erupted into cheers and congratulations. This was followed by several toasts, some serious and some just for fun.

Finally, Dorothy raised her glass high. "Here's to a romance that was planted then forgotten many decades ago. May it blossom and grow, coming into beautiful fruition for many decades to come. God bless!"

They all echoed with a hearty "God bless!" Then Leroy turned to Brynna and sealed it with a kiss.

Turn the page to read the first chapter of another
heartwarming contemporary romance
from Melody Carlson.

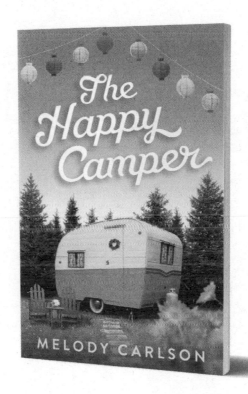

Chapter 1

Dillon Michaels was fed up—but it wasn't with dinner. In fact, she was ravenous. And Brandon was late. Again. Dillon hadn't eaten since breakfast, but her appetite wasn't simply a desire for food. Despite the tantalizing aroma of mussels and garlic from her favorite house special, *cozze in padella*, Dillon realized she longed for something more . . . something intangible.

"Will your date be here soon?" the waiter asked—for the third time.

"I hope so." Dillon forced a smile while she reached for her phone. As the waiter refilled her water glass, Dillon grimaced to see the time. "I'll text him again," she muttered. Too embarrassed to look up, she shot Brandon her fifth message.

WHERE R U?

But what she really wanted to say was, *Why are you ALWAYS late?*

Of course, that raised another question: *Why do I always put up with it?* She set her phone down, trying to relax as she sipped her water. She was well aware that Brandon was a pro at concocting plausible excuses. But why did she automatically accept them? Why didn't she believe she deserved better than this? Dillon glanced around the restaurant's crowded patio. Other couples and families visited congenially, enjoying this unexpectedly warm evening in Colorado

Springs. And seated among cheery flower boxes and merry strings of lights at DeMarco's was the perfect place to celebrate the start of summer. Such a happy scene . . . but Dillon's frustration was quickly turning to fury, bubbling straight to the surface.

She'd had enough. Snatching up her things, she stood and laid a small tip on the table, signaling the waiter that she was leaving. And seeing relief in his eyes, she ducked her head and hurried out of the popular Italian restaurant. She was nearly to the parking lot when she heard Brandon call her name. With her cheeks still warm from embarrassment, she turned to face him.

"Where are you going?" He frowned. "I thought you made the reservation for—"

"I made the reservation for 6:45," she shot back. "It is now 7:35 and I am going home—thank you very much."

"But what about our table, Dillon?" He gave her his feel-sorry-for-me look. "What about dinner? What about me?"

"What about you?" She glared back at him, bracing herself for a showdown. "I've had it, Brandon. I'm done waiting on you and—"

"But I couldn't help it. I was—"

"Save your breath, Brandon. You know this happens *all the time*. Do you have any idea what it feels like to be the one waiting and waiting and waiting? Why is it that you are *never* on time? *Never!*"

"I'm really sorry, Dillon. But I was tied up with a client and we had to get the deal wrapped up before the weekend and it—"

"Yes, that's what I thought you'd say." She took a deep calming breath. "And I'm sorry for sounding so angry right now. But I just can't do this anymore—"

"Do what?" he demanded.

"*This.*" She wildly waved her arms as if that explained everything. "I'm done, Brandon. I'm not going to keep waiting for you. I'm moving on. I'm finished with you."

"Oh, Dillon." His tone turned placating. "You're hungry and tired. It's been a long, hard week at work and you just need a nice evening of—"

"No!" She held her palms toward him. "I'm finished, Brandon. I mean it. Don't try to talk me out of—"

"Fine," he snapped. "If that's how you want it. *Fine!*" He turned, and she could tell by the way he clomped the heels of his good calfskin loafers, he was vexed. But she really didn't care. She'd meant what she said. She was done with him—finito!

But as she got into her car, she felt a mix of conflicting emotions. On one hand and to her surprise, she was relieved—how incredibly freeing to put an end to a two-year relationship that appeared to be destined for nowhere. On the other hand, she felt a shaky sense of uneasiness. What had she just done? What if she woke up tomorrow morning and regretted this? What if she had to eat her words? To beg his forgiveness . . .

As she drove home, Dillon had no doubts that multitudes of women would consider Brandon a great catch. And maybe he was—if anyone could actually catch him. Good luck! Sure, he was good-looking, had a decent job, was responsible, owned his condo unit, drove a nice car, and even went to church. But Mr. Perfect was afraid of commitment. How many times had he told her that very thing—acting as if she were the key to unlock that door? But she didn't want to wait ten years for it!

Dillon would turn thirty-four this summer. And although she'd never confess it, she could hear her biological clock ticking faster and faster each year. She knew this was a by-product of being an only child with a single mom. Since girlhood, Dillon had dreamed of becoming a wife and mother . . . someday. But someday just got farther and farther away. And even if she couldn't admit her outdated fantasy out loud, she couldn't deny it either. Not to herself.

As Dillon parked in her apartment complex lot, she couldn't help but notice how many spaces were vacant tonight. Tenants were probably relishing the beginning of a summery weekend. Maybe her roommates would be out too. Dillon hoped so. Right now she just wanted to be alone—a pity party of one. As she headed for the apartment, she realized Brandon had been right about a couple things. She was worn out from a long, hard week—and she was hungry too. Microwaved lasagna wasn't the same as mussels and pesto pasta, but it would do in a pinch. Fortunately, she'd stocked up on Lean Cuisine a few days ago.

Dillon heard music as she unlocked the apartment door. That probably meant that Reba was home tonight. Hopefully her boyfriend wasn't here too. Dillon never knew what to expect from her roommates. They were best friends and she was always the odd one out. It was a good setup a few years ago when she'd gotten a job with the software company. Cheap rent and close to work. But she'd never planned to stay this long.

"You're home." Reba sounded disappointed. "I thought you were on your standard Friday night date with Brandon Kranze."

"I thought so too." Dillon dumped her bags into a chair then quickly explained about the impromptu breakup.

"You're kidding!" Reba's eyes grew wide. "I thought you guys were about to get engaged."

Dillon shrugged. "I guess I thought so too . . . or I used to. But I gave myself a serious reality check tonight. Brandon has no interest in marriage."

Reba's brows arched. "Well, I'm hoping that Jarrod does." She pointed to the clock on the stove. "And he'll be here in a few minutes. He's bringing pizza and we planned to watch a movie."

"Oh . . . nice." Dillon opened the freezer part of the fridge. "I'll just nuke some dinner and lay low in my room." She poked around, looking for her frozen meals, but only saw a half-empty carton of licorice ice cream, a crusty bag of mixed vegetables, and a frost-covered guinea hen that had been there since Christmas. "Hey, what happened to my Lean Cuisine meals?" she asked Reba.

"Val started her swimsuit diet this week." Reba chuckled. "She probably ate them."

Dillon removed the ice cream and firmly shut the freezer door. "Figures!" Grabbing a spoon, she took the carton to her room and changed into her "comfort jammies" before pulling her auburn hair back into a ponytail. Then, even though she disliked licorice, she plopped down on her bed and proceeded to consume every last drop of the gooey, sweet, charcoal-colored ice cream. As she plunked the soggy container into her wastebasket, she caught a shocking glimpse of herself in the closet door mirror. Her licorice-blackened lips and grayed teeth looked strangely stark against her pale skin, which hadn't seen sunshine due to long work hours. And with her hair pulled tightly back, her dark blue eyes looked even larger than usual—resulting in an image that could easily land her a zombie role in a horror flick. *Attractive.* Hearing Reba and Jarrod out in the living room, Dillon didn't want to frighten them by going to the hall bath to brush her teeth and wash her face, so she simply crawled into bed and turned out the light. Feeling pathetic and hopeless and lonely, she cried herself to sleep.

The sound of her phone's jingle dragged her back into consciousness. Assuming it was the wee hours of the morning, she felt a jolt of concern as she grabbed up her phone—was it Brandon? Was he sorry? But seeing Margot's name on caller ID, Dillon braced herself for bad news. The last time her mother had called late at night was to inform her that Grandma had passed away.

"Who died?" Dillon demanded without even saying hello.

"No one died, silly Dilly." Margot's tone was light. "Why would you even say such a thing?"

"Well, it's the middle of the night and—"

"Middle of the night? Good grief, it's not even nine o'clock yet."

"Oh? Well, uh, I thought it was, uh, later." Dillon turned on her bedside light.

"Don't tell me you were already in bed. What are you—like, eighty?"

"Funny." Dillon didn't hide her irritation. "So why are you calling me? What's up, Margot?" She'd called her mother *Margot* for as long as she could remember. She couldn't even imagine calling her *Mother.* That would be just plain weird.

"Maybe I simply want to hear my little girl's voice."

"Right . . ." Dillon rolled her eyes. Margot rarely called for any reason—certainly not to hear Dillon's voice. "How's Grandpa doing?"

"As a matter of fact, that's partly why I'm calling."

Dillon sat up in bed, concerned. "Is he okay?"

"Well, I don't know—"

"What's wrong?"

"Nothing's wrong exactly, Dilly. But I think he misses your grandma."

"I'm sure he does. It's only been about eight months. But I'd hoped he was getting over it."

"I'm not so sure . . . I think he's depressed and I'm worried about his health. His diet is atrocious, he's letting the farm go and staying in bed too long."

"That doesn't sound like him."

"Well, he is getting old. Do you realize he'll be seventy-seven soon?"

"I know—I already got a birthday card for him. But he's always been so active and energetic and young for his age. I can't imagine him sleeping in when the sun is up."

"You haven't seen him lately, Dilly. Don't forget, you didn't even come home for Christmas."

"That's because I'd taken that time off for Grandma's funeral in the fall. And I couldn't get more time for Christmas—"

"I know, I know. I also know you're a hopeless workaholic, Dillon. I just don't understand how it happened, though. I certainly didn't raise you that way."

"That's for sure." Dillon was assaulted by an unwanted flashback from her childhood—a sad snapshot of herself and Margot living on child support, food stamps, and government handouts. It wasn't until Dillon moved to her grandparents' farm as a teen that she eventually quit worrying about her next meal.

"Well, there are things more important than work, Dilly. Like having a life. Do you ever think about *that*?"

"Yeah . . . right." Dillon wanted an excuse to end this conversation.

"So how are things with Brandon? Any wedding bells yet?" Margot's voice tinkled with sarcasm.

"For your information, we broke up." Dillon instantly regretted disclosing her personal news.

"Broke up? But I thought he was your Mr. Right."

"More like Mr. Not-Right-Now."

"Well, I'm sorry to hear that, Dilly."

Unwilling to continue down this path, Dillon inquired about her mother's boyfriend. "Are you and Don still together?"

"Just getting ready to celebrate seven years."

"Congratulations. And I can probably assume you're not hearing any wedding bells either." Dillon knew that Margot and Don had no intention of marrying—ever. Just one more irritating element of her mother's nontraditional lifestyle.

"Don and I don't need a piece of paper to prove our love for each other, Dilly. You know that."

Dillon rolled her eyes again, but she'd asked for it, so why cringe over Margot's worn-out answer? "Back to Grandpa—do you really think he's depressed? Should he see a professional or something?"

"You mean like a shrink?" Margot laughed. "Can you imagine your stubborn grandfather talking to a shrink? Or taking antidepressants?"

"No . . . not really. But I hate hearing that he's unhappy. I wish I could come out there to see him. Maybe for his birthday." Even as she said this, Dillon knew it was unlikely. It wasn't that she couldn't afford the airfare, but after recent layoffs and cutbacks, getting a few days off work was a major challenge.

"Oh, that'd be sweet, Dilly. He'd love to see you. He was just saying how much he misses you."

"Tell him I miss him too. Give him my love." Dillon felt close to tears again. So much for thinking she'd been cried out.

"I'll be sure to tell him. And I hope you're not feeling too miserable over Brandon. I never wanted to say anything, but based on what you've told me, he sounded too good to be true. I'm glad you found it out before it was too late."

Even though Margot was partially right, Dillon wasn't ready to hear those words just yet—especially from a woman who had never committed to a marital relationship. So Dillon told her goodbye and shut off the light. Lying there in the darkness with only the muffled noise of an action movie for company, she longed for an escape. But what exactly did she hope to escape? After all, she'd already jumped ship from a two-year relationship with Brandon. Shouldn't that be enough for one day?

But she still longed for something more. Or maybe it was for something less. She wasn't quite sure. Maybe she simply wanted to escape from herself and her dreary little life for a while. Thankfully it was the weekend, but even the thought of some time off brought no comfort. As she lay there, listening to the thumpity-thump of the film's explosives in the living room, she realized she was stiff as a board, clenching her fists, and probably would be grinding her teeth before long. Her dentist had warned her this was problematic and had recommended a bite guard for sleeping. Although she promised to think about it, she'd also started to practice calming exercises before bedtime.

But deep breathing and happy thoughts were not working tonight. So she turned to prayer, begging God for some serious help. It was the first time in a long time that she'd asked God to direct her path—but that's exactly what she said. Because Dillon had no idea where her life was headed—for all she knew it was about to go over a cliff. Admittedly, it wasn't much of a prayer, but it was heartfelt, and when Dillon whispered amen, she felt slightly more at ease. Like Scarlett O'Hara said, tomorrow was another day.

Melody Carlson is the beloved author of well over two hundred novels. She has been a finalist for or the recipient of many awards, including the Romantic Times Career Achievement Award. She lives in central Oregon.

A Story of Love, Restoration, and Starting Anew

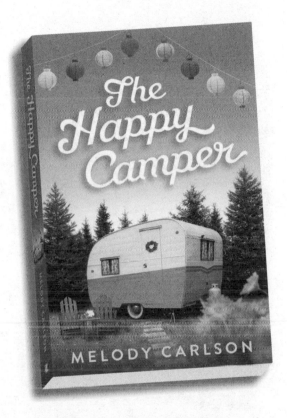

When Dillon Michaels returns home after a breakup, her grandfather gifts her a vintage camp trailer that needs restoration. Intrigued by the work, and the charming hardware store owner, she's hopeful for a fresh chance at love—until a surprise visit from her ex-boyfriend turns everything upside down.

No One Is Too Old to Change Their Life—
OR FIND A NEW LOVE

George Emerson doesn't want his predictable life to change, but free-spirited ex-hippie Willow West has other plans for him. They may soon discover that no one is too old to change their life—or find love.

MEET
Melody

MelodyCarlson.com

MelodyCarlsonAuthor   AuthorMelodyCarlson